Life Rage

L.L. Soares

First Edition

ISBN: 1-938644-03-4
ISBN-13: 978-1-938644-03-0

Nightscape Press, LLP
http://www.nightscapepress.com

For Laura

CONTENTS

ACKNOWLEDGMENTS

Once you write a novel, the path from that point to actual publication can sometimes be longer and more convoluted than you expect. But I am overjoyed to finally see LIFE RAGE, the book. I want to thank all those who helped this become a reality, especially:

To Gregory Lamberson, who read the book early on and constantly encouraged me to keep sending it out and not lose faith.

To my wife, Laura Cooney, for her constant support, patience and love.

To my buddy Peter Dudar for his encouragement, advice, and for those late night pep talks. You were a big part of why things happened the way they did, and I appreciate that.

To William Cook, an excellent artist who provided an amazing image for the cover for this novel.

And to my publishers and editors at Nightscape Press, Robert Shane Wilson and Mark Scioneaux, two terrific guys who have made the entire process a positive one, and kept things exciting throughout.

Thanks.

Prologue

It sounded like the deep, raw cough of an old woman, but when Sam turned to look back, he saw a young, attractive girl, covering her mouth.

She noticed his stare and took her hand away. Forced a smile.

Sam realized he was staring right at her, right into her eyes, and the sudden consciousness made him tear his gaze away. He looked up, above her head, at an advertisement for a local community college. Some acne-scarred student smiling next to a quotation in big, white letters, about how wonderful education was.

There are stairs. That go upstairs. Only, there's nobody there.

A tune was playing in his head that he just couldn't shake, and the lyrics made no sense. He tried to empty his mind.

When he turned to look at the young woman again, she was standing up, moving toward the train doors, getting off at the next stop.

It couldn't have been her who made that noise, who coughed like that, Sam thought. *Must have been someone else.*

He tried to concentrate on the newspaper, but there was nothing in it that interested him. He watched the woman's back, her ass, as she disappeared from view, and the subway doors closed, and the train began to move again.

And there's nobody there. No matter how long I wait. Nobody at all.

The next stop was his. He got out and tossed the unread paper into the nearest trash receptacle. He let the other people around him provide the current, and swam along with them, letting their movements dictate his own.

He thought of the pretty woman with the cough. Wondered what her cunt felt like. What noises she made during sex. What her mouth would feel like wrapped around his cock. What her asshole felt like.

Another day.

Nobody at all. There are stairs. That go upstairs.

PART ONE
THIS SHARED RAGE

CHAPTER ONE

Back when she was fourteen years old, Colleen used to carve words into her arms with razor blades.

Funny she should think about that now, riding the subway.

It wasn't something she did all the time, but it occurred often enough for her mother to get very concerned and make her see a psychiatrist. An odd, mostly emotionless woman with her hair tied in a severe bun behind her head.

Colleen had tried to make it very clear that she was not suicidal. That the razor was her way of dealing with being alive. It wasn't always clear what she was feeling, or what she was trying to say, and the razor helped her to focus sometimes.

The psychiatrist had promptly put her on anti-depressant drugs, and urged her to express what she was feeling.

Colleen decided she would rather not talk, and the sessions consisted of hours of silence. Her mother did not seem to mind that she was wasting her money. Colleen had stopped cutting herself. She eventually stopped going to the psychiatrist's office and stopped taking the drugs.

That was because Colleen had found *boys*. They focused her in ways that the razor just couldn't compete with.

But that didn't mean that sometimes she didn't miss the feel of the razor cutting into her flesh. Spelling out feelings she just couldn't articulate.

Maybe I'll take this stop, she wondered as the train slowed down. Then again, maybe not. I have a lot of time to kill.

On the days when she didn't sleep late, she often rode the subway for hours at a time. Today, she wasn't sure if there was anywhere she really wanted to go. But she didn't want to spend time in her claustrophobic apartment, either.

Maybe I should look for a job, she thought. A _real_ job.

But she knew she wouldn't. Not today, at least. She wondered if she would ever get motivated enough to try. How much longer would she just scrape along?

She thought about the man who had been staring at her earlier, on that other train. He was attractive enough, but something about the way he looked at her scared her. In different circumstances, she might have tried to talk to him, and see where things led.

Then again, maybe not. She did follow her instincts after all. That's how she was able to survive this long. By her wits.

She felt a tickle at the back of her throat. She hoped she wouldn't start coughing again.

Maybe I should quit smoking, she thought.

* * *

"Calm down," Sam found himself shouting.

Richard Croix was standing up now, waving his arms, and shouting as well. In fact, he had started it all. His anger filled the room, and Sam was afraid that Carla would call the police this time. But he'd told her not to do that, ever. He could handle it.

"Sit down!" Sam said, getting up from his own chair.

"The fucking asshole," Croix was saying. "He just sat there in his car, grinning at me, like it was some kind of a fucking joke. He sped away before I could pull him out of his car and tear his fucking head right off."

"Richard," Sam said, loud enough to get through to him, but trying to stay calm. "Richard, get a hold of yourself."

Croix was practically foaming at the mouth. He wasn't just telling the story, he was clearly reliving it, as angry now as when the incident originally occurred.

"Smirking at me, like some fucking retard, daring me to do something! I wanted to just rip his car door off and cut him in half with it."

Sam put his hands on Richard Croix's shoulders, like some kind of healing priest, and stared right into Croix's eyes. Trying to take control of the situation, trying to exert some kind of dominance over Croix's anger. Something a lot like electricity tingled in Sam's hands and arms. It traveled. He could feel it in the back of his neck, and then reaching the circumference of his skull.

"Sit down," Sam said, quietly. "Sit down and get a hold of yourself. It's over now. It's not happening anymore. It's all in the past."

Croix stopped shouting. The silence happened so quickly that Sam swore he could hear a faint hiss and crackle of electricity in the air around them, in place of the shouting. Filling the void.

"You're losing it, Richard," Sam said. "You're letting it run away with you. Don't let that happen. Don't let it control you. Control it. You're the master here."

He pressed down on Croix's shoulders, and the larger man did not resist as he dropped back into his seat, staring up into Sam's eyes.

"That's better," Sam said. "You're yourself again."

"I was shouting again," Croix said after a few minutes.

"Yes, you were," Sam said. "And I had to stop you."

"Thank you," Croix said softly, noticeably shamed by this news. "I'm so sorry."

"It's over now, Richard. You're back in control again."

"It's just that the whole thing got me so angry."

"And isn't that why you're here, Richard? The anger? You can't let go of the anger, even days after it's ignited. You can't break its hold on you. Even talking about it makes you lose control."

"I'm sorry," Croix said, fumbling for words. He seemed so helpless, so child-like now. So unlike the roaring Vesuvius of a man who had just been shouting at the top of his lungs. "I can't help myself."

"No, you can't. Not yet. But you will, Richard. That's why you're here. That's why *I'm* here. To help you."

"Help me," Croix said, not so much pleading as repeating Sam's words. His head wasn't clear enough yet to plead.

"You've come to the right place, Richard. You know you have. This is my specialty, after all. I am a rage specialist."

"It was so real," Croix said. "Just telling you what happened, made it so real again."

"Sounds to me like it was lucky that guy drove away before you could reach him. Who knows what you would have done if you had gotten your hands on him."

"I would have killed him," Croix said, softly but confidently. There was no question in it.

"Yes, you probably would have. I find it remarkable that you haven't killed anyone yet, Richard. It's amazing that you have any control at all."

"It wasn't always this bad," Croix said, then thought about it. "But it's always been bad. I don't know how I haven't killed anyone, either. I came close a few times."

"I bet you have," Sam said.

"Are you going to prescribe something for me?" Croix asked. "Like the other doctors?"

"No, Richard. That's why you came to me. Because you need a different kind of treatment. Drugs don't change anything, they just mask the anger. The behavior. And that doesn't solve anything. You came to me because you really wanted to change. You wanted to *alter* your behavior."

"The drugs I've taken before, they affected me badly. Made it hard to think. I couldn't do my job right."

"I know. You've had bad side effects from all of the medications you've been prescribed. That's why I can help you. There will be no medication in this therapy."

Croix looked at him, holding his hands out. He didn't even realize he was doing it. "I've been like this for so long. I almost can't imagine it any other way."

"I know," Sam told him. "But don't lose hope."

Richard Croix sat there, quietly, seeming lost and alone.

Sam Wayne glanced at his watch and then looked into Croix's eyes. And smiled.

"Our session is done for today," he said. "I'll see you again tomorrow."

Croix got to his feet. For a moment, he almost stumbled, as if the act of getting up had made him light-headed. A sudden light-headedness almost overcoming him.

"Tomorrow is fine," Croix said. "If you can fit me in."

"I insist on it," Sam said. "Tomorrow, same time. I look forward to seeing you again, Richard."

"Thank you," Croix said, and left the room.

Sam watched the door close. A bead of sweat trickled down his forehead.

The air in the room was oppressive. He found he was having a hard time breathing.

What the fuck am I doing here? Sam wondered.

And then, as if in answer, an adrenaline rush washed over him. It was then that he felt the most alive. He felt like he could do anything, heal anyone. This sensation filled up something inside him that remained empty most of the time. Unfortunately, he knew this quickening would be fleeting. It never lasted long enough, and always left him wanting more.

CHAPTER TWO

*H*ot pink murmuring.

Colleen woke up to the neon sign that said, "Open All Night," in big pink letters on the wall of her bedroom. A joke gift that had long since lost its humor. But for some reason she hadn't taken it down.

There was someone in bed with her. Someone she didn't recognize. Not that it was such a shock. It happened too often these days to offer any surprise.

Her life was turning into a really bad joke.

She got out of bed, holding back the beginnings of a cough, to go to the bathroom. She kicked an empty whiskey bottle along the way, and it went spinning under the bed. Where it would no doubt find companions.

She tried to pull the sheet off the bed, it was cold in the apartment, but her new "companion" was too wrapped up in it and wouldn't budge. She shivered as she made her way through the humming pink light to the door of the bathroom.

Once inside, she covered her mouth as a coughing fit broke free from her mouth. It seemed to get worse when she stopped smoking, so she lit up a cigarette and took a drag. That seemed to quiet her down a bit. Sitting on the toilet, listening to her piss rain into the

- 10 -

bowl, she tried to think of who the stranger was. Surely they'd been introduced before they got down to the whole fucking business.

There was a window in the bathroom, aglow from a streetlight just outside. She didn't need to turn on the bathroom light because of this, and she stared out the window while she pissed and smoked. She had a view of the roof across the way, and the top of a lighted sign that read, "Martin's," flashing on and off.

There's too much neon in my life, she thought, as she wiped herself. Wondering how much alcohol content there was in her urine these days.

The slow-motion roar of snoring cut through the air then, and she knew, at least, that her friend for the night was alive. Which she almost regretted.

Colleen resisted the urge to turn on the shower and step inside. Instead, she finished her cigarette and threw the stub in the toilet. Then she went back out to her bedroom and got back into bed.

She turned her back on the snorer. Somehow, her coughing hadn't woken him. She was not even curious to see his face. It didn't matter.

Knowledge wouldn't change anything. Not now.

* * *

The subway train stopped and the lights flickered, then went out. Sam was wedged between a squat, round woman who looked to be wearing two sets of clothing over her already substantial bulk, and a large man in a suit who must have had an equal amount of body fat, if not more. To make matters worse, the car was full of people. They covered every available square foot of floor. He couldn't get up right then, even if he had to.

That hadn't stopped the old woman in front of him from glaring at him since the last stop, no doubt pissed off at men in general, and men who didn't get up and offer their seats to old women in particular. Not that the idea of offering his seat hadn't crossed Sam's mind. It was almost a reflex, drilled into him since he was a little boy by his mother. *Always give a lady your seat, and that goes double for the elderly.* But Sam had been feeling a little nauseous, and he *never* got a seat on the subway. He might be selfish in his refusal get up, but that was tough shit. Sometimes you had to look out for your own well-being and comfort.

Besides, the woman's reaction had been so obnoxious, so blatantly hostile, that he wouldn't have accommodated her anyway. She turned to the woman next to her and said, "Men today have no manners at all," and then made it a point to turn her eyes to Sam and glare.

Well, fuck her! He wasn't her fucking lap dog, to jump up to attention just because she had been on the Earth a few decades more than he had. And if men like him, *middle-aged white men* specifically, because there was no fucking way she would have made that comment if he had been a different color or if he didn't look so goddamned safe, lacked manners, then what about old women with snide comments and glares, and the expectation that the world owed them something for being alive? Where were *her* fucking manners?

And then the train had slowed down and come to a halt between stops. And the lights went out.

He could hear the old bitch breathing. And he closed his eyes, imagined hitting her repeatedly in the face, until her wrinkled head was the color of plums. And that would just be the beginning....

Before he could take his fantasy further, the lights came back on. The unscheduled stop wasn't going to last an hour after all. The train rattled and hissed and then started moving again.

Sam felt like a steer in a slaughterhouse, shoulder to shoulder with other doomed souls, pushing forward, ever forward, to certain death.

But then he reminded himself, it wasn't as grim as all that. He was going home after a long day.

CHAPTER THREE

When Colleen woke, it was early afternoon, and her latest visitor was long gone. There wasn't much sign he'd been there at all. Just a half-smoked cigarette stubbed out in one of her cheap metal ashtrays. And two rolled-up twenties on the nightstand.

She hadn't asked him for money. She never asked any of them. But most of them left some behind, anyway. She was grateful for small tokens of gratitude.

The clock radio on the nightstand said it was exactly 2:07 in glowing pink letters. The shades were all down and the room was still dark, with just a line of light coming in from the slit of space above the shades. She wrapped the sheet around her and walked to the bathroom again, then dropped her covering on the bathroom floor and took a seat on the porcelain.

While wiping herself, there was a knock at the door. She hesitated getting up. She didn't get many visitors. Unless it was some former fuck-mate who was interested in a repeat performance, but even that didn't happen very often, and never this early.

Not ambitious enough to search for clean clothes, Colleen picked the sheet off the floor and wrapped herself up like the Bride of Frankenstein, her hair probably looking just as bad, and moved as if in slow motion toward the door. The knocking did not stop.

She put the chain lock on. Not that it would protect her much. The door was old and thin and would probably shatter to bits if someone with any strength kicked it in. But it was like a symbol of security. The slightly rusted chain. And when it was in place, she opened the door a crack.

"Yeah?"

"Colleen?" asked a voice she recognized. "How you doing?"

She closed the door, slid the chain off and opened it again.

Turney slid inside and grinned at her as he moved toward the bed and sat down. "What's up, girl?"

Seeing him made her glide deeper into her melancholy mood. Another lost one. She hadn't seen him in weeks, and had even considered that he might be dead. But here he was, like a ghost that refused to stay buried.

They'd gone to high school together. While she had barely graduated, he'd dropped out the year before, and began his descent all the sooner. If she was a loser, then he was a hardcore loser. A junkie, who, despite a few attempts at getting clean, would probably die someday soon with a needle in his arm. Who wasn't above selling his body to the lowest bidder. Turney still had a specter of his former personality. Enough to be sad and likable, and capable of bringing out whatever maternal instincts Colleen harbored.

"Where the fuck have you been?" she asked him. "I haven't seen you in ages."

"Been around," Turney said, smiling sheepishly. Shrugging his bony shoulders.

She remembered when she'd first met him, in her freshman year. He was a class ahead of her. He seemed like just another normal kid, except he wore clothes that were too tight and was too shy to say much. Then, as the years went on, he loosened up and got involved with the druggie crowd. *Burnouts* was what everyone else called them. Since then, she'd learned he had horror stories of his own, and his self-medication seemed more than justified. But it was funny how she'd been witness to his metamorphosis. It made her feel all the more close to him.

Even though he was a year older than her, he still looked like that scared, skinny high school kid. Even though they knew each other much more intimately now than they had back then, he still seemed shy a lot of the time. Some things didn't change.

"So what brings you here?" she asked. "Besides saying hi."

He looked around the room. "Hadn't seen you in a bit. Wanted to make sure you were okay."

"I'm okay. Hanging on. Same as you."

Despite his skinniness, he looked healthier than the last time she'd seen him. He'd had a cold then that he wasn't able to shake. She was sure that it would turn into pneumonia. Somehow, he'd gotten past it.

"Can I stay here tonight?" he asked. "I hate to ask, but…"

"Sure thing," she told him. She thought about the one time they'd done it, or tried to. About a month or two after she'd been on her own. He'd come over and they got to talking about how miserable their lives were. They'd even cried on each other's shoulders. It was kind of like what she thought it must be to go to college, stay in a dorm, and share all-night talks with new friends or a roommate. Except everything they had to say was miserable. After a good cry, they'd taken off their clothes and tried to do it. It had happened spontaneously. But he couldn't get hard, and it was just one more addition to the misery pile. She'd done all she could to convince him it didn't matter, and after a while, he seemed to handle it okay. Now that she looked back on it, his inability to perform was probably more due to junk sickness than anything else.

"Sorry to impose," he said, looking bashful. Like when he was a kid. "I'll be gone in the morning."

"Stay as long as you need to," Colleen said. "Nobody cares. It's not like this is a luxury hotel or nothing. As long as I get the rent paid on time, they don't care what the fuck I do."

Somehow, she'd been able to keep the rent payments up. And she'd been able to keep herself somewhat fed. It could have been worse. She was doing okay.

"Thanks, Colleen," Turney said.

She sat down next to him. Put her arms around him. "No problem, kiddo."

For some reason, she was feeling sentimental. And she had so few friends left, that it was a relief to see him again. To see a familiar face that wouldn't condemn her.

They rocked back and forth on the bed. And then they fell back, and she held him down, and kissed his cheek now and then. He tensed in her embrace, but made no move to get away.

She started crying before she even realized. And he eventually put his arms around her as well. And they got through it.

* * *

Sam woke in the middle of the night, shaking and breathing hard. He'd had one of his dreams again.

He turned to look at Maggie, who was still asleep beside him.

Well, if he'd made any noise, at least he hadn't woken her. Not that it would have been the first time. The nightmares had been bothering him on and off for years now.

It had been a while since the last one, though, and he'd hoped that maybe they were over, but no such luck. He tried to remember the events of this dream. He remembered seeing blood splashing against a wall, and there was a scraping sound he couldn't place. And of course, someone was screaming. But it wasn't clear where he was or what was happening.

The nightmares weren't always the same, but they were linked. They were all violent dreams. Something horrible was happening. And there was always the screaming. But it was never clear who was being harmed, and who was doing the harming.

Am I the victim in these dreams? he wondered. *Or the perpetrator?*

There was always such a strong sense of dread when he woke up from them. He was so sure he was in danger.

But they were only dreams.

Maggie moved slightly beside him, and he thought she was waking up, but she didn't.

He put his head back down on the pillow and closed his eyes. He could feel his heartbeat slowing down. It wasn't pounding in his ears anymore.

It didn't take long to get back to sleep.

CHAPTER FOUR

"Let's get out of here," Colleen said. "We need some air."

They had fallen asleep awhile in each other's arms.

Turney pulled away and sat up on the bed, silent. She could see the fear in his eyes.

"What are you so afraid of?" Colleen asked him. "You've been out on your own for years now. Out on the streets. Why are you so afraid all of a sudden?"

Turney shrugged.

"Did something happen to you out there? Did someone hurt you?"

He took a moment, as if in thought. Then shook his head. No.

"Well, then, let's get out of here. I don't know what's gotten into you."

She went to the door. Opened it and looked back at him.

He was still sitting on the bed like a lost puppy.

"Come on," she said. "There is no way I'm just staying here."

Turney hesitated, then got up and went past her, out into the hall. He stood there as she closed the door and locked it.

She noticed that someone had replaced the bulb in the hallway. *Every once in a while something actually gets fixed around here*, she thought.

She walked past Turney. He didn't move.

"Come on," Colleen said. "It will do you a world of good."

He was just standing there, looking down at his shoes. Clearly, he would have been content to just stay in her room forever. Like a kind of sanctuary. But the thought of staying there reminded Colleen of a prison cell. Night had fallen, and she had to get out into the world. She had to *move*.

She turned and looked at him. Really looked at him in the harsh light of the bare bulb that hung above them. While his face still looked as youthful as she remembered, when they were both back in school, there were wrinkles around his eyes now, faint markings on the cheeks, that gave away the fact that even Turney was getting older.

"Well?" she asked. Her hands on her hips. "Are we going outside?"

He hesitated.

"I wish you'd open up to me," Colleen said. "If I'm letting you stay here for free, that's the least you could do in return. You could let me know what's got you so spooked."

Instead of answering her, he moved away from the wall, and passed her, going down the stairs. She sighed and followed him.

Outside, the air was crisp and invigorating after the staleness of the apartment. Colleen laughed and spun around in front of him, illuminated by an overhead street lamp. In the corner of her eye, she could see the grin on Turney's face.

"Isn't it great to be alive?" she asked him. "If you *really* think about it?"

"You're not serious," Turney said. "Who are you supposed to be? Fucking Mary Tyler Moore?"

* * *

Croix was back again. It was funny how the days almost blurred together.

This time he seemed calmer. He was able to talk about incidents from the past that angered him. Random incidents that should have been long forgotten. People cutting him off in traffic and following them until he was able to get some kind of grip on himself and let them go. People who had bumped into him on the sidewalks and he had grabbed, and had been inches away from striking, before he'd been able to maintain some semblance of control. But he did not raise his voice. He did not rise up out of his seat this time.

"Do these things still bother you?" Sam asked. "You do not seem particularly agitated today. You're not losing your temper."

"I'm not, am I?" Croix asked, suddenly surprised, like it hadn't even crossed his mind until that moment. "Yeah, I'm pretty calm today."

"One positive thing from these past incidents," Sam said. "Is that you were able to gain control of the situation. You were able to prevent things from escalating further."

"I'm a civilized man," Croix said. "I have a wife. Kids. A good job. I can't let all that fall apart. I just can't. But it's been harder and harder to maintain control."

"Have you ever struck your wife, Richard? Your kids?"

Croix lowered his head. The flesh of his face reddened. He did not answer.

That told Sam all he needed to know. This was a man crying out for help. A man losing control of his life. He had already started to shatter the flimsy barriers he had been using all these years. Who knows? Perhaps the violence in his home had been going on for a long time now, and he'd never had the guts to talk about it. Even now, he wasn't articulating it.

"It's okay, Richard," Sam said. "That's why you're here. There is no way you can help yourself if you won't admit your problems. The things that are tormenting you. And, as you know, everything said in here is completely confidential."

Actually, he should have reported any actual abuse, but Sam didn't care about Richard Croix's family. He only cared about the man himself, and the sessions.

"The pills the doctors prescribed," Croix said, still looking at the floor. "They didn't solve anything. They just doped me up, made it hard to think."

"I know, Richard. That's why I told you, I won't be putting you on any medication. That's not how I operate."

There was a soft sob. Croix was crying now. It was a sadness tinged with anger at himself. Self-loathing.

Sam stood and went over to him. Standing before the seated man, he put his hands on Croix's shoulders. There was complete silence in the room. Croix had even stopped his sobbing. Sam closed his eyes and emptied his mind. Croix did not move.

It was easier this time. No resistance. Earlier, Croix had been less cooperative. But that was the same with all new patients. They had no idea what was happening, and weren't sure how to react, much less how to make the process easier. But this time, Croix surrendered to him, and it happened much easier.

There was still a lot of anger inside the man and Sam took a little more of it away this time. Unfortunately, the easier it got, the less satisfying it was as well.

In truth, Sam did not even have to touch them to take something away. He could have done it from his seat, across from Croix. But there was something about the healing power of touch, a human element that added an extra sense of comfort to the process. It worked so well; Sam had adopted it as part of his technique.

Croix's head slowly swiveled on his thick neck, and he looked up into Sam's face. He seemed slightly confused, but also relieved. His tears had stopped.

"Is that better?" Sam asked, softly.

Croix nodded, not wanting to break the silence with a reply.

Sam removed his hands and went back to his seat. The air was charged around them, but it wasn't as pronounced as the previous visit. It was more relaxed, comfortable. More like a heightening of the senses. There were no visible sparks.

"Tell me more," Sam said. "The healing works better if you talk. It makes the whole process more complete."

"It doesn't happen all the time," Croix said. He spoke like a man in a trance. "Just sometimes, when the anger gets too hard to hold inside. I get home, wanting so badly to relax, and they yammer at me. Their voices are like the squawking of birds. And I can't hold in the anger anymore..."

"And, either out of love or fear, they do not fight back."

"They just look at me with these sad eyes, afraid of what I can change into. Like I'm a monster they have no defense against. And I don't want to see that look in their eyes anymore. I don't want them to have to make excuses for their bruises anymore. I don't want to be a source of fear in their lives."

Croix's voice had no trace of anger in it. And he wasn't crying. His voice was calm and level.

"You won't be a source of fear anymore," Sam said. "I will teach you how to make the barriers stronger. How to have more control of yourself."

"I believe you," Croix said softly, and it was probably the most truthful thing he had ever said in his life.

CHAPTER FIVE

Colleen watched from the bar. Turney had gravitated to a tall blonde, and they were in a dark corner, kissing. She felt weird watching. There was a slight tinge of something like jealousy, but she had never thought of Turney in a romantic way. Not really. Even that night when they'd tried to make love. He was just a friend.

As it was, she only saw him about once a month, sometimes less, when their paths crossed. And he was often so quiet and secretive. It was usually too much effort to get inside his head.

And now, she was giving him a place to stay. They were up close and personal. Here she was, even watching him being intimate with another woman.

"You want some popcorn?" the man beside her asked. "It might help you enjoy the show a little more."

Colleen turned, tried to smile. "I was just thinking about something."

"Thinking about that guy?" the man said. "I was hoping you'd think about me."

She looked into his eyes, tried to smile a little wider. "Well, I think that can be arranged."

She didn't know his name. Didn't want to know his name. *Ever.*

"Let's say we go somewhere else," the man said. "Somewhere quieter."

Colleen looked down at her glass. "Let me just finish my drink."

"Sure thing," the man said. He had dark hair that was going slightly gray at the temples. And a long face. He was dressed a little slicker than most of the men at the bar. Seemed a little cleaner. His smile told her he had caps, so he probably had money. But he came here, to this place, to get away from his life. From people who might know him. Colleen guessed that he probably led some kind of double life.

The bar was pretty full. There were people at the tables and lots of people standing at the bar. It was beginning to be a popular place. She went to different places every night. Some of them were quiet and dark, but sometimes she needed a place like this. The human contact.

She finished her whiskey sour and stubbed out what was left of her cigarette, and found herself looking in the corner for Turney, but he and the blonde weren't there anymore.

"You ready?" the man asked. His hand gently squeezing her arm.

"Yeah, sure," Colleen said. "Why don't we go to my place? It isn't very far from here."

* * *

Sam felt as if he'd done a good day's work on the way home. Another anguished soul would find peace, finally, thanks to him. It made the job worthwhile.

The subway car opened, and he held back a minute before he entered the fray. So far, it had been a good commute, and he didn't want to tempt fate. He let an old woman cut in front of him on the way out, thinking about the lady who had glared at him the day before, but feeling generous.

Once he got out on the platform, a teenager behind him was in a rush and slammed into him from behind. In hindsight, the kid didn't seem to have done it maliciously; he was just in a hurry and wasn't watching what the fuck he was doing.

But Sam whirled and grabbed the kid by the arm of his jacket. He couldn't have been more than fifteen. Sam held him tight, jerked him forward, and raised his other fist, ready to do some extensive damage to the kid's face.

But he stopped himself.

In his mind's eye, he saw the bones of the kid's face crushing in, spurting blood, as he struck him again and again.

But in reality, he stopped the fist. Did not let it surge forward. Maintained control.

"Hey, Mister," the kid said, pleading. "I'm sorry."

Sam stared deep into the kid's eyes. He felt his jaw tighten into a scowl of anger. He must have been quite a sight.

Sam hesitated. Then said, "Yeah, it's okay," and released his grip on the kid's jacket. The kid hurried past to join up with his friends, who had been just as surprised, and who had been too caught up in the moment to offer assistance. As soon as the kid reached them, the moment passed and he turned to shout a loud and quick, "Fuck you, Mister," before they moved in a group toward the escalator.

Sam stood on the platform, watching them go. Sorry that the incident had happened. But at the same time, wanting to run after them, and pound the whole group of them down into the concrete. Make them bleed and scream and beg for mercy.

Mercy that he found less and less within himself.

CHAPTER SIX

By the time he got home, Sam had stopped shaking.

Maggie was stretched out on the couch. She'd kicked her shoes off, removed her nylons, and was drinking a rum and Coke.

"Hard day?" Sam asked, plopping into the love seat beside her.

"Is there any other kind?" Maggie asked. "Shit, at least you stay put in the same office all day. I've got to run around the city like a chicken with its head chopped off."

"Believe me, the office isn't so much better. Sometimes it's downright claustrophobic. I feel like a prisoner. And all I ever see are people with problems. I keep worrying it's going to rub off on me."

"Okay, okay," Maggie said. "We both have it rough. Make yourself a drink and relax."

"Sounds good." He put his briefcase down beside the loveseat and went over to the kitchen. The rum was in the refrigerator. He put two fingers it in a coffee mug and then covered it with cola.

He sat back down. "At least you get to drive. I am getting real sick of the subway."

"Driving's worse. Traffic's been horrendous. You'd start getting migraines again if you drove."

"But the people on the subway. They're assholes. And there's so many of them. I go from a claustrophobic room to a claustrophobic train car. It's like being shipped off to Auschwitz every morning and afternoon. At least at night I know I'm coming home, so I can deal with it better."

"At least you've got your own practice. You're your own boss."

"You don't have it much different. You can do whatever you want every day. No one checks up on you."

"But I'm in sales. If I don't bust my hump each day and get as much done as possible, then I won't get a good commission. You have patients who need you, who come regularly. You don't have to sell yourself every day."

"You have regular clients, too. After all these years, people know you. You don't have to hustle like you used to."

"Hustle is right. Some times I feel like a whore or something."

"Come on now," Sam said. "It's not as bad as all that."

"Sometimes it really bothers me, gets to me," Maggie said.

"Then why do you do it? I make enough for both of us. You could stay home if you wanted to."

"And do what? Climb the walls. At least I'm good at selling. It comes natural. Even if I do hate it sometimes."

He knew she'd stay home in a minute if she had a reason to. If she had someone to take care of. A child. There was a time when they'd tried and tried, until the doctor told them what the problem was. They could have gone the fertility treatment route, or the adoption route. But she avoided both ideas, for some reason. Said it didn't matter. She wasn't the mother type anyway, she'd say. She liked to stay on the go. But he knew that if she really wanted to, there were other ways to become a mother. But he didn't push it. She'd come around to it in her own time.

Besides, he wasn't sure if he was ready to take the step toward parenthood, either.

"Want to eat out tonight?" Maggie asked. "I sure as hell don't feel like cooking anything."

"Sure. Or we can just get something delivered. That would be even easier."

"Sounds good," Maggie said. "My feet are real sore."

"Want to hear something? I was getting off the subway today, and this kid banged right into me. Didn't even say a word. And I grabbed him, and I came so close to hitting him, it was so weird. To be that close to losing it. I almost knocked the kid's head off."

"Fucking kids," Maggie said. "It probably would have done him some good. Shown him he couldn't just slam into people and get away with it. He probably knocks old ladies over, too."

"I know. But the funny thing is, I'm always so hung up on being in control, and I came real close to losing it. Pounding this kid's face in. It was something I really wanted to do. Something tempting."

"But you didn't. You stayed in control."

"But I *wanted* to lose it. I *wanted* to smash his face in. I really did."

"We all feel that way sometimes. It's totally normal. You were totally justified."

"I guess so," Sam said. "It was just funny. Here I am, making a living helping other people handle their anger, and I almost give in to my own and beat some stupid kid senseless."

"You're exposed to it every day," Maggie said. "It's bound to affect you on some level. And besides, you're still human. You have emotions just like anybody else. You aren't some kind of robot."

"I still thought it was funny. Funny *weird*. You don't know how close I was to giving in to it. It kind of scared me."

He took a long gulp of his drink.

"Don't worry about it," Maggie said. "You're entitled. I've felt the same way myself, a lot of times. You should see some of the asshole drivers I have to deal with on the road. If I had a gun, I would have probably killed someone by now."

"All the road rage out there," Sam said. "You're probably lucky no one's killed you, either. Some of the people driving today are animals. I should know. I treat a lot of them."

"Road rage," Maggie said, and laughed. "It's funny that there's a word for it now, isn't it? It's almost like we're giving people an excuse to act like crazies. Oh, don't worry if you overreact to someone cutting you off and try to kill them, you just have road rage. Everyone's got it."

"I know. I feel weird using the phrase myself. It sounds like bullshit. And maybe it is. But it's just so damned prevalent."

"I think it's just plain old rage. These people are angry all the time, not just when they're driving. And when we name it, make it a separate thing, we're giving them a way out. An excuse."

"Yeah," Sam said and drained his mug. "Hey, you want a refill?"

"Sure," she said, giving him her glass. "Why don't we order a pizza? I'm in the mood for one tonight."

"Sure," he said. "That sounds good. We can have it delivered."

* * *

Colleen opened the door to her apartment and turned on the light.

"Looks like we've got company," the man said. He was probably smiling, finding it funny, but she didn't look at him, she was looking at *them*.

Over in the corner, on the floor, Turney and the blonde were fucking. They were so caught up in themselves that they didn't notice the intrusion.

Colleen turned, "Let's go somewhere else."

"No," the man said. "We don't have to do that. They left us the bed free, after all."

She hesitated. He grabbed her arm and led her over to the bed.

At first it was awkward, but then, as they listened to the sounds Turney and the woman made on the floor, it actually got exciting, and they soon got lost in their own passions.

CHAPTER SEVEN

It was late, and Sam sat in his car, staring at the red light. Maggie had fallen asleep early, and he'd been finding it harder and harder to get to sleep himself. For some reason, driving around at night relaxed him.

Maybe I should start driving to work more often, he thought. Although it was always a hassle finding somewhere to park. And the traffic was murder during rush hour, not like now when there was hardly anyone one else on the road. He was just getting so sick of the subway. There was a feeling of freedom that came with driving, and he wouldn't have to go underground. Into the subterranean caverns below.

He also wouldn't have to deal with the assholes down there. Despite the convenience time-wise, sometimes he felt so trapped in subway cars. There were so many assholes in the world.

When the light changed to green, he didn't hesitate to step on the gas, and it became readily apparent that all the assholes weren't below ground. A car pulled out in front of him, from a side street, and cut him off. It was something he'd heard his patients bitching about a million times before. Most recently, Richard Croix had complained of a similar scenario. He said he'd almost cracked his dashboard, pounding on it in rage.

Sam found himself speeding up a little, to keep up with the offender. He didn't really feel angry. He just didn't want to lose the guy so quickly. He wanted to toy with him. Make him nervous.

The car took a right. Sam took a right as well.

When they stopped at another set of lights, Sam got out of his car and walked slowly over to the stopped car in front of him. He leaned over and looked in the window.

The driver was a middle-aged woman. She looked very tense, staring up at the lights. In her mind, she was probably praying for the light to change. Or trying to decide whether to drive right through it.

Sam stared in at her. And smiled. He was not going to lose his temper.

He motioned for her to roll her window down. She pretended not to notice.

He threw his fist forward, into the glass, shattering the window.

The light turned green, and the woman sped away as fast as she could.

Sam looked at his hand. There was some blood. Not much. He wrapped a handkerchief around it.

He non-chalantly got back in his car. There hadn't been any witnesses.

This didn't happen, he told himself.

He stepped on the gas and made a U-turn. Then he got back on the road that would take him home.

* * *

I don't know you, Maggie thought, as she stared at Sam's sleeping back. You would think after all these years that I'd feel some kind of comfort, in knowing who you are. But there isn't anything close to comfort here.

Sam was oblivious, asleep. He didn't know that Maggie was awake, watching him, thinking about what they had, and didn't have.

She thought about getting out of bed, then decided against it. She had nowhere to go. Not this time of night. She wasn't hungry and she didn't have to go to the bathroom. Why not just stay here, waiting for sleep to take her?

Waiting, until it just wore her out and left her exhausted.

It wasn't until recently that she had realized that she was afraid of him again. Not that there was any real reason for the fear. He never hit her anymore, rarely even raised his voice, and even then, he was so apologetic afterwards. So regretful that he had lost control.

Maybe that was it. His almost obsessive sense of control. He always seemed so tightly coiled. Like he was afraid that if he let his guard down, even for a moment, he might explode.

What did I see in you? she wondered. *How did we end up together like this?*

What was it about you that attracted me in the first place?

There was something about his intensity that was attractive. She had found his strong, silent personality very sexy at first. A man of few words and oh, so passionate in bed. And he was very good looking. It probably sounded shallow, but she couldn't deny that his looks were what really caught her attention, the first time they'd met.

There was always a sense of mystery about him. Sometimes, he could go days without uttering more than a handful of words. Other times, he'd go through phases when he got very talkative and he could barely bring himself to stop. Like earlier that evening, talking about the kids on the subway. But it didn't put her at ease. She could still sense something was wrong.

The conversation tonight had been a fluke. Even though they'd mainly just bitched about work, and the commute, it had given her a moment of hope. That maybe this thing was salvageable. But she knew it wouldn't last.

She resisted the impulse to wake him now, to barrage him with questions. Who was he really? What did he think about? How did listening to other people's troubles day in and day out affect him?

Why did he often go for long drives alone? Why did he work so late sometimes? Did people really go to see him at the office so late? She'd thought that maybe there was another woman, but she had a hard time believing that.

She wondered if things would have changed if she had been able to get pregnant; if that would have somehow brought them closer together. If it would have inspired him to open up more and share his feelings with her. Probably not. In fact, he might have grown even more distant. And she really wouldn't want to subject a child to an absentee father. She'd gone through that when she was a kid, and knew how painful it was.

She thought about getting up and getting a drink. But instead she turned over on her side, her back to him, and closed her eyes. It would be just a few more hours until morning, and she really needed to get some sleep.

* * *

Colleen woke up hot, naked and entangled in sheets. Her "date" for the evening was long gone. She sat up and saw Turney lying in one corner of the floor, wrapped up in the girl he'd been fucking. They were both sound asleep.

Colleen disentangled herself and got to her feet. As quietly as possible, she gathered some fresh clothes together and softly walked to the bathroom, but she started coughing once she reached the door. She covered her mouth as she went inside and closed the door, and turned on the shower.

She had a pack of cigarettes stashed in the bathroom, on the floor behind the toilet. She opened the pack and lit one up. *I guess I'll never be able to quit,* she thought as she puffed. *Every time I stop, the cough gets worse.*

When she got her coughing under control, she looked at herself in the bathroom mirror. There were creases around her eyes, and they were blood shot.

I'm looking old, Colleen thought, contemplating her reflection. *It's like I'm aging before my very eyes.*

Her gaze inevitably fell to her breasts. They were small. A-cups. And yet she had never had trouble attracting men. Her mother used to always tell her that a pretty face was the best thing a girl could have, and she had that. She had toyed with the idea of getting breast implants a few times, but there was never any need to touch her face. Looking at herself now, she was glad she had never gone the implant route. Not that she could afford it, anyway. She'd had moments where she felt insecure about her breasts, especially when she was growing up, but she'd learned to accept her body.

Got to do something about the eyes, though, she thought. They're bringing me down. Maybe I just need more sleep.

She stared at the water spraying from the shower and slipped under the spray. The
water washed her sweat away. The sweat that was starting to stink more and more of alcohol. She lathered herself up, and rinsed it all away. Then she lathered up again. It took a lot more scrubbing to get clean these days.

She found herself wondering if she'd had an orgasm the night before. There were faint memories, images of what they'd done, but the memories weren't tinged with any sense of pleasure. She couldn't remember the last time she'd felt anything really memorable.

She was turning into a *fucking machine*. Just going through the motions night after night, knowing how to move, how to sound, how to please, but reducing herself to some kind of robot in the process. A mechanical receptacle for come.

It felt nice, the touch of her fingers as she washed herself. So much different from the clumsy, rough touch of the men she brought to her bed. Her fingers were gentle, soft. *Her sex was like a soft flower opening to her touch*, she thought. Then she almost laughed. *That sounds like something out of a fucking romance novel.* But there was something oddly romantic about the moment. It reminded her of the first times she'd been aware of her sexuality, of pleasure. The first times she'd ever touched herself.

God, she thought. *To turn back time and start all over again.*

She closed her eyes and let herself get lost in the sensations. As she felt an orgasm approaching, she pressed her back against the shower stall and rode it out, breathing loudly.

You'd think I'd be sick of the lower half of my body by now, she thought afterwards. That I'd used it as much as I could. But instead, it's like I can never get enough.

But that wasn't really true. Quantity didn't equal quality. Random sex with faceless men didn't replace the level of intimacy she yearned for.

She bit her lip as the hot water softly stung her like a thousand gentle bees.

* * *

When she was done, she got dressed and slipped out of the apartment. Turney and his friend were still asleep on the floor. Lost in dreams.

CHAPTER EIGHT

After Sam had left for work, Maggie dropped her briefcase and went over to the redwood cabinet in the living room. She pulled open the door and looked at the liquor bottles within. Sam rarely drank anything but the occasional beer. Sometimes a shot of Scotch. The bottles were mainly gifts from the holidays. Most of them had remained full for years. Until recently.

She could not really explain the urge to drink. It had come upon her suddenly. It wasn't as if she had been an advocate for temperance before. She had always had that glass of wine to unwind with after a day of work. And her college days were almost a blur, because of so much alcohol consumed and pot smoked. Hell, it had started in high school. But, once the college days ended and the working world began, she had cut down a lot. Limited the amount of alcohol that entered her system. She was a married woman, after all. A responsible adult. She'd loosen the restraints a couple of times a year, at Christmas parties, on vacations. But the drunken incidents were few and far between. And she always regretted them afterwards. Especially if she'd gotten sick.

This was different. She was actually waking up, getting ready for work, the whole time thinking only about that first drink of the morning. Once Sam was gone to his practice, she was alone. And free to indulge. She grabbed the brandy decanter and sat down on the white leather couch. She kicked off her shoes, and opened it. She didn't even bother to get a glass. Drank it right from the bottle.

The taste didn't bother her anymore. She could drink anything.

This wasn't the first time she'd stayed home from work to get drunk. It was happening more often lately. After the first drink, she'd call in sick, and then she'd kick back and get sloshed, making sure she had enough time to sober up and take another shower before Sam got back home.

It had been an occasional thing at first. When she just couldn't face the world and she decided to take a day off. This was the first time she'd done it two days in a row. How much longer before it became a problem with her job? Before they fired her? Before she didn't bother to sober up and Sam caught her?

She couldn't say. But she knew it was going in that direction. And, honestly, she didn't care.

She had showered and dressed, but now she took off her dress and put it back in the closet, on a hanger. She went back to the couch, in her underwear and took a long drink from the brandy. Then she went to the phone and called her office.

"Hello, Mary?" she asked, hearing the receptionist's voice. "This is Maggie. I'm still feeling pretty awful and I won't be able to make it in today. Can you cancel my appointments for me?"

Mary said she would take care of it, and Maggie hung up the phone.

Then she went back to the couch and the bottle.

It was like there was a snake inside her, coiling around her insides. That's really what it felt like. *A snake that only got nourishment from alcohol.* That hungered for it.

A snake, or maybe more like a drunken tapeworm. Demanding sustenance.

It wasn't like her at all to do these things. She wasn't the kind of person to stay home and drink all day.

But she *was* becoming that kind of person, slowly but surely.

* * *

Jonathan Williams sat very tensely in the leather chair. His bandaged hand resting uncomfortably on his lap. Staring at the man's hand, Sam thought about the incident at the red light. When he'd struck the car's window. Strangely, his hand seemed to have healed overnight. It mustn't have been badly hurt after all. But there was a subtle, probably psychosomatic stinging along his knuckle line now, as he stared at the man's bandage.

"I don't know what came over me," Williams said. "I just lost my temper."

"These things happen," Sam said. "If you were the only person this ever happened to, I'd be out of a job."

There was a slight change in how Williams was sitting. Sam's last statement had made him relax a little. It was always comforting to know you weren't alone in feeling a
certain way.

"Start at the beginning," Sam said.

"It was Tommy, my son," Williams said. "He was playing ball near the house and almost broke the kitchen window. I told him to get away from the house, maybe three, four times, and he just wouldn't listen to me. He's at that awkward age, you know. No longer a child, but not really an adult, either. I can't blame him for being volatile. But if he lives in my house, I have to demand that he listen to me. Don't I?"

Sam nodded, but didn't speak.

"So he came real close to hitting the window. It bounced off the wall. But I was outside, you see, watching him, ready to yell at him. And his defiance, throwing the ball when I was standing right there. It just infuriated me."

"So you broke the window yourself," Sam said.

"How did you know? Yeah, I got so furious, I smashed the window with my fist. And I told him 'Is that what you meant to do, you little shit?' It scared him so much, he ran away. And for a moment, I felt good about that. Victorious, you know?"

Sam nodded.

"But then I looked at my hand, and saw all the blood. So much blood. My wife had to drive me to the emergency room. It took something like thirty stitches. I realized then that I had to do something about my temper. This just isn't rational behavior, is it?"

Sam thought about how it had felt, punching that woman's window. Seeing the spider-webbing cracks in the glass. Knowing that in that moment, she was not sure if she would live or die. And how he had let her live.

Sam leaned forward. "I don't want to pass judgment on your behavior, Jon. I really don't need to, do I? You realize that there's a problem here. You don't need me to tell you that. You've already identified the problem, so I won't waste your time. You came here for help. That, I can give you."

"I sure hope so."

"Is this the first time you've done something like this?" Sam asked.

"No, not really. I've broken things before. But I never hit my son. I never touched him. It was always objects, things."

"You're afraid that might change one day."

"Yes."

"Then I'm glad you came here. I can help you, John."

"I really do hope so."

"Tell me about some of the other incidents," Sam said. "As many as you can remember."

* * *

When Colleen got back to the apartment, Turney was taking a shower. His "companion" was nowhere to be found.

She sat down on the edge of the bed and waited for him to get done. She had been out walking, thinking about their situation, and she had decided that he had to leave. She knew she'd told him he could stay indefinitely, but she realized now she wanted her own space, and she was uncomfortable sharing it with him.

The sound of the shower stopped. The bathroom door was open. Turney got out and started drying himself with a towel. Colleen could see part of him, his side, but he was not yet aware she was back. Or, if he was, he didn't let on.

He came out into the bedroom, dragging the towel behind him. It was the first time she had seen him naked. *Really* seen him. She'd seen him tangled up with that girl on the floor the night before, and there'd been that time they'd tried to do it, but for some reason he'd insisted they kept the lights off then. She had never really seen him standing before her like this, totally exposed.

He was radiant.

There were a few scars, but they were the only evidence of a life spent mostly on the streets. His body was mostly free of fat, and there was definitely a muscle tone that contradicted the thought of him being malnourished. His nomadic lifestyle had not reduced him to an empty shell.

She found herself looking at his arms. Looking for tell-tale signs. Track marks. But they weren't there. If he was an addict, he wasn't into needles, or he'd kicked it long enough for punctures to heal. There was something about him that said addict to her, but she hadn't seen one sign to confirm it since he'd come to stay with her. She hadn't seen any sign of paraphernalia, either. No crack pipes; not even the discarded butt of a joint.

"Oh, Colleen, I didn't know you were back," Turney said, sounding embarrassed, but she couldn't tell if it was real, or him trying to act like he thought she wanted him to.

"Turney, we've got to talk."

"Can I get dressed first, Col?" he asked.

"Sure," she said. Watching him go over to the corner of the room, where his bag was. He started pulling out clothes. He made no attempt to cover his nakedness with the towel. In fact, he left the towel in the middle of the floor.

She could not help staring at his cock. It looked larger than she remembered it being. Unscarred and half-erect. He was enjoying putting on a show for her.

He had never seemed so beautiful before.

He pulled on a shirt, making sure to leave his lower body exposed. And turned to look at her. A knowing smile on his lips.

She tried to remember him in high school. A quiet, morose kid. Always sneaking away to smoke pot with his loser friends. She was one of the few girls who found that scene attractive. Who had hung out with them sometimes, when she wasn't hanging out with her own clique, other girls who had the label "slut" tattooed on their foreheads in the minds of the other kids. Strangely, though she had smoked pot and hung out with him sometimes, even having long marijuana-fueled conversations with him, Colleen had never fucked Turney back then. Had never even seen him as a sexual being.

Even that one time they'd tried to do it, years after they'd known each other in school, it just didn't seem real. It seemed like they'd done it more out of curiosity and for something to do rather than because of real desire. And of course, it had ended disastrously.

This was the first time she'd looked at him and really *wanted* him sexually.

He pulled some jeans up over his naked ass. "What did you want to talk about, Col?"

"It's about this place," she said. "It's kind of small for two people."

He sat down beside her on the bed, bounced a few times, smiling at her.

"It's kind of homey," he said. "I like it."

"Turney, I've been thinking about it," she said. "And I'm sorry, but I really need my space."

He did something then that surprised her. He reached under her skirt. He got a surprise, too, and grinned when he realized she wasn't wearing panties.

When he looked over at her, they were both smiling.

He rubbed her with his fingers. Staring into her eyes.

Then he pushed her back, kicking his jeans off. He pushed up her skirt. She did not resist. He climbed on top of her, penetrating her immediately, his cock now fully engorged.

She stared up into his face while he was fucking her. He had his eyes closed in concentration. His jaw was clenched tight.

He had no stamina. He came too fast. But she was on the verge of coming when he finished, and she finished herself off with her hand.

He rolled over on his back, panting softly, watching her.

CHAPTER NINE

He looked across at her. Her eyes were welling up with tears. They were entering some touchy territory. This was the original reason she'd come to him, after all. The time she'd struck her daughter in a fit of rage. It had resulted in a broken arm. Who knows what could have happened next, if she hadn't come to him for help?

There was a time when it was too painful for her to talk about. But enough time had passed for them to confront it again. Sam was sure she was strong enough now.

"I didn't know what had taken hold of me," the woman said, covering her eyes, and lowering her head in remembered shame. "I didn't want to do it. It was like someone else was doing it."

"No, Brenda," Sam said. "It wasn't someone else. It was you."

He had to make her face it. Head on.

"I know," she said.

"How do you feel now?" Sam asked. "These days? Do you still worry about flaring up? Are you still afraid of the rage inside you?"

"No," she said, between sobs. "Not anymore."

Of course not, Sam thought, almost smugly. *Because I'm a fucking miracle worker.*

"It's so much better now," she said. "It's easier to control the anger."

Sam almost smiled as he grabbed the tissue box and handed it to her. She plucked a tissue from the box and dabbed at her eyes.

"So you've made substantial strides," Sam said. "You should be proud of yourself."

"I have you to thank, Doctor Wayne," she said.

"I'm your guide. The actual journey is all yours."

Sam could feel a slight adrenaline rush.

He rose to his feet. "We'll talk in more detail about this next time. I'm sorry to say our time is up for today."

"Of course," she said, and stood.

He escorted her to the door, and opened it. She gave him a weak smile as she went to the lobby, still dabbing at her eyes. Croix was in the waiting room. Staring at Sam in the doorway.

"You can come in now, Mr. Croix," Sam said, glancing over at his receptionist, Carla, who had started talking to Mrs. Carlisle about her bill.

Sam stood aside and let Croix enter. He was a big man, and when Sam first met him, he thought he'd be a tough nut to crack. But, like all the rest, he was a rather easy victory. Already the man's body language was different. Gone was the stalking-animal walk that he used to dominate whatever room he entered. And he had simply stared when Sam came into view. On earlier visits, he had glared. He probably hadn't even realized he'd done it.

Sam thought that the man's eyes looked different. A clear sign of change.

Croix sat down in the chair Mrs. Carlisle had just vacated. Sam sat where he always sat.

"So tell me how you've been getting along," Sam said, opening the door to their conversation.

As the session began, Sam could feel the adrenaline rush again. Where it had been subtler with Mrs. Carlisle, it was more pronounced now. Sam could feel the hair on his body standing on end.

"I've been sleeping better," Croix said. "I can't remember how long it's been since I've really slept."

Sam smiled. "That's a good sign. Do you remember any of your dreams?"

As Croix spoke, Sam only half heard him. He was distracted with the energy he felt inside. Then he found himself looking around the office. It was so many steps up from his humble beginnings. The expensive carpeting, the furniture, the fine draperies that framed the windows. The sheer size of the office, compared to former ones he'd had. Even the waiting room was impeccable. Business was good.

Other people's rage had rewarded him well over the years.

* * *

There was some tension between them, despite the intimate connection. In fact, that unexpected interlude just made things more uncomfortable. Colleen still wanted Turney to move out, to give her space, but now she felt more reluctant to push it.

The place was too small for two people, and if Turney was down on his luck when he first showed up, there was no sign that this was going to change. He was not trying to change his life at all. He was not looking for a job. He never spoke of moving on.

I hope he doesn't think that we have some kind of relationship now, she thought, almost shuddering at the idea. Not that Turney was all that horrible. He was nice enough to look at. But he was so devoid of ambition, so content with his meaningless lot in life,

that she was afraid it was going to rub off on her, and make her even less likely to "take hold" of her life — as her mother had always been so fond of saying — and try to act like the adult she was.

She was afraid Turney would drain away what little ambition she'd been able to muster lately. Like some kind of ambition vampire. Like a walking, talking joint, always lit and always filling the air with sweet smoke, threatening to take you away to "I Don't Care" Land. That image almost made her laugh.

He'd gone outside for a while. When he came back, she had resolved to tell him once and for all; he had to move on. Maybe she'd take him out for a drink first, and soften the blow a little. But it had to stop now. Before it was too late.

Before she just gave up completely, and became like him. One step away from being homeless. In fact, he had gone through periods of homelessness, and would no doubt go through them again, maybe right after she gave him the heave-ho. But she couldn't think about that too much, couldn't worry about what happened to him. She had to be more concerned about what happened to *her*. She couldn't handle being out on the streets, without a place of her own, a sanctuary. It would drive her mad.

She sat on the edge of the bed, dressed to go out, and waited for Turney to get back from his adventures. Who knew what he was doing out there? Fucking, scoring drugs, looking for people he knew to hit up for money, maybe even panhandling.

He got back around seven-thirty. She was still sitting on the bed. It was dark, but she hadn't bothered to get up and turn on the lights. He was surprised to find her there.

"Whatcha doing?" he asked. "Sitting there in the dark?"

"We have some stuff to talk about," Colleen said. "How's about we go for a drink?"

"What kind of stuff?"

What was he thinking? Didn't he know she was going to ask him to leave, or did he have some half-baked idea she was going to declare her love for him?

"I don't want to talk here. I've been here awhile now. I want to go out."

"Yeah, sure," Turney said. "Just let me take a piss first."

It was like he just came back to use the bathroom. She didn't say anything as he walked past her. He didn't close the door. She still made no attempt to turn on the lights.

CHAPTER TEN

"So tell me," Sam asked. "How's the anger?"

Croix lowered his head and his mouth twitched. "It's better," he said softly.

"Good," Sam said, sounding truly thrilled. "That's very good news, isn't it. I mean, when you first started coming here, it sounded like anger ruled your life, and now, you say it's better. How much better?"

"I can't explain it," Croix said. "It just isn't there as much as it used to be. It's easier to breathe now."

"See, I told you there would be progress, that you would notice it right away, and not after years and years of therapy. I told you it would happen quickly, didn't I?"

"Yes, you did," Croix said.

"And you've already seen a big change. That's wonderful, Richard."

"Yeah, it's pretty good. The wife's noticed, too. She says I seem much calmer."

"Exactly. She couldn't help but notice. You were a hissing cobra before, always ready to strike. I'm surprised you never killed anyone, or got yourself killed. All these years of anger. I don't know how you got through it all unscathed."

Croix shrugged, not sure what to say.

"You're making remarkable progress."

"Thanks," Croix said, softly.

There was a noticeable change. This man used to be a ball of angry energy. His hands were always clenching and unclenching, always on the verge of becoming fists. His muscles were always tight. His jaw tight. His eyes glared. He had trouble speaking, expressing what he felt.

Now, he was noticeably calmer. He hesitated when he spoke and wasn't so quick to lose his temper. He was *tamed*.

Sam had done it so many times now; he just took it for granted. And it was taking less and less time.

I'm a bronco buster, Sam thought with hidden glee. *I tame wild horses for a living.*

Sam asked Croix about the past few days, and they had a quiet, calm conversation, until the session was over and it was time for Croix to go.

Sam leaned forward and shook the man's big hand. "You're making incredible progress, Richard. We'll beat this yet. Keep up the good work."

Croix smiled, pleased with himself.

He thinks he's doing it himself, Sam thought. He thinks I'm giving him the tools and he's doing all the work. He doesn't realize he is just clay for me to mold. *A wild horse for me to tame.*

The two men stood and Croix left the room. Sam closed the door and sat down in his leather chair.

"Remarkable," he muttered to himself.

* * *

They were out on the street. There had been more than just one drink. There were many drinks. They weren't walking very steadily. Early on, she'd explained about her need for space, her wanting him to move out. He seemed amiable enough about the whole thing, and suggested they enjoy one last bash before they parted. He even had money for a few rounds.

They had talked about high school, about how he'd always had a crush on her when they were kids, how surprised he was that she let him stay at her place. He really didn't try to change her mind, though. He seemed okay with her decision. It was just that the drinks brought up this wave of nostalgia and sentimentality. In both of them.

At first they were walking arm in arm, then they drifted apart, walking back toward the apartment. Colleen had agreed to let him sleep it off there, and he had sworn to move on come morning.

They didn't notice the man until they were upon him. At first, Colleen just saw him in her peripheral vision, and thought he was going to bump into Turney, but instead he grabbed Turney by the arm, held him, looked right into his eyes. Turney had a horrified look on his face. It was almost as if they knew each other.

The man's face was bright red with rage, and he was sneering. As he stood there, and Colleen stared at him, she got a sharp image in her head of two rattlesnakes biting each other over and over again. And something else, just out of sight, that she knew was even worse. It didn't last long, but the vision was so strong that it almost made her fall over, and it left her with a sharp pain in her head.

Turney struggled to get away but could not. Colleen couldn't really grasp what was going on, what with the pain and the alcohol and the shock.

The man squeezed tightly, and Colleen could hear the snap of bones breaking, and suddenly the man ripped one of Turney's arms free and threw it into the street. At first, everything seemed to happen in silence and then Colleen realized Turney was screaming. She was frozen, watching, her back pressed up against a wall.

The man grimaced as he gripped Turney around the throat and proceeded to crush his windpipe. The bones of his throat and spine were crunching beneath the man's fingers like an empty aluminum can, and then the hands ripped Turney's head free and the man raised it up, above his own. It was all so unreal. There was no way it could be happening. Turney, despite his lifestyle, was still young and strong. He was not easy prey. But here he was, helpless as this man tore him to pieces. Human bodies just didn't come apart that easily. Turney's blood gushed onto the sidewalk.

The man threw Turney's head at the wall beside Colleen, and she jerked away. It rolled near her feet. She imagined it spasming down there, the eyes blinking repeatedly, the mouth open as if gasping for breath, but she couldn't be sure if that was really happening. When she really stared at it, the head was very still.

Colleen tried to contain her fear. She looked right at the man who had done this thing. Who had killed Turney. She could see his face clearly.

Despite his rage, he seemed confused now, as if he were blind. Like he could sense someone else was there, but couldn't see her.

She felt a tickle in the back of her throat. The beginning of a cough. If she coughed now, he'd find her for sure.

She ran.

When she was a good distance away, she turned back, to see the man standing in the same spot. He was sort of looking in her direction, as if listening to the sound of her shoes hitting the street, but did not pursue her. Whatever the reason, Colleen considered herself lucky and continued to run as fast as her legs would carry her.

PART TWO

THIS GROWING RAGE

CHAPTER ELEVEN

B RUTAL MURDER SPREE CLAIMS FIVE, the headline read.
Sam had woken early enough to go down the block to the twenty-four hour convenience store to get a coffee and a newspaper. He even had enough time to read some of it. He felt awake and refreshed and better than he had in weeks.

The headline caught his eye. He read further.

The bodies were all found within the same six block radius. All had been brutally dismembered. The victims, two men and three woman were all found with their arms and legs ripped out. They were all decapitated. Several of the victims had been sexually violated.

Sam felt a shiver of revulsion go through him. *Horrible stuff,* he thought.

This is the third such incident in the last year and a half. Because of the brutality of the attacks, the killer has been referred to as "The Shredder." The police have not released any information as to whether they have any leads. The only witness to these horrific events said that he saw a man, but could not give any definite details.

The Shredder, huh? Sam thought. *If this murderer is so full of rage, perhaps he should come to me. I might be able to help him. Who knows, maybe he's already one of my clients.*

This thought made Sam laugh out loud for some reason. Hell, I should offer the police my services to help calm down violent cases. Not that it would pay as well as private clients.

But the thought intrigued him. He had been able to prove he had the talent. Even seemingly hopeless cases had bowed before his abilities. People with violent tempers that destroyed their lives. He had been able to change them, take the rage away.

Maybe what he really needed was a challenge. A real challenge.

"Sam," Maggie said, coming up behind him. "You're up early."

"Got lots to do today," Sam said.

She stood across from him. She looked so tired. "Are you leaving early today?"

"Might as well get an early start. I've decided to take the car today. I hope that's okay. I might as well get a jump on the traffic."

There was something odd about her this morning. Something he couldn't put his finger on.

"You sure you don't want me to give you a ride to work?" Sam asked.

"No, I can take the train for a change."

"Are you feeling okay, Mag?" he asked.

"Sure," Maggie said. "I feel fine."

"Well, I'm off," he said, rolling the paper to take with him. "Have a good day at work."

He kissed her briefly, grabbed his briefcase and headed out.

* * *

Maggie waited until he had driven away. The minutes seemed to last forever.

An early start, he had said. That's what she thought as well. There was a bottle of bourbon in the closet, and the seal hadn't been broken yet.

* * *

Jeremy sat back on the sofa, the leather sticking to his ass. His bathrobe had slipped open, and he resisted the urge to tie it up again. It never stayed tied for very long anyway.

The big-screen television was playing some inane talk show. People he didn't recognize were interviewing some pop star he'd never heard of and didn't care about. But he noticed he had an erection, and it was throbbing. Absent-mindedly, he reached down and grabbed it.

With his free hand he grabbed the remote control. He kept flipping channels, looking for something good, but it was the usual morning fare. Poorly drawn cartoons, stupid talk shows, infomercials for products he'd never use, reruns of old sitcoms he hadn't watched the first time they were on, old movies that had already started, more stupid talk shows.

He hadn't seen anything interesting by the time he was about to come. He dropped the remote control and grabbed the glass ashtray on the coffee table in front of him and ejaculated into it. His ashes floated in his semen. He squeezed out the last drops and put the ashtray back down on the table. He'd clean it out later. He wiped his dick on his bathrobe.

Jeremy grabbed the remote again and kept flipping. Nothing worth stopping for. He got up and lit a cigarette, then walked to the bathroom for a shower.

There was really no reason for a shower, for getting dressed. He had nowhere to go. But it was a ritual as old as time, and he had cultivated it because he wanted to retain at least the semblance of a real life. He remembered a time when he'd be out all night, drinking the best champagne and dancing with supermodels and movie stars. Now, he'd see an old conquest on television and try to remember what it was like fucking her. Wondering if she even knew he was still alive.

He stood in front of the big bathroom mirror, and looked himself over. Some days were tougher than others. Seventy percent of his body was covered in scars; even with the best plastic surgeons money could buy doing the work on him. But most of them were faint, he convinced himself. Hell, he was lucky to be alive. The plane crash had been a bad one. Everyone else involved had died instantly. But somehow he'd lived through it.

But was this living?

The only part of him completely unscathed was his dick. But how often did he get a chance to use it these days? His face was like some kind of mask of his former self. Enough of the handsome features of his past to make it clear who he was. But it was distorted now. A grotesque parody of who he had been. His lips were so thin, they were practically non-existent. Even now, he got accumulations of saliva on the side of his mouth when he spoke, which was distracting and humiliating. His eyes were too large. His nose bent a little to the left and looked misshapen. Skin grafts could only do so much.

One time he had been rich and appeared in the society pages. Now he was still rich, his one remaining blessing, but he had been absent from the newspapers for years. The crash had been news when it happened, but who really remembered it now? Most people probably thought he was dead or a recluse like Howard Hughes had been. Afraid to touch doorknobs or go outside.

When, really, it was pride. Pride over who he'd been. And shame over what he had become.

Look at me, he thought. *I'm fucking Frankenstein's monster.*

He stopped looking at himself. It was getting him depressed first thing in the morning. He turned on the shower and slipped inside.

* * *

Colleen got off the bus and started walking. She had been traveling blindly for hours. First, after Turney was killed, running away as fast as she could, then, once she had reached the terminal, she got on the first bus heading out, not caring where it was going as long as it was away from there. She wasn't out of the state, but she was far enough from the city now to start feeling safe.

As the bus groaned and drove away, she realized that she could see the ocean from where she stood. Along the street were large, ornate beach houses, built far apart from one another. The water behind them was so inviting.

She had no idea how she looked. In her flight, she had been on autopilot, oblivious to everything but the need to get away, to get to safety. Now, in a rare moment of lucidity, she looked down at her torn dress, spattered with tiny droplets of blood. It was obvious she had been up all night. She was surprised no one had tried to stop her or question her. Not that she would have been in any kind of state to answer questions.

Now, looking around, she was reminded of trips to the beach with her mother and sister, some of the few good times she could remember from her childhood. There was safety in that feeling. She tried not to think about Turney.

She wandered along the road. Some of it was covered with dirt and loose gravel. Colleen had a sudden impulse to jump into the water and wash herself clean. She cut across the lawn of one house, a lawn devoid of grass and covered with brightly colored tiles, and ran until she reached sand. Until she could see the water in front of her, beckoning.

She ran toward it. Her arms rose like those of a child, and she was crying out despite herself.

CHAPTER TWELVE

Jeremy was out on the back porch. He'd put on a pair of pants and a silk shirt, but his feet were still bare. There was something about the ocean that distracted him, calmed him. Something very necessary about it. He had to be here, near it.

He was smoking a cigarette, occasionally drinking from a glass of Scotch. Enjoying the brightness of the day and the brilliance of the water.

Suddenly, a woman darted out from beside the house, and ran toward the beach.

She was fully dressed and waving her arms around, shouting at the top of her lungs. Like a playful child. He was quite in awe of her. So much so that he didn't care that she was trespassing on his property, despite the clearly marked signs out front.

She ran into the water up to her waist and was jumping around. It looked like she was washing herself, washing her clothes.

He decided he wanted to know more, and walked down the porch steps to the sand, towards her, even though he had grown reluctant to interact with strangers since his accident.

When he was at the edge of the water, he called out to her, "Excuse me," he said. Then again, louder, "Excuse me?"

Colleen stopped her thrashing and turned to face him. She seemed very confused. He wondered if she was mentally disabled.

"I don't know if you noticed the signs," he told her. "But this is private property."

He took a long drag from the cigarette, followed by a gulp of Scotch.

She stared at him, and he couldn't be sure if she was trying to determine whether she knew him, or if she was scrutinizing his damaged face in curiosity. Her eyes on him made him feel uncomfortable.

"Are you okay?" he asked, wanting her to say something, wanting her to get her prying eyes of his face. "Do you need help?"

Her eyes seemed to become more lucid, as if she hadn't been aware of who or where she was at first, and then the knowledge slowly came back to her. She saw him staring and pulled her gaze away, looking embarrassed.

"S-sorry," she said, looking down into the water. "I didn't know."

She began to move toward shore. He suddenly felt very guilty that he'd intruded upon her private moment. That he'd sounded like the voice of authority, telling her *No*.

"No," he said. "It doesn't matter. Stay where you are. It's my property, and I don't have any problem with you staying in awhile longer. When you're done, come up to the house. I have some dry things there, and some cognac to warm you up."

Then he turned, and moved back toward the porch. The sand was warm against the soles of his feet.

When he got back up to the porch and looked out, he saw that she was still out there. She hadn't moved since he turned his back on her. Then, seeing that he was looking out at her, she submerged. She stayed under for several minutes, then broke the surface and emerged. She did that a few more times.

He watched her with curiosity, wondering how she had gotten here. Why she had chosen his part of the beach to dive into. Who she was, and if she was truly crazy.

Jeremy went inside and opened the bottle of cognac and poured her a glass. Then he got one of his clean robes and laid it across a chair. When he turned to go back out on the porch, he saw that she had left the water and was coming in the direction of the house.

He waited as she ascended the stairs with mild anticipation. She walked across the white planks of the porch and crossed the threshold of the glass sliding doors. He had an odd thought that she had just arisen from the dead and crossed this threshold into his world. The world of the living. Well, the *semi-alive.*

"You're soaking," he said, taking on a maternal, or rather *paternal,* tone that was alien to him. He hadn't heard himself talk that way before.

"Yes," she said, taking the robe from him, and putting it on.

"Take those wet things off first," he said. "The robe won't do you any good otherwise."

Like a somnambulist, she slipped her clothes off and let them drop to the carpet, then she put the robe back on and tied it. He took her things and went out to the porch and hung them on the rail. The sun would dry them quickly enough.

When he went back inside, she had found the glass of cognac, and was drinking greedily from it.

"I wasn't expecting you," he said.

"I know," she said. She smiled then. It was a good sign. "I want to thank you for your kindness."

"What made you go into the water like that?"

"I don't know. I've been traveling a long time, and when I got here, the urge just overtook me. I'm real sorry. I didn't mean to trespass."

"No big deal," he said. "Would you like a refill?" He nodded toward her glass.

She nodded, and he got the bottle.

"What's your name?" he asked.

"Colleen," she said.

"I'm Jeremy," he said. "Jeremy Rust."

He said his full name like it was something important. Like she should recognize it. And surprisingly enough, she *did.*

"*The* Jeremy Rust?" she asked, her eyes lighting up. "I used to read about you all the time...." She stopped. He assumed she remembered an account of the accident.

"I guess I was pretty notorious at one time," he said. "But that was a long time ago."

She brought the refilled glass to her lips. Jeremy had never seen someone so young and pretty gulp down alcohol so freely. It was like she was drinking milk.

But it did seem to calm her, and that was the desired effect.

While there was a certain thrill to being remembered, *The* Jeremy Rust and all that, there was also a certain sadness. What had he been known for, after all? Being young and rich and dating models and actresses. A celebrity by association. Sure, there had been some acting, awful acting at that. Mostly walk-on roles on bad TV shows. Roles given to him because of who he was more than what he was able to do. And that brief stint in the music biz, that hadn't amounted to much. But he had never been famous in his own right, not really.

He still had all the tabloids with his pictures in them. Back before he had become a parody of himself. They were all in chronological order in one of the closets. He would take them out sometimes to reminisce about what had been. There was a time when he appeared in their pages just about every week. The media always on the look out for who he was dating next.

Now he was a hermit, hiding out in a beach house. Afraid to show his face.

He watched Colleen as she drank the cognac. She was drinking too much, wasn't she? She would be drunk in no time if she continued at that rate.

But it really didn't matter. She was safe here. And it would be nice to have someone to take care of, even for just a little while. To keep his mind off what had happened to him. And she didn't seem too disturbed by how he looked now.

She was sitting on the leather couch, the glass in her hands, looking up at him. He realized he had been lost in thought.

"I can't believe it," she said. "Here I am, with Jeremy Rust."

"It's not that big a deal," he said. "My fifteen minutes ended a long time ago."

"What happened to you?" she asked. "Where did you disappear to?"

He smiled. With that practically lipless mouth of his. He could feel his bulging eyes watering again, and wiped them with his handkerchief.

Could she really not have heard? he wondered. *I thought it was everywhere. My most famous moment.*

"I got tired of all the public scrutiny," he lied. "I took myself out of the picture."

"So who did you end up with? Cindy? Naomi?"

"Unfortunately, my jet-setter days are over. My life's been very quiet these past few years."

God, he thought. *I would be shocked if any of them called ever again. It's like I've dropped right off the face of the fucking world.*

"Do you have a cigarette?" Colleen asked.

He tried to guess her age. Twenty? Twenty-two? He wondered if she went to the nearby college. But something made him think she was from much farther away.

"Sure," he said, searching for his Silk Cuts, the ones he got imported from England.

He walked over and put a cig in her mouth. She was very receptive. He lit it for her with his silver lighter in the shape of a mermaid.

The corners of her mouth formed a smile and she sucked in the smoke.

He refilled her glass with cognac. It was a pleasant feeling to be a host again.

"Would you like some ice?" he asked.

"No thanks," she said. "But I could use an ashtray. I don't want to get any ashes on this nice couch."

He handed her an ashtray, then noticed it was the green glass one with his semen inside. It was dried now, mixed with ashes. An odd-textured crust lining the bottom. He didn't care enough to wash it out. He handed it to her, and she was too buzzed to notice anyway, as she flicked her ashes inside.

"This is so nice," she said, and surrendered to a fit of the giggles. A sure sign that she was reaching her limit. Her eyes were half-closed.

Jeremy smiled and went out onto the deck, to look out on the water. When he returned, Colleen was asleep on the couch. Looking even younger and more innocent than she had awake. Luckily, the cigarette was in the ashtray. It was mostly ash and had burnt out.

He swept her up in his still-strong arms, (he certainly had enough time to work out regularly these days) and carried her to his bedroom, where he laid her on his king-size bed, surrounding her in pillows. Then he left the room, closing the door behind him.

He hoped she wouldn't vomit on his sheets.

CHAPTER THIRTEEN

Viv looked into the man's eyes, and it was clear to her that he wanted to die.

The motel room was unkempt. The sheets seemed clean, but little else. The cleaning woman was clearly dissatisfied with her work.

He sat on the bed, looking up at her, trying to smile.

Viv unbuttoned her blouse. She contemplated doing a kind of striptease, but he waved her over. He wasn't interested in preliminaries. He wanted to get right to the action. And his eagerness was catchy. Actually, it was more like desperation.

By the time she was down to her panties, he was naked, and stretched out on the bed. He had an erection and motioned for her to come over. To get on top of him.

She slipped off her panties and complied.

While they were fucking, she looked into his eyes and saw behind the desperation of his actions. Despite his current zest, something there told her that any fight he had in him had vanished. That he had lost the will to live.

She was on top. She was fucking *him*. She was in control.

They had not kissed. He had not even touched her breasts. All he wanted was to fuck. Cock to cunt, the only real contact left to him.

She did not even know his name. Not that it really mattered.

There came a time, there always did, when something changed. When it wasn't just about sex anymore. Usually when her lover felt the first signs of impending orgasm. They were the most vulnerable then, and they would look into her eyes, and something would *change*.

And the whole world would flip upside down.

Viv could not really explain it. It was a feeling, like she was mentally searching for a lock, a lock she had a key to, deep inside the person she was fucking. Deep in their very soul. And she would insert the key, and turn it. Just like she did now.

The man's face, on the verge of pleasure, contorted. This wasn't the way an orgasm felt. This was something different. Something more. A new level of pleasure. With the turn of the key in the lock of his soul, new sensations flooded his senses. The orgasm was at the center, but these new sensations emanated from that, outward like waves. Building, emphasizing, then glowing red hot.

There was a point when she got inside their heads, where she could feel what they felt, and see glimpses of thoughts, but emotions were much stronger.

The man's face looked almost in pain. She had seen it so many times before. But it wasn't pain. It was just the look of too much pleasure. More than was humanly possible to assimilate.

"It's okay," she said softly, still on top, still pumping. "It's almost over, now."

He did not try to speak. He just closed his eyes and got lost in the feelings. The orgasm became a snowball, rolling and getting bigger and bigger. So big that he didn't believe he could contain it, but she could.

It was at that point, that he knew it was an unstoppable force. That there was no coming back from it. This was what it felt like at the very edge of death.

"Thank you," he said, so softly she wouldn't have heard him if she didn't know to listen closely. If she hadn't leaned in and pressed her ear to his lips.

The lock inside him opened completely then, and the floodgates poured forth, and he felt pleasure like he never had before. Overwhelming ecstasy.

And then he was dead.

At that moment, her own orgasms began, one after another, and she held him tight as the sensations rippled through her. As she absorbed his soul. She clenched her teeth tightly, but sounds still escaped as she rode them out.

When it was over, she closed his glassy eyes and slid off him. The amount of semen he'd ejaculated at his last moment was phenomenal. His pubic hair was thick with it. She needed a long hot shower, right away.

In the shower, she closed her eyes and remembered when they had met, in the bar. He'd told her that his wife had just left him, and she'd taken the kids with her, and he didn't want to go back to an empty house. He had been trying to make it work, but it just wasn't happening. He used to have a horrible temper, but he didn't anymore. It was amazing how forthcoming he had been, but they'd had a lot to drink before they came here. It was funny how, even talking about such intimate things, they hadn't exchanged names.

After her shower, Viv got dressed and then went through his things. There were some credit cards in his wallet, but she didn't touch those. There was some cash. Two fifties and five twenties. She took the twenties, and left the fifties behind. Most importantly, she found out his name. *Richard Croix.*

She felt no guilt over what had happened, as she cleaned up after herself, removing all the traces she could that she had been there. She did not like to be in the same room with corpses for very long. She pulled the sheet up over him.

Viv pulled her cowboy hat down over her eyes and left the motel room. She walked down a stretch of road until she reached a gas station. She took her time. There was a phone booth there. An old-fashioned one, with a real closing glass door. She called the number of a local taxi that was in big yellow letters on a sticker attached to the phone.

Ten minutes later a cab came to take her away.

CHAPTER FOURTEEN

"I got so angry," Brenda Carlisle said. "And my first instinct would have been to strike out, to hit her, but I didn't. I maintained control. I grabbed her, and hugged her instead."

Sam sat across from her, watching her as she spoke with her eyes closed. It was so emotional for her to relate these events. She couldn't distance herself in the telling. It was like she was reliving them all over again.

"Wonderful," Sam said. "Amazing progress."

"I know," she said. "And I have you to thank for reaching this point."

"We have reached that point *together*," he said. "I was merely the guide. You did all the hard work. It is your achievement, Brenda. Completely yours."

She was crying. "I am so happy. It's so hard to control myself."

"You've come a long way, Brenda," he said. "It's bound to be overwhelming."

She lost the ability to speak. Her words replaced with sobs.

He sat there, uncomfortable, watching her. It was satisfying to see he could help these people, but it was so awkward sitting across from them when they broke down. He just didn't know what to do with himself.

He watched her breasts quiver as she sobbed. He imagined taking her here, right in his office. Tearing her clothes off and fucking her until she screamed. It was an image that passed quickly.

She wiped her eyes. "I'm sorry. It was just such an incredible moment."

"I totally understand. You should feel good about it. It was a definite leap forward."

"I don't know how my temper got so out of control. But I can't thank you enough for helping me find my way back."

He almost blushed. He wasn't sure if it was because of her words, or because of his rape fantasy.

"You've made incredible progress," he said, knowing damn well it was all because of his abilities, and growing very tired of this session. It was good that his talents really worked. But did he really have to sit here and listen to his patients slobber?

He looked at his watch. "Time's almost over," he said. Then, "I'm sorry. Take some time to compose yourself."

She wiped her eyes. He almost smiled. He really didn't need to see her anymore. He'd cured her. Rather, she'd gotten to the point where she no longer interested him. But he had to make a living, so he'd use this progress to keep her coming. He knew it would be tough, each time he saw her, keeping himself from throwing her down onto the carpet and ripping her clothes off. Stabbing her repeatedly with his cock. It was the only thing left she could possibly offer him.

But, he was, after all, a professional.

She maintained some kind of composure and stood up. "Thank you, Doctor," she said. He did not correct her. He'd never gotten his Ph.D. But then again, he didn't need it. He could do more than psychiatrists could, with their degrees and their pills. Sam had *the talent*. Had the ability to *really* heal. What did medication do? Just mask the symptoms. He fucking *healed* his patients from within. If anyone deserved the title doctor, didn't he?

"You're welcome," he said. "You're very welcome." He took her hand and squeezed it, ever so reassuringly, and led her to the door. He opened it for her, and led her out to the lobby.

He brought her over to Carla's desk. "Please confirm Mrs. Carlisle's appointment for Thursday." He smiled at both women and went back to his office, ignoring the other patients waiting.

* * *

When Colleen woke up, she was alone. She was in a ball in one corner of a large, king-size bed, rolled in the sheets like a burrito. She was still wearing the bathrobe, too.

Faint light came in from a partially-open window. A mild sea breeze wafted in. She could smell the salt. There was a lamp near her, beside the bed, and she reached out and turned it on.

The room was a mess. There were clothes strewn on the floor, hanging on a straight-backed wooden chair in front of a closet door. There were magazines and newspapers in piles against the wall. Large, oversized, leather-bound scrapbooks that looked like the family albums her mother had kept stashed away for nostalgic sojourns. And books. Stacks of books.

As she sat up, she remembered how she'd gotten here. She remembered Jeremy Rust. She remembered her excitement at meeting him, after reading about him for so long in the tabloids, in the celebrity magazines.

As her feet reached the floor, and she stood up, a sharp cramp and a hint of moisture made her realize that her period had arrived. There was a bathroom at one end of the room. She tied her bathrobe closed and headed there, closing the door. After she switched on the light, she hurriedly sat on the toilet and looked around the room. She was amazed at how big it was. The fixtures were shiny brass. The shower stall had ornate angels carved above the entrance.

Where's my purse? she wondered as she wiped herself. *Did I even remember to stick some tampons in there? I must have seen this coming.*

She rolled up a wad of toilet paper and put it between her legs. She'd stained the robe. These kinds of things didn't happen to her as often as they did when she was a teenager, but they always unnerved her. Being caught unawares always made her feel small and stupid. Vulnerable.

She scrubbed the spot on the robe, only succeeding in making it a bit fainter.

She didn't even have a change of clothes. When Turney was murdered, she'd just run away as far as she could. Without a second thought. Without really stopping to think and plan what she was doing. It was like she had suffered a tiny nervous breakdown, and lost all sense of reason for twenty-four hours.

I don't belong here, she thought. *I'm an intruder.*

And, at that instant, she suddenly became very afraid that she'd left a stain on Jeremy's bed.

She threw open the bathroom door and ran to the bed, lifting the sheets to examine for stains. There were a few drops, and she went to the bathroom and got a wet paper towel and wiped furiously at the spots. It wasn't that bad. He probably wouldn't even notice them.

I wasn't even wearing any underwear, she thought. *And where are my clothes?*

She searched through his bureau and found a pair of briefs to slip into.

She went to the door that led out of the room and hesitated before she opened it. She had a strange premonition that Jeremy would be standing there on the other side, waiting for her. But he wasn't.

The house was dark.

She went down the hallway and then she turned and could see through the sliding glass doors that led out onto the beach. She could see the rolling waves.

"You're up," Jeremy said, surprising her. He seemed to appear out of nowhere. "I was worried about you. You've been asleep awhile."

"I'm sorry," she said. "I didn't realize."

"No problem," he said. "I think it did you good."

"I didn't mean to stay so long," she said. "I didn't mean to take advantage of your kindness."

"Not at all," Jeremy said. His eyes were watering. He dabbed at them with a tissue. "I appreciate the company."

"I've got to go," she said, not knowing where she could go. She didn't want to go back to that neighborhood, where she'd seen Turney die. But she'd have to go back and get her stuff eventually; she couldn't put it off forever. Another option was to go to her mother's house for a while, but that filled her with just as much dread. There were too many bad memories of that place. What she really wanted to do was stay here for as long as she could. Far away from all the things she feared. She felt safe here.

"You don't have to," Jeremy said.

She just stood there, not knowing what to do next.

"You seemed *so* upset before," Jeremy said. "So out of sorts. You really don't have to hurry out, do you? You can stay here awhile. Take a break before you go back."

His kindness touched her on a level that almost made her cry.

"I really shouldn't," she said. But then remembered how long she had traveled, how far away this place was from where she lived. And night was falling.

"I insist," Jeremy said. "If you want to, I really want you to stay."

"I didn't bring anything with me," she said. "I don't have any other clothes."

"Don't worry. Viv might have something."

Viv? she wondered. *Who is that? I thought he lived alone.*

"Did you notice if I brought my purse with me?" she asked. "Where are my clothes?"

Just then, someone was outside the sliding glass doors, looking in.

"Viv's back," Jeremy said. "Please stay and meet her."

She really didn't want to go out into the night. It would take forever to get back to her apartment. And maybe Turney's killer was looking for her. The buses ran so seldom at night. She wasn't even sure what time it was.

"Okay," she said, as Viv opened the glass door and came inside.

As the door opened, Colleen could hear the roar of the waves outside.

CHAPTER FIFTEEN

The kid was very tense as he sat across from Sam. He looked like a cornered animal. There was an odd look in his eyes. Clearly, he wasn't here because he wanted to be. Normally, Sam didn't see patients so late in the day, it was already getting dark outside, but the boy's mother had insisted it was urgent they start sessions right away.

"So Charlie," Sam said, debating the best way to start. "Your mother tells me you have a hard time controlling your temper." *Might as well get right to the point.*

"She's a liar," Charlie said. He adjusted his long hair, and it hid his eyes for a moment. His mouth was a scowl. "There's no reason why I should be here."

"Well, I'll tell you Charlie. You don't seem real calm to me."

"I don't want to *be* here, don't you see? Who's going to be calm somewhere they don't wanna be?"

"Makes sense," Sam said. "I'd feel the same way."

"That bitch lied to you. We've been having problems, sure we have. But there ain't nothing wrong with my head. I don't need to see a shrink."

"So you really don't see any point in being here?"

"You got that right."

"Well, why do you think your mother would lie about that?"

"Who the fuck knows? She's the one who should be here."

"Do you think your mother's crazy, Charlie? Do you think there's something wrong with her?"

"How the fuck do I know? I got some fancy degree?"

"You can't tell by the way she acts? The way she talks?"

Charlie stared straight ahead. "I don't want to talk about her. This is a fucking waste of time."

"You know, you might be right. But I have to at least pretend like I'm trying to help you, don't I? Can't go taking money for nothing, can I?"

"Fuck I care."

"Stand up," Sam said.

Might as well stir things up, he thought.

"What?"

"You heard me. Stand up."

"What the fuck for?"

Sam got up from his seat and went over to where Charlie was sitting. He looked down at him. "Stand the fuck up, Charlie."

"You fucking with me?"

"You got that right."

Sam felt something crackling just under his skin. This was exhilarating.

Charlie stood up, right in front of him. Their faces almost touched.

"You wanna start something right here?" Charlie asked. Something in his voice told Sam he was waiting for a word. An excuse to strike out.

Sam smiled. There was a tingling along the length of his spine. He wasn't sure what to do next, but he didn't want the feeling to end. The air was crackling around them and Charlie felt it, too.

Charlie reached under his jacket, and pulled out a knife. "Get away from me, or I'll cut you!"

"Put it away," Sam said, stepping back a bit. "And let's talk about how you're feeling right now."

"Fuck that. *Don't you dare put your hands on me.*"

"Calm down, Charlie, I'm not going to hurt you."

"You bet you're not!"

Charlie lunged at him. Sam first disarmed him of the knife, then he had Charlie in a tight hold. The kid was struggling.

"I thought you didn't have a bad temper?"

"Fuck you!"

"Calm down, Charlie," Sam said. "And let's talk about it."

There was an electric transference. Something was subtracted from Charlie and added to Sam. Sam felt Charlie go limp. It only lasted a moment, but it was enough to take the fight out of him. Sam put him back in his chair.

He stood there, watching. Charlie seemed subdued, and a little dazed. Sam could feel a tingling throughout his body. He hesitated a moment before he went back to his own chair.

"So we had our little confrontation," Sam said. "You knew it was going to happen sooner or later. Better sooner, I say. Now that we have this bullshit out of the way, we can talk seriously about why you're here."

"Fuck you." Charlie said again, softly this time, his eyes looking glazed over.

"You've got a temper, Charlie. It's so obvious that it's a joke to deny it. The first time I laid eyes on you, I saw it. The anger. The only way to get it under control is to learn to deal with it."

Sam felt a sudden rush of adrenaline wash over him. He tried to resist smiling, since it might antagonize Charlie more, but it felt so good. He tried to keep his face rigid.

"I don't wanna talk about it."

"I don't care *what* you want, Charlie," he said, finding it difficult to talk, to concentrate. "You're here to learn how to control yourself, and I'm the guy to teach you."

Charlie stared at the wall, saying nothing.

"Why all the anger?" Sam asked. "What do you have to be angry about?"

Charlie laughed. "What do I have to be angry about?"

"Yeah."

"Man, I got so much anger inside of me, I can't even get away from it in my sleep. It's like I'm always wound up tight. I don't know how to fucking turn it off." The dazed look in his eyes was gone now, replaced by the fire. He was himself again. A match always on the verge of being struck.

"Tell me more, Charlie."

"I hear all this bullshit about road rage, air rage, black rage, white rage, male rage, female rage, kid rage. Fuck, man, I got fucking *life rage.* Just being alive makes me pissed off all the fucking time."

"How long have you felt like this?"

"All the fucking time I can remember. When I was a little kid, I was mad all the fucking time. They gave me some bullshit pills to mellow me out, but it never changed anything. It just kept me dopey. Then I get older and they say I'm too old for those pills, time to grow up. But the rage, it's still there, you know? It didn't just go away."

"You must get in a lot of fights."

"Fuck, yeah. People get in my face; I make them wish they hadn't. I've even been arrested a few times."

"Are all these fights justified? Do these people always do something to you, asking for it? Or do you ever attack anyone for minor offenses? Petty shit?"

"What's petty shit? Someone fucks with me, that ain't petty. Someone gets in my face, that's enough to justify my actions."

"I hear you attacked an old woman once. What did she do to you that deserved you putting your hands on her?"

"She was yelling at me. Waving her arms like she was going to touch me or something. I didn't give her the chance, the fucking bitch."

"Sounds scary," Sam said. "Some old woman. Lucky she didn't kill you."

Charlie looked at him. "Shut the fuck up."

"You always so fucking articulate?" Sam asked. "This the way you talk to people in day to day life? Your teachers, your mother?"

"I talk to people how they deserve to be talked to."

"Well, that's all going to change, Charlie. You just need some guidance, that's all. It's a good thing your mother brought you here. I'm an expert in these things. She told me you almost went to jail for a few years. Somehow, you got out of it. But I don't see that lasting. You'll have another run in with the law soon enough. If you keep up like this, they'll lock you away for a very long time."

"What the fuck do you care?"

"I'm here to help you, Charlie. And that's what I'm going to do."

Charlie said nothing. Sam sat there, watching him. Neither of them said a word for a while.

Then Sam looked at his watch. "The session's over. You can go now."

"That's it?"

"Well, it's just the first visit. It's just an introduction, that's all. We'll do some real work next time."

"There won't be a next time."

"You'll be back. If you don't come back, you won't have a chance in hell. You'll end up in prison or dead. This is your only other choice."

"I'll take my chances," Charlie said and stood up. Sam stood as well. Charlie hesitated, like he wasn't sure if Sam would push him back down again.

"Where's my knife?" Charlie asked.

"I'll hold on to it. You come again, you'll get it back."

"Fuck that."

"Good bye, Charlie. We're through for today. You won't be needing that knife today."

"It's mine."

"So go buy another one. You come in here from now on, you leave any weapons outside. I don't want that shit in here."

Charlie looked around, on the floor, and then shrugged and went to the door. He opened it and turned around. Sam was standing where he had been. He hadn't moved.

Charlie scowled and left the room. Sam watched the door close.

Then he actually jumped up and down. He had never felt so energized in his life.

This is going to be good, he thought.

* * *

"Colleen," Jeremy said. "This is Viv."

Viv removed her hat, and, right away, Colleen noticed something strange about her. A glow. It was similar to the glow that surrounded the killer who had torn off Turney's head, but instead of filling her with fear, this glow was less threatening. And yet, it was there. It wasn't like she saw such things every day. In all her life, she had only seen two. First, Turney's murderer, and now, Viv.

For a moment, deep in the glow, there was a vision. A pattern. Like strands of ivy entwined upon her brow, and then the pattern was gone. The glow remained, but it was fainter now. Colleen could see Viv's face clearly. She was very pretty; possibly she'd been a model at one time. With short, blonde hair.

"Is something wrong?" Viv asked.

"Colleen," Jeremy said. "Are you okay?"

"Sorry," she said, realizing she had been staring intently. "I thought you looked familiar for a moment."

"Hmm," Viv said. "Sorry. I don't remember you."

"No, it's my mistake," Colleen said.

Viv turned to Jeremy. "Well, nice to meet you and all, but I've really got to get some rest. I haven't slept in *days*." She moved past them and down the corridor.

At the end of the hall, a door closed, almost a slam.

"I'm so sorry," Colleen said. "I didn't mean to stare."

"It was kind of an uncomfortable moment," Jeremy said. "Is something wrong?"

"No, not really." Colleen said. "I don't want to talk about it. You'll think I'm nuts."

"No I won't," Jeremy said. "Really. I want you to talk to me."

She sat down on a chair in the darkened living room. Very conscious of feeling physically uncomfortable. "Can I please have my clothes?"

"Of course," he said, and went out onto the porch. Her clothes were drier, but still a bit damp.

"Did I have a purse with me?" she asked.

"You don't remember?" he said, then, "No, I don't think so. I can look around. Maybe you left it down by the water."

"You don't have to do that," she said, but he had already gone outside. The open sliding doors letting the sound and the smells of the ocean in. She could see him from where she sat, moving down the beach.

What am I doing here? she wondered. *How did I get here?* But at the same time, she was glad she'd made it here. That she'd met Jeremy. He seemed so nice.

He came back in, holding her purse. "It's wet, I'm afraid. It was floating against some rocks."

She took it from him. "Thank you."

"You're not serious about wanting to leave, are you?" he asked. "It's late, and I really wish you'd at least stay here until morning."

There was nowhere else she wanted to be. "Okay," she said. "Thank you."

"What were you going to tell me?" he asked. "Before I went to get your purse?"

"It's been so horrible," she said. "I don't know where to begin."

"Start wherever you want. Wherever you can remember."

"Okay," she said. "But I really need to go to the bathroom first."

* * *

"I saw my friend killed right in front of me."

She was wearing her clothes now, and she'd found some dry tampons in her purse and had been able to replace the toilet paper. *That* made her feel a little less self-conscious at least.

Jeremy was sitting on the sofa, across from her. "Sounds like the kind of thing that would shake you up a bit."

"This guy, he grabbed Turney, my friend, and tore him apart right in front of me. Ripped his head right off." She took a long drag of her cigarette. She could feel her heart beat faster even thinking about what had happened to Turney.

"I remember reading about something like that in the paper. Some kind of psycho. Sounds almost unbelievable, someone being able to physically do something like that."

"After it happened, I just ran and ran. I didn't want him to grab me next. I just remember running, getting on a bus. It's all a blur now. But somehow, I ended up here."

"It makes sense now," he said, softly. Then, "Why did you have such a strange reaction to Viv?"

He said it almost as if he were concerned about the answer. As if he thought it was possible Viv had been involved somehow in the horrors Colleen had endured.

"The man who killed Turney," Colleen said. "He had this strange glow around him. I'd never seen anything like it before. And, for a moment, I had a vision. There was something superimposed over his face. Rattlesnakes."

Jeremy poured her a glass of red wine, handed her the glass.

"When I first saw Viv, she had a glow, too. And I saw another vision. But it was different, kind a weird pattern. Viv's wasn't threatening. She was more...I don't know. But the fact that it was similar; it scared me."

Jeremy watched her drink.

"I'm so sorry," Colleen said. "I didn't mean to insult her."

"I don't think Viv will even remember," Jeremy said. "She was tired. I haven't seen her for days. I think sleep was all she had in mind."

"Is she your wife?" Colleen asked. "Maybe I remembered her from one of those magazines. Is she a model?"

"She modeled for a little while. I don't think she liked it much," Jeremy said. "But no, she's not my wife."

"I'm sorry," Colleen said. "I'm saying all the wrong things."

"Not at all," Jeremy said. "No reason to chastise yourself. You just assumed we were *involved*. She does live here after all, when she wants to."

"So she's not your girlfriend?" Colleen asked.

"Not that I haven't thought about it," Jeremy said, with a slight smile. "But she won't have anything to do with me."

CHAPTER SIXTEEN

Maggie was asleep on the couch when he got home. He had seen it once before, and thought it was odd. This time puzzled him even more.

She normally got home from work just before he did. Usually, she'd be caught up in a flurry of activity: changing her clothes, getting something to eat, checking the answering machine.

He walked over to her, softly. There was something on the floor beside her. An empty bottle. He'd kicked it with his foot before he noticed it. He bent down and picked it up. It was a bottle of Macauley Brothers' bourbon.

Sam was tempted to shake her awake. But instead, he let her sleep. He put the bottle on top of the coffee table. It would be the first thing she'd see upon waking.

Then he went into the bedroom to change.

When he was in more comfortable clothes, he came out. She was still asleep. He was hungry and decided not to disturb her. He was tempted to take her pulse, check her breathing. But he could see her chest moving. She was still alive.

In order to get in this state, she had to have enough time. Chances are she hadn't gone to work at all.

They had an argument once, when his practice started getting successful. He had told her she didn't need to work anymore. She had insisted that she wanted to, that the life of a housewife would drive her crazy with boredom. In the end, he had given in to her, agreed she should keep her job. He didn't remember why it was so important to him that she stay at home. Some kind of misguided concept of gender roles. He was finally successful and wanted her to reap the rewards of not having to work anymore. He had worked his whole life, and while it could be a pleasure now, like his session with Charlie today, it could be tedious too. And he'd had enough jobs in the past where he couldn't wait to leave; he'd just assumed she felt the same about hers.

The argument hadn't lasted long. And he'd given in readily enough.

But now, to see her like *this*.

This was a side of her that she'd somehow been able to keep secret. A side of her that disturbed him.

The last time he'd caught her asleep in the middle of the day, she'd said she was sick. It was plausible enough. He didn't remember smelling alcohol on her that time, and there hadn't been an empty bottle on the floor beside her. Now he wondered if this was the start of a regular thing. If he had simply failed to notice the warning signs.

My wife is a drunk, he thought, watching her sleep.

He could have easily made a scene and confronted her. But this was not the time. He simply decided to go out to eat. She probably needed the sleep.

He went out to the car. Despite his training, he wondered how he should handle this. After all, she wasn't one of his patients. She was his wife. And how he handled this one would affect him as well.

* * *

I wonder if he thinks I'm nuts, talking about glowing and visions and everything, Colleen thought. *But he didn't even question me when I said it. He really seemed to believe me.*

The television was on. One of those big-screen plasma numbers. An old movie called *All About Eve* was on. She'd always wanted to see it, but never had. He seemed happy to show it to her.

But she wasn't really paying attention. She was too wrapped up in her thoughts. Going over the conversation they'd had in her mind.

She was on the sofa now. He was asleep on a big, leather chair. It had to be almost midnight.

Viv was still in her room. The door was closed. She hadn't come out to eat or anything. And she didn't make a sound. Colleen assumed she was sleeping, too.

Colleen didn't feel tired at all. The nap she'd had on Jeremy's bed had been more than enough. She was wide awake, but having difficulty focusing on the movie. Not that it was bad. At first she'd been very interested. She really liked Bette Davis. But so much had happened in the last twenty-four hours that there was no way she could just sit still and watch a movie.

She quietly got up off the sofa and moved toward the sliding glass doors. She wanted to be outside, near the water. She wanted to walk along the beach, and get away from her thoughts.

Slowly, she opened the door and slipped outside. She slid the door closed behind her. She'd brought a pack of cigarettes with her and lit one as she stood on the deck. There was a breeze. She took a drag and descended the stairs.

The moon was almost full and the beach at night was beautiful.

* * *

Sam woke up sweaty and breathing hard. He'd had one of his nightmares again.

Not that he remembered any of it. There was just a jumble of blurred images. While he was actually *dreaming*, though, it had been horrible. He could still feel the terror. His chest felt tight.

He turned over. Maggie was sprawled beside him, oblivious. She'd come to bed some time during the night. There was a time in their marriage when she'd wake up when he had his nightmares. When she'd hold him close until he went back to sleep. Sure, there was something Oedipal about all that. Having Mommy close by when he was afraid. He wasn't afraid to face his Freudian demons right in the eye. But that didn't make it any easier to lose that comfort. To see Maggie unconscious and oblivious to his needs.

He wondered if she'd snuck more drinks before coming to bed.

What am I going to do? he asked himself. *Subject her to daily urine tests?*

He wasn't going to do anything to rob her of her dignity. But he couldn't just sit by and watch her descent into the maelstrom. He was a therapist, after all. He had to confront her on this, talk to her. Get her to tell him why she was acting this way.

They'd grown apart these last couple of years, since his practice started growing by leaps and bounds. His success seemed to coincide with her decline. Was this some sort of strange competition? Or was she merely crying out for his attention?

It's like she's giving up, he thought, hoping he was wrong.

She gently stirred in her sleep. One of her hands absently rested on the side of her mouth as she half-turned.

He moved up close to her and wrapped an arm around her. Despite the current distance between them, he still loved her. He could still remember what had drawn him to her, the way he felt about her back when they were both younger. And how those feelings grew.

Sam wasn't going to let her fall. He wasn't going to let her hit bottom.

"I'm here," he said softly, squeezing her. Could she even hear him?

He lay there, awake, his arm around her. Hoping his holding her while she slept gave her some kind of subconscious comfort of her own.

He closed his eyes, trying very hard to keep his mind blank until the alarm rang.

CHAPTER SEVENTEEN

When Colleen came back inside, Jeremy was still asleep in his chair, unperturbed by the noise coming from the television. *All About Eve* was over, and there was some kind of shoot-out on the screen now. Colleen grabbed the remote and switched it off.

She wanted Jeremy to go back to his own bed, but she knew he wouldn't. That he would insist that she take it. She didn't want to argue with him. He looked so peaceful.

She didn't have the heart to wake him.

Maybe I should go back to bed, she thought.

She could see down the hallway from where she stood, down to the room where Viv was. There was light coming from under the door.

Maybe she's awake, too, Colleen thought. Either that, or she's afraid of the dark, which didn't seem too likely. Colleen had only met her for a few minutes, but Viv did not seem like the type who would scare easily.

And there was that strange vision she'd had. Did it mean something? Was there some kind of link between Viv and the guy who had killed Turney? Colleen hoped there wasn't. But she'd never seen those kinds of things before. And now, twice in two days.

I wonder what she's doing in there, Colleen thought.

She slowly walked down the hallway, making sure she didn't make any noise. She took great care in each step. Softly putting each foot down.

When she reached the door, she bent down. It was one of those old-fashioned doors with a keyhole. She could see Viv clearly.

She was nude, sitting in the middle of a wooden floor in the lotus position. Her mouth moved, like she was chanting, or maybe saying her mantra, but Colleen couldn't hear anything.

She must be meditating, Colleen thought.

Sweat glistened on Viv's shoulders and forehead. Colleen could see that Viv had a very good body. Small-muscled and fit. She certainly looked like she could have been a model at one time. Her breasts were slightly larger than Colleen's, and firm. Her whitish-blonde pubic hair, what Colleen could see of it behind her folded legs, appeared to be trimmed into a very precise, tiny triangle.

Like a topiary hedge, Colleen thought. She almost laughed at that.

Suddenly, Viv's eyes opened.

Not knowing if Viv could see her looking, Colleen resisted the urge to run away. It would make too much noise. And if Viv didn't know she was there now, the sound of her running would be a dead giveaway.

Softly, Colleen stood up and slowly walked away from the door.

The whole length of the hallway, she dreaded that the door would open behind her, that Viv would accuse her of spying.

But there wasn't a sound. By the time Colleen got back to the living room, she was convinced that Viv hadn't known she was outside her door, looking in.

Jeremy was still asleep.

Quietly, Colleen went down the other corridor, back to his bedroom, and closed the door. She was already barefoot (the cool sand of the beach beneath her feet had felt wonderful), and she stretched out on his bed in her clothes. Her head against the fluffy pillows.

She closed her eyes, convinced she would just lay here until dawn, and then maybe she'd get up and see about making breakfast. She thought about how nice Jeremy had been to her; how she'd been able to open up to him so quickly and tell him what had happened to Turney. How she felt safe here. And even though Viv had seemed kind of odd, Colleen didn't feel threatened by her.

She had these thoughts, and then, without warning, she fell into a deep sleep.

* * *

Riding on the subway to work, Sam's thoughts drifted to Charlie. The kid was only seventeen, and he already hated the whole world. Already had a police record and a history of rage. *He is going to be a hard case,* Sam thought. *I wonder if he'll show up today, or if he'll stay away for a week or two.*

Either way, Sam knew he'd be back eventually. Sam was his only option to control that temper of his. Otherwise, the kid's future probably amounted to iron bars and maybe even a lethal injection.

I've got to save him, Sam thought. *It's clear nobody's tried to reach him, help him before. I've got to be the one.*

And, like tiny rockets, those thoughts led him to think about Maggie, asleep through the alarm, refusing to get out of bed. He wondered how many days she'd gotten drunk and missed work. Did she even still have a job at this point? And was it to the point where alcohol had taken over as the most important thing in her life?

He'd seen the symptoms before. He couldn't stand seeing her this way, and found himself more perplexed about how to deal with her.

He thought about calling her office, checking up on her, but that might just make matters worse. Chances were she wasn't there and his inquiring about her might make it all that more difficult for her to take her life back, once she realized how bad things were.

He would have to really consider the best course of action in dealing with her. After all, he still loved her. He wanted to help her. Wanted to save her from as much pain as he could.

Why did this happen? he wondered. She used to be so stable. So confident. What made her fall apart like this? Was it _me_? Did I contribute to this fall? And why did it take me so long to see what was happening? Are we *that* distant these days? Am I really that self-absorbed lately that I didn't see what must have been so obvious?

He couldn't be sure. But he refused to think about it further. For now.

He was so wrapped up in his thoughts that he almost missed his stop. He managed to get off just before the train doors closed.

CHAPTER EIGHTEEN

Colleen woke up coughing. She was wrapped up in the sheets again. There was a return-to-the-womb quality about the entanglement that she would have recognized if she thought about it deeply enough. But she didn't. Instead, she just freed herself from the sheets and got up. She was still dressed. She lit a cigarette and took a long drag. Then, she went and changed her tampon before she left the bedroom and went out into the hallway.

She was greeted by the sound and smell of bacon sizzling. When she reached the living room, she turned to look down the other hallway that led to Viv's room. The door was open. Jeremy was in the kitchen, in his white and red striped robe, cooking breakfast. No doubt he'd spent the rest of the night sleeping in front of the television.

"Ah, *there* you are," he said, clearly pleased to see her. "I was hoping you'd wake up before the food got cold, or burnt."

She didn't say a word as she sat down at the kitchen table. A round Formica number that reminded her of her childhood, even though she'd never had a table like this. But it seemed so familiar. Was it because of the TV shows she'd watched so religiously as a child?

He put a plate in front of her soon after. Scrambled eggs, bacon, fried tomatoes, buttered toast.

"I hope you aren't a vegan," he said, as he looked down, seeing if she'd eat.

"Nope," she said. She stubbed out what was left of her cigarette and grabbed a fork. Jeremy poured her a glass of fresh orange juice, as she eagerly dug into the food. "You must have been tired," he said. "I *knew* you'd gone back to sleep after your walk on the beach."

She was sure he'd been asleep when she'd done that, but maybe he was a lighter sleeper than she'd assumed. Then she remembered the way she'd spied on Viv. Had he seen that, too? There was no point in dwelling on it. And she *was* starving.

"I'm glad you like it," he said. "There's plenty more if you want it." He poured her some coffee.

"I'm fine," she said between mouthfuls of eggs.

"We have a big day ahead of us," he said, smiling. His lips didn't match, but that was okay.

She looked up from her plate. "Huh?" she asked.

"We're going to go to your old apartment, and gather your stuff," he explained. "You're moving in here today."

She didn't know how to answer that, so she continued eating. She had already intruded enough on this man's life and really had no right to be here. But another part of her wanted to get as far away as she could from what had happened to Turney. Wanted to embrace Jeremy's offer of a safe haven.

Better to simply give up all responsibility, she thought, *and let him make up my mind for me.*

He sat down across from her. There was a glass of orange juice in his hand, and she just knew it was spiked with vodka for some reason. The glass kept going to his non-matching lips, then away again.

"You've been through a lot and need a sanctuary," he told her. "Fortunately, I can give you that. We've got plenty of room here."

She didn't argue with him.

* * *

Maggie smiled at the bartender. "Another martini please," she said.

"I'll have the same," a woman's voice said beside her.

Maggie looked over at the attractive woman beside her. Her hair was an almost whitish-blonde, and she had the most beautiful violet eyes Maggie had ever seen.

"Hi," the woman said, noticing Maggie's gaze and smiling.

"Hi," Maggie said. She was sure when she'd first entered the bar that she wanted to be alone. But now she wasn't so sure.

"My name's Viv," the blonde said.

"I'm Maggie," she said, grabbing the martini glass by the stem and bringing it to her lips.

"Cool," Viv said, taking her own glass and swallowing. She paid for both of the drinks, and Maggie let her. "You come here often? Haven't seen you here before."

Her words washed over Maggie like a warm geyser spray. There was something very soothing about her voice.

Maggie realized she'd been there awhile already, even though it was only around one in the afternoon.

"On and off," she said.

Viv took a long draw from her glass. "Good to meet ya."

Maggie, who had never flirted with another woman before, suddenly found that she was very attracted to *this* woman for some reason. In *this* setting, no less.

"You wanna' go somewhere?" Viv asked, absently touching the ring in her left nostril.

"Where?" Maggie said, determined to play it dumb.

"Anywhere but here."

"Okay," Maggie said, tapping into a part of herself she never would have had access to if she had been sober. She was actually excited, agreeing to Viv's suggestion.

More excited than she'd been in years. "I'm game, if we can pick up something to drink on the way."

Viv smiled. "Sure."

After they finished their drinks, they got up, arm in arm and slightly tipsy, and left the dark interior of the unnamed bar for parts unknown.

* * *

He sat in his office, on the soft leather chair he always sat in when he addressed patients, waiting.

He resisted the impulse to get up and ask Carla if Charlie had canceled. It was obvious the kid wouldn't have picked up the phone to call.

Shit, he thought. *I could have predicted this would happen. This kid is going to be a special case, deserving personal attention.*

He looked through his old-fashioned Rolodex. Carla had recently updated it for him. He looked through the J's and stopped at *Jarrold, Charlie.*

He looked at the phone number written there, and hesitated.

What good is calling going to do? he wondered. *If he picks up, he'll probably just hang up on me. If his mother answers, I'll just get him in trouble. Which will make it more difficult to establish a bond of trust between us.*

The decision didn't have to be made, though, because just then the phone buzzed.

"Yes, Carla."

"Charlie Jarrold is here. Shall I send him in?"

"I'll be right out," Sam said.

He put down the phone and took a deep breath. Then he got up and went to the door. Charlie was standing by Carla's desk, looking disheveled. He refused to look at Sam.

"Come on in, Charlie," Sam said, standing in the doorway.

Charlie walked past him, into the office. The kid sat down, his legs spread apart, his body language giving off hostility.

Sam closed the door and sat across from him.

"We had an appointment, Charlie. For half an hour ago."

"I know," the boy said, not looking up from the floor. "I had to take care of something first."

"Well, that leaves us with a very short session. However, I'll have to charge your mother for the full hour."

"Do what you want."

"I thought you were going to try, Charlie. That you were going to take this seriously."

"You're lucky I came at all," Charlie said.

"It doesn't matter to me, Charlie. If you don't want to come here, I can't make you. This is for your good, not mine."

Charlie didn't say anything. Just kept his head down.

"Did you get in a fight, Charlie?"

No answer.

"That's why you're late, isn't it?"

"Why would you ask me that?"

"It doesn't take a detective, considering your temper is why you're here. Besides, you're out of breath, and you seem very agitated."

"Well, you don't know shit," Charlie said. It was almost a whisper.

"I was waiting here for half an hour. I thought you weren't going to show. And I almost called your home. But I didn't, do you know why?"

"I don't care."

"Because if your mother answered, she would be very upset to hear you were blowing off these sessions, considering how badly she thinks you need them. But I had no intention of letting her know that you weren't here."

Charlie said nothing.

"I want us to get along, Charlie. I want us to trust one another. I knew you'd show up eventually."

"You thought I wasn't coming."

"I knew it was very possible you were just late."

"Look, I don't give a fuck what you do. Call my mother. It doesn't matter to me."

"I think you're wrong, Charlie. If it didn't matter to you, you wouldn't have come at all."

Charlie said nothing. His head still down. Refusing to look Sam in the eyes.

Sam looked at his watch. "Time's almost up. But this session hasn't been wasted, Charlie. Do you know why?"

"No."

"Because you came here. You made the effort. You showed me you want my help."

The boy said nothing.

"Are you sure you don't want to talk about what happened today?" Sam asked.

Charlie continued to stare down at the floor. For a few minutes, they said nothing to each other. Sam watched him, waiting for the kid to say something. He could feel the tingling inside himself. *The energy.* He could feel the anger coming off the boy. It was the most intense energy he'd ever felt from another person before, and it didn't seem to dissipate as quickly as the others, either. He sat there, letting it wash over him, feeling compelled to move closer, like a moth to a flame, but somehow he resisted.

When it was clear there was no getting through to him, Sam forced himself to look at his watch. He didn't want the session to end, but he had to maintain some control.

"You have to go now, Charlie. I have another patient to see. But next time, try harder to get here on time. These sessions will only do you good if you're here."

Charlie finally looked up as he rose from his seat. Sam could see the swelling around his eye.

"I know you're trying. Don't give up on me yet, Charlie."

"My knife," Charlie said.

"Huh?"

"My knife," he repeated. "You said you'd give it back to me if I came back here."

"I did make that particular deal with you, didn't I?"

Sam went to his desk and took the knife out of the top drawer where he'd put it. He handed it back to the Charlie.

"But I don't want you ever bringing it back here again."

The kid muttered something and went out to the lobby, leaving the door open. Sam sat in his chair, watching him go. Wanting so badly to call him back. To tell his other patient to leave. To give Charlie however much time he needed.

But he just watched as Charlie stood by Carla's desk. She was telling him when his next appointment was. The boy took a card with the information and left, not looking back.

Sam looked over at the woman who was waiting.

"Mrs. Huston," he said, looking into the woman's eyes and trying his best to feign interest. "Please come right in."

CHAPTER NINETEEN

It felt strange to be back in her apartment. It had only been two days since she'd left, but already it seemed alien to her. There was her bed, looking smaller than she'd realized. There was a blanket on the floor where Turney had slept his last nights.

"You lived here?" Jeremy asked, hovering near the doorway. "It seems too small for a mouse."

"It's all I could afford," Colleen said, feeling a tinge of embarrassment. "It's not like the cash was flowing in."

"All the more reason to come with me. Get your stuff together and we'll go."

Looking at this place now, there was no way she wanted to stay here. And there wasn't anywhere else she could turn. Not to her mother, her sister. It would have hurt more to beg them to take her in. Jeremy was the best choice she had right now.

She got her suitcase out from under the bed. She started filling it with clothes from the closet, from the drawers of the old dresser, with its scratches and peeling paint.

Jeremy closed the door and leaned his back against it. "You know you'll be much happier at my place."

Which was true enough. If she could just get over the guilt she felt, relying on him like this. He was just a stranger after all. Sure, they'd talked a lot since she appeared at his place, and she really liked him. But how much did she know about him really? And how much did he know about her?

There were lots of things about her past that she wasn't proud of.

"Can I help you at all?" he asked.

"There isn't really very much to pack," she told him. "All I really have is my clothes, and the furniture is mine."

"I can have someone put it in storage for you."

She looked around. "You don't have to do that," she told him. But then she thought about the future. She couldn't assume she'd stay with Jeremy forever. Something would probably go wrong eventually—it always did for her—and she might still need the furniture. "Oh, I guess I better keep it, just in case, but not the bed. I won't be needing that old thing ever again."

"I can have someone put that out in the trash."

"That would be great."

She went around, grabbing up little odds and ends. She went into the bathroom to get her stuff that was in there.

"Do you want me to get some of the boxes out of the car?" he asked her.

"I guess we could use a couple of them."

"I'll be right back," he said. It was obvious he couldn't wait to leave.

She threw a bunch of things on the bed. Then went over to the blanket where Turney had been sleeping. She didn't think he'd left anything behind. It wasn't like he had a lot to begin with. But she found his backpack on the floor, under the blanket. There were some odds and ends in there. An old Walkman with a piece of masking tape holding the battery compartment closed. Some old cassette tapes. It had been a long time since she'd seen any of those. An old sandwich wrapped in cellophane. Random things he'd picked up here and there. Nothing all that interesting...except for a diary.

She lifted it, opened it. But could not bring herself to read it.

These are the last worldly possessions Turney ever had, she thought. *I can't bring myself to just throw them away.*

She put his diary in her suitcase and zipped it up. She knew that at some point, when enough time had gone by, she'd be able to read it. To find out more about who Turney was. Who he had been. There was so much about him that she didn't know.

She put his backpack on the bed. She'd bring that along, too. She knew she would rifle through it in more depth later. After all, there wasn't anyone else he could have left it to. She'd use it to look for the clues of his all too brief life. But she needed some time to put his death behind her, to grieve, before she could even think of doing such a thing.

Jeremy returned with some folded boxes. He started opening them.

"This is about it," she told him. "I told you it wasn't very much."

His eyes looked misty. She couldn't tell if he was reacting to all this, if he felt bad for her, or if his eyes were simply watering. They seemed to do that a lot. He pulled a handkerchief from his pocket and wiped at them.

She started filling the boxes. The car waited for them downstairs.

"I spoke to your landlord," he told her. "I paid up your rent. There's nothing to keep you here."

She nodded.

"I'll make sure someone comes for the furniture," he said, then paused. "Except for the bed, of course. I'll make sure that's disposed of."

He grabbed a box and started going downstairs. She grabbed her suitcase. On the way out, she noticed the pink "Open All Night" sign on the wall. She considered leaving it behind, a symbol of her life before she'd met Jeremy, but she decided she couldn't part with it. She knew it was silly, and she should just let them take it when they came to get the furniture, but she didn't want to risk them forgetting it. She wanted it with her.

She put down her suitcase and removed the sign from its hooks on the wall, and unplugged it. She wrapped the chord around it and put it under her arm. Then grabbed her suitcase handle with the other hand and started down the stairs to the waiting car.

It was still difficult to think of Turney as being dead. But he was never coming back to sleep on the floor or to beg her to let him stay just one more night. He was just a memory now.

How could anyone rip another person apart like that? The whole thing had been so unnatural, unearthly. Even now, she couldn't be sure it wasn't a nightmare. Descending the stairs, she half-expected Turney to come running up, asking her where she was going. But she knew that wasn't going to happen.

She found herself remembering his touch. The way they made love. She would much rather remember him that way than the way he died. She didn't want to keep the images in her head of his being torn apart, his blood splattering across the sidewalk.

It was almost too much to bear. She felt slightly dizzy, almost lost her footing on the stairs. As she wavered, she leaned against the railing, and saw Jeremy coming up

toward her, putting his hand on her.

"Are you okay?" he asked her. "You looked like you were going to faint."

"I'm okay," she said, her voice sounding like an echo to her. "I just didn't know it would be so tough coming back here. After what happened."

"You don't have to ever come back here again," Jeremy said. "I'll take care of you, now."

Driving away, they passed the place where Turney had been killed. Colleen looked out the car window. All that was left of him was a chalk outline on the sidewalk, and probably some bloodstains. She wondered if there were other outlines for where his head landed, where his limbs were strewn about.

* * *

Maggie stretched out on the twin bed, wondering what convinced her it was okay to come to this place. Sam would kill her if he knew she had let a strange woman pick her up and bring her to a motel room. Then again, Sam probably wouldn't care. He seemed to have very little interest in her life these days.

She was convinced she drank because she was unhappy, and that her unhappiness was in no small part caused by Sam's indifference to her. To be honest to herself, she had to admit that the drinking was at least partly a final attempt to get Sam to notice her again.

But she had been thinking about a lot of things way too much lately, and this wasn't exactly the time and place to be soul-searching.

"What are you thinking about?" Viv asked her.

"I want a drink," Maggie said.

"Not now," Viv said. "You don't need that anymore. I'm here now."

Maggie smiled. "I've never done anything like this before?"

"Come to a motel room?"

Maggie nodded.

"With a strange woman?"

"That's the one."

"Well, I hope I'm not all that strange, Maggie. Or else I would think you shouldn't have come with me. Unless your judgment is clouded by the alcohol. In which case, I'm taking advantage of you."

Maggie stared up into Viv's eyes. They were violet and reminded her of Elizabeth Taylor's.

"You have such beautiful eyes," Maggie said.

"Thanks."

"Please be gentle."

Then she thought about what she said, and laughed.

Viv laughed, too.

"Why don't you get out of those things, and we'll push the twin beds together."

"Can I have the bottle back?" Maggie asked.

"No, I'll give it back to you later. I want you to be aware of what's going on. Otherwise, you'll be no use to me."

"Okay," Maggie said softly, and smiled again. Then she leaned up and kissed Viv's lips. Maggie closed her eyes, like a schoolgirl. Viv kept her eyes open.

Their lips parted.

After a bit, Viv pulled away. "Get undressed," she said. She got off the mattress and pushed the beds together. Maggie sat up and started pulling her clothes off.

She saw the bottle on the floor, at the foot of the bed, and almost reached down for it, but she resisted the urge.

Viv stood before her, smiling, and did a little striptease act. It took Maggie's mind off the bottle.

She removed her panties and lay back in the bed, watching Viv.

Viv removed the last of her clothes and then crawled beside Maggie, kissing her again.

And then things progressed from there.

* * *

Maggie had the bottle in her hand again. She handed it to Viv. "You want any?"

Viv hesitated, then took it from her and took a gulp of vodka. She handed the bottle back to Maggie.

While they'd made love, Viv had come close to unlocking the place inside

Maggie, the part that set her free. But she resisted, because there was something about Maggie that made her want to keep her around a little bit longer. Viv couldn't bring herself to make this their one and only time together.

If she hadn't finished off Richard Croix so recently, she wouldn't have had much of a choice in the matter. The part of her that unlocked people would have done its thing without her consent, and that was that. But since she'd been satiated recently, there was the ability to resist the need. For today, anyway.

It was a lot like eating. And she was full enough to keep satisfied for now.

This time with Maggie had been one of the more intimate experiences she'd had in a while. And it had a happy ending. A welcome change to the fucks she'd had with people who weren't alive anymore. It felt good to get really close to someone, to feel really human. It wasn't something she got to enjoy very often.

There was a time when she'd wanted this kind of intimacy with Jeremy. She'd been tempted lots of times, but she'd vowed never to let it get that far. Never allow him to get that close. She couldn't risk losing him.

She almost felt like making a similar vow about Maggie. But she knew she wouldn't be able to keep it this time. Something about Maggie told Viv that it was hopeless. Maybe the way she kept holding onto that liquor bottle.

Maggie was drifting off to sleep. If anything, it might do her some good. At least she couldn't drink while she was sleeping. Viv took the bottle away from her, gently, and screwed the top back on. Maggie murmured softly and snuggled up on the bed.

Viv stretched out beside her and held her close, trying hard not to feel the pain emanating from her. Trying not to let the pain touch her too deeply and force her to do something she wasn't ready to do yet.

* * *

All the way home, Sam found himself thinking about Charlie. There was something different about this kid. He'd never seen someone who was so much like a raw nerve. Charlie took offense at everything and everything made him uncomfortable and combative. It was amazing they'd been able to hold organized sessions at all. The whole time they sat in his office, Sam had the idea this kid wanted to lash out at him, knock him off his chair. Take him down a peg or two.

Charlie was more cautious now. Their first visit showed him that Sam wouldn't be a pushover. That there would be resistance. And while that did not make Charlie back down in attitude, it made him less likely to act out physically, on impulse. Then again, he might be completely unpredictable. The moment when Sam assumed he was calm might be the exact moment Charlie had waited to strike.

Sam found the whole dynamic intriguing.

Would it make any sense to introduce Charlie to one of his group sessions? Probably not. The kid barely trusted *him*; there's no telling how he'd react around a bunch of strangers. Although being around strangers might rile Charlie up, make his anger flare up and come to the surface so Sam could feed off it. But no, he couldn't rush things and he couldn't risk things getting out of control so soon. He had to take this slowly. He had to have patience. Besides, the groups were usually for people whose anger levels had diminished. People who had made some progress. And Charlie wasn't even close to that point yet. Sam thought of what it would feel like to have a whole room full of Charlies and the amount of tingling and adrenaline he would feel *then*. It excited and scared him.

Just the thought of the way Charlie affected him, scared him. Usually other people's anger was something he absorbed in short bursts. Intense sensations. But it never lasted long. He'd absorb, and they'd relax. But with Charlie it was different. Not only was the anger coming off him stronger, it lasted longer. And even now, thinking about it, Sam wanted *more*.

He tried to convince himself that it was a mutual process, that he gave as much as he took. He healed people who couldn't manage their rage, and in return they filled a hunger inside him. The perfect synergistic relationship. But down deep, he knew. Their healing wasn't important to him. It was simply the reason why they kept coming back, their only hope of overcoming the anger that enslaved them. But at the same time, the more he healed them, the less they had to offer. The less satisfying their interactions became.

But he had to make a living, and as long as they came back, this whole thing *worked*, and he'd be damned if he examined it too closely.

Sam remembered being a child, small for his age and often bullied. Except the bullying never lasted much more than a day or two. Then the bullies would lose interest, grow lethargic. Whatever fueled their taunts and jabs got leeched out of them. Sam knew early on that it was he who did these things. Other kids weren't so lucky. They were taunted mercilessly, day in and day out. But not him. Nobody stayed angry around him, and nobody stayed interested in tormenting him, for very long.

Even then, the more disoriented they felt around him, the better he felt inside. The ability became stronger over time, but that was just the beginning. The first stirrings. He felt a strangeness inside himself. A tingling that he could neither fathom nor explain. His young mind didn't have the knowledge to investigate the matter, and he wouldn't have bothered if it had.

There was a time, early in his career, when some people came to him for depression, but he could only tolerate them for a short time before he had to admit he couldn't help them. He'd referred them to colleagues who were better equipped than he was. His specialty was anger and he tried to make that quite clear. There were so many angry people in the world, so much rage all around us. Did he really need to be able to do anything more?

He pulled the car up into the driveway, and as he stopped in front of his house, his thoughts turned from Charlie to Maggie. Poor, lost Maggie. He had to do something to help her.

Shutting off the engine, he thought about his options. It was probably best to confront her about this. If he continued to ignore it, she would never feel the need to change her behavior. While this might have been easier with a patient, with his own wife he found it was a tremendous weight upon him. He had no desire to rub her nose in it. But he had to say something.

Sam got out of the car and walked across the lawn to the house. He fumbled for his keys and let himself inside.

"Maggie," he called out before he had even shut the door. "Are you home?"

An exploration of the house revealed that she wasn't. Which was totally unlike her.

Maybe she went to work today, he thought. Maybe she's working overtime and got caught in traffic.

He went over to the answering machine, but there weren't any messages.

He sat down on the couch in the living room, searching the floor with his eyes to see if any stray liquor bottles were around. But there was no trace of her problem.

Maybe she resolved this herself, he thought. *Maybe right now she's attending an AA meeting.*

He knew it was a foolish thing to think. But if it were true, that would mean he wouldn't have to deal with it. He wouldn't have to confront her at all.

Yes, he thought. *She took care of things herself. I just know it.*

CHAPTER TWENTY

There was no turning back, now. Not only would Colleen be living in this house for the time being, now her old apartment was no longer available to her.

She carried her suitcase inside. Jeremy brought in the rest. He put her boxes on the floor.

She looked around the living room. "Do you want me to sleep on the couch?" she asked, then instantly wished she hadn't; she was afraid he'd misinterpret her comment and think she was hinting at getting the bedroom again. But she didn't want to inconvenience him any further, and certainly didn't want to kick him out of his own bed.

"Don't be silly," he told her. "There are other rooms. It's just that I wasn't prepared for company when you first arrived."

There were two hallways. One led down to Viv's room. The other toward his own. But the halls held other rooms than these. Closed doors lined the corridors. Jeremy took her in the direction of his room. He stopped halfway, and opened a door.

"Here you go," he said, leading her inside.

The room was in disarray. Boxes were here and there. Big hardcover books were scattered on the floor. Items wrapped in brown paper and plastic covered the desk and the bed. "Just let me clean this up a bit."

"Let me help you," she said, putting down her suitcase.

"It won't take long at all," he told her as he started taking things away to another room across the hall. In a much shorter time than she expected, the room was cleared of debris and available for her. She went over and sat on the bed when it was uncovered. It had an old comforter on it, musty with age.

"Don't worry about the bed sheets. I have fresh linens in the closet."

She looked around the room. There was even a chest of drawers for her to put her clothes in, and a closet, which had been hidden behind boxes.

He stopped and sat on a wooden chair next to the desk.

"Well, we got a lot accomplished today. I told you there was plenty of room for you."

"This house is bigger than I thought it was. *So many rooms.*"

"A lot of them are just storage areas now, for the most part. I'm a real pack rat, you see. Always collecting something. At one time it was art, then it was books. It's amazing how things accumulate in here."

"When was the last time someone stayed in this room?"

"Hmmm," Jeremy said, half-closing his eyes. "It's always been considered a guest room, I suppose. But I think only one or two people ever slept in here. So it has a very innocent history, I'd think. At least in my lifetime."

"I'm surprised you don't have a maid or anything," she said.

"I never was much for servants. Too protective of my privacy, I suppose. Although I can't for the life of me tell you what I'm protecting." He laughed. "I only use half the rooms here; there really wouldn't be much for a maid to do. Besides, it really isn't *that* big."

"Did this used to be your parents' house?"

"One of them, a long time ago. Even when they were alive they didn't come here very often. They weren't much for the beach, I suppose. They preferred being in the city proper. They bought this place when I was a child, and I remember only weekending here once. They might have come back a few times without me. This is actually rather small compared to our other homes. This place was pretty much ignored, until I came here after the accident, that is."

He stopped. He was clearly uncomfortable talking about the accident. Colleen had made sure not to bring it up, even though she had read all about it in the tabloids. She'd heard about the tragedy, as well as the glamour. The way he acted when he brought it up made her feel even more uncomfortable talking about it. It was like a secret they had both agreed not to mention.

"Are you okay?" she asked.

"Yes, I'm fine," he said. "Where was I? Oh yes, after the accident, I came here as an adult for the first time. The house had been left to me in their will, but I'd avoided it for years. And now that I've lived here, I can't understand why I didn't come sooner. It's everything I'd want. A private, comfortable house by the ocean. Now, I can't imagine having lived anywhere else."

Even now, he could not bring himself to talk about the crash in detail. He was surprised he even mentioned it to her at all.

"There was a time when this house seemed very isolated. And I have to admit, for a while there, that's exactly what I wanted. But now it's coming alive again. And it's all because of you. It's like winter's over and spring's finally begun."

"I can't thank you enough for asking me to stay here," she said.

"Nonsense, I'm more than happy to have you. Especially when I saw your old place. How could anyone live in such a small room?"

"I didn't have much choice," she said.

"Well, don't worry about that anymore."

"I won't stay forever," she said. "Only until I can afford a new place of my own."

She stopped. She knew it was nonsense and couldn't bring herself to continue. After all, where was she going to get the money for her own place? The best room she could afford was the place she'd just left.

"Colleen, I really don't care. Stay as long as you like. Nobody is rushing you out the door."

"Can I ask you a question?" Colleen asked.

"Sure."

"What is it between you and Viv?" she asked. "You never did tell me. I guess it wasn't any of my business before, but now that I'm going to be living here, maybe I should know what to expect."

"There's nothing between us," Jeremy said. "Not from lack of trying. When Viv met me, I was at a very low point in my life. She has been very important to me since. She accepted my offer when I told her I wanted her to move in with me. She'd been going through some apartment troubles herself at the time. I can think of once or twice when I thought something might happen. But she always had this line she drew between us. And she never crossed it."

"Do you know why?"

He hesitated. Clearly there was something he hadn't told her.

"Maybe, one day," he said. "It's kind of a long story, and personal. I don't know if Viv would want me talking about it. It's nothing that should concern you, though."

"So she isn't a predatory lesbian or something," Colleen said, with a little laugh to break the tension.

He laughed, too. "No, not at all. It's nothing for you to worry about. Let's just say that Viv and me, we just weren't meant to be, okay?"

She wondered why he wouldn't confide in her. She'd told him so much. Even about Turney's murder. The strange red-faced man. Even how she'd seen those strange auras. She was more than a little disappointed. It must have shown.

"Don't pout," Jeremy said, and smiled. One side of his mouth seemed to turn up higher than the other, so that his grin was lopsided. "I'll tell you one day. I promise." he said.

"Okay," she said. "It's like a rain check, then?"

"You could say that."

She stretched out on the bed. "Hey, this isn't too bad, considering nobody's slept here for so long."

"It's a nice room. It's just that I'd had no reason to clean it out before. But I'm glad I have a reason now. I'm really glad you're here."

"It seems like Viv isn't here very often," Colleen said, then yawned.

"She comes and goes a lot. Sometimes I don't see her for days on end. And she rarely tells me if she's going to be gone for a long time."

Colleen laughed, "Jeremy, you sound like her mother!"

"I do, don't I? That's strange, because if there's one person I think I don't need to worry about, it's Viv. Believe me, that's one woman who can definitely take care of herself."

He got up off the chair. "How about something to eat? We've been on the go so much today, we forgot to get a bite."

"Sure, what have you got?"

"I know this really nice seafood place, down the road from here. It's not the fanciest place in the world, but the food's really good. It's convenient at least."

"Sure."

"Give me a minute."

Jeremy got up and went down the hall to his own room.

She lay back on the pillow and looked up at the ceiling. It was strange to find herself back here, not some distraught girl who wandered on the beach anymore, but someone who was going to *live in this house*, with, of all people, Jeremy Rust. It was like living a dream. To go from a tiny one-room apartment in a horrible neighborhood to this beautiful house by the beach.

She wondered what it would be like to live in this house forever. Despite a tinge of guilt, she knew she might end up testing Jeremy, to find out just how generous he really was.

He came back and stuck his head in the doorway. "Are you ready?"

* * *

When Maggie got back to the house, Sam was gone. But there were telltale signs that he'd been there. His briefcase beside the couch. The clothes he'd worn to work were draped over a chair in the bedroom. The smashed mirror in the hallway.

Had he smashed it out of anger, because she wasn't home? There had been times when he'd been the jealous type, years and years before. She'd thought he'd gotten over it, but who knew anymore? While he claimed to be some expert in human behavior, she never had.

She poured herself a glass of wine. There were still some bottles on the wine rack on the kitchen counter. Somehow she'd been able to resist them so far. Mostly because Sam would notice if they suddenly disappeared. But right now, she didn't care.

I have to buy more wine. She looked at the wine rack. *Replacement bottles.*

She thought about Viv. How strange it was to meet another woman who made her feel this way. At first, she figured it was just impulsive. She'd been drinking and wanted someone to talk to more than anything. Someone who would actually *listen*. Not that she'd had much important to say. Bitching, mostly. And rather slurred bitching at that. At first, even in her hazy state, she had known enough to protect her privacy, not say too much. Not name names, so to speak. But she had to say something. It was all building up in her so much, that she thought she would start screaming soon without some kind of release.

And Viv had listened to her tales of woe. The neglectful husband, the unsatisfying job, the disillusionment with life itself. The desire for a child she couldn't have.

She was sure it had sounded like the kind of self-indulgent diatribe you'd hear on a soap opera. The pathetic whining of an unhappy wife. But she'd felt such a need to let it out.

She would never have told any of this to her friends. They weren't much help when it came to the real painful stuff. She didn't want them to see her that vulnerable. She didn't want them to know she had flaws, weaknesses, so she'd been avoiding them. At first she had made excuses when they'd tried to make plans to get together. Now, she didn't return their calls at all.

She'd thought of going to a therapist, but she was always afraid they'd know Sam and she couldn't betray him, despite their problems. She resented therapists anyway, the whole lot of them, because of him. Because of what Sam had become over the years. On the surface, he was a man on a mission to cure the world of mental illness, wanting to suck up all the anger around him and replace it with a great Age of Calm. On that level, he was an altruistic, good man. But she saw the other side of it, too. He was obsessed with his patients, and his cause. To the exclusion of all else. *Even her.*

She didn't want to spill her guts to someone like that. Someone who would view her as just another pathetic patient to be cured.

And, even more so, she would never discuss things with *him*. There was a time when she would have. When she would have at least tried to trust him, and respect his opinions about things. But the wounds were too raw now. And since many were attributable to him, she had no desire to let him know just how deeply he'd been hurting her.

She didn't want to be put under his microscope.

She resented his work, saw it as her rival, and had no desire to become *part* of it.

Viv, on the other hand, was removed from all this. She was not part of the problem. The fact that she was a stranger made her even more attractive. Made her all the easier to talk to.

It would be only a matter of time before she opened up completely. Revealed her soul. It was so easy talking to Viv, and at least she tried to make the right noises to comfort her.

The sex had been a surprise. Not that Maggie hadn't seen the look in Viv's eye when they left the bar together. She knew what Viv's agenda was. The surprise was that Maggie had gone along with it so easily. At first, she attributed it to the booze. To the letting down of her curtain of inhibitions in an inebriated state. That, mixed with her vulnerability and desire to do something for Viv in return, for being there for her. For listening.

But it was more than that. Maggie had experienced fantasies, after all. She had toyed with the idea of being with another woman. Surely she wasn't the only one. The media almost made you think that every woman had those tendencies on some level, but Maggie didn't believe it was that widespread. That was probably some kind of lascivious myth perpetrated by men to make women more open to sexual experimentation. If a woman didn't go that way, all the marketing in the world wouldn't change her mind. Either you were attracted to the same sex, or you weren't.

But Maggie had always had a part of her that toyed with such ideas. She never acted on them, of course. But they were a mental game she played now and again. There were at least two of her friends she'd fantasized about at some point, or she'd had dreams, which, after all, are completely beyond our control.

Viv made her feel at ease, free, and it didn't take much convincing on her part to

get Maggie to go along for the ride. It had been so easy.

She looked forward to seeing Viv again. In fact, she'd wanted to stay longer in that motel room, to continue exploring each other's bodies, so alike and yet different. But she'd come to her senses for some reason, and realized she should be home. That Sam would be concerned. Would wonder where she was.

She had enough presence of mind to still think of such things. But she could see a time in the near future where she simply forgot completely, giving in to the binging and the impulses. Their marriage was becoming more and more empty, and she was less inclined to maintain the illusion anymore.

Which made her think of the broken mirror in the hallway, and the early years of their marriage, when an angry, jealous Sam had tried to control her comings and goings. In those times, it was not uncommon for Sam to break things, to lash out at inanimate objects. To lash out at *her* on occasion. But he always gained control again before things got too bad. She always wondered if that would continue to be the case, however. She lived in fear that someday he would snap completely. That he might even kill her in a fit of rage.

That was the past, though. Sam had learned to take control of his temper. *Physician heal thyself,* and all that. Which was a good thing, because she wouldn't have stayed in the marriage if he hadn't gotten his act together. As it was, she'd lived in fear longer than she'd planned to. She'd thought about leaving him so many times, but could never seem to bring herself to do it. Perhaps she really had loved him, and hadn't wanted to accept that their marriage was unsalvageable.

Now, saving their marriage seemed like an utter waste of time. Save it for *what?* Sure there were some good years in between. He'd started making good money and was less prone to outbursts, and they'd started really enjoying themselves again. But the closeness didn't last more than maybe five years, and then it became a kind of hollowness. Not really worth the trip at all.

At one point, she'd tried to get pregnant. She'd had some misguided idea that having a baby would save their marriage. That was before she'd gone to the doctor who'd told her she was infertile. But she knew now that a child wouldn't change him, that it would have just complicated things further. She was glad now she hadn't pursued other options.

Yes, the broken mirror reminded her of the old days. Things would get broken a lot back then. Clearly, it was a message to her. Sam was angry, and when he returned, it might get ugly.

It had been so long since she'd had a reason to be afraid of him.

She wished she could go back to the motel room, to Viv. But the room would be empty now. And she had no idea how to contact her. She hadn't even gotten her phone number. Or her last name.

The bar where they'd met? Maggie thought about it, but was too tired to leave again. She just wanted to bring this bottle with her to the bedroom, turn on the television, and roll up in a ball on the bed. Wanting so badly for the wine to numb the pain, and maybe she could even get some sleep.

If she slept, she wouldn't worry about Sam. Wouldn't dwell on what their relationship had become. And that it was getting worse.

I've got to make plans, she thought. *I've got to plan my escape from this house.*

CHAPTER TWENTY-ONE

Sitting alone in the motel room, in the dark, Viv found herself feeling conflicted about Maggie.

There had been a kind of instant rapport between them, and once they had come here, to this room, Maggie had felt so comfortable with her, so at ease, that she had poured her heart out to her. Not that the alcohol had hurt much.

It wasn't the first time something like that had happened to Viv. She had a way about her that put people at ease, that made people trust her. If not, she wouldn't be as effective at what she did. It was a gift. A spider had its web. She had the ability to comfort people.

When they made love, Viv knew it was Maggie's first time with a woman, but that made it all the sweeter, that she would give herself to her. Not only had Viv been attracted to her from the start, but this surrendering of herself really touched Viv in a way she hadn't felt in a long time.

For once it hadn't just been a matter of fucking.

But then again, it never really was *all* about fucking. It was about something a lot more. Feeding. But usually all Viv cared about was giving them a good time, while she rode them out to oblivion.

This time, she had felt more, and it scared her.

She knew that if she hadn't recently fed on that Richard Croix guy, she would have taken Maggie's life today. The desire was still there, and while they made love, she could feel that predator inside her feeling around inside of Maggie, trying to find the lock that her key fit, and she came really close. But chances were slim she could resist it again.

Now that she was aware of Maggie's pain, she wouldn't be able to ignore it next time. Once they'd had sex, the process had begun. That was why she had never gone that far with Jeremy. She didn't want to be put in a situation where she had to take his life. Not after all he had done for her. She felt closer to him than she ever had to any other person. And even then, she was quite sure that he felt distanced from her. Because her *closest* was still not close enough for normal people.

But now that she had a taste of what was making Maggie hurt, she wouldn't be able to stop what was meant to happen. They would meet up again, and then Viv would have to let things run their course.

It hurt her very much to realize that. She almost cried. But she hadn't cried in so long, that she had forgotten how.

She could still smell their scents in the room, their musk. Maggie's presence was still very much here, even though she had left.

I wish I could protect you, Maggie, she thought. *But I was put on this earth to end your pain. And there's no turning back now.*

In most cases, Viv felt like she was performing a service. Ending the pain of those who were suffering. But in Maggie's case, she just felt miserable.

* * *

I saw Colleen again today. It's been so long, I didn't know if I'd ever see her again. I remember her saying that she was going to go to Hollywood and become a movie star. But she never did. I was so glad to see her again.

Some ashes fell on the page and she brushed them away.

Colleen was stretched out on her bed, reading Turney's diary. When she first opened it, breaking the little lock, she felt weird. But it wasn't like she was invading his privacy. Turney was dead.

I was probably as close to him as anybody, she thought. And he talks about me in here, so why *shouldn't* I read it?

His family had moved away years ago, and she had no idea how to reach them. Not that she would know what to say if she could. If Turney had a wallet and some form of identification, it was on him when he died. Because there was nothing like that in his bag. The only truly personal thing he had left behind was his diary.

Which she had opened and was now reading.

The police must have notified his parents by now. They had ways of finding out stuff like that. So, it was out of her hands.

Luckily, they hadn't come looking for her. Since there were no other witnesses that night, there was probably nothing to link her to what happened. Unless anyone had seen them together before that. The police might want to talk to her at some point. But she hoped they would never be able to find her here.

Back in high school, I really thought I loved Colleen, but I never told her. Sometimes I wish I had.

She read the words, feeling even more lost and alone. Sure Jeremy was right down the hall, but despite all his kindness, he was still a stranger to her. She had known Turney for years. Even when there were long stretches of time when they hadn't seen each other, she used to hear things about him. It sounded like he was having a worse time than she was, getting through life. But he'd seemed like he was getting back on track when she saw him last. Maybe she was deluding herself about this, but he didn't seem messed up or using when he came to stay with her. And they did talk a couple of times about life. About how sometimes life seemed to be going nowhere.

No matter how much he said, though, he always seemed to be holding a lot back. She suspected that there were some things he never told anyone.

Except, maybe, his diary.

She remembered that thing she used to say in high school, about going away to California, and being a star. It seemed so stupid now. It almost made her laugh that Turney had actually believed it. It would have been kind of funny, except that it was too sad now. She'd never have gotten the nerve to move so far away, but he didn't know that. She wondered what would have happened if she had gotten the nerve, though. She probably would have ended up acting in porno movies or something. It wasn't like she had some kind of real *talent* she could cash in on. There was no way she could really act. Or sing.

But *fucking*. She could do that.

She remembered this guy once who had paid her a hundred bucks to take some pictures. At the time, she thought they were just for him. But now, she wondered if maybe those pictures were published somewhere. Hell, they were probably all over the Internet at this point. She was glad she didn't have a computer.

There had been one or two guys who had tried to talk her into fucking on video, but she had always found a way to avoid it. The truth was, she didn't like the idea of being captured on film. To be there for anybody to see, whether she knew about it or not. The idea made her feel very uncomfortable.

She flipped through the diary. A lot of the entries were short and mundane. Stuff about people she'd never heard of, and most of it wasn't very interesting. She scanned the pages for mentions of her name. But there were only a few at the beginning, and some at the end. In between, there wasn't much reason to mention her.

The ones at the beginning, though, showed that he thought about her sometimes, even when he hadn't seen her. Which made her feel good. It sounded like he'd never really gotten over her.

I wish you'd told me, Turney, she thought. At the same time, she knew it would have been uncomfortable for her. She didn't share his feelings, after all. But who knows, over time, she might have felt the same. Maybe she could have helped him get off the streets. Could have turned his life around.

Yeah, right, she thought. *What really would have happened is we would have both ended up in the gutter.*

The diary started a few months back. Which made her wonder if there were other, earlier books. She wondered where he would have kept them. Maybe in a locker somewhere? Maybe this was the first one he'd ever tried to write. Maybe this whole diary thing was new to him.

Early on, there were some mentions about a psychologist he was seeing. Some guy called Dr. Wayne. There was something about the man that scared Turney. After about three visits, he stopped going. But there weren't a lot of details about why the man scared him.

I wish you'd gone into more detail, Colleen thought. Don't you know you're supposed to reveal *all* in your diary?

But, as in life, Turney was guarded in his diary. He gave some clues, but very little in the way of details.

She wondered if the doctor abused him in some way. Maybe the guy came onto him.

Then she thought about the way he was acting when he first asked to stay at her place. He seemed to be afraid of something. Something he wouldn't tell her about. Could it have been this doctor?

Well, there was no proof either way.

She flipped toward the back.

Colleen and me made love last night. It was great. All these years I'd thought about it. We were sitting on her bed, and I just kissed her. I couldn't help myself. And she was into it. I couldn't believe it finally happened. And no problems this time.

Colleen could feel her eyes getting misty. She hadn't realized he had such feelings for her. She'd just assumed it was something that happened. Not that it was something he'd wanted for so long.

And then, despite her trying to block it out, she saw his death in her mind's eye again. It was something she played over and over in her head. Like picking at a scab. She didn't want to think about it, but it kept returning. Seeing Turney torn apart in front of her. His head being thrown, bouncing off the wall. Landing at her feet.

And the man who did it. His face full of rage.

She would never forget that face as long as she lived.

CHAPTER TWENTY-TWO

Maggie woke in the middle of the night. She could hear a sound in the darkness. It was water running. The shower.

Normally she would have slept through such a subtle sound, but something woke her this time, and she realized she had to go to the bathroom anyway. So she slipped out of bed and walked softly to the door. She opened it and walked down the hall toward the source of the sound.

The bathroom door was closed, but not completely. It was open a crack. Softly, she pushed it open, forgetting about the cracked mirror in the hall. Forgetting about the chance that Sam might be angry with her for getting home late.

She could see his silhouette in the shower curtain. She knew it was him. As her head cleared, she found herself wondering why he was taking a shower so late. It was still dark, not yet sunrise. It was then that she looked down at the floor, then that she took in the whole picture.

There was blood on the floor, and blood on his discarded clothes, in a heap in the corner.

"Sam?" she said softly, finding herself suddenly concerned for him. Wondering what had happened while he was gone. Had he gotten hurt somehow? A car crash, maybe?

"Sam?" a little louder.

She could see his shape behind the shower curtain. He shut off the water. The sound stopped.

"Sam, are you okay?" she asked him, louder now, wanting to go to him, to pull the curtain aside, but she was so afraid of what the blood on the floor might mean. It made her stay where she was.

"I thought you were asleep," Sam said. His voice was calm.

"Sam, the blood. Are you okay? Are you hurt?"

"Go to bed, Maggie."

"Sam, do you need me to do anything?"

He was suddenly angry. "Go to fucking bed, Maggie."

"What's wrong, Sam?"

He pulled the curtain aside now, and stared out at her. At first, she had a really hard time focusing on his face. When he finally came into focus, the way he was looking at her made her remember the fear again. She remembered the way he used to be, before he got control of his temper. When he used to hit her.

"Don't make me get out of this shower, Maggie," he told her. "Don't give me a reason."

She was frozen, staring at him. The way he looked at her, she just wanted to get very far away from him, but it was as if she'd forgotten how to move.

"Just go back to bed," he said, softer now. Regaining control again. "Just get out of here."

He turned the shower back on.

She stood there, not knowing what to do. Her eyes kept being drawn to the blood. But he hadn't looked injured. Not that she'd been able to examine him or anything. But he certainly didn't seem incapacitated in any way.

Who was this man she shared a house with? If she felt before that he was a stranger, that feeling was worse now. With his late night sojourns to unknown places. His bloodstained clothes.

She didn't even use the toilet; she'd forgotten about her bladder. Instead she went down the hall, back to the bedroom, where she got under the covers and wrapped herself up in them. Rolled herself into a ball and closed her eyes, hoping it had all been just a dream, and the blood hadn't been real.

But sleep did not come, and the fear would not go away.

* * *

About an hour later, Sam came to bed. He slid in next to her, but he did not touch her. She tried to avoid coming into contact with him, but did not want to tip him off that she was still awake.

She tried to control her breathing, but realized that the more she thought about it, the closer she was to hyperventilating. Somehow, she was able to blank her mind and get control of herself.

Maggie wondered if there were any traces of blood left in the bathroom.

She found herself waiting for the sun to rise. Hoping that Sam would leave soon.

* * *

Colleen woke to find the light still on. She had fallen asleep reading Turney's diary. She closed it and slipped it under her pillow.

She could hear movements in the house. It was probably Viv. She came and went at such odd times. It was hard to think of her as living there at all. She was pretty enough, but Colleen wondered what Jeremy really saw in her that he felt they had such a strong bond. What kept Jeremy so loyal to her?

The sounds stopped. Colleen resisted the urge to get up and investigate. It wasn't like it was some great mystery after all. And besides, if it was trouble, what was *she* going to do about it?

She wondered if Jeremy was still awake. She had the urge to go to his room, slip into bed with him and hold him as he slept, but she knew she wouldn't act on this urge, at least not tonight.

She reached over to shut off the light, when there was a knock at her door.

"Come in."

Jeremy popped his head in. "I saw your light was on. I thought you might be awake."

"I was just reading," Colleen told him. "But I probably should turn in."

"Do you have a minute?" he asked her. "I wanted you to hear something."

"Okay."

She got up and followed him out into the living room where the stereo was. She lit a cigarette as he found an old 45 record and put it on the turntable. She hadn't seen a turntable in *years*.

"I just wanted you to listen to this," he said. "Tell me what you think."

There was a brief crackle and then the song began. It was something she had definitely heard when she was younger, on the radio. The tune was very familiar.

Then the voice began singing.

There are stairs. That go upstairs. Only there's nobody there.

"I know this song," she said.

"That's me," he told her.

"What, singing?"

"Yep, I was about seventeen there. My father owned a recording studio. I used to be in a band back then and he let us cut a record. Somehow some record label got wind of it and turned it into a minor hit. But we never made another song. We were definitely one-hit wonders."

"I can't believe that's you," she said, and then got very quiet, listening to his voice at seventeen.

"I actually think it's kind of embarrassing," he said. "I've only played it for one or two other people. I guess it's something I'd rather time forgot."

"But I used to love this song when I was a kid," Colleen said.

"When you were a kid? When was that, last week?"

"I'm not *that* young. I remember hearing this song on the radio."

"You know, I still hear it played, even now, every once in a while," he said. "It's always unexpected, and it always sends a chill through me. To think I once sounded like that."

"Why didn't you pursue a career in music?" Colleen asked.

"I don't know. It just wasn't meant to be. After our taste of success, the band broke up. We were all too young to appreciate it, and we just couldn't get along. After that, I dabbled in all kinds of things over the years. Never did find something I was really good at."

"I bet you're good at plenty of things," she said.

"Maybe. I didn't mean to drag you out of bed. I just got this whim to play the song for you. It kind of made sense at this late hour for some reason."

"I'm glad you shared it with me."

"Just don't tell anyone else about it," he said. "Or else."

She laughed. "Your secret's safe with me."

He shut off the stereo. "We both better get some sleep now," he said. "We have a big day tomorrow."

"What do you have planned, Jeremy?"

"I don't know yet," he said. "But it will be something good."

* * *

"So tell me about your childhood," Sam said, putting on his best therapist face. Trying to set the boundaries between doctor and patient, and finding it increasingly difficult.

"What about it?" Charlie asked, not getting the question at all. "What do you want to know?"

Everything, Sam thought, but knew that to voice it would confuse Charlie more. If someone had asked *him* such a question, it wouldn't baffle him in the slightest. He'd simply catalog every slight and grievance he could think of, and take it from there. But Charlie clearly needed guidelines.

"Well, is there anything in particular you remember? Anything that left a big impression on you? A joyful event? A trauma? Usually the really bad stuff takes a while to unearth, but if you are feeling particularly helpful today, I'll go with it."

Charlie didn't laugh. Sam had never seen the boy so much as crack a smile, and he really didn't expect that to happen anytime soon. But there was a calmness about him now that wasn't there before. All his patients went through this transformation at some point. Sam was surprised that it didn't take long for it to wash over Charlie, although it was far from complete. After all, the boy's eyes still had the look of a caged animal, looking for a way out. The boy's anger was far from gone, but it was more subdued now, controllable. The fidgeting was reduced to a minimum. And he didn't seem so confrontational now. No suddenly revealed knives. No threats and challenges. Charlie sat in his seat and listened. He actually seemed on the verge of actually *answering* something, if he could just think of the right words.

"How about my eighth birthday?" Charlie volunteered.

"Sure, great," Sam said. "It's a beginning."

"When I was eight, I had this party in the back yard. All my cousins were there. Some kids from school. And we ate ice cream. Played tag. Shit like that."

"So it's a good memory?"

Charlie hesitated. "After everybody left, my father pulled out his belt and beat me, because I left some gift wrapping on the lawn. He hit me right there, in the back yard, for all the neighbors to see."

The source of Charlie's rage was so obvious, it was almost laughable. But Sam didn't really care about the source. It was less than insignificant to him.

He almost said, *And how did that make you feel?* Another therapist's cliché. But he couldn't bring himself to do it. All this talking was such bullshit, really.

"So it's a bad one," Sam said. "A moment of pain, humiliation. Does it still make you angry to think about it now?"

Not that *Does it still make you angry to think about now?* was any different than *How did that make you feel?* He found himself falling back to the clichés, for lack of anything else to say. He almost hated himself for it.

"Not really," Charlie said. "It doesn't bother me too much now."

"Are you sure about that, Charlie? Are you sure that it doesn't hurt at all?"

"Yeah."

"No anger at all?"

Charlie thought about it. "Nope."

"Do you feel like it happened to somebody else? That it wasn't you? When you look back, is it like standing outside yourself, watching it happening to a stranger?"

"Maybe. I'm not sure."

"It's important that you're able to discuss this, Charlie. But emotionally, you're cold to it. You're distancing yourself. And that's part of the problem."

"Whatever. I thought that's what you wanted."

"It *is*," Sam said, trying to sound as positive as possible. "It's *exactly* what I'm

looking for. And so much sooner than I expected. Most people can't face these things so early on. You're doing fine. My point is that the way you remember it, it points to the problem here."

"How?"

"You don't feel anything, Charlie. You've shut off your reaction to what your father did to you. And it's those emotions we want to get at. If we can get at *them*, we can get to the heart of your anger, Charlie. Then real changes can begin."

Charlie half-nodded. Sam was sure the boy had no fucking idea what he was talking about. But he was trying.

"So," Sam said. "What kind of relationship do you have with your father now?"

Charlie half-glared at him. It was part reproach, part disbelief that he would ask him such a thing.

"He left us years ago. Good riddance, too," Charlie said. "I hope he's dead."

"You haven't heard from him in years?"

"I don't want to talk about him anymore. He's gone and that's all that matters now."

The tone of Charlie's voice told Sam that this was suddenly dangerous territory. He normally would have pursued it anyway, because it was at least stirring up emotions, breaking the calmness. But their session was coming to a close and there wasn't time to explore it properly.

"Charlie," Sam said. "I wanted to ask you something before you left today. I hold a group session every Tuesday and Thursday night. And I was wondering if you'd be interested in attending."

"Group? You mean you want me to talk about things in front of a bunch of strangers?"

"I think it would be good for you to be around other people who have the same problems. People who can relate to you."

"You're lucky I show up at all," Charlie said. "No, I don't want to go to no group sessions."

"Okay, I just wanted to ask. I thought it might do you good."

"Fuck that."

Sam saw in an image in his head. The back of his hand connecting with Charlie's face. But instead, he forced a smile. "Enough of that, Charlie."

"Is it time for me to go?"

Sam made a big production out of looking at his watch. "Yep, it is. You're free again."

"Good," Charlie got up and went to the door.

"See you again tomorrow, Charlie."

"Maybe," the kid said, and left the room.

Sam knew that there were other patients waiting outside, but he didn't want to see them. He had too many things on his mind.

He thought about the night before. Going home in a kind of daze. He remembered showering before he went to bed, but not much else. He thought Maggie had come into the bathroom at some point, but he couldn't be sure.

This morning, he'd tried to wake her, but she'd complained of feeling sick. So he let her sleep.

In the old days he would have considered staying home with her, taking care of her. But he had an obligation to his patients. Especially Charlie. He had to get through to that kid.

Another thing he had found upsetting was the obituary he'd found in the back of the paper during his commute to work. *Richard Croix dead at age 42. Apparent heart attack.* That bothered him. The man had seemed healthy, strong. And he had been making such good progress.

Sam felt a wave of remorse over losing another one. It always hurt to spend time helping someone, and have them flicker away like a burned-out bulb. Well, at least it didn't appear to be a suicide. That would have been a real failure.

Sam wondered if anyone would be calling the office to tell him Croix wouldn't be coming anymore, his wife perhaps? Probably not. She would be too caught up in her own grief. Calling the therapist was a low priority when funeral arrangements were being made.

Should I go to his funeral? Sam wondered. *No, I didn't know him well enough, and certainly not on a personal basis.*

At least Croix felt like he was getting his life back together before he died, if that was any consolation, Sam thought. *I helped him get some control over his anger. Made his life a little better.*

Oh well, Sam thought, getting up from his chair. *I've got other patients to see.*

CHAPTER TWENTY-THREE

"I want to get away from here," Maggie was saying as she led Viv inside. She closed the door after them and locked it.

"Why, is he coming back soon?"

"It was so weird last night," Maggie said. "He was acting so strange. And the blood. There was blood everywhere."

Maggie led her to the bathroom, which had since been cleaned. Maggie was able to find a few neglected spots here and there, though, which could have been blood.

"I guess you didn't dream it. But maybe there was a good explanation."

"You don't know how it's been," Maggie said. "He's been acting so strange lately. Coming and going at all hours of the night, and never telling me where. When he thinks I'm sleeping, he slips out. At first I thought there was another woman, but now I don't think it's that at all.

"When I saw the blood, I got to thinking some pretty terrible things. And the way he acted when I came in here, it scared me. I really don't know what to think."

"He didn't attack you?"

"No, but he had that look in his eyes. Early on, when we were first married, he'd get that look sometimes. And he did hit me a few times then. I thought that was all behind us now, but it's like everything's falling apart."

"Calm down," Viv told her. "You're getting upset."

"I just don't want to stay here, Viv. I don't feel safe here anymore."

"How did he act this morning, when he tried to wake you?"

They both went out into the hallway. Maggie led the way to the kitchen. There she opened a bottle of wine and didn't even bother finding a glass.

"He seemed okay, I guess. Like nothing ever happened. He sounded concerned when I told him I felt sick. Not concerned enough to stay, thank God."

"You're sure it wasn't a dream? Maybe those spots in the bathroom are something else."

"It wasn't a goddamn dream, Viv! I swear it wasn't."

"Okay, I believe you. I'm just trying to figure this out. It's a strange story. You're sure he wasn't injured somehow. Maybe he got in an accident or something."

"I thought that at first, too, but he didn't seem hurt at all. He was just angry. You should have heard the tone of his voice. I really thought he'd kill me if I didn't leave him alone."

Viv moved closer, put her arms around Maggie. "You've got to calm down. You're a wreck."

"You've got to take me away from here, Viv. Please."

"Isn't there anywhere you can go? Your mother's place maybe."

"I really don't talk to her much anymore. It's a long story, but she married this horrible guy a few years ago. There's no way I'm going there. And I really don't want to involve any of my friends. You're all I've got, Viv."

"Maggie, we just met. How can you expect me to take you away?"

"Maybe I could stay at your place for a while. Until I figure out what to do."

"No, my roommates wouldn't go for it. There's no room there."

Maggie put down the bottle and hugged her close. "Viv, you've got to help me."

Viv had been surprised when Maggie showed up at the bar again. It was true that she had gone there, hoping to see Maggie again, too, but she didn't think things would happen so fast. In fact, she'd wished Maggie wouldn't come back. She'd purposely not given Maggie her phone number or her address. There was no way Maggie could find her if she didn't want to be found. But there was also this soft aching inside Viv, this growing need, that made her go where Maggie might find her.

If she were the kind who prayed, Viv would have prayed that Maggie would stay away from her. But she had appeared like a sudden ghost, materializing out of thin air, as Viv sat in a corner booth with her morning screwdriver. She'd sat down across from her and told her how she was terrified of her husband. How she had to get away.

Reluctantly, Viv returned to the house with her. They could talk there, Maggie had said. But there was always the chance her husband could return, or something could go wrong. Viv never liked to go to their houses. It was better to meet in anonymous places, so nobody could trace her. And there was no way she'd bring someone back to *her* place.

Maggie was crying now. The tears were warm on her shoulder. Viv rubbed the back of her head.

"You really need to calm down," Viv said. "You're worrying yourself sick here."

"Please take me away," Maggie said. "Anywhere. Anywhere at all."

"Okay," Viv said. "We'll go somewhere where he can't find you. And then, when you get a hold of yourself, I'll help you in whatever you decide to do."

"Do you promise?" Maggie asked, pulling away, and looking at her through tear-stained eyes.

"I promise."

"Oh, Viv, you don't know what it means to me, to have you here. I don't know who else I could have turned to about this."

"Gather up some of your things," Viv said. "And we'll get started."

Viv had no idea where they were going, but her car was just outside. She had an idea that anywhere would be okay, as long as they didn't have to stay here.

Maggie went to pack her clothes. She brought the wine bottle with her.

Viv stayed in the living room. On a hearth, there was a framed picture of Maggie and a man, holding each other. Smiling. It had to be her husband. They made a nice couple. Viv tried to imagine him covered with blood, with rage in his eyes. It was a difficult image to conjure.

"There was blood everywhere," Maggie had said. There was no real evidence of such a bloodbath now. Just a few miniscule drops in the bathroom, which could have been anything. But she believed Maggie. There was no reason to make up a story like that.

Not that it mattered much. Even if Viv hadn't come along, Maggie would have left anyway. Better to go with her and keep an eye on her. Because at this point, if Maggie slipped away, it would be torture trying to find her again. The pain inside her was growing, and it couldn't be ignored much longer.

And there wasn't enough time to find a suitable substitute at this point.

* * *

"So what do you want to do?" Jeremy asked. "We can do anything you want. Anything at all."

"I don't know."

"We could go for a drive somewhere, get something to eat."

Colleen fidgeted. "I'll go along with whatever you say."

"It's so nice to have someone to do things with again," Jeremy said. "It's been such a long time. There was a time when I could count on Viv to do things with me, but she's hardly ever here anymore."

"Where does she go all the time?"

"I have no idea," he said, and she could tell he was holding something back.

"Seriously, what do you want to do? I'm game for anything," she told him.

"Is something wrong?" Jeremy asked.

"I don't know," she said. "It's just kind of strange. One minute I'm in my own apartment. Sure it was as big as a birdcage, but I'd lived there for years. And now, here I am, in this big house by the beach. It just takes getting used to, I guess."

"It's not me, is it?"

"Why would you say that, Jeremy? You've been nothing but wonderful to me. I owe you so much. I've never met anyone like you in my whole life."

He leaned over the back of the couch, beside where she sat. "I sure hope you feel that way. I didn't rush you out of your old place, did I? I just thought you wouldn't feel safe there anymore."

She leaned toward him and kissed him. The watery eyes didn't bother her. The slight spittle that occasionally collected in the corner of his slightly malformed mouth didn't stop her. He wasn't the hideous creature he obviously thought he was. She was determined to make him realize that."That was nice," Colleen said. "I've been wanting to do that for a long time now."

"Really?"

"I used to have such a crush on you, when you were in the magazines. You don't know. And now to be here with you. It's hard to believe."

"Colleen, I know I don't look exactly like I used to then. I want to be honest with you, right from the start. There was a plane accident. It was one of those little planes. I was flying, taking some friends for a ride, and we'd all been drinking. I just lost control. Everyone died but me. It was horrible."

"I think I read about it somewhere," Colleen said. "It was a long time ago."

"You don't hate me?"

"Of course not. What a horrible thing to go through."

"The guilt was unbearable. And there was so much reconstructive surgery. Even now, I feel so strange sometimes. Especially my face."

She leaned toward him and kissed him again, to quiet him.

"I really wanted to thank you for everything you've done for me," she said. "I guess I didn't know how to say it until now."

Jeremy was speechless. She started unbuttoning his shirt. He swept her up and carried her down the hall to his bedroom.

* * *

Sam was driving around, with no idea where he was going.

After he'd taken the subway home, he'd been surprised to find the house empty. He'd waited awhile, but he could tell something was wrong. He called Maggie's cell phone, but she didn't answer. He even called her work, but the office was closed for the day and he only got a recorded message. Considering Maggie's recent behavior, this got him worried, so he took the car out to look for her.

The problem was, he really didn't know where he could find her. A bar perhaps? A liquor store? He'd gone to a few of them near the house, but she wasn't there. He'd started checking some of the bars further out, toward the city, but still no luck.

He'd stopped for something to eat and then just kept driving. More to keep his mind off of things than to really find her. He knew he should probably go home soon to check if she was back yet, since he'd been gone for hours.

As he drove along a long stretch of road, he saw a girl illuminated in his headlights. She wore a red jacket, and was carrying a suitcase, which she appeared to be having trouble with. For the briefest of moments, he thought it might be Maggie, but it wasn't.

Sam pulled over to the side of the road and rolled his window down.

"Having trouble?" he asked.

The girl hesitated, then moved closer to the car. She looked him over. He could see the apprehension in her eyes, and then see her relax. "Someone was supposed to meet me, but they never showed up. And this suitcase is pretty heavy."

"Well there's no reason why I can't give you a ride where you're going. Why don't you get in? Put your bag in the back seat."

He opened the back door for her. She put her suitcase on the backseat and closed the door. Then she got in on the passenger side. She was a pretty blonde.

"Lucky thing you happened to come along," she told him. "I don't think I ever would have made it otherwise."

"I saw you were having trouble," Sam said, with a smile. "I couldn't just pass you by. So where are you headed?"

"The center of town is fine," she told him. "I can find a friend of mine there."

"Sure."

The road was lined with trees on either side. Then the trees got fewer. He smiled at her.

"It sure would have been a long walk for you. I don't know how you could have done it in the dark."

"God, I had no idea."

He suddenly struck her in the side of the head. It was hard and fast, and she slumped over against the passenger side door.

He took a side street, away from the main road. He knew a quiet place. The sun was already starting to go down.

After he parked, he leaned over her, and hit her again. Then he opened his car door and got out. He went around and opened the back door, pulled her suitcase out, and put it in the trunk. Then he opened her door, got her out, and put her in back.

She didn't move as he stretched her out on the backseat.

He straddled her, looking down at her face. She was young. Probably on college break. His receptionist Carla was maybe a year or two older. It was funny, him thinking of her at a time like this.

She had some bruising on the side of her face already. And there appeared to be a tear in her left eye. He hadn't even had time to find out her name.

He sat there, his crotch against hers, and started to unbutton her blouse. Then he stopped, looking down at her.

What the fuck am I doing? he wondered. But he was already starting to drift into a haze, into another mindset. Even though he asked the question of himself, it was already too late to really ponder it. To really consider the consequences of his actions. He was already outside of himself, an observer.

He undid the last button. She was wearing a white bra.

"Bitch!"

He rammed his fist into her head.

"Cunt!"

He hit her again. His balled up fist ramming her skull. There was bruising, blood.

"Whore!"

She made soft sounds, strangled sounds, like she was struggling with all her might not to regain consciousness.

He just kept hitting her, and about the fifth time, he heard a crunching sound, the cracking of bone. Part of her face was collapsed, the cheekbone shattered. But he still kept pounding.

He wasn't happy until her head was a bloody mess, devoid of features. It wasn't a human face at all anymore.

The rhythm of his punches overtook him, became the entire focus of his existence. He wasn't Sam anymore. Sam had long since left.

Sam was no longer in the car.

When her face was so much pulp, he finished tearing away her clothes, and fucked her still-warm corpse.

CHAPTER TWENTY-FOUR

They were in another motel room. Viv was sure she'd been here once, a year or so ago. She tried not to repeat herself too much, but it was bound to happen sometimes. Motel rooms offered a neutral ground, so people didn't have to die in their homes. When Viv came to places like this, she was almost always left alone. She tried to remember details about the last time she had been here. Who she'd been with. She tried to remember the room number back then. Was it the same room? There was something very déjà vu about this place.

Had someone else died in this same room, because of her?

No, it wasn't her fault. The desire was within them. She just brought it to fruition.

She and Maggie had gone drinking, Viv trying to postpone the inevitable. Then, when they came here, they made love. Viv had made sure it lasted awhile. She didn't want to rush this. But the ache inside her was getting worse.

Maggie was stretched out on the bed, now. Viv watched her drift in and out of sleep.

"What are you looking at?" Maggie asked sleepily, and smiled.

"Nothing," Viv said.

"Come back to me," Maggie said.

For someone who had never been with another woman before, Maggie was certainly very eager to learn. She had a lot of passion and it wasn't like Viv had to lead her by the hand every step of the way.

Although hands were involved.

At one point, when Maggie was in the midst of an orgasm, Viv had almost reached out to her mind, tried to find that lock only she could open. But she resisted it with all her willpower. It was still too soon.

Viv was greedy and wanted a little more time with her, before the end.

"What are you looking at, sweetie?" Maggie asked again.

"Just you, angel." Viv would never have allowed herself to use such a silly word before. But it seemed fitting here.

Maggie smiled wider. "Come back to me."

There was a tear in one of Maggie's eyes, and it was then that Viv knew there was no turning back. No matter how painful this would be, she had to go through with it.

"Okay."

Viv crawled across the bed and snuggled up beside Maggie.

I could get used to this, Viv thought. *I could even see myself falling for this one.*

But she knew that was a mistake. Her hunger came first. Just like any job, she had made a promise to herself long ago not to get emotionally involved. But there were bound to be times like this, when that promise became so very difficult to keep.

Viv kissed her, then ran a finger along her brow. "You're really enjoying this, aren't you?" she whispered.

"Yeah."

Viv looked right into Maggie's eyes and they felt like magnets, holding her gaze.

"Do you know where the bottle is?" Maggie asked, suddenly breaking their staring contest to look around on the bed, on the floor.

The booze. Well, if nothing else, it would make things easier. The alcohol made Maggie seem more pathetic, and maybe it wouldn't hurt as much to take her life. *Yeah*, Viv thought. *Who am I kidding?*

"One minute," Viv said and pulled away to look for the bottle. There were actually two of them. One was empty and had rolled out of sight. Another one was half empty and near the foot of the bed. Viv snatched it up off the floor and brought it to Maggie's waiting hands.

"Thank you," she said, perking up, and unscrewed the cap. She brought the bottle to her lips and took a long drink.

Might as well let her enjoy it, Viv thought. *It'll be her last.*

Viv watched her drink, then took the bottle away and put it on the floor. She kissed Maggie again.

"Enough of that," Viv said. "I'm starting to get jealous of that bottle."

"What do you think Sam is doing right now?" Maggie asked her. "Right this minute? He must be home by now. Do you think he's going nuts wondering where I am?"

"I thought you didn't care about him anymore."

"I don't. I was just wondering. Do you think he misses me at all? That I ever was important to him? I don't care, but I wish I could see for myself."

Viv put a finger to her lips. "Sssh. You're with me now."

Viv kissed her deeper, and let her fingers go exploring. They shifted on the bed.

This time, while they were in the midst of exploring each other with their tongues, Viv zeroed in on the part of Maggie's psyche that wanted to die. The sad part of her soul.

"Oh, Viv," Maggie moaned softly beneath her.

Viv turned the key that unlocked Maggie's soul, slowly. She didn't want it to happen too fast. Maggie started to thrash beneath her.

"Oh, my God," Maggie said, louder now. "Oh, Viv!"

Viv was getting caught up in the passion, too, and wanted to enjoy it as much as she could before Maggie was gone to her.

"Oh Viv, that feels so fucking good!"

Viv slid up her body, so that she could see Maggie's face. She let her fingers continue what her mouth had been doing. She looked Maggie right in the eyes.

Maggie's eyes were half-closed as she looked up at Viv. She had stopped thrashing about.

"Oh, that's so good," Maggie said, softer again. "I can feel myself fading."

"I know."

"I'm dying. That's right, isn't it, Viv?"

"That's right," Viv said.

"It feels so good," Maggie said again. But her voice was getting fainter.

Maggie smiled, and then she was dead.

In those last moments, inside Maggie's head, Viv could feel the waves of love emanating from her. The overwhelming emotions.

And, as Maggie died, Viv found herself in the throes of ecstasy. She rolled over onto her back and surrendered to the sensations. Letting them move her like a puppet.

When it was over, Viv could not be sure what had actually *fed* her. She took it for granted that it was Maggie's soul, but she could never be certain about such things. Even after all these years of feeding, it was still a mystery to her in many ways.

"I'm sorry, Maggie."

Viv got up and went to the bathroom to shower. When she was done, she got dressed and cleaned the room as best she could.

She left Maggie there, on the bed. At least she didn't have to say good-bye.

* * *

"What was that?" Colleen asked, sitting up in bed.

"It's just Viv come back," Jeremy said.

She lay back down. "Sorry, I forgot we're not here alone."

"I probably should go out and talk to her," Jeremy said. "I haven't talked to her in a while. She does live here, too, after all."

"Are you ever going to tell me why you two never did it?" Colleen asked playfully. "It's not like you're not good in bed."

Jeremy blushed. "I guess a thank you would be in order."

"Thank you," Colleen said, grinning.

"I meant me," he said. "It's been a long time. I had a lot of time to make up for. It's not like I'm the stud I once was." He laughed at that one.

"Well, you were. I saw you in the papers. Always with a different model. Or an actress. Talk about variety. And to think I'm sharing your bed. How many famous women were right where I am, right now?"

"Enough," he said. "I'd be lying if I said I didn't enjoy myself back then."

Jeremy slid out of bed. "I'll be right back." He grabbed his robe off the floor.

"Well, at least I know Viv isn't competition," Colleen said. "At least I hope not. You haven't been lying to me about her, have you?"

"Of course not," Jeremy said, putting on his robe. "But we're still friends, after all. I want to see how she's been doing."

Despite the fact that Colleen was in the midst of her period, they'd been unable to control themselves and had been making love most of the night. Which was something odd for Jeremy. In the past, he'd mostly dated women who were very self-conscious about those kinds of things. But Colleen wasn't concerned in the least. All she suggested was he put a towel under her during sex, to protect the sheets.

She put her panties back on and got back in bed. Jeremy looked down at her.

God, she's beautiful, Jeremy thought. *Like a downpour after a drought.*

Colleen returned his gaze, and blew him a kiss.

Jeremy smiled and left the room, closing the door behind him.

Colleen stared at the door, and used her fingers to bring herself to orgasm. Something Jeremy had just barely failed to do. Not that she'd let him know that. She faked an orgasm perfectly for him. His self-satisfied air told her that. But Colleen was not about to give up after getting so close.

As she touched herself, she tried to keep from thinking about the scars on his body. She had never seen anyone before with so many. He had been so self-conscious about them; it had been kind of touching how vulnerable they made him. But now, unable to keep her mind off them, she almost found them exciting in some weird way.

She gasped, staring at the closed door.

* * *

"Hi," Jeremy said, entering the kitchen. Viv was eating some cold lasagna and drinking a beer.

"Hello stranger," Viv said. "Where's the kid?"

"Hey, she's over twenty-one," Jeremy said. "Barely."

They both laughed.

"It's good to hear you laugh," Viv said.

"So where have you been lately? I haven't seen you in ages."

"I know," Viv said. "A lot of shit's been happening lately."

"You're still feeding then?"

"You know I don't have a choice in the matter."

"I'm surprised nobody ever caught on," Jeremy said. "I mean, I'm thankful. But after all the people you must have sent to the great beyond…"

"Do we really need to talk about this?" Viv said, and shoveled a big spoonful of pasta into her mouth.

"I'm sorry," he said. "I didn't mean it that way."

"Sure you did," Viv said. "You're afraid I'll get busted at some point, and I'll bring some trouble back here. Don't worry about it. I cover my tracks. Besides, they can't prove anything. They die of natural causes. It's not murder."

"How can you be so sure the coroners will decide that way?"

"Because I know," Viv said. "There's no proof of foul play at all. I've been doing this a long time."

"I hope so."

"Don't worry so much."

"Are you okay? You seem kind of down."

"A rough one today. I actually had feelings for her. That's bad when you do what I do."

"Which is why you never did it to me, even when I begged you to?"

"I couldn't do it to you. It would be painful. Shit, it was painful enough doing this one, and I only knew her a few days. She was pretty special, though. Kind of like you."

"You know, you could have saved me a lot of suffering."

"I am not going to have this conversation again," Viv said. "Besides, if I'd done that, you wouldn't be enjoying your new girlfriend right now."

"True enough," Jeremy agreed. "I guess time does make it easier."

"I told you so."

"Pretty ironic coming from you. The mercy killer."

"Not now, Jeremy."

"I'm sorry. That was crossing the line, wasn't it?"

"What if she were to hear you. You haven't told her, have you?"

"No," Jeremy said.

"But you will."

"Not if you don't want me to."

"You'll slip in a moment of passion. You'll tell her whatever she wants to know. Just make sure you can trust her first. Or at least warn me, so I can move on."

"I don't want you to go."

"What you want doesn't matter, Jeremy," Viv told him. "My survival means that I leave when things get unsafe here. You spill the beans, and she blabs, I'm gone."

"I won't say anything."

"I know you, Jeremy. When you fall for her, it will be hard."

"It's been so long since I was involved with anyone, Viv. You know that."

"Exactly what I meant; you're vulnerable. There *is* something endearing about her, though, I'll give her that. But there's something about her I don't trust. Maybe that will change as I get to know her, but for now, I'm going to be very careful."

"You don't have to worry about her."

"I hope you're right."

"Oh, I almost forgot. She told me that when she first met you, she saw some kind of vision for a moment. Some kind of pattern. Remember how she kind of zoned out? Staring at you? That's why."

"That's weird. What does she think it means?"

"She doesn't know exactly. But guess what? You're not the first one. She saw somebody else like you."

"What?"

"Well, not exactly like you. Someone murdered her friend right in front of her. She saw a vision around him, too."

"Another one?"

"Sure sounds that way, although she did say his was a lot different than yours. It was kind of threatening, which would make sense. I don't think she found yours threatening."

"Who,   where?"

"Back in the city, where she used to live," Jeremy said. "Like I said, someone who killed her friend right in front of her. It sounded bizarre, the way she described him. His face bright red. Able to tear a man apart with his bare hands."

"Really?"

"A relative of yours, perhaps."

"I don't do anything like that."

"You just feed on their souls. That's how you described it to me."

"Do we really need to talk about that now?" she asked. "Do you think she's afraid of me?"

"Not really. I think you freaked her out for a moment when she first met you, the whole vision thing. But she doesn't seem particularly disturbed by you now. In fact, she's really embarrassed about the way she reacted to you."

"Well, I certainly don't want to disturb anyone. You don't think I should move out?"

"Not at all," Jeremy said. "I told you, she's cool. So do you think you and that other guy are linked at all?"

"Well, it's not Grif, I know that much for sure. But I want to know more about this guy. Do you think she'd tell me?"

"I don't know."

"You could get her to."

"Maybe, at some point, but it's still painful for her to remember."

"Well, if there is a link, and there's somebody else like me running around, I want to know more about it. "

"Makes sense."

"By the way," Viv said, then shoveled a chunk of lasagna into her mouth.

"Yeah?"

"I can smell blood on you."

He tried to keep from blushing, but it felt like he failed. "It's that time of the month," he said and then trailed off, not wanting to go into any more detail than he had to.

Viv chuckled.

Jeremy got two bottles of beer from the refrigerator.

"So, are you going to be okay?" he asked.

"Yeah, sure. I'll live. I can feel the exhaustion coming on. After I eat I'll head to bed. I'll be real quiet for a day or two, as usual. Locked away in my room."

"I understand. Nobody will bother you."

"Thanks for being so understanding, Jeremy. I doubt many people would be as supportive as you've been."

"You got me through some tough times, Viv. I can't imagine not returning the favor."

"I know you feel that way, but thanks anyway."

He moved closer and kissed her on the cheek. "I still regret not taking our relationship to another level, though. Even if it meant the death of me."

"You say that now," Viv said. "But I had your best interests at heart."

"Well, if I find out I have cancer or something someday, let me go out with a smile, okay?"

"Sure thing."

He took the beers down the hall, back to his room. Viv finished eating.

* * *

Sam returned to a dark, empty house. His first instinct was to take a shower, get cleaned up. There was some blood on him. This would have disturbed him, especially since it was becoming more and more common, but he was still in somewhat of a daze. Like coming out of a trance.

As he was taking a shower, he started thinking about Maggie.

When he was done, he made his rounds of the house he shared with her, looking in every room. He even looked in the closets and under the bed, which made no sense at all, but there was no sign of her. And there weren't any messages on their answering machine. No words, spoken in her voice, to tell him where she was or put his mind at ease. No messages on his cell phone, either.

"Strange," he said softly to himself, his head still slightly fuzzy. "This isn't like her at all."

He figured she must have gone on a drinking binge, and was at a bar, or worse, passed out in the gutter somewhere. Maybe someone even took advantage of her. This last thought made him shudder.

I remember searching for her, but not much else, he thought. Who knows? *Maybe I went on a binge of my own.*

But he felt too good. In fact he felt *very* good, energized. The more his head cleared, the more he could feel the energy surging within him.

What the hell was I doing all night? he wondered. *Clearly, if I'd found Maggie, I would have brought her back home with me.*

He saw the clock radio on the bedside table in the bedroom. It was after midnight. It was like he had been out sleepwalking. He wasn't even sure if he'd ever been a sleepwalker before, but there were lots of clues that seemed to point in that direction now. The whole idea disturbed him; not having control over his own actions.

He stretched out on the bed, wondering what to do next about Maggie's disappearance. Should he call the police now? Should he go out and look for her again?

Instead, he drifted off to sleep.

CHAPTER TWENTY-FIVE

Alone in her room, Viv sat cross-legged and naked on the floor, trying hard to empty her mind. She should have been asleep by now. Usually, the exhaustion would take over a few hours after she "fed," but for some odd reason her mind was sharper than ever.

Even though she tried to wipe her thoughts clean, she saw Maggie's face, beatific in the midst of orgasm, thanking her for the peace that opened up before her. She saw the moment when life vanished from Maggie's eyes, turning them to glass.

She also found herself worrying.

In the past, she was able to refrain from feeding for weeks at a time. Sometimes, she could go a whole month without having to find a victim. But lately, this had changed. It had only been a matter of days between Richard Croix and Maggie. Was her hunger getting stronger? Was she going to have a harder and harder time resisting the urges that welled up inside her? As she grew older, she thought the needs would diminish with time, that eventually she could resist the urge completely. But the exact opposite seemed to be the case. Her appetites were stronger than ever now.

I've got to cleanse my mind.

But the images were so vivid. The worry so nagging.

Eventually, the exhaustion came and took over, and she couldn't concentrate on anything anymore.

She slid onto her mattress just before dawn, finally able to sleep.

* * *

Sam woke to the ringing of the telephone. He sat up in bed, franticly looking around the room. His eyes fell upon the clock beside his bed. It was almost noon and he'd forgotten to set the alarm for work. Then he realized that it was Saturday.

The phone continued to ring. Grabbing for the receiver, he knocked the phone onto the floor.

He picked it up. "Hello?" he said, before he'd brought it to his ear.

"Mr. Wayne," the man's voice said on the other end. "Sam Wayne?"

"Yes." He had hoped it would be Maggie's voice. But this man, asking his name. *It couldn't be good.*

"Mr. Wayne, my name is Detective Ben Carroll. I have some news about your wife, Maggie."

"Oh God, I was just going to call the police. She's been gone all night. Is she okay?"

"I'm sorry to have to tell you this, but I'd like you to come with me down to the city morgue and identify a body we believe might be your wife."

"What?"

"I'm sorry to have to tell you this way. A woman was found dead in a motel room this morning, and she had your wife's identification. Margaret Wayne, right?"

"Yes, that's right."

"Do you have a pen handy? I'll give you the address."

"One minute," Sam said, pulling open the drawer of his night table and rummaging around for a slip of paper and a pen. When he had it, he told the officer on the other end, and then wrote down the address the man gave him.

"I'll be there as soon as I can," Sam said.

"I'll be waiting for you, Mr. Wayne. Once again, I'm sorry for your loss, if it is her."

Sam hung up the phone.

He tried to figure out what he was feeling at that moment. All he could really come up with was *numb*. There was a chance, after all, that it wasn't Maggie. But everything seemed to point to the possibility that it probably was. She was missing. She hadn't called or tried to contact him in any way. And her behavior had been very erratic lately.

"Oh, Maggie," he said, wanting so badly to cry, but it just didn't seem real yet. It felt as if he were still dreaming, or in a bad TV movie.

He got his clothes together and went to take a shower. Maybe the water pounding on him would wake him up a bit. Maybe then he'd realize that this wasn't really happening.

CHAPTER TWENTY-SIX

"So it's your wife?"

"Yeah," Sam said, staring down at her. The coroner had opened one of the long, metal drawers and, there, lifeless before him, was Maggie. It was strange how death transformed people. Just because he was looking at her body didn't mean that it really felt like her anymore. She seemed so alien to him now.

He looked at her face. Almost angelic, but also weird, like a mask. He wondered what was beneath the sheet? Had they cut her open at all? Performed an autopsy?

"I'm sorry," Detective Carroll said, nodding to the coroner, who closed the drawer.

"What happened to her?"

"Appears to have been a heart attack," the coroner said, looking into Sam's eyes. He was older than Carroll, and where the detective was stocky and intense, the coroner was thin and seemed bored. "No sign of trauma."

"She was found in a motel room by a cleaning lady," Carroll said. "There doesn't seem to have been any foul play, but we're investigating it. She seems to have died peacefully."

"Thank God."

"On the phone, you said something about her being missing. That you were just about to call the police yourself?"

"When I got home from work yesterday, she wasn't home. I had no idea where she was. And she didn't come back all night. I was worried, but I had no idea something like this had happened."

"So you really had no clue where she'd gone? If she was with anyone?"

"None. I just told you that. *Was* she with anybody?"

"Your wife was the one who got the room key, and she did it alone. We've been asking around and someone saw a woman near the room. Walking away. And I hate to say this, but there appears to have been sexual contact. But there was no evidence of force. There's no sign of a crime." Detective Carroll didn't wait to get Sam's reaction to his wife's infidelity. "Did you know your wife had a heart condition, Mr. Wayne?"

"No, I didn't," Sam said.

"Well, sometimes people have one and don't even know it. I guess that's what happened here. It's strange that a doctor never caught it at some point."

Sam could feel the tears welling up in his eyes. He tried to hold them back.

"I'm sure she died without much pain," the coroner said. He led them down the hall, back to his office.

"You can tell?"

"There are signs," the coroner said.

Sam suspected there was no way to be a hundred percent sure about such things. That the coroner was trying to put his mind at ease.

"Can you fill out these forms, Mr. Wayne?" Carroll asked him, indicating some papers. "They just confirm that the body in there is your wife?"

"Yes, of course."

Sam skimmed the papers quickly, then signed them.

"You should probably make arrangements to have someone come get her," the coroner said. He sucked his back teeth and acknowledged Sam's blank state. "You know, a funeral home or something."

"Oh. I hadn't even thought about that."

"That's because you're in shock, Mr. Wayne," Carroll said. "It's totally understandable. This would shake anybody to the core."

"What about the woman someone saw leaving the room? You think they were lovers? Do you know who she is?"

"You didn't know anything about it?"

"No," Sam said. "I don't have a clue who it could be."

"Our witness said it was a blonde woman. Beyond that, she wasn't too helpful. She said it was difficult to see the woman's face. Does that mean anything, Mr. Wayne?"

"She has a few friends, and I know one or two of them are blonde, but nobody out of the ordinary. No one who would hurt her. She'd been kind of keeping to herself lately, anyway, from what I can tell. She's been missing a lot of work."

"I see," Carroll said.

"Do you think it's relevant?"

"I'll look into it."

"I want to thank you for calling me, Detective. For letting me know."

"I'm sorry I had such bad news," Carroll said. "But I guess somebody has to do these things, right? What else can you tell me about your wife's health, Mr. Wayne? Was there anything else, any illness she'd had recently?"

"Not really," Sam said, then thought about it. "Well, I had this suspicion that she'd been drinking a lot lately. I was going to try to stage some kind of intervention, but I didn't have a chance."

"The autopsy did show alcohol in her system. But she didn't die from that. You see, the reason why I'm taking such an interest in all this is, there have been a few deaths like this, recently. Strange deaths. Seemingly healthy people just up and dying. No sign of a struggle at all. Nothing suspicious. But the deaths themselves are suspicious. To me, anyway."

"I understand," Sam said.

"I'll be in touch if I find out anything more," Detective Carroll said.

Sam nodded. "Is it okay to go now?"

"Of course," Carroll said. "Thanks for coming down here. I wish it were different circumstances; that it wasn't your wife. Once again, I'm sorry for your loss."

Sam nodded and made his way down the hall.

* * *

After that, Sam didn't remember very much. He must have wandered out of that place in a real daze, and somehow he'd ended up in the park.

"You blind bastard," someone shouted. It took Sam a moment to realize it wasn't directed at him. It came from behind some trees. He moved in that direction. There was a baseball diamond on the other side. A little league game was going on.

"Enough of that," an umpire was saying to a parent in the stands. "Watch your language."

"You blind fuck," the father said. "You made the wrong call."

Sam could feel the tension. He saw one of the kids tense up, probably the irate father's son. The air around Sam was crackling.

"I told you to watch it," the umpire said. A coach came over to try to defuse things.

"You asshole," the father said and jumped off the bleachers, running onto the field. He grabbed the umpire.

Everyone seemed to freeze at that moment. Like a still photograph. Sam saw the father grab the umpire, his other fist balled up and ready to strike. He saw the coach preparing to grab his arm and try to restrain him. But everything had stopped.

Then, everything sped up.

Fists were thrown, the umpire was on the ground, and the coach was grappling with the father. But then something strange happened. Everyone's attention was focused on the altercation. Everyone in the stands, all the kids in the field.

And then, something snapped.

Fights broke out in the stands first, and then the violence spilled out onto the field, as the kids and coaches started fighting with each other. In no time at all, everyone in the stands surged toward the field.

Sam watched as it became a massive brawl. Everyone lashed out at whoever was closest. People were crying out, fighting, bleeding.

Sam stood there, watching, taking it all in.

There was a full-blown riot breaking out right in front of him. A kid struck a woman in the face, knocking her to the ground. A grown man attacked the kid, punching him over and over. Everybody was attacking someone. Children were beating mothers, fathers were punching each other. A pregnant woman was on the ground, being kicked in the stomach by a pack of kids. Their faces were red with rage.

Sam walked away, back toward the trees.

He felt strangely serene as he disappeared into the woods. He could hear police sirens in the distance.

* * *

Viv woke covered in sweat. She'd had a nightmare, strong enough to wake her, but once awake she couldn't remember any of it.

She looked around the mostly bare room. She was alone. She could not remember the details of her dream, but there was a feeling that she was under attack. It was such a strong feeling, that even now she was struggling to regain her composure.

After she fed, Viv would usually be completely exhausted for a good twenty-four hours. Sometimes longer. She usually came back to Jeremy's place to hide away and recover. She'd learned a long time ago that it was better not to fight it, that the best thing she could do was to sleep it off.

As the feeling of dread left her, it was replaced with a sense of physical well being. As if Maggie's energy had been sucked into her. That always happened afterwards. She just didn't think about it very much. She definitely didn't want to think about it *now*.

In fact, there was a lot about her needs that she did not understand at all. She took them simply on faith. What really happened when she found "the lock" inside people? How did she take their lives away? And was it really "feeding"? It felt that way, as if something were leaving them and entering her. Their souls, perhaps? Since it happened to her at the moment when the others died, that's what she always thought. But Viv wasn't sure if she believed in souls. There was definitely *some* kind of energy exchange, though.

At first, after the other person died, she felt euphoric, but it eventually gave way to exhaustion. After she got some rest though, and assimilated what had happened to her, she felt a different kind of pleasure. She felt whole. Satiated. She positively glowed.

Like right now.

She wouldn't let herself think about the fact that the energy making her feel so good now was a direct result of Maggie's death.

What really concerned her, though, was the *immediacy* of Maggie's death. She usually didn't need to feed so soon afterwards. There would be an aching inside her, and she would put it off for as long as she could, before she had to seek out her next *victim*. Was that the right word? Was she like some kind of vampire who sought out victims? She saw it coming. Viv knew before they went to that motel room that Maggie would die there. She also knew that she would be unable to resist it.

Some people had such a sadness in their core, that they were irresistible to her. Maggie was like that. There was something deep inside her that begged Viv to release her. That was why she couldn't resist the urge.

It was inevitable that they would meet, that Viv would take her life away.

But why so soon? Viv wondered, sitting up in bed. *Why couldn't we just have a few weeks together?*

She knew deep inside that it would have made things worse. If she felt this guilty now, what would she have felt if they had been even closer? As it was, she had been on the verge of falling for Maggie. On the verge of breaking her own rule, to never get emotionally involved with a victim. It was intimate work she did, and such intimacy always brought with it the risk of pain.

Viv remembered Maggie's face the last time she saw her. Maggie was stretched out on the motel room bed, her face so peaceful and angelic. Viv's victims were nothing if not grateful for what she bestowed upon them. They all wanted release. But Maggie's face had been even more beatific than most. Like she had seen the face of God before she died. And who knows, maybe she did.

Or maybe Viv had simply been able to make Maggie's last moment alive as pleasurable as possible.

Viv got out of bed and began her exercise regimen. She had all this energy to burn, why not use it constructively?

* * *

"How does it look? Colleen asked, modeling the outfit for Jeremy, who looked on approvingly.

"It looks great."

"Oh, I've never worn anything this nice in my whole life."

"Then it's yours," Jeremy said. "You can wear it to the fundraiser."

"What fundraiser?"

"There's an AIDS charity next month. I get these invitations all the time. I guess I used to go to a lot of those kinds of events, before the accident. I've been itching to get back into the swing of things. This would be the perfect excuse, if you're interested that is."

"And you want *me* to go with you?"

"Who else?" Jeremy asked her.

"Oh, that sounds wonderful, Jeremy."

"I'll reply to the invitation soon, then." He smiled. His grin was slightly lopsided. "I have to admit, I'm pretty nervous about the idea, though.

"Don't worry," Colleen said. "I'll be there, right beside you."

Right then, Turney's death was the furthest thing from her mind. She was finally starting to feel normal again.

"The dress is beautiful," Colleen said, hugging her arms.

Jeremy laughed.

CHAPTER TWENTY-SEVEN

Sam stopped in front of a house. He'd wandered through the park and found himself in a neighborhood he didn't recognize. In shock, aimless, he simply kept walking. The neighborhood was unfamiliar, but the house he stopped in front of seemed to spark some sense of recognition in him. He had been here before.

He walked up the steps and stood in front of the door. Instinctively, he pulled out his keys. There were a few new keys there he hadn't noticed before. Keys he didn't recognize. He put one in the door and turned.

The door opened.

Slowly, cautiously, he went inside. It was like part of him knew already what he would find in there. But the part of him that was conscious, aware, didn't have a clue.

Sam locked the door behind him. All the shades were down, and there was a distinct odor in the house. The house was in a shambles, everything in disarray.

He wandered from room to room, flicking the light switches, but the power must have been shut off, because none of them worked. But he moved around as if he were very familiar with the layout of the house.

Then, in what was probably one of the bedrooms, but was devoid of furniture, he stumbled on something. He went over to the window and raised the shade.

There were bodies, strewn across the floor.

He lowered the shade again and sank to his knees, as the realization hit him that he was somehow responsible for the horrors that unfolded before him. And on some other level, unrelated but just as devastating, was Maggie's death. A tremendous wave of grief washed over him.

His body was wracked with sobs. The tears came without warning, mercifully blocking out the carnage before him.

PART THREE

THIS CONTAGIOUS RAGE

CHAPTER TWENTY-EIGHT

L ITTLE LEAGUE RIOT CLAIMS 10!
  He'd already read the article three times, but something compelled him to read it again. Perhaps it was the description of the incident as "an eruption of pure rage." The possibility of such a violent free-for-all seemed far-fetched, even by today's standards, and yet, here was the proof. Children, parents, coaches all involved in some bloodthirsty melee. Ten people dead, including several children, as well as a pregnant woman and her unborn child. She had been kicked in the stomach and ribs repeatedly.

What fucking animals, Sam thought, amazed by what he read. *I guess rage management really is a necessary profession these days.*

The incident had happened a week ago, but for some strange reason, he couldn't bring himself to throw the paper away. There were still daily updates. A couple of kids who had been in the hospital had finally died. There were still some in critical condition, and the doctors weren't sure if they'd make it. A woman suffered severe brain damage.

Charlie had an appointment for nine that morning, but he was late. Earlier in the week, his mother had called to say he wasn't feeling well. Sam could tell she was lying, but even if it had been the truth, he should have been better by now. He'd already rescheduled the boy twice. Sam looked at his watch. It was a couple of minutes before ten. The session was over.

He isn't coming back, Sam thought. *Does he really think I'm going to just forget about him?* I'm going to have to go see him sometime soon and try to talk some sense into him.

Sam thought they had an understanding, but he had been wrong. This showed him that Charlie had no respect for him or his abilities at all.

He's not coming back.

The phone buzzed and Sam picked up the receiver. It was Carla.

"Would you like Mrs. Carlisle to come in now?"

"No, Carla, give me a few more minutes. I'll come out when I'm ready."

There were photographs in the newspaper on his desk of the police trying to break up a crowd of people who were intent on killing each other. A man with a bloodied face was off in one corner, trying to cover his head. A woman appeared to be lifeless on the ground beside him. It seemed more graphic than what the papers usually printed.

It hadn't happened very far from where he sat now. Almost a stone's throw away. In the park. He walked by there almost every day at lunchtime. In fact, he'd seen baseball games being played there all the time during the summer months.

He looked at his watch again. Inwardly, he cursed Charlie for not showing up. Then he got to his feet and went to the door of his office. He opened it and went out into the lobby.

"Mrs. Carlisle, I'll see you now," he said to the woman seated on the other side of the room. She got up from her chair, put down her magazine, and followed him into the office.

"Please take a seat."

She did as she was told. She was one of his success stories. Her volatile temper was a thing of the past. She was calmer now. She didn't even feel the need to smoke anymore, an unexpectedly pleasant side effect of his treatment.

"Dr. Wayne, did you read about that awful riot in the park?" Brenda Carlisle asked him. She was about thirty-five, brunette hair, slightly stocky build. She dressed tastefully, but not expensively. She was an executive assistant in an office. She was taking time off from work to be here, and yet she didn't have any trouble making it to her appointment on time. *Unlike Charlie.*

"I saw," Sam said. "It was pretty horrible."

"Too bad you couldn't have helped those people," Mrs. Carlisle said. She was not particularly old looking, nor was she unattractive, but there was something matronly about her. He had a hard time thinking of her as Brenda. Mrs. Carlisle seemed to fit better, for some odd reason.

"Thank you for the vote of confidence," Sam said. "But unfortunately, I can't help everyone. Only those who come to me. Like you."

Mrs. Carlisle smiled.

"How have you been doing, Brenda?" he forced himself to use her first name, as she had requested in past sessions.

"I've been doing wonderfully, Doctor," she said. He was going to correct her and say that he was not a licensed psychiatrist, that he was a *psychologist*, but he saw no point in saying it. In her healing process, she had seen him as an authority figure, a doctor. Many of his patients did. He did not correct them, if their mistake helped them define his role in their minds.

"In fact, I wanted to talk to you about that."

"Of course, Brenda. Please go on."

"I've been doing so well lately, thanks to you of course, that I wanted to stop coming here for a while. To see how I can do without the sessions."

"Hmmm," he hummed.

"I don't mean it as an insult, Dr. Wayne. In fact, it's the opposite. You've done such a good job, I feel like I can handle this myself from now on. Or, at least I hope I can. You know, I used to come three times a week, and now its just once a week. I know things are a lot better. I was just thinking maybe it's time for the next step."

It was funny how she'd demanded he call her Brenda, and yet she continued to call him *Dr. Wayne.* She wanted him to be the dominant figure and had no desire for them to be equals.

He had an image in his mind of her on the floor. Her clothes torn off. He was trying to force a pen into her rectum.

The image bothered him. He tried to put it out of his mind. Instead, he thought of Charlie skipping his session.

"Doctor Wayne?"

"Yes, Brenda. I think you're right. I think we've made a breakthrough, and your desire to move on is definitely a healthy one. I won't stand in your way on this. In fact, I totally agree with you."

"You do?"

"Yes, you've made incredible progress over the last year. And I think it's become very clear that you are not the same woman you were a year ago. You are in control of your life now. You are free of the confines of your temper."

"I owe it all to you, Doctor."

"You owe it mostly to yourself. I simply provided the tools. You had to want to heal yourself; you had to make the effort. And you did. A year is actually quite remarkable, you know. Some people take many years to reach the point you have."

Which was only partially true. While most therapists did take years to heal someone like Brenda, he found that his methods were much more effective, and worked much quicker. He was able to heal most of his patients in a very short span of time, considering the severity of many of their maladies. The thing was, most of them didn't know when to move on, and continued to come long after the sessions had lost any effectiveness. He didn't tell them otherwise, because he had to pay bills, after all. But it was nice to see someone come to the realization on her own.

Besides, the ones like her, who had been coming for a while, had nothing to offer him anymore. The adrenaline rush he got from patients when he first started seeing them always fizzled out over time. The thrill was diminished the more he healed them.

"Thank you for agreeing with me, Dr. Wayne," she said. "And thanks for making a difference in my life."

"All this praise," Sam said. "I'm not used to it." Which was a lie. He'd had many grateful patients who had showered praise on him in the past. Too many.

"I mean every word of it, Doctor," Mrs. Carlisle said.

"Well, thank you. I have grown so used to seeing you every week that I have to admit, I'll miss you, Brenda."

I'll miss your perfume, and the curve of your thigh, Sam thought. And I'll always wonder why I didn't make a move on you when you made it so obvious that you were interested.

She smiled at his compliment. "Well, thank you, Doctor. I'll miss you, too."

"So there's really nothing else to say at this point. You can tell Carla on your way out that this was your last session."

"Don't we have anything else to talk about?"

"I think that about covers it."

She looked disappointed. Perhaps she really did want him to at least try to seduce her. He couldn't be sure. Those kinds of signals were often wasted on him. It wasn't because he was a professional, although he did try to uphold the integrity of his profession. Was it because he was a married man? *Had been* a married man, he corrected himself. Maybe he still felt a loyalty to Maggie, after all these years. But an even bigger reason was because he just had a kind of awkwardness about these things. Here he was a confident, sophisticated adult, a professional healer, and even now he had vestiges of the feelings he had back in high school when a girl would flirt with him, and he'd get all tongue-tied, not sure how to respond. It was a wonder he ever got beyond that enough to have relationships at all, much less find someone like Maggie. *And now she was gone.*

The image of Mrs. Carlisle on the floor, on all fours, and him exploring her orifices with his gold pen, came back to him.

She stood up. Her skirt rode up for a moment as she rose, revealing a brief glimpse of a thigh. "Well, I guess this is goodbye," she said.

She hesitated, then held out her hand.

She clearly was as clueless about this moment as he was.

He shook her hand. "I am very proud of you, Brenda. You have proven to me how strong you really are today. But please, if things get difficult again, don't ever hesitate to come back. It is not a sign of failure to need help. In fact, realizing you need help is the first step to victory."

As he said the words, he knew it sounded like so much bullshit, but he felt the need to say *something*, and he just couldn't bring himself to ask her if she wanted to fuck right then and there on the dark green carpeting.

"Thank you, Dr. Wayne."

They released hands. He saw something in her eyes that told him he'd had a chance at something this morning. A chance he'd let slip by.

It's not a big deal, he told himself. It's not like she's a knockout or anything. And Maggie just *died*, for Christ sake. They just buried her this week; I was standing over her grave as they lowered her coffin in the ground. There was a proper amount of time to grieve, after all.

He watched Mrs. Carlisle go. She closed the door after her, and he was alone in his office again. He wanted to just grab his coat and leave, go to Charlie's house, talk some sense to the kid before it was too late to save him. But he had responsibilities here.

Carla had told him he should take a few more days off, it being so soon after Maggie had been laid to rest, but he couldn't stand to stay in that empty house alone. His patients needed him. And he needed to be as far from that house as possible.

The phone buzzed. It would be Carla to ask if he wanted to see his next patient now, since Mrs. Carlisle had left early, or if he wanted to wait until the appointed time. He stared at the phone, unable to bring himself to answer it. After three buzzes, it stopped.

He stared at the newspaper headline again, wondering why the story bothered him so much. Sure, it was a horrible thing that had happened. But why did he feel so close to it all?   He didn't know anybody who had been there, who had been hurt.

And then he noticed the date. It had happened the same day that he'd identified Maggie's body. Maybe *that* had something to do with his fixation.

He sat back in his brown leather chair and closed his eyes, trying to empty his mind and failing miserably.

CHAPTER TWENTY-NINE

"What do you got?" Detective Ben Carroll asked, finishing his fourth cigarette of the morning.

"Wait til you get a load of this, Carroll," Fred Chapin told him, leading him to the site. "A guy was walking his dog through the park and his dog noticed something strange, I guess, and tried to dig it up."

They went behind some trees. There was a mound of fresh-dug dirt on the other side. And a pit. In the pit, were *bodies*. Actually, *bodies* was the wrong word. There were pieces of bodies. Body *parts*. Hands and feet, legs and arms, upper and lower torsos, heads. All mixed together like some gigantic, obscene salad, mixed in with the dirt. Forensics was trying to sift through it all.

"So far, we've counted twelve bodies. There are probably more."

"What kind of fuck could have done something like this?" Ben asked, crushing his half-smoked cigarette underfoot. "It looks like a fucking holocaust or something."

"They've been here awhile. Months, maybe. But Frankie seems to think that someone capable of doing this—this might not be all of it."

Carroll nodded, watching passively as body parts continued to be removed from the pit and put in bags.

"We're dealing with some kind of fucking *animal* here, Ben," Fred said, clearly frazzled by the whole thing. Carroll had been doing this long enough to know how to keep his emotions in check. Some guys never learned how to do that. But he had to admit, even he hadn't seen anything like this before.

"You think it's the Shredder, or whatever they called that guy?"

"Could be," Carroll said. "It's the same kind of carnage. But the last time he went wild, there were maybe five people tops. Now, who knows how big this thing is."

He was past the point of wondering how a human being could have been capable of such violence. There were witnesses after all, even if they were no help in identifying him. At first, Carroll was sure the tearing asunder of human flesh had to be the work of a real animal, or some kind of machine, but people had seen the Shredder, or whoever this guy was, rip people apart with his bare hands. Something that really defied logic, but they'd seen his handiwork, and for now, there wasn't much else to go on. Somehow, a man with superhuman strength was going around tearing people to shreds.

"This is fucked up," Fred said.

"Yeah." Carroll lit up another cigarette. "You can say that again. Sure is some spooky shit."

"You got any leads on that guy yet?"

"We got jack shit, Fred. Nobody got a good look at him. We can't even put a sketch together. A guy just goes wild in the streets and nobody can even identify him."

"Sorry to hear it. Well, there's not much you can do here right now. Things are under control. They're collecting all the evidence, and I have some other guys making the rounds, asking questions. But you know there won't be any leads. If the bodies have been here that long, and nobody's spoken up yet, it's a lost cause at this point."

"I know," Carroll said. "Keep me informed. Get me copies of any paperwork. I want to be totally updated on this thing."

"You bet."

"Thanks, Fred," Carroll said. He just wanted to get away from this place. He went back to his car and sat there, feeling very ill despite his calm exterior in front of the men. He had two strange cases. On the one hand, he had these strange deaths in anonymous motel rooms that seemed benign enough—just really strange. And on the other hand, he has a serial killer who specialized in total carnage.

Two bizarre cases. Two extremes.

He closed his eyes, and he could still see the severed body parts. Legs, heads, torsos. Like some kind of gigantic tossed salad of human remains in there.

This is fucking *sick*, he thought. He felt some vomit about to surge up inside him, but was somehow able to hold it back.

He started the engine and drove away from the park.

CHAPTER THIRTY

When Colleen woke, she was in the bed alone. Jeremy didn't need much sleep and always got up hours before she did. But he was so quiet, she never even noticed. It was something that took getting used to. She was used to men being gone when she woke up, but she didn't care about them. She didn't miss them. Jeremy, she missed. Every time she woke up alone, she had to remind herself that he wasn't gone. He was just in another room.

The cough started as soon as she moved to get out of bed. She covered her mouth and ran to the bathroom. In her hurry, she almost opened the door to the closet by accident, but stopped herself. She turned on the light and went inside and then coughed up a hunk of phlegm, which she spat into the toilet.

She poured herself a glass of water. That calmed the cough down a bit, but the best thing she could do was light up a cigarette. She found her purse and pulled out the pack. She went back to the bed and lit one up.

The first cigarette of the day always tasted so good.

Colleen got up and went to the bedroom door. She could hear Viv and Jeremy talking out in the kitchen, but couldn't make out the words. The last couple of days, Viv had been around more, and didn't even spend all her time in her room like she did when Colleen first got here. Colleen thought Viv was an odd, secretive person back then, but now she actually seemed pretty nice. Friendlier, but there was still a kind of coldness about her. Like she was holding back, afraid to get too close to anyone.

She wanted to open the door a crack and listen to what they were saying, but she had to pee.

Sitting on the bowl, puffing on her cigarette, she couldn't help looking around. She had been in this bathroom a dozen times or more since coming to this house, but it still amazed her. The marble walls, the fancy fixtures. The *size* of the bathroom, with big open space all around her. There was even a bidet beside the toilet, but she wasn't sure how to use it and was too shy to ask. She'd have to take Viv aside at some point and ask her about it.

There was something strange about all of it; from this ornate bathroom she now found herself in, to her budding relationship with Jeremy. It all seemed so unreal. Like a fairytale princess finding her Prince Charming. She almost pinched herself. And Jeremy had been taking her on shopping expeditions all week. For once in her life, she had been able to get the clothes she really wanted, *and shoes*. At first she had felt so guilty, taking his money, his gifts. But now she was starting to enjoy it all. And it felt wonderful.

To think of all the bad years spent confused and alone. Despite the parade of strangers who filled her life, she always felt totally alone. That's what was missing now, that loneliness. She didn't feel it anymore, and she didn't miss it.

When she was done, she went back to the bedroom door, to listen to the murmur of voices from the other room, but they were silent now.

Realizing she was dressed only in her panties, Colleen snatched up her robe and put it on. Then she opened the door and went out to the kitchen to greet them.

It was a new day.

* * *

"Cancel my appointments for this afternoon," Sam said. The lobby was empty, except for the two of them, and he wanted to take advantage of the break. "If anyone shows up, tell them I'm not coming back the rest of the day."

"Of course," Carla said, ready to pick up the phone and start calling. He knew she thought this was about Maggie's death. About a need to take more time off to mourn. No harm in letting her think that.

"You don't need to say why, do you?" he asked.

"Not at all," Carla said, ever the understanding employee. "I'll just tell them something came up and they will have to reschedule. There's no reason to go into any more detail than that."

"Thanks, Carla."

Sam went back into his office and looked up Charlie's address, and wrote it down on a slip of paper.

CHAPTER THIRTY-ONE

An hour later, Sam was driving to Charlie's house. He parked across the street and checked the address against the slip of paper he'd brought. It hadn't been difficult to find the place. He'd only taken one wrong turn during the course of the trip, and he'd caught that soon enough not to end up too far out of the way.

It was almost three in the afternoon. Sam walked across the street and up the lawn, seeing no sign of anyone. He went up to the front door and rang the bell.

The second time he rang it, Charlie's mother answered the door.

"Hello, Mrs. Jarrold," Sam said. "I've come to see Charlie."

"Of course, Dr. Wayne," Charlie's mother said. He didn't correct her. "I think he's out in the back yard. Right this way."

"I've been concerned," Sam said as she led him toward the rear of the house "He hasn't been in all week. And we were on the verge of making real progress. We can't take it any further if he doesn't show up."

"I assumed he'd been going to his appointments," she said. "I'm so sorry."

She led him through the kitchen. It was a nice house, but nothing too fancy. Clearly Mrs. Jarrold worked hard for her money.

In fact, he suspected that Charlie had been sent to him only as a last resort, that they really couldn't afford the sessions.

She opened the door leading out to the back yard. Sam thanked her and went outside.

There was an old swing set in the yard. The metal was rusted in places. Charlie was sitting on one of the swings, just staring off at the sky. Clearly he'd outgrown them years ago, but they'd never bothered to take them down. And probably didn't have the time or urgency to have someone else do it.

"How are you feeling, Charlie?" he asked.

"What are *you* doing here?"

"I was concerned about you. I haven't seen you in a while."

"I've been sick."

"Really? What's wrong with you, Charlie?"

"I don't know. I just haven't been feeling good. Didn't my mother call you?"

"Nobody called me," Sam said. "So I thought I'd come check on you."

"You don't have to do that," Charlie said. "I'm just not feeling good, that's all. It won't last forever."

"I hope not."

Sam did not sit on the swing beside him. He stayed standing.

"Are you sure you're coming back at some point, Charlie?"

The boy said nothing.

"I thought we were so close to making real progress," Sam said. "I thought we'd come to a real understanding. That you were starting to trust me."

"Bullshit," Charlie said softly.

"What do you mean by 'bullshit,' Charlie?"

"I'm not coming back, okay? I didn't think you'd get that bent out of shape about it. I had no idea you'd actually come *here*. But that whole therapy thing, it's bullshit. I don't have time for it."

"Yeah, I can see how busy you are."

"That kind of stuff doesn't work," Charlie said. "It's a waste of time. And you're just ripping my mother off, taking her money. I told her I don't need to see you anymore. That you said I was normal."

"I don't believe you Charlie. But I do believe we have a lot of work to do. And refusing to see that won't do you any good. Surely you've noticed a change in your behavior, however slight, since you've started coming to me. Don't you want to learn to control your temper, Charlie? Don't you want to be the master of it, instead of letting it control you?"

"I don't give a shit anymore."

"You'll end up in prison, you know. If you don't control this temper of

yours now, you'll end up really hurting someone. Maybe even killing somebody. Or they'll kill you. I really don't see much good in denying you have a problem."

"But you see, that's it. I *don't* have a problem. It's everybody else that has the problem. People fuck with me, that's *their* problem, not mine. I just take care of myself, that's all. I can't see how you can help me with that. I know how to handle myself."

"Clearly you don't, or you wouldn't get in so much trouble."

"Like I said, it's all bullshit. What you do is a scam. I see right through it."

"Is that so? So I guess nothing I can say or do will convince you to come back, right? You've made up your mind?"

"You got that right."

"Well, I guess I misjudged you, Charlie. I thought you were a smart kid, who really wanted to change. I guess you fooled me on that one, because I really believed in you. But that's just because I'm gullible, huh?"

"Must be."

"But you're not. You see right through me."

Even here, between where Sam stood and Charlie sat on the swing, Sam could feel the transfer of energy. The spark of electrons around him. The adrenaline rush. Charlie was getting angry again. His bewilderment at Sam's appearance here, at his *home*, was giving way to real anger. And Sam found that the angrier Charlie got, the more energized he felt.

"Can you go now?" Charlie said.

"Yeah, sure," Sam said, not wanting to move from the spot. He looked up at the clouds, wondering what was so fascinating about them that Charlie remained focused up there and refused to look at him directly.

"I'll go, Charlie. But if you change your mind, you know where to find me. If that temper of yours gets the better of you and you start feeling like maybe you want a little more control over your life, remember that I am available to you. Call me."

"Yeah, right."

"It's too bad," Sam said. "I'd hoped you and I had connected on some level."

"Bullshit," Charlie said again, refusing to look at him.

Sam did not go back to the house. Instead, he left Charlie sitting on the swing and walked around the house to the street. He sat in his car for a moment, trying to think of something that would change Charlie's mind. But he couldn't think of anything.

Instead, he started the car and drove away.

* * *

Viv answered her cell phone on the third ring. There weren't too many people who knew the number. And, of those few, most of them were dead.

She hesitated a moment, then said softly, "Hello?"

"Sis, that you?"

She hadn't heard Grif's voice in such a long time, she almost didn't place it at first.

"It's been too long, Grif."

"I hear ya," her little brother said, sounding as thrilled as she did. "I'm sorry about that."

"Where the hell *are* you, you little bastard?"

"I'm at the train station. In your neck of the woods. With my few earthly possessions. Waiting for a ride from my dear old sister."

"You're *here*?"

"So close you can almost touch me. But I won't be staying for long. I got in a little trouble and I'm trying to stay one step ahead of the storm. Since I was passing through, I figured it wouldn't hurt to make a pit stop and say hello."

"Shit," Viv said. "How many years has it been?"

"Four, five," he said. "Too long."

"I'll be there soon. You okay otherwise?"

"I'm as good as good can be. Except for the complications I mentioned."

"You get a good head start?"

"Real good, but I want to keep it that way. That's why my visit is going to be brief but unforgettable."

She left her room, phone to her ear, and walked out to the front door. No sign of Jeremy and Colleen. Either they had left or were otherwise indisposed. "I'm heading out to the car now. I should be there in about twenty minutes."

"Sounds like a plan. See you then."

"You bet."

He hung up first. She got into her car, the silver BMW Jeremy had gotten her three years before. One of the *presents* she'd been the recipient of over the years. There was so much she felt she needed to repay him for. There was no way to even begin. She wished she could have given in to his desires so many times over the years, but she knew how easy it would have been to find that special spot inside him, the one that wanted so badly to die. And if she found that weak spot, like a tongue probing a cavity, she wouldn't be able to leave it alone. And he would end up very dead.

She couldn't bring herself to risk that. She'd explained it all to him one night a long time ago, when they'd both had too much to drink. And he seemed to understand. Hell, the fact that he believed her at all was enough to make her love him all the more. He'd been so incredibly kind to her, and even respected her rule about no sex, even though she'd wanted to grab him and fuck the life out of him so many times (*literally*). It had been rough on both of them.

She was racing down the narrow street that provided the path to and from the ocean-side properties. Not another soul on the road. She felt the wind caressing her short blonde hair.

Grif! It had been so long since she'd seen him. They were only two years apart, but she always thought of him as her *little brother*. The one she'd had to protect when they were growing up. Sensitive little Griffin. It was funny how much he'd changed over the years. He'd grown up into such a man, but she'd never been able to abandon the image of him she'd had when they were kids. It was something she had to curb. He surely didn't want to be treated like a child again after all these years.

She got to the train station in fifteen minutes. Grif was sitting in a dark corner, reading a magazine, but she spotted him immediately. They shared a kind of sense for each other. Could feel if each other were in the same room, the same house. How many parties had they both attended and not even known until they both got there, sensing each other from opposite ends of the room.

She stood before him and snatched the magazine from his hands. "I knew you were there all along," he told her.

"Sure you did."

He got up and grabbed his bag. "We going back to your place?"

"Naw, there's nothing to see there. There's a bar not too far from here you might like, and they'll be open by now. I figured you might like a few drinks and we can catch up on things."

"Sounds like a plan," he said. He said it all the time, and she didn't expect him to stop now. It was nice in small doses, because it was like his signature in a bizarre way, but if he was around too long, it got tiresome fast. She almost told him to get a new catch phrase, but she was just so happy to see him, that she didn't have the heart.

"Follow me," she said, leading him out of the station to the parking lot.

"You still living with that Rust guy?" Grif asked, following her out the door.

"Yep."

"Am I finally going to meet him?"

"I don't know. Will you be able to behave yourself?"

"Don't I always?"

"I won't answer that."

"This guy's real important to you, isn't he?"

"That's a way to put it."

"So this bar is close by?"

"It's a spin around the block. You think you can last that long?"

"I'm not sure. I'm pretty thirsty."

"I better get you there before you collapse," she said and laughed.

CHAPTER THIRTY-TWO

"Is it the same stuff," Ben Carroll asked.

"Well, it's older, and it's mixed with dirt. But yeah, there are traces," Jasper Eng said, leaning over the microscope. "Sure as shit. That same weird fucking alien sperm."

It sounded like something out of a bad science fiction movie, but there was no other way to describe it. On many of the Shredder's victims, male as well as female, there were traces of a substance that seemed similar to semen, but, up close under the microscope, it looked nothing like human sperm at all. Jasper was unable to identify it, and neither were any of his colleagues. They'd come to call it *alien sperm* as a kind of joke, but it was as likely an explanation as anything else.

"So those bodies in the mass grave," Carroll said. "They're all his work."

"I think that's a pretty safe assumption."

"And we have no leads. Nothing to go on. Even people who actually *saw* him can't offer us any kind of clear description. Nothing that makes sense."

"I know, Ben. It's frustrating."

"Fuck that. It's downright torture. To be so close to nailing this guy over and over, and having nothing concrete to go on. I can't even get a decent description of the son of a bitch. His face is always blurry or obscured or some shit. They can't even tell me how tall he is or what he's wearing."

"If he's wearing anything at all."

"How the fuck does he do it?"

"It's like that old radio character, *The Shadow*," Eng said. "You know, *he has the power to cloud men's minds.*"

"That's not half funny, Jasp. Sounds close enough to the fucking truth to be credible."

"You think he can hypnotize people, even from a distance?"

"Who the fuck knows? It's just that we can't find any credible witnesses. And this monster is getting away with what's starting to look like genocide. What does this bring the body count to, Jasp?"

"Including the ones today? Well, we're not done counting, Ben, but I'd say the number is almost forty at this point. Over the last year or so."

"And who knows how many were before *that*. Maybe he's been on a killing spree across the country, and has killed thousands by now. For all we know, he could have moved on already. How long ago were these people killed?"

"The ones in the pit? Two, maybe three months ago."

"That's fucked up," Ben said. "So he could be long gone?"

"I know as much as you do, Ben. He could be long gone, or he could be killing more people right now, as we speak. The only thing we know is that he's male and that he rapes most of his victims. And that his sperm doesn't seem to be human."

"Shit."

"Kind of freaks you out, hearing these were his, huh?"

"Not really. I mean, I knew it when I saw the condition of the bodies. But the sheer number, Jasp, that's what freaks me out. This kind of mass slaughter going on right under our noses. And not a witness to be found."

"Seems like any witnesses would be dead."

Ben Carroll faced the wall. Took a deep breath.

"I never saw anything like this before. I don't even know how to process this kind of information. I don't know what's harder to accept, that he's killing this many people and getting away with it. Or that fucked up sperm you keep finding."

"I sent it for analysis, Ben. It's just that nobody else can figure it out, either. It's a mystery."

"Have there been other killings like this. In other parts of the country?"

"I haven't heard anything yet. But I suspect we will at some point. With something this big, something's bound to turn up sooner or later."

"Well, let me know if you hear anything."

"You know I'll do that, Ben. Anything at all."

"Thanks, Jasp. I better head out. I just don't know how to process this shit anymore," he said, shaking his head. Eng knew exactly how he felt.

CHAPTER THIRTY-THREE

They were walking along the beach, the water crawling along the sand, reaching for their feet, and always retreating soon after touching them. The smell of salt was strong in the air around them. They were walking hand in hand, and Colleen should have been happy.

She was thinking about Turney. About the night he was killed right in front of her.

She was thinking of the man's face. The man who killed him.

Colleen hadn't thought about that in days now. She thought she'd finally gotten past it. But the image was haunting her again. There had to be something she could do about it.

Once she'd been able to think about it clearly, she suggested to Jeremy that maybe she should go to the police after all, but he seemed visibly distressed by the idea. At first she thought that he was afraid for some reason, but that didn't make any sense. He hadn't been there that night; he had no reason to be afraid of anything. Then again, maybe he was afraid that the killer would somehow come after *her*.

And he'd looked distressed when she'd told him about the vision she'd had. Like the one she'd seen on Viv. That meant something to him. Something he wouldn't tell her.

Colleen wanted to know so badly what it meant.

"Jeremy," she asked him. "Can I ask you a question?"

"Sure."

"Remember that night I met Viv, the time I told you about the vision I'd seen."

"Not this again, Colleen."

"And I told you I'd seen something similar around that guy who killed Turney."

"I remember."

"What do you think it means?"

"I have no idea," he told her.

"But you had a reaction when I told you about it. Like it bothered you."

"I just thought it was odd, that's all. Especially when you said that you'd seen it on Viv. I've known her for years, Colleen. There's no reason to be afraid of her."

"I know. What I saw on her was different. It didn't seem dangerous. I was just wondering if it made any sense to you at all."

"No, of course not."

"You'd tell me if you knew something, wouldn't you?"

"Of course I would."

She couldn't tell if he was lying to her.

"Maybe there's something at the library, or on the Internet. Something that would explain that kind of thing."

"Maybe."

"You think I hallucinated the whole thing, don't you?"

"I don't know what to think, Colleen," he said. "You were traumatized that night, when your friend was killed. Who knows how that affects a person?"

"You still don't think I should go to the police, do you?"

"I fear for your safety," Jeremy told her. "That's why I moved you out of that apartment. If he found you, then you might be in danger. There's no way he'll trace you out here. I really think you should stay here until they catch him."

"But don't you think I could help the police? I saw his face, after all. When I read the papers, it said that there hadn't been any witnesses who could describe him."

"I know, Colleen. But I really think you should just stay here with me. I can't explain it, but I have a bad feeling about all this. I don't want you to put yourself any closer to danger."

"You still have a bad feeling about it?"

He hesitated. "I don't know. Maybe it's safer now. But we can't be sure. I haven't heard anything about them capturing him yet."

"I know."

"Do we really have to talk about this now, Colleen? It's such a nice day."

"I was reading Turney's diary last night. I just felt so bad about what happened to him. He was such a sweet guy. Really, he was. I wish there was something I could have done to help him."

"I know you do, Colleen. I know this whole thing is really bothering
you."

He squeezed her hand. "Really, I just want to keep you safe."
"I know."

"I've been meaning to ask you. I noticed you tend to have a really bad cough in the morning."

"I know," she said. "It's the cigarettes. I know I should quit."

"Once you're up awhile you seem okay, but in the morning it just sounds so bad. I was really concerned. And you smoke so much. Have you ever *tried* to quit?"

"Yeah, a few times. It's tough."

"You know, there are a lot of ways to do it these days. I'd be more than happy to help. Maybe you could see my doctor."

"When I've tried to quit in the past, the cough gets worse. So I just gave up. But I'll try whatever you want me to."

He smiled. "Don't do it for me, do it for *you*. Hell, I'll even quit along with you. But we can talk about it more later. It's so warm today. This might be the last day of Indian summer. Don't you want to do something today? Maybe we could go to the city and do some more shopping. There must be something you need."

"I don't know."

"Well, maybe if you see it you'll realize you need it," he smiled that crooked smile of his. She could still see the handsome face that used to be on newspaper covers. It was still there, slightly altered but not gone at all.

And she was here, with him.

It was so much like a dream.

"So you want to go back to the city again today?"

"Why not? And afterwards, we can go somewhere really nice to eat. You don't know how tired I am of being locked up in this house. I'd been hiding away from the world for so long, and now I want to go out again. With you, Colleen."

"Aren't you afraid for my safety?" she asked.

"We won't be in any one place long enough to be in danger," he said with a laugh. "Besides, you're with me. I'll protect you."

Despite the accident, he looked in good physical shape. He had no doubt been working out regularly all these years in solitude; there was a personal gym in the basement. But could he do anything against the man who killed Turney? A homicidal maniac?

Something about Jeremy did make her feel safe, though.

She smiled and closed her eyes. "I'll go wherever you take me, Jeremy."

* * *

After he left Charlie's house, Sam did not go back to the office. He'd told Carla to cancel all his appointments for the afternoon, so there was no reason to go back there.

And there was no reason to go back home. Maggie was dead. The house was empty. There was nothing for him there, either.

He resisted the urge to stop at a bar. Alcohol made him think too much of Maggie.

He wondered about the blonde woman the police detective had mentioned to him. Sam realized that he didn't know any of Maggie's friends from work. She tended to keep that part of her life separate. And the friends she'd had before they'd gotten married, well, they were mostly on the west coast. She hardly spoke to them at all toward the end.

And this woman, whoever she was, was it true that Maggie had been having some kind of lesbian affair?

Sam had been driving around randomly since leaving Charlie's house, and his gas was getting low. He'd have to stop at a gas station soon.

What can I do about Charlie? Sam wondered. What can I do to get through to him so that he doesn't end up as another casualty, like Maggie?

And Richard Croix.

Too many people he knew had been dying lately. People he'd been trying to save. People he felt responsible for in one way or another.

And he felt responsible for Charlie, too. He was sure they'd established some kind of connection between them. That the boy wanted to reach out to him, to ask for his help, but something held him back. Pride, perhaps. Or maybe the kid was scared to spill his guts. Maybe there were things he was holding back and felt he couldn't tell anyone.

One thing was sure; Sam had never seen anyone so full of anger before. It was like Charlie was constantly holding back the floodgates. The tension coming from him was so tangible. And yet so invigorating.

There was a gas station up ahead. Sam got in the right-hand lane.

I've got to save Charlie, he thought as he drove up next to the gas pumps. *I can't let him die as just another statistic.*

* * *

They were seated at a dark table at the back of the bar. The waitress clearly knew Viv and was flirting with her. Grif was impressed.

"You always were able to make friends easily," he told her.

"I wouldn't go that far," Viv said. "I've actually been trying to keep a low profile these days."

"Why bother? And what about your sugar daddy?"

"He's not my sugar daddy. He's a close friend."

"So you haven't fucked him?"

She stared at him, but did not respond.

"There's something wrong with him then, am I right? Something that puts him at risk?"

"Shit, Grif, you must have found out by now. *Everybody* has something that puts them at risk. I haven't met a person yet who didn't have some part of them that wanted to just give up and die.

Most people are able to cover it up under layers of denial, but there is a seductiveness to death. It's just closer to the surface with the real vulnerable ones. That's why you learn early on to avoid getting too intimate with the people you really care about."

"I haven't been really close to anyone in a very long time," Grif told her. "Not since we were younger and had each other to lean on. I have to admit, it's been pretty lonely sometimes."

"I've been there."

"Even with your friend in the same house?"

"I don't want to talk about him anymore. But no, his being there doesn't take away the loneliness. I still feel it. I feel it because I can never be as close to him as I want to be. Because I can't be really close to anybody. But he's involved with someone now, and it's a little uncomfortable. I feel like an intruder when I'm there. I try to be at the house as little as possible."

The waitress brought their drinks. A draft beer for Viv, and Scotch for Grif.

Grif drank half his glass then put it down. "So, does he know about you? The *real* you?"

"Do you mean did I tell him what I do? What I am?"

He nodded silently.

"Yeah, he knows."

"Amazing. I thought you were the one who told me it was better to keep it our secret."

"He wanted to know why I wouldn't sleep with him. He thought there was something wrong with him, and I couldn't let him think that. Not if I wanted to stay living there."

"You could have always moved on."

"I need him as much as he needs me," Viv said. "Or I used to. I'm not sure how much he needs me anymore. Like I said, he's got someone new."

"It was bound to happen. He couldn't wait for you forever."

"Like I said, I told him about me. He wasn't waiting anymore. He knew there was no real future between us."

"I wish I had someone like that to confide in. Someone who could understand. He must be pretty special."

"He is, Grif. And he's been through so much pain. If I ever gave into the desire, it would be torture to keep from taking him. And he wouldn't be any good to me dead."

Someone new entered the building and headed over to the bar. Grif was sitting against the wall and had a good view of the place.

"That guy has cop written all over him," Grif said.

Viv resisted the urge to turn and look. "A problem?"

"I don't think so. He's just so obviously damaged goods. A lot of them end up that way. On the verge of suicide every time they wake up in the morning. I've never seen such a sad lot. You must have taken a cop or two in your day."

"Yeah, sure. I know what you mean. I was just wondering if he had something to do with the reason you're passing through town."

"Naw, he's not looking for me," Grif said. "I'm safe here for a little while.""So what happened?"

"I maybe took a few more lives than I should have," Grif said, quietly, as if talking into his glass. "I've had this insatiable hunger lately."

"Me, too. I've been trying to resist it, but it has been worse than usual."

"Well, I don't resist things, as you know. And some cops started sniffing around the trail. And I realized if I wanted to stay ahead of these dudes, I'd better move on."

"So you got sloppy."

"I didn't get sloppy so much as greedy. But I regret it now."

"My most recent one was this really sweet woman I met in a bar just like this," Viv said. "I think I was almost falling in love toward the end. It broke my heart when I couldn't resist the ache anymore."

"How long did it last?"

"Not all that long, but I tried to put it off until I couldn't anymore. I find that makes it even sweeter. But I started to have real feelings for her. After I did it, I felt so horrible afterwards. I still do. Even though she was practically begging for me to do it."

"I try to never get emotional, but I've been on the verge a few times. It gets rough."

"Tell me about it."

"So what else have you been up to? Just feeding and relaxing around his house?"

She took a pull from her beer. "Not that much relaxing. I'm afraid I might have to move on myself sometime soon."

"Because of his new girlfriend? Just get rid of the bitch."

"I can't do that, Grif. First of all, he really cares about her. And secondly, she seems really nice. I can't bring myself to harm what they've got. I really want him to be happy. Besides, what do I really have to offer him? I mean, I've kind of added to some of his misery over the last few years."

"You could have ended his misery at any time."

"I know that, but I didn't want to. And I don't think he did, either, even though he sometimes tells me otherwise."

"So what are you going to do?"

"I don't know yet. I'm thinking about it. But, it's not every day I see my little brother. So let's forget about that for now. How's about a fresh drink?"

"Sounds like a plan," Grif said. "Hey, see that guy at the bar? That cop? It's torture watching him like this. He's so obviously depressed."

"Not tonight, Grif. You know, you really have to start learning some self-control."

"But I need it," her brother said. "And he's so ripe for the plucking."

The waitress came back. "How is everything?"

"Just the tab," Viv said. "We've got to go."

"Hey, we just got here," Grif said. "I don't want to go yet."

"You're visiting me, remember? I want to move on, so you're coming with me."

"Some hostess you are."

"Look, I haven't seen you in years. And all you want to talk about is if someone's ripe. Don't you want to catch up on my life? I know I want to know about yours. I don't get a call from you in months, and all of a sudden you ring me out of the blue and say you're in town. And you're passing through. So who knows how much time we have together."

"Don't give me that. I know I make you nervous, and you can't wait for me to leave."

"You make me nervous because you don't know how to control yourself. You never did. That's why you're in trouble now. I mean, how long does it take for this shit to start sinking in? Are you incapable of learning anything?"

"That hurts, sis. You know it does."

"I want it to hurt. I want you to wake the fuck up."

"So glad I called. Maybe I should take the next bus out of here tonight."

Viv took a deep breath. "Look, I don't want to you leave so soon. I'm glad to

see you, really I am. But after all this time, I want some time for *us*. I don't want you half-listening to me while you scope the place."

"I know that kind of shit pisses you off. But I can't help it. I've been so *hungry* lately. It's like having this itch that just won't go away."

"I know what it feels like, Grif. And you know I sympathize. But you have to be stronger than this. You have to control the need. Not let it control you."

"But that's why it's called a *need*. I've got to have it. You know that."

Viv rolled her eyes, on the verge of giving up.

"If we go somewhere else, I'll just keep looking around. If you don't want to see it, then maybe I should just go off on my own for a while."

"You really can't control yourself for one night?"

"Let me put it this way. Do you want to bring me back to where you live?"

"I seriously don't know."

"Well, if I scratch this itch, it'll be safe for me to go back there with you. If not, it will be dangerous."

"So maybe we'll just crash in the city tonight. Find a room. I don't *have* to bring you back there."

"I know. But I'd like to meet this Jeremy guy. You've told me so much about him. But I don't want to be hurting the whole time I'm there."

"I'm telling you right now, Grif. If you do anything to Jeremy—"

"I know, I know. I'm just trying to talk some sense into you."

The waitress came back with the bill. She put it on the table in front of Viv. *Is it that obvious I'm the responsible one here?* she wondered. She got out her wallet and paid the tab.

"So we're really leaving here?"

"I don't know what the fuck I want to do at this point," Viv said. "But I sure as hell don't want to hang around and wait for you to scratch that itch."

"Maybe it was a bad idea to come here, the way I've been feeling. It's not fair to you."

"Look, you were in town. I want you to call me if you're coming through. We see each other so rarely as it is."

"I know."

"Come on, let's get some air. It's too hot in here anyway."

Grif drained his glass and grabbed his bag. Then he followed his sister out.

CHAPTER THIRTY-FOUR

Brenda Carlisle jumped when she heard a loud bang against the side of her house. She was sitting on the couch, watching her favorite soap opera, which she'd recorded earlier in the day. She'd had to work late and was starting to nod off in front of the television. But the noise woke her right up.

"What the hell is that?" Brenda said out loud, feeling her muscles tense up. She was on her own after all. Her husband had split years ago, and there hadn't been anyone new in a long time. Between work and raising Jessica, there didn't seem to be *time*.

There was another bang. Terrified, she didn't even want to get off the couch and look. But Jessica woke up this time and started crying. After all the time it took to get her to fall asleep!

Should I call the cops? Brenda wondered. *But what if it's just some teenagers throwing a baseball against the house or something?* She could take care of that herself. She was a woman alone, but she wasn't helpless. She could yell at some kids if she had to.

Brenda went to the kitchen. There was a drawer by the sink, where she kept her knives. She took out the biggest one she could find, just in case. She looked out the back window, but it was too dark to see.

Getting up her nerve, she flicked the switch above the microwave. Suddenly, the back yard was flooded with light.

But no sign of any people. Big, little or otherwise.

Maybe it was a raccoon, she thought, starting to relax. Then again, it could have been the plumbing or something. There had been other times when the house made strange noises. It wasn't the most well constructed place she'd ever lived in. Which was her ex-husband's fault again, getting them a crappy place like this that seemed to be put together with glue and sticks sometimes, for all the repairs she had to have done.

She hoped he was dying of syphilis somewhere.

After switching off the back yard light she went and sat on the couch. A glass of zinfandel was on the coffee table, on top of the latest copy of *Soap Opera Digest*. She picked it up and took a healthy gulp.

Jessica had stopped crying and settled back to sleep. Brenda hadn't even considered going in there to comfort her daughter. Not that she was a bad mother, but she had just been so groggy at first, and then so scared, it hadn't crossed her mind. She felt bad about that. Then again, Jessica seemed to fall back to sleep pretty quickly. If she'd kept crying, Brenda would have gone to check on her.

It wasn't like I didn't know why she was crying, Brenda thought. The noise scared me *too*.

If she went in there now, she'd just wake her daughter up all over again.

Sometimes she wished Jack had taken the kid with him when he left. It made her feel horrible to think that. It made her feel like an unfit mother. Maybe she was. She really didn't know why she had had such trouble bonding with her daughter. At first she'd thought it was post-natal depression. But Jessica was four now, and she just resigned herself to the fact that some people were born for mothering, and some people just didn't have that much of it in them. She was just happy that she'd taken enough control of her life so that she didn't feel the urge to hit Jessica anymore. It wasn't her little girl's fault that her father was such an irresponsible bastard who'd ruined both their lives and ran away, leaving them to fend for themselves.

God, she hated that man. Even when she'd sometimes hit Jessica in the past. She really wanted to be hitting him. Wanted to make *him* hurt. Not Jessica.

It was good to know she was past that now. Thanks to Dr. Wayne. That man was a miracle worker, the way he helped her. And for the first time in her life, she felt like she was in control again, despite being alone and having a hyperactive four-year-old. Well, she was as in control as she could be, considering the circumstances.

She grabbed the remote control and turned her show back on. It was right in the middle, and the story was just on the verge of a big revelation.

There was a crash. The sound of glass breaking.

Brenda jumped from the couch. She whimpered, but her voice sounded like it was coming from someone else. She was afraid to go in the kitchen and see what had happened. She looked for the cordless phone and saw it on the carpet. She picked it up, moving slowly toward the kitchen.

The back door was smashed in. Glass was all over the linoleum floor. But she didn't see anybody outside. She flicked the light back on. There was nothing to see.

She was about to push the buttons for 9-1-1, when something leapt at her through the smashed back door. She dropped the phone. It looked like a man. A naked man, knocking the door off its hinges, spraying more glass across the floor.

The man stood before her, breathing hard. She could not make out his face. There was a shimmering about him that made his features indistinct.

But there seemed to be something familiar about him.

Despite the shimmering, she could see that he had an erection. It was impossible to miss.

She did not move or say a word.

Then, without warning, he leapt upon her, wrestling her to the ground. Grabbing at her and clawing her body, and hurling chunks of her flesh across the room. She cried out beneath him, struggling to get away. The last thing she heard was Jessica shouting in the other room, and then she lost consciousness.

* * *

There was the deafening blast of a shotgun, and then nothing.

Colleen sat bolt upright in bed to find herself in a dark room and breathing hard. Her heartbeat was loud.

Her movements were so sudden they woke Jeremy, who had been dozing beside her.

"What is it?" he asked, half-waking. "What's wrong?"

Sitting up, she realized that the shotgun blast hadn't really happened at all. That it had been a dream. But that didn't do much to calm her.

"I had a nightmare," she said. She could hear and feel him squirming beside her. "Go back to sleep."

Jeremy sat up beside her. "You're shaking. What did you dream?"

"Nothing," she said. "It's over now."

He rubbed her arms. "It sure doesn't sound like nothing. You sure you don't want to talk about it?"

She could feel him in the darkness, but couldn't see him. His arms were around her, holding her close. Her shaking came to a stop as he enveloped her.

"I dreamt about a gun going off," she said. "I thought it was real for a moment."

"I've had dreams like that," he said. "They can really shake you up. They seem so vivid you could swear they really happened."

"Yeah," she said, enjoying his embrace, and trying to forget the way the dream made her feel.

"Was there anything else besides the gunshot? Anything leading up to it that you can remember?"

"Does it matter?"

"It might. Have you ever had a dream like that before?"

"Sure, lots of times," her voice got quieter.

"So this isn't the first time then. How long have you had these dreams?"

"You're starting to sound a lot like Sigmund Freud or something. What are you going to do, analyze my dreams?"

"I was just curious."

"I know what the dreams mean," she told him. "And I don't want to think about it."

"Just trying to help. You sure you don't want to talk about it?"

"No, Jeremy."

"You know, you can tell me anything."

"I really don't want to go there again, Jeremy. Not yet."

"Okay, I'm not going to pressure you."

"Why don't we just go back to sleep," Colleen said. "And pretend this didn't happen."

"If that's what you want."

They both lay back down, nestling their heads on the pillows. His arm went around her, pressing against her chest, pulling her close to him. She could feel his breath on her shoulder.

"Jeremy?" she said softly, after they got settled. She was afraid he might have fallen asleep again.

"Yeah?"

"When I was a little girl, my father killed himself. He put a shotgun in his mouth and pulled the trigger. I saw him do it."

"My God."

"That's what the dreams mean. I really don't want to think about it, but the dreams kind of force me to. I didn't want to talk about it, but I wanted to tell you."

"Thanks for trusting me."

"I wanted to be honest with you. But let's not talk too much else about it, okay?"

"Sure."

"Now we can go back to sleep."

"Do you think you'll have that dream again?"

"I should be okay for tonight."

"I hope so." He kissed her shoulder. "I'll have to hold you extra close."

"That sounds good," she said.

CHAPTER THIRTY-FIVE

Charlie was awakened by something clattering on the roof.

In his half-conscious mind, he thought, *Is it Christmas already?* The image of some drunken Santa Claus up on the roof was in his head.

He sat up in the dark. Everything was quiet. He'd had a hard time falling asleep. On the other side of the wall behind his bed, his mother had been fucking her latest boyfriend, and they made a hell of a racket. He'd really had to restrain himself from pounding on the wall.

But they weren't making any noise now. And they sure as hell weren't up on the roof.

He cocked his head and tried to listen carefully.

Nothing.

And then it started again. Clattering down the side of the house.

"Charlie?" he heard his mother calling out from behind the wall. "What's that noise?"

"I don't know, Ma!" he shouted into the darkness. "It's not me."

He slipped out of bed and pulled his underwear on. He'd slipped it off earlier, when he jerked off to the sounds from the other room.

He pulled on his jeans and turned on the light.

He stopped at the door. Listened again.

All was quiet.

Charlie went back to his bed and grabbed underneath it for the aluminum baseball bat he kept there. Just in case.

He opened his bedroom door and went out into the hallway. He got to the kitchen and looked out the window into the back yard. The sun was just starting to rise. There wasn't any sign of life out there.

"What is it, Charlie?" a masculine voice said behind him.

He turned. It was his mother's new guy. Some jerk named Phil. A big, dumb-looking guy who switched on the kitchen light and was holding a gun.

Charlie was fascinated by the sight of the weapon in the big man's hand.

Shit, I wish I had a gun like that, he thought. *Think of how many assholes I could wipe off the planet with a big-ass gun like that.*

"I don't see anything out there," Charlie said.

"Well I heard someone on the roof," Phil said. "You heard it, too, didn't you?"

"Yeah, I heard it. Might have been a tree limb banging against the house or something." All the time, Charlie did not take his eyes away from the pistol.

Phil looked out the window. "Could have been. But you can never be too careful. There's a lot of fucking nuts out there, you know."

"Where did you get a gun like that?"

Phil smiled. "You like it, huh? Maybe I'll take you to the firing range sometime and you can try it out yourself. How does that sound?"

"Sounds great," Charlie said. Suddenly Phil didn't seem so bad.

"I'm going to go outside and check things out."

Phil opened the door and went out into the yard.

"What is it?" Charlie's mom said, coming into the kitchen. "Is there somebody out there?"

She was dressed in an old bathrobe, but she hadn't tied it up and he could see her breasts through the sheer fabric of her nightgown.

"I didn't see anybody. Phil went out to check it."

"That was so weird. Sounded like someone was on the roof."

"Yeah."

Charlie was feeling real uncomfortable and wished he could just go back to bed.

But he wanted to find out what the noise was all about. He wanted to go outside, too, but for some reason he felt like he couldn't move.

Phil came back in. "Looks okay. Must have been a tree limb or something, like Charlie said."

"Is that what you think, Charlie?" his mother asked.

"The tree's right next to the house. It makes sense."

"That sounded like a person to me," Phil said. "Sounded like they scrambled down the side. But I don't see anybody, and I went all around the house. Believe me, if they were out there, I would have taken care of them."

"You went outside with that gun?" Charlie's mother asked. "What if the neighbors saw you?"

"It's not even dawn yet," he said. "Besides, I was protecting you two, I don't give a shit who saw me."

There was a crash in front of the house.

"What the fuck?" Phil said and ran down the hall.

"Oh my god," Charlie's mother said. "What the hell is going on?"

"Stay here," Charlie said, and was running after Phil. He couldn't help hoping something would happen. Something horrible.

Before he even got to the living room at the front of the house, he got his wish. He heard a shot go off. Phil finally had a reason to use his gun.

He could hear Phil struggling with someone and turned on the light. Phil was on the carpet, on his back, and someone was on top of him, punching him over and over in the head.

A naked man.

The gun was a foot or two from Phil's out-stretched hand. There was a crunching sound each time the naked guy's fists pounded into Phil's skull.

Charlie raised the baseball bat and screamed. It wasn't a sound from fear or horror. It was a cry of rage.

The man who was pulping Phil's head looked up. But for some strange reason, Charlie could not focus on the man's face. It was blurry, like looking through an out-of-focus lens. He couldn't even tell what the man's reaction was to his screaming.

Charlie ran at the man, swinging the bat.

The man stood up and grabbed the bat in mid-swing. He tore it from Charlie's hands and threw it across the room. Then he slapped Charlie with the back of his hand.

Just once. But once was all it took.

* * *

Charlie's mother entered the room then. The naked man stood over her son, looking down at him, when he noticed someone new had entered the room. He looked at her with his out-of-focus face.

She didn't scream. She didn't make a sound.

She noticed the gun on the floor and tried to decide whether she should go for it.

The intruder leapt at her, using the weight of his body to force her to the ground.

She didn't have a chance to cry out.

CHAPTER THIRTY-SIX

Viv turned her key in the lock. "Now be really quiet. They're probably sleeping."

"Okay, okay," Grif said softly.

It was against Viv's better judgment to bring her brother here. He had a real knack for causing problems. But he needed a place to crash, and she didn't have the heart to make him go to a hotel or something. Besides, it didn't seem like he could afford very much these days.

They went inside. The kitchen light was on, but there was no sign of anyone awake. Viv led Grif down the hall to her room.

She closed the door.

"Now please don't make any noise," she told him.

"What, do you live in a museum or something?"

"You know damned well what I mean. We're not the only ones here."

Somehow, she'd been able to get his mind off his *need*. Or at least she thought she had. Who knows what he had done out of her sight, like when he'd gone to the bathroom at the clubs they'd hopped. Well, if he *had* done anything, she didn't want to know. She was just grateful he had stopped talking about it. It was making her antsy.

They'd both had too much to drink, but Viv was better at hiding it. She was terrified that he'd raise his voice too loud and wake the others.

She started taking off her clothes. Grif looked around at the room. There was a mattress in one corner. A small stereo sat on the floor not far from it, plugged into the wall. There were a few books, and a trunk in another corner, but most of the floor was bare. He noticed a small laptop computer tucked behind the books.

"You don't go for much furniture do you?" Grif asked. "Living the life of a monk these days?"

"I need space to work out."

"You always were into discipline. I always wondered why you didn't join the Marines or something."

She stripped down to her sports bra and panties. He just stood there, by the door, watching her.

"Well, are you going to go to sleep?"

"I'm hungry," he said, seeming to revert back to the child he once was in her eyes. *Her little brother.*

She gave him an angry look.

"No, I mean food."

"Fuck it," she told him. "It's real late. Just get some sleep."

She went to the mattress and pulled back the sheet. Normally, she would have done some yoga before going to sleep, but there wasn't enough room with him there.

"Okay, okay," he said. He kicked off his shoes and unbuckled his belt. As he got undressed, she was stretched out beneath the sheet, watching.

"You having fun?" he asked her. "Should I dance around more?"

"You sure are taking your fucking time."

"Look, we're adults here. This isn't some kind of fucking pajama party, where we have to worry about the parents busting us if we stay up too late. You sure are acting weird about this whole thing."

"I'm tired. I would sleep a lot better if I knew you were going to stay out of trouble. I brought you here against my better judgment. Don't make me regret it."

"What is it you think I'll do that's so horrible?"

"You really don't want me to answer that, do you?"

"You think I'm going to do something bad to your precious Jeremy, or his girlfriend?"

"Cut the bullshit, Grif. We both know you're not very good at controlling your impulses. If some whim should come over you, who knows what the fuck you're capable of."

"I'm really insulted, sis. To think that you have such little faith in me."

"Grif, don't play games with me."

"You know, if I wasn't so tired and drunk, I'd leave right now and go find somewhere else to spend the night."

"Big loss," Viv said. "Now come to bed."

He stood there, naked. "So how do I look?"

"Fine," she said. Her voice indifferent. He spun around slowly.

"Like what you see?"

"Knock it off."

"I know I liked what I saw. You're as hot as ever. But then again, I guess you and I have real incentive to stay looking our best, right? Sounds like you have to work at it more, though. I am able to stay nice and trim, with no effort at all."

"Lucky you," Viv said. "Shut the light off when you come to bed."

"What's with the mattress on the floor, anyway? Jeremy too cheap to spring for a proper box spring?"

"I like it this way. I like to be low to the ground, okay?"

"Whatever," he switched off the light and half-stumbled in the dark toward her. She reached out a hand and grabbed his leg when he got close enough. Then he squatted down and let her guide him under the sheet.

"Now get some sleep."

"You know, I can't stay long. I really have to get out of town soon."

"I know," she said. "You already told me several times."

He was drunk and babbling.

"Chances are we won't see each other again for a long while."

"It was a long time since I saw you last. It always is."

He snuggled up against her. "We don't have much time. You sure you just want to sleep?"

"Yeah, I'm sure."

"Come on, Viv," he said, and tried to find her with his lips. She turned her head away.

"Go to sleep, Griffin."

* * *

Colleen woke up in the middle of the night, hungry and curious. She'd heard Viv get in earlier and could have sworn she heard two voices, hers and a man's. That was about two o'clock. Now it was three and she was wide-awake.

Jeremy snored gently beside her. It wasn't loud enough to be a problem at all. In fact, the sound was kind of reassuring. She slid out of bed, careful not to wake him, and grabbed the robe at the foot of the bed. It hadn't been knocked onto the floor after all. She wrapped it around herself, and opened the door.

The light was still on in the kitchen. She'd suggested leaving it on in case Viv returned. Jeremy hadn't seemed to care either way. Not out of indifference toward Viv, but because he said she had a knack for staying away for days on end, and he wasn't sure if she needed it.

Well, it will come in handy for *me*, Colleen thought, walking down the hall. She could see the light up ahead and to the right. A beacon, allowing her to pass through the shadowy hallway without having to turn on any other lights.

The house was quiet. Colleen lit a cigarette and then opened the refrigerator and looked inside. Jeremy sure kept it very well stocked. There were so many items to choose from, that she wasn't sure what to take first.

"Anything good?" a man's voice whispered.

She turned, startled, but tried to maintain her composure. He stood there in the light, dressed only in black bikini briefs. His well-muscled torso caught her attention first. This must have been the man Viv had brought home for the night.

His face was something more than handsome. And at first, she smiled. But then there was the glow and a momentary overlay of latticework; so similar to the vision she'd had when she first met Viv. Like vines, except this time the vines seemed almost snake-like, the way they moved.

"What is it?" he asked her. "Am I that ugly, that I scare you?"

"No," she said, as the vision passed. "Not at all. I just thought I was the only one awake in the house."

"I haven't had much to eat all day and couldn't wait anymore. I can't sleep with my stomach growling the way it's been. Could you spare a few morsels for a man in need?"

Colleen decided to disregard the vision she'd had. After all, Viv had also had an aura like that, and as far as she could tell, Viv was no threat. Not like the man who had killed Turney. His aura had been much different. Scary.

This guy wasn't like that at all.

"It really looks like I've startled you," he said, looking down at himself. "Maybe it's the way I'm dressed. I'm sorry, I didn't even plan to get out of bed. It was an impulse. I guess you're lucky I put on anything at all. But maybe I should go back and get some clothes."

"No, it's not that," she said, and turned to look back into the refrigerator. "What are you in the mood for?"

He grinned slyly. "I'm not fussy. Whatever you were going to have, I would be more than happy to share."

She didn't want to take out anything that needed to be heated up. The microwave would make noise. She took out some sliced ham and cheese. "How about sandwiches?"

"Sounds like a plan."

She started taking things out and putting them on the table next to the bread. Mayonnaise, tomatoes, lettuce. Then she got some knives. "Help yourself," she said.

He started putting the ingredients together. "Do you have any mustard, instead?"

"Sure," she said, and got it for him. "Have you known Viv long?"

He smiled, taking the mustard jar from her. "Long? I've known her all my life. She's my big sister."

"Really?" Colleen asked, wondering why he was sleeping in her room, dressed only in those briefs. Maybe it was silly of her to wonder about that.

"I really don't know Viv very well," Colleen said. "But she seems nice. Are you going to be visiting her long?"

"Not really. I have some pressing business I have to take care of. I'm actually just passing through town, and thought I'd look sis up."

They quietly put their sandwiches together. Colleen started putting jars and packages back into the fridge. "Would you like a beer?"

"Actually a soda would be fine," he told her.

She grabbed a can of Coke and handed it to him.

"I'm Colleen, by the way."

"My name's Griffin, but you can call me Grif for short."

He was really quite handsome. If Colleen thought that Viv was attractive enough to be a model, then she was even more sure about Viv's brother. With such strong good looks, there's no way he wouldn't have found a way to use them to earn a living. It would be a crime if he didn't.

"Are you a male model?" she asked, blurting it out before she could decide against it.

He laughed. "Hardly."

"I think you'd be a natural for it."

"Thanks, but I'm too restless for that. I can't see myself standing still long enough for anyone to take pictures of me. That sounds like such a drag."

He took a bite of his sandwich. "Thanks for the food, though. I really needed
this."

"Didn't you get anything to eat with Viv tonight?"

"Actually we did, but I haven't eaten much the past few days, I've been so busy. I guess my hunger is still catching up with me. Besides, we did a lot more drinking than eating."

"Has it been long since you two saw each other last?"

"Years," he said. "That's why I'm sad I can't stay longer. We have so much to catch up on."

He washed down his food with soda. "You're Jeremy's girlfriend, right?"

She smiled. "Yeah, I guess you could say that. Do you know Jeremy?"

"Never met him. But Viv has told me so much about him. He sounds like a great guy."

"He is."

"Viv told me about you, too. Only nice things, of course."

"Really?" Colleen said. "We haven't had much chance to talk. I really had no idea what she thought of me."

"Well, you don't need to worry. She likes you just fine."

"Would you like some chips?" Colleen asked.

"I'm fine."

She was leaning up against the counter by the sink. He was standing near the dining table.

"Have you known Jeremy long?" Grif asked.

"I've only known him for a few weeks," she said. "It's a long story." She really didn't want to talk about the night Turney died and how she got here.

There was something new in his eyes. Something she could not identify. A subtle change in his demeanor. As if he had suddenly seen something he hadn't noticed before. Something he found attractive in her.

"No problem. I don't need to know every detail. Do you like it here?"

"Oh, yeah. It's really nice here. Much nicer than where I was staying before."

"You're really cute, by the way. Jeremy has good taste."

"Thank you," she said, wondering if she was blushing. She could feel heat on her forehead.

He moved closer, leaning on the counter beside her.

"This sandwich is actually pretty good," he said, finishing it off. "It really hit the spot."

"Good," Colleen said. She could faintly feel his breath on her. He was that close.

Without warning, he leaned in and kissed her. His tongue was just about to explore her mouth, when someone cleared their throat.

Grif pulled away. They both looked over at Viv, who'd entered the kitchen. She was in her underwear. Looking at them both, now, Colleen could see similarities in their features. For a second, she caught sight of the ivy auras again. This time in stereo. It made her jump.

"I thought you were going to get some sleep?" Viv asked Grif. She seemed genuinely upset to see Colleen and Grif huddled together.

"I told you I was really hungry," Grif said. "And I heard someone else moving about. I figured it wouldn't hurt anything to ask for a bite to eat."

"I was more than happy to make something for him," Colleen said, feeling guilty. "I was hungry, too."

"So I see," Viv said. "Are you done in here Grif? We've got a long day ahead of us tomorrow."

"I know," Grif said. "Yeah, I'm done here."

He winked at Colleen, "Nice talking to you. I guess I should get some sleep, though."

"Nice to meet you," Colleen said, not knowing what else to say.

Grif and Viv went back down the other hallway, to Viv's room. She heard the door open and close again.

Colleen did not move from where she was still leaning against the counter. She could still feel Grif's kiss.

I wonder if she'll tell Jeremy I was kissing her brother, Colleen thought. It was bad enough it had happened at all, when she was supposed to be involved with Jeremy. But to have a *witness*, too. And she knew how protective Viv was of Jeremy.

She stood there, frozen. Unsure of what to do. She wanted to go back to Jeremy's room and pretend nothing happened. But now, she wasn't sure what to expect in the morning. She didn't know Viv well enough to predict how she'd react. Were she and Jeremy so close that she'd tell him what had transpired? Or would she forgive Colleen a momentary indiscretion, especially since her brother was so very good looking?

Things like monogamy were so new to Colleen. She hadn't even resisted when Grif kissed her; the thought hadn't even entered her mind. Was she really suited for a real relationship? Or would she break Jeremy's heart the first chance she got?

Maybe Viv should tell him, she thought. *Maybe I don't deserve to be here at all.*

It was then that she heard sounds coming from Viv's room, just loud enough to attract her attention away from her thoughts. Voices, too, but the words weren't clear.

Slowly, Colleen moved away from the counter and walked around the refrigerator. She stood at the end of the hall from Viv's room. The hallway was empty, but there was light coming from the room, through the keyhole.

She wanted to walk away, back to Jeremy's bed. But her curiosity was too strong. The sounds were familiar, but she found it difficult to believe. She had to see for herself.

As quietly as she could, she moved down the hall, toward the room. She did not make a sound. She squatted before the door and looked inside.

Viv and Grif were on the floor. They had removed their underwear. Grif was lying on his back and Viv was on top of him, moving. They both were breathing hard.

The kinds of sounds people made when they were trying hard to keep from making noise.

They both had such attractive bodies. She could have watched them forever.

Oh my god, Colleen thought as she watched them. They're brother and sister, and they are *fucking.*

Suddenly, she wasn't so worried about Viv telling Jeremy anything about that kiss. She had her own story to tell, should the need arise.

* * *

"There's a man's here to see you," Carla said when Sam came into the office. He had a severe headache and had almost called in sick. The last thing he needed was an unexpected visitor in his lobby.

"He doesn't have an appointment, right?"

"He's a police detective," Carla said. "He was very insistent."

"Really?" Sam said. He looked over at the man sitting across the room, who was looking expectantly in their direction. He was obviously waiting for them to finish talking before he got up from his chair and introduced himself, but Sam recognized him already. It was Detective Carroll from that day at the morgue.

"Mrs. Addleson won't be here for another hour. Would you like me to try to call her and reschedule?"

"Hopefully it won't take that long," Sam said.

Carroll rose from his chair and was coming over.

He held out his hand. "Dr. Wayne? I don't know if you remember me, but I'm Ben Carroll," he pulled out his badge.

"*Detective* Ben Carroll. Could I have a few words with you in private?"

"Sure I remember you," Sam said. "Can I ask what this is about?"

"Some patients of yours, Dr. Wayne."

"You realize that there is confidentiality between a therapist and his patients?"

"Please, Dr. Wayne, hear me out. This is rather serious."

Sam looked over at Carla, then back at the detective.

"Okay," Sam said. "Let's go in my office."

Sam led the way. Once they were inside, Sam closed the door.

"Please sit down, Detective," he said, motioning to the chair where his patients usually sat. Carroll went over and sat down.

"I really don't want to bother you, Dr. Wayne, but this is a very grave matter."

"First of all, I'm not a doctor," Sam said. "I'm a therapist."

"I'm sorry. I just assumed."

"No problem," Sam said. "I just wanted to make that clear. I'm a psychologist, not a psychiatrist."

"Of course."

Sam sat in his usual chair, across from him.

"So what seems to be the problem?"

"It's about two of your patients, Mr. Wayne. Brenda Carlisle and Charlie Jarrold."

"What about them?"

"They were both attacked last night. Mrs. Carlisle is dead. Horribly mutilated. Charlie is missing. But his mother and her boyfriend weren't in very good shape, either."

"That's horrible," Sam said.

"Horrible isn't half of it. If you saw the crime scenes, they would probably scar you for life."

Sam lowered his head, and tried to regain his composure. The news really shocked him.

"Mrs. Carlisle had been seeing me for a while. I didn't know Charlie very long. What can I do to help you?"

"Did either one of them ever say anything about having enemies who would want to hurt them like this? You see, I'm desperate for any leads I can get on this case. It's so horrible, that I want to catch the perpetrator as quickly as possible. When I found out that they both saw you professionally, I thought maybe there might be some clue to what triggered all this."

"I can't discuss their sessions here, Detective, but I can say that neither one of them mentioned anyone who would want to do such a thing to them. And I don't believe they knew each other, although I could be wrong about that."

"Are you sure they never mentioned anyone who wanted to hurt them? Either one of them? Anything that might be relevant?"

"No, nothing at all. In fact, Mrs. Carlisle had nothing but good things to say the last time she saw me. She had made enough progress so that she was going to stop seeing me for the time being. I was very pleased to hear it, actually. You always hope you can help your patients get back to a healthy, normal life. As for Charlie Jarrold, well, he'd just started coming here. I could tell it would be a long process. It would take me a long time just to gain his trust, you see. But I didn't get to know him well enough for him to confide anything to me. If he was in danger, he never let me know about it."

"I see," Detective Carroll said. "I guess that will do for now. I really appreciate your cooperation in this matter."

"I haven't betrayed any confidences here. I just answered your questions. I must admit I find this news very disturbing, though. For such awful things to happen to two people I know. I think anybody would be disturbed by that kind of news."

"Of course. It's only natural," Detective Carroll said, getting to his feet. He fumbled with his wallet and pulled out a business card. "I would like to stay in touch if you don't mind. Some coincidence that both of them were patients of yours, don't you think? Chances are I won't have to bother you again, but I'd like to know that if I need to, I can call on you."

"If I can help," Sam said. He took the card.

"Thank you. And please, if you think of anything at all that could help, please don't hesitate to call me. There's a very dangerous man out there, and he can strike again at any time. We really need to stop this as soon as possible."

"Yes," Sam said. "If I think of anything important, I'll call you."

"Good," the detective said. "I must be going now. You have no idea how much work cases like this are."

Sam escorted the man to the door, and opened it.

"Good-bye, Mr. Wayne," Detective Carroll said, holding out his hand. Sam shook it.

"Thanks again for your cooperation."

Detective Carroll smiled at Carla and then went out the door, leaving the lobby.

"What a spooky guy," Carla said. "Was it something serious?"

"Just some awful news about Mrs. Carlisle," Sam said. "It seems she was murdered last night. And Charlie Jarrold is missing."

"Oh my God."

"You know, I've had this splitting headache ever since I got up this morning, and this news doesn't help. In fact, I feel awful. Can you do me a favor, Carla?

Can you call all my patients for today and reschedule their appointments? I really can't do this today."

"Of course," Carla said. "I'll take care of that for you."

"And after you make the phone calls, you can take the rest of the day off, too."

"That is awful news about Mrs. Carlisle," Carla said. "And Charlie. Do they think he was murdered too?"

"It didn't sound like they had a lot to go by. I hope the boy's okay."

"Me, too."

"I really have to go back to bed," Sam said, rubbing his temples for added effect. "Let's try this all again tomorrow, shall we?"

"Sure thing, Dr. Wayne."

He didn't correct her. Everyone just seemed to have this need to call him *Doctor*, even Carla. And he was starting to like it.

He went back into his office to get his briefcase. He thought about Detective Carroll. There was something about the man that made him nervous. It was probably normal to feel that way about a policeman asking questions. Then again, it didn't help that seeing him again reminded Sam of his trip to the morgue. He could still see Maggie's lifeless, mask-like face.

And to think I once considered offering to help the police with violent cases, Sam thought. The way he felt right now, the police weren't people he wanted to spend much more time around.

Then he left, waving to Carla as she talked on the phone.

CHAPTER THIRTY-SEVEN

When the doorbell rang, Colleen's mother hesitated a bit before answering. She wasn't expecting company, and didn't often get any. Unless it was Maryann come to check on her.

She was shocked to see through the window that it was Colleen standing on the front steps, looking fidgety and nervous. Dressed better than her mother had ever seen her before. New, fancy-looking clothes. But even that wasn't the biggest shock.

The biggest shock was the car idling in front of the house. A big black limousine.

Colleen's mother opened the door and embraced her daughter.

"Oh, Colleen," she said. "So good to see you."

"Hello, Mamma. I can't stay long."

Colleen looked around. She hadn't been here in a long time. It wasn't a big house, but it was clean. Everything in its place, just like always.

"What happened to you?" her mother said, unable to restrain her curiosity. "You're like Cinderella going to the ball. And is that car out there for you?"

"Yes, the driver's waiting, which is why I can't stay too long. I'm meeting someone for lunch in the city. But I hadn't seen you in a while and I wanted to stop by on the way and check on you."

Her mother's face beamed. "You came to check on *me*?"

"You're my mother, aren't you?"

"*Of course* I'm your mother!"

"So how have you been? Feeling okay?"

"Did you hit the lottery or something, Colly?"

"I met this great guy, Ma. He treats me so good. I've been waiting all my life for someone like him. It is like some kind of fairy tale."

"Who is he? Do I know him?"

"No, Ma. But he was in some magazines awhile ago. He used to go to movie premieres and date models. That sort of thing. His name is Jeremy, and he's the most wonderful guy."

"Is he famous, Colly?"

"I guess he was kind of famous for a little while. But I don't think you would have heard of him. His name is Jeremy Rust."

"No, I don't remember him," her mother said. "How did you meet him?"

"It was all so strange. I don't have time to go into it now. But I'm happy and he spoils me so much with clothes and jewelry, and limousines. This is what I was born for, Ma."

"I told you, it's all like something out of Cinderella," her mother said. "Let me look at you."

And she did. She looked Colleen up and down in her new dress.

"It's just amazing. The last time I saw you, you were living in squalor."

"Isn't destiny amazing sometimes?"

"I could have sworn you'd hit the lottery or something, but I hadn't heard anything about that. When I looked out the window and saw you dressed like that, with a limousine waiting, I didn't think it could be anything else."

"How's Maryann, Ma? I was going to visit her today, too, but I just don't have time. Has she been doing good?"

"She's okay. The last time I saw her, all she did was complain about the kids. You know how it is."

"I really better go," Colleen said. She didn't dare go any deeper into the house. She just wanted to make an appearance and be on her way.

"So soon? You have to tell me more about this Jeremy."

"I'll call you soon, Ma, we can talk more then. But I really have to go. The driver's waiting."

Her mother looked strangely sad. Her eyes were welling up with tears.

"What is it, Ma?" Colleen asked. "Why are you crying?"

"I'm just so glad to see you doing well. After all these years, I thought you were going to be miserable all your life. And I thought it was all my fault."

You certainly didn't give me much of a childhood, Colleen thought, but didn't say it. Instead, she opened her purse.

"Ma, I know things can be tight sometimes. Do you need any money?"

"Oh, how sweet of you to want to share your good fortune with me."

Colleen took out her wallet and opened it. She withdrew a hundred dollar bill.

She glanced up and saw her mother staring expectantly.

"How would *this* be?"

"Oh, Colly, you don't have to do that," her mother said. "You're much too generous."

Colleen resisted the impulse to agree with her. To put the hundred back in her wallet and give the old woman a ten instead. She really wanted to torment her mother and make her beg, for all the times she'd had to endure the woman's criticism and abuse. For the awful childhood she'd had, feeling unwanted and unprotected from the lechers that her mother brought into the house on a regular basis. Colleen wanted to humiliate this woman standing before her, to pay her back for all the misery she'd given her throughout her life.

But she didn't do that. Despite all her bad memories, Colleen couldn't be that cruel. Somehow, there was a part of her that still loved her mother. To be able to come here, and show off her good fortune, was revenge enough.

Colleen handed her the hundred-dollar bill. Her mother snatched at it eagerly, like a homeless beggar. It would have torn in half in Colleen's hand, if she didn't let go of it in time.

"Thank you so much, Colly. You'll call me soon, won't you."

"Yes, Ma. I'll call you in a few days and we can talk more. But I really have to get going now."

Her mother stepped forward and hugged her. Really *hugged* her. If Colleen hadn't just given her the hundred, she would almost have believed it was sincere. That her mother really loved her.

Colleen hugged her back. Tightly. Wanting so badly for this to be a real mother-daughter moment.

Then Colleen pulled away and went out the door. She walked as fast as she could to the waiting car and got in the back door before the driver could even get out to open it for her.

"Where to, now?" the driver asked.

She gave him the name of the restaurant where she was going to meet Jeremy for lunch. Then she looked out the window as the car pulled away from the curb.

Her mother was still standing in the doorway of her house, waving. Waving as if she would really miss her youngest daughter. As if her leaving really mattered.

Colleen found that she was crying uncontrollably.

* * *

Jeremy looked out the car window, watching the scenery rush past. He glanced ahead at the driver, who had tufts of graying hair sticking out beneath his cap. He turned his attention back to the window.

Imagine, Jeremy thought. Paying for *two* limos in one day.

It almost made him laugh. There was a time, not too long ago, when he hardly ever left the house. So this had to be an improvement. It felt good to have a reason to spend money again.

All those years cloistering himself in the beach house like some kind of monk, having minimal interaction with the outside world. He had felt so ugly then, so repulsive. He didn't want anyone to see him. And with his money, he didn't have to deal with anything. Everything that could be delivered, was. And he had people to take care of his private affairs. That was the one great thing about money, if you wanted to distance yourself from the world, you could.

Even when Viv came to stay, it didn't give him much inspiration to go outside. Sure, they went to bars a few times. But he always felt strange there. He never enjoyed himself and he never had the courage to approach a woman. Especially one he knew.

He hadn't wanted anyone to see him this way. Even after five operations, he just wasn't the same, and he'd had the hardest time confronting that.

Better to not confront it at all.

Which was why this thing with Colleen was so strange. He felt that his time of exile was over. He actually felt the desire to go back into the world again. It was as if fate had brought her to him that morning when she appeared on the beach. Sure, she'd been traumatized and needy, but so had he. They provided something for each other that neither one could explain.

She was the best thing that ever happened to him. She made him want to live again.

He wondered where Colleen was right now. She'd insisted that she had so many things to do before she met him for lunch. She'd mentioned something about seeing her mother. He'd almost half-hoped she would invite him along on that one, but on second thought was kind of relieved. He'd only known Colleen a couple of weeks now, and he certainly wasn't ready to meet her mother yet.

He'd had things of his own to do, but he'd gotten them done early. Now, he had nothing to do but wait. So he'd had his driver take the roundabout route.

Jeremy found himself wondering about Viv. She'd been rather distant lately, which wasn't all that strange. There were times when she was there for him, when she was the only one who was. But then there were weeks when he wouldn't see her at all. She'd come and go without a word of explanation. He'd just gotten used to it over time.

Drifting in and out of sleep the night before, he could have sworn he'd heard a male voice out in the kitchen. Viv wasn't the kind to bring men home. In fact, she never brought *anyone* back home with her. He'd have to ask her about that.

He'd noticed that Colleen had gotten out of bed at one point, too. Maybe she'd just gotten hungry in the middle of the night. She had strange sleep habits. She tended to get up in the middle of the night fairly often, from what he could tell. He wondered if she was capable of sleeping through a whole night without interruption. Some people were just like that.

Jeremy looked at his Rolex. Colleen would be meeting him in the city in half an hour.

"What time should we get there, Jack?" Jeremy asked the driver.

"I can take the turnoff here if you want to save some time. It would take about twenty minutes."

"Yeah, do that. I guess I've wasted enough time today."

"Sure thing."

Jeremy stared at the other cars, half-hoping to see Colleen's heading in the same direction.

He hated being apart from her for very long.

CHAPTER THIRTY-EIGHT

V iv sat in the lotus position, trying hard to empty her mind. But it kept going back to Grif. She opened her eyes, and watched him sleeping. He had to be faking by now. Nobody slept that much. Unless he really was as exhausted as he'd said.

She was too distracted to do her morning workout. For some reason she felt uncomfortable doing her exercises with him in the room. She was so used to being alone, that she was very possessive of her privacy.

She thought about the night before. Grif and Colleen. It had made her really nervous at first, seeing the two of them together. That was the exact thing she'd hoped to avoid. But Grif was so impulsive. She never knew what he would do.

She had never warned Jeremy about Grif. She felt bad about that, but she saw Grif so rarely that she didn't see the need. And besides, Jeremy hadn't woken up the night before. So it hadn't become an issue.

But Colleen. Viv didn't know very much about her, but what little she did know made her think that Colleen was as flighty and impulsive as Grif was. Which was a bad combination. Grif had a tendency to take advantage of people like that. Despite his promise to her, she knew that he would not be able to resist it if someone too willing came into his orbit. She almost trembled at the thought of what could have happened if she hadn't woken up in time. If she hadn't intervened.

And then there was the sex. Viv had long since rejected any guilt associated with having sex with her own brother. It wasn't like they were normal siblings, able to sustain any kind of normal relationships with other people. No, intimacy with them could mean death. And the only partners who were one-hundred-percent safe, without the chance of someone dying, were each other. Viv had come to it from a more cerebral point of view, and Grif had been more than eager to play along.

They'd first made love in their early twenties, the first time they'd been reunited since Viv left home. They'd even lived together for a brief period, but it just didn't work out.

At first the sex had seemed very strange. Kind of dirty. Viv remembered throwing up after the first time (although she never let *him* know that). But over the years, it just lost any sense of taboo it could have had. It was something they did out of necessity, a desperate attempt at real intimacy, and it was strange how they'd come to trust one another—to feel more at ease and comfortable with each other's bodies than with anybody else. Sex with Grif offered Viv a chance to totally let her guard down, to truly enjoy the act itself, and she was sure he felt the same way, although she'd never expect him to articulate it. However, no matter how enjoyable it was, it never reached the levels they felt when they were *feeding*.

She'd had an ulterior motive in seducing him the night before. To get his mind off Colleen. Viv knew Colleen would have been putty in Grif's hands. That he could have made her do anything he wanted. And with Jeremy right down the hall.

So she'd seduced Grif to save Colleen. It sounded so noble when she put it that way. But it wasn't so clear-cut. She'd wanted to fuck Grif ever since he came back. He was good in bed, and it really felt great to not have to worry about whether there was enough pain inside a partner to entice her to kill them.

Because she just couldn't ignore pain. And if someone had a death wish, she was more than happy to oblige. In fact, it wasn't even a conscious thing. If they had a self-destructive impulse, then she could not stop herself from acting on it. There was a line that, once crossed in the midst of intimacy, she could not turn back. Even if she wanted to.

And it had struck her as almost funny that Colleen had watched them fucking through the keyhole. Yeah, she'd sensed that and she knew it wasn't the first time Colleen had peeked through that keyhole at her. She'd been tempted to call her on it, to embarrass her, but she didn't care enough to take it that far.

Let her watch, Viv thought. *Maybe she'll learn something*.

And what did Colleen think watching Viv fuck her own brother? It didn't really matter very much, did it? Who was she going to tell? Jeremy? After Viv had caught her kissing Grif? Probably not. Her secret was safe. Not that it was much of a secret. Viv wasn't one to feel that she had to answer to anyone else. If Colleen had problems with what she saw, what she *spied on*, then fuck her.

Viv got up and opened her trunk. She took out some underwear and jeans. Then she went to the closet to get a shirt.

She stared at the mattress on the floor. At Grif, with his head on a pillow.

One of his eyes opened. He smiled.

"God, that was the best night's sleep I've had in a long time," he told her.

"I'm glad. It was getting late, but I didn't want to wake you."

"Afraid that I might leave?" he said, sitting up.

"You said you couldn't stay long."

"Yeah, I better move on. But it was nice to be here. With you. You know, there's a freedom I have with you, that I can't share with anybody else on the planet."

"I know," she said, realizing this was the first time he'd ever tried to put it into words. She'd put it into words a hundred times before, in her head. Maybe he had, too.

Maybe she didn't give him enough credit for smarts.

"Thanks for letting me stay here," he said. "Were you going to take a shower?"

"Yeah."

"Mind if I join you?" he asked, staring across the big room at the bathroom door. That was one thing really nice about staying in Jeremy's house. She had her own bathroom.

"Why not?" she asked and smiled.

He rose naked from the mattress and walked over to her. He took her in his arms.

"I really love you, Viv," he said. "I know I hardly ever say it, and I know I must really seem like a total fuck-up to you. But I share a bond with you that I can't with anybody else."

"I know."

She'd planned to chastise him when he woke, for toying with Colleen the night before, especially since it could have hurt Jeremy. But now, with him close, she only wanted to enjoy his being here while it lasted. He would be gone soon, and she would miss him again, despite herself.

She led him into the bathroom and turned on the shower.

* * *

Ben Carroll sat at the back of the bar, drinking a beer. It was only the middle of the day, but he'd already started drinking in earnest. There used to be a time when he cared whether anyone could smell it on him, but those days were long past. If he got too drunk, he'd just call in sick.

He looked around for the blonde from the night before. The one with the short, punky hair. She'd been with a guy then, or else he would have approached her. He'd seen her here before a few times, and he'd seen her leave with other people. Men and women.

He found himself thinking, When will it be *my* turn?

Maybe it just wasn't meant to be.

He looked down into his beer, at the swirling islands of foam, and he wondered about what had brought him here so early in the day. Why he felt so defeated lately.

There was this philosophy that when you're green at this job, you're not prepared for the kinds of things you will see. And over time, your skin gets harder, your stomach gets stronger, and you're able to handle anything that comes your way.

But that wasn't always the case.

For years, Ben seemed to get harder. To handle more. To get through bloody crime scenes and random atrocities without losing his humanity too much. He could even remember a time when it didn't make him sick; when it made him angry. And the anger was the fuel that kept him going.

But the anger was an ember that had long since died out. The tough hide had shed itself. All that was left was the sickness. *The horror.*

I can't do this anymore, he thought. I'm going to take early retirement and get out of this shit.

Right after this case is over.

The sheer numbers made him think of old newsreel footage he'd seen of the concentration camps. But this was different. It was happening *now*, and under everyone's noses, and nobody seemed to know how or why? There wasn't a Dachau you could go to, to find the killers. No death trains whistling into the night.

How were so many people being systematically slaughtered?

He thought of the mass grave in the park. It was difficult to believe someone dismembered all those people and buried them all together in pieces. And yet, he'd seen the proof of it. How much bigger was it than what he'd seen?

And did one man really do all this? It had to be the work of more than one person. Even after listening to the eyewitness accounts of the Shredder, he found it hard to believe just one killer did this all by himself. And why couldn't any of the witnesses describe him? How could a mass grave fill up in a public park, totally undetected, until now? Until a man's dog found a human ass cheek, leading to the discovery of the horrors.

All his years on the force, building a tough skin, were meaningless in the face of this.

Some of the others he worked with were able to maintain their composure. He'd tried his best as well. But it was getting harder and harder.

He drained his beer, caught the waitress's eye and signaled for another. It didn't take very long. He was one of the few customers at this time of day, and she would glance in his direction now and then, anyway.

Will I go back to the office today? Will I respond if I get another call on the radio about another murder scene?

The waitress put a fresh glass in front of him, took the empty one away. He asked her for a Scotch this time, to go with the beer.

And why did he keep thinking about that psychiatrist, Sam Wayne? Aside from being the doctor of two of the victims, nothing else linked him to the crimes. Yet, something about him would not let Ben Carroll forget about him. The first time they'd met had been in the morgue, when Wayne had identified his dead wife. Even then, something strange about the man set off his radar.

The second time, in Wayne's office, it had been even worse.

Why?

I need to do some more research on Mr. Wayne, Carroll thought. Maybe he *is* involved in this, somehow.

Ben Carroll had learned to trust his instincts. A couple of times, they'd led to dead ends, even though he was sure he was right. Sometimes, the pieces just don't add up, no matter how sure you are.

But he had to solve this one. It wasn't like the rest.

It was bigger than them all. And it would keep getting bigger, until it was stopped.

CHAPTER THIRTY-NINE

"Let me go," Charlie said.

Dr. Wayne just stood there, near the doorway, staring down at the floor. Charlie was tempted to shout again, but the last time he did, the shrink had struck him hard across the face and threatened to put the gag back on.

Charlie hated the gag. And he hated being tied to a chair like this. The ropes were so tight, he could barely move at all. His legs were starting to go numb.

It was obvious his comfort was not on Wayne's agenda right now.

"Why did you bring me here?" Charlie asked. Trying to keep his temper in check, because it would not help him here.

The man looked up at him. He looked as if he really wanted to say something, but the words wouldn't come out.

Dr. Wayne started walking toward him. Slowly. As if it was something he didn't want to do.

Charlie looked around at the trash-strewn floor, the graffitied walls. *Where is this place?* he wondered. *And how long have I been here?*

"Why can't you tell me anything?" Charlie asked. "Why won't you let me go?"

Dr. Wayne stopped in front of him.

"I can't," he said softly.

"Why the fuck can't you?" Charlie said, his temper flaring up again. He struggled at the ropes, trying to break free. The chair fell over on its side, but he was no closer to freeing himself.

His captor grabbed the back of the chair and put it right side up. Charlie tried to move his head forward and bite him, but there were ropes holding his shoulders back. Dr. Wayne grabbed the gag that hung loosely around his neck and put it back in his mouth. Then he tightened it.

As Charlie struggled, he stared into the man's face. It was no longer clear to him. It was unfocused, *shimmering*. Charlie blinked but Dr. Wayne's face still did not come back into focus.

The man pulled a handkerchief from his pocket and wrapped it around Charlie's eyes, returning him to the darkness.

* * *

Sam stood there a few minutes, adrenaline rushing through his brain the more Charlie struggled. The hairs on the back of his neck stood up. He was even shaking slightly.

He could feel himself getting energized.

When it reached a high point, Charlie suddenly went limp. The energy had been sucked out of him. Sam walked out of the room, and locked the door from the outside.

He kept walking until he got outside the house, and he locked the outside door as well.

He felt as if he were walking in a dream. As if he were locking doors inside a dream. Charlie really wasn't inside this house at all. As he walked to his car, Sam became disoriented, not really sure where he was or how he had gotten here. At least he recognized his car. He unlocked it and got inside, trying to get his bearings. These kinds of things were happening more often, and they were really starting to scare him.

* * *

"So how did things go with your mother?" Jeremy asked, knowing how anxious she had been earlier in the day.

They were in a restaurant at the top of a skyscraper. They had an incredible view from up here. They could see most of the city.

"It went better than I thought it would," Colleen said, taking the menu from the waiter. "It felt so good to have the upper hand for once."

"What do you mean?" he asked.

"You know, the limousine certainly didn't hurt. And the new clothes. She was really impressed. All these years she'd kept telling me how much of a failure I was. How I'd end up in an early grave and all that."

"Pretty upbeat, huh?"

"You said it. Well, it was so nice to show her how I wasn't a failure — and to rub her nose in it."

Colleen started laughing uncontrollably. It took a couple of minutes to regain her composure.

"God, you should have seen her face when she opened the door. Her jaw literally *dropped!* She stared at me, then the limo out front, and she just couldn't think of the *words.*"

"Sounds like a success, then."

"You don't know how long I wanted to do something like that. My whole damned *life.* All I ever heard were such negative things, about how I was wasting my life. And then to do that. It felt *wonderful.*"

Jeremy found himself laughing, too. "So maybe it was good I didn't go along to take away from your triumph."

"I know you didn't want to go, Jeremy. I'd told you such awful things about her, and we've only known each other such a short time. I thought it would be unfair to spring her on you so soon. But you should have seen her face. If you'd been there, it would have just been icing on the cake. I know she would have recognized you from the magazines and it would have astounded her to no end. I was only afraid that if you'd gone with me at this point, it would have seemed like I'd arranged it all. Like it was some kind of prank. As it was, she couldn't stop asking about you."

"What did you tell her?"

"I told her you were famous, and wonderful, and the best thing that had ever

happened to me."

"You really told her that?"

"Of course I did."

He reached across the table and grasped her hand. He squeezed it.

"You should have seen her. At the end, she couldn't stop crying."

"The poor soul."

"What about all the times she'd made me cry? And those weren't tears of joy, like hers supposedly were today. No, that woman made my life miserable for as long as I can remember, always crushing me with her words."

She didn't tell him about the money she'd given her mother. Not because Jeremy would have disapproved of it, but because she thought it might have sounded sadistic to add how pleased she was to have her mother begging for money for a change. It was a private pleasure she'd decided to keep to herself.

When the waiter returned, they ordered. Or rather, Jeremy ordered for the both of them. He ordered things she had always wanted to try, but never had the luxury of eating before. It was a feast fit for royalty. She could tell he enjoyed ordering it all, almost like he was showing off for her.

An expensive bottle of champagne was the first item brought over, in an ice bucket. The waiter popped the cork for them.

"You know," Jeremy told her. "You really do look beautiful today."

She blushed. "Oh, Jeremy."

She watched him across the table, and remembered something her mother had said, about her being something out of Cinderella. That's exactly how she felt now. She kept waiting for the clock to strike and everything to disappear. Jeremy, the food, the beautiful clothes she was wearing. She kept waiting to go back to that one-room apartment, waking up to another miserable day.

That life was so far behind her now.

She drank champagne and laughed and ate wonderful foods, and held Jeremy's hand across the table. It was like something out of a romance novel.

When they were done, Jeremy signed his name in a fancy book the waiter brought over, and then they left. Jeremy had dismissed her limousine before lunch, since there was no longer need for two cars.

"Where would you like to go now?" he asked her, as she walked toward the waiting limousine. "Do you want to stay in the city for a while longer? We could shop, and wait until the nightclubs open."

Colleen stopped in her tracks. "Oh, my God."

"What is it?" Jeremy said, noticing the discomfort on her face.

"It's him, Jeremy," she said softly. "The guy who killed Turney right in front of me."

Jeremy turned to look. A man was across the street, walking past them, quickly.

"That man there?"

"Yes, Jeremy. It's him. I'm sure of it."

"Well, we can't let him get away," Jeremy said. "Let's follow him."

"He's dangerous. Are you sure we should?"

"We'll stay far enough away to stay inconspicuous," Jeremy said. He stuck his head into the passenger side window of the limousine. "Can you wait here awhile? We'll be back as soon as we're able," he told the driver.

"Yes, sir."

"It would be kind of conspicuous to follow him in a limousine," Jeremy told her. "Maybe we should get a cab instead."

Jeremy stepped into the street and hailed a cab. She had never seen anybody get one to stop so quickly. Perhaps it was because they were so well dressed. They got inside.

"We're trying to catch up with someone," Jeremy told the driver. "So I might have some odd directions."

"No problem," the cabbie said. "Which way we going now?"

"Straight ahead," Jeremy said, "but not too fast."

* * *

Viv had just seen Grif off at the bus station and was feeling low, so instead of going right home she had the cab drop her off at the bar instead. She'd been there the night before with Grif, but there was a different bartender behind the bar now. A slightly older man than the guy who served drinks at night.

"I'll have a shot of tequila," she told him. "And a beer. Whatever you've got on draft."

The man nodded and went about getting her order.

"Hi," a man's voice said not far from her.

She turned. Someone was sitting down her beside her. He looked familiar. Then she remembered. He'd been here the night before, too. He was the depressed guy who Grif had wanted to seduce, until she'd talked him out of it. The one Grif thought was a cop. There was something of that about him, and it made her unsure of how to respond.

"Sorry, I didn't mean to startle you," the man said. "My name is Ben. Ben Carroll. I come here pretty often and I've seen you here before. I just never got the nerve to come up and talk to you. Until now."

She saw it then. The wound within him. The ache behind his eyes. It made her relax a little.

"Well, I'm glad you did," she told him. "I'm Viv."

He hesitated extending his hand, like he was surprised it was so easy to engage her in a conversation. "Nice to meet you."

She returned his handshake. "What are you drinking, Ben?"

She noticed he'd brought a glass of beer with him, but it was almost empty. He must have come from one of the tables toward the back.

"I should be asking *you* that," he said. When the bartender brought Viv's glasses over, he insisted on paying, and ordered a fresh beer and Scotch for himself.

"Oh, so you're a two-fisted drinker, too, are you?"

"Same as you," he said, and laughed.

"We must be quite the sad pair, sitting here in a bar in the early afternoon, drinking like this."

"Well, I'm not so sad now that I've met you," Ben said, lifting his glass of Scotch. "Here's to us," he said.

They clinked glasses. He downed his Scotch and she downed her tequila.

"So what has you down today?" Ben asked.

The idea that he might be an undercover cop pumping her for information about Grif crossed her mind, though she didn't believe it. She was pretty good at reading people.

"I saw an old friend I hadn't seen in ages," she told him. "And he had to leave this morning. So I guess that's got me down. I usually don't drink this early. How about you?"

"My job's getting me down," he said. "And I've been thinking about quitting."

"What do you do?" she asked. This was his chance to lie to her, if he wanted to keep his cover.

"I'm a detective. Homicide. You wouldn't believe the stuff I've seen."

She relaxed a bit more. He didn't ask her anything about her friend. And he really seemed depressed by his job.

"Pretty horrible stuff?" she asked him.

"You got that right," Ben Carroll said. "I guess I've just about reached my limit. And I'm wondering if I should just hang up the badge forever."

It was clear that something had seriously affected him.

She had made a pact with herself not to pick up cops anymore. It was a good way to avoid trouble. But for two reasons, she decided to leave with Detective Ben Carroll.

First of all, was the fact that he was hurting so badly that she couldn't resist him. She was like a shark getting a taste of blood before a kill. The sensation was uncontrollable.

The other thing was that, like Grif had mentioned to her the night before, she'd noticed the ache was bothering her again. Where, in the past, a kill would last her a few weeks, now they only lasted a day or two. And then she wanted more.

She needed *more*.

And Ben Carroll's pain was like an aphrodisiac to her, making the ache even stronger.

He drained his beer. "Do you want another one?" he asked her.

"Ben, I was wondering. Would you like to go somewhere else? Someplace more, I dunno, more *intimate*."

He seemed surprised at her suggestion, but it made him smile. He was almost handsome when he smiled. "I'd love to," he said.

She smiled and finished her beer. "Let's go."

She took his hand and they got up from their stools, and went out into the afternoon sun.

CHAPTER FORTY

"Stop here," Jeremy said to the cab driver. The man pulled over to the curb.

They'd stayed a good distance back from the man. The growing traffic made that easier.

"Do you want me to wait?" the driver asked.

"Just drive around the block and come back," Jeremy said. "And then we'll head back."

He opened the door. "Do you want to stay here?" he asked Colleen.

"No, Jeremy. I want to go with you."

"Dressed like that?"

"You're not exactly a homeless man, yourself."

"We don't really have time to change," Jeremy said. "And this could be dangerous."

"I want to go with you, Jeremy."

"Okay, but we won't get too close. I just want to see where he's going."

They could see him across the street. He went into a wide alleyway, which appeared to open out onto a court of some kind.

They got out, and the cab pulled away from the curb. They crossed the street and headed in the direction of the alley's mouth.

"Stay here," Jeremy told her, looking around. "Hell, this isn't exactly the best part of town. We better make this quick."

"Jeremy, shouldn't we call the police?"

"By the time they got here, he'd be gone. I want to see where he goes. Maybe he lives around him, and we can give the police the address."

He was about to move away from her, then hesitated. "You better come with me."

"Okay."

He grabbed her hand and they approached the alley. It led out onto a courtyard between buildings, and there were neglected gardens on either side. It had obviously been a fancy part of town at one time, but had been allowed to get run down and ignored.

"Any sign of him?" Colleen asked softly.

"No. I think we lost him. Which means this whole thing was a waste of time."

"Not really. We could still tell the police he came here. Maybe they could find him."

"There are a lot of buildings here. He could be in any of them. For all we know, he could be long gone by now."

"Maybe this wasn't such a good idea," Colleen said.

"This man has to be brought to justice," Jeremy said. "We had to at least try to find out where he was going."

They journeyed a little deeper into the courtyard. Jeremy looked up and around at the surrounding buildings. It was easy to see that, in another era, they had contained luxury apartments.

It was then that the man attacked him. He came without warning, with a speed that defied description. He leapt and crashed into Jeremy, pushing Colleen to the ground. She tried to stand up, but the force of the collision left her feeling disoriented for a moment.

The attacker, the same man they had been following, was pounding Jeremy with his fists, ripping at him with his hands. Then the man bit down into the meat of Jeremy's throat and ripped out a huge chunk of flesh, spitting it to the ground, as he continued to rip Jeremy's body apart.

It reminded her so much of what had happened to Turney. It was happening all over again.

She somehow got to her feet, hearing Jeremy's screams as he was torn apart by his attacker. She wanted so desperately to scream, or to hurl herself at this maniac, but she simply stood there, frozen in time, unable to respond to the horrific tableau before her.

Jeremy's screams didn't last long, and then the man was standing there, awash in blood. What was left of Jeremy was only pieces on the ground.

He was breathing hard as he stared in *her* direction.

It was the same red, raging face she'd seen when Turney was murdered. The mouth twisted into an unnatural grin that wasn't amusement at all, but uncontrolled anger. The glaring eyes, the flared nostrils.

And then she saw another vision. This time, instead of rattlesnakes, she saw an animal roaring without sound, nothing familiar, just pure ferocity. Something beyond classification or time. The image was superimposed over his face, and then was gone. His real face was even worse, contorted in a mixture of anguish and fury.

He didn't stare her way for long. Soon he was frantically searching in several directions. A puzzled look crossed his face. It was clear that he was as confused as she was.

Something was holding him back.

She found the ability to move again, and ran out of the courtyard. Her high-heeled shoes threatening to topple her, but she kicked them off and kept running.

She ran down the block. A horn blared at her. It was the cab.

She flung the back door open and got inside.

"Where's your boyfriend?" the driver asked her. "What's the matter?"

"He isn't coming," she told him. She spoke as if she were in a trance. She gave him an address and he pulled away from the curb.

As they drove by the alleyway, she was terrified that the man who killed Jeremy and Turney would leap out at them and tear the taxi apart with his bare hands. But he did not. He wasn't anywhere she could see.

* * *

"You wouldn't believe the kind of shit I've seen," Detective Benjamin Carroll said as he unbuttoned his shirt. "It's enough to send a normal person around the bend."

Viv nodded her head. This place made her uncomfortable. It was the same motel she had brought Maggie to that last time. She wasn't certain, but this could have even been the same room. The one Maggie died in. She never brought her prey to the same place twice, but he'd insisted they'd come here. She couldn't exactly tell him, "I killed someone here recently, can we go somewhere else?" Besides, the way she felt right now, the quicker they got this over with, the better.

Since Grif had left that morning, she had found herself in a profound funk, and this was just what the doctor ordered to relieve the sadness that draped over her like a shroud. This sad, weary man had practically begged her to end his life.

He had a good build for a man his age. Viv guessed he was in his mid-to-late forties. He didn't have much of a gut, and he had good muscle tone. *He must work out regularly,* she thought. Some of the older ones like him had a tendency to let themselves go to pot.

She knew. She'd taken her share of policemen's lives away. There were a lot of depressed men on the force, and she'd exploited that when she'd been younger. But they were a little too easy, and they could draw the wrong kind of attention for someone trying to keep under the radar.

Ben Carroll's stomach was pretty tight. His arms were hard and muscular. His face, on the other hand, betrayed him. The tired eyes with the glassy stare. The tell-tale wrinkles in the corners of his face.

And the smell of desperation on him. Desperation and too much cheap whiskey and beer.

She imagined he had probably been a handsome young man once. Maybe a football hero in high school. Smart but aimless, he'd found his way onto the police force. He'd been intelligent enough to excel to the rank of detective.

But he clearly found that unconsoling. Pointless.

As he got undressed, so did she. She was stretched out, wondering again if she'd been on this particular bed before. They all felt the same in this motel. Hell, there were other places just like this that felt the same, too. The same hard mattresses and weak box springs. The same blankets that you knew were never cleaned regularly.

So many telltale stains if you inspected them closely enough. The evidence of a thousand fucks.

"But enough about me," Carroll said, pulling off his underwear. He wore briefs. She noticed things like that. She would have thought he was a boxer man. She was already naked and spread on the hard mattress that creaked every time she moved. "What about you?"

"You know," she said. "I really didn't come here to talk about myself. I came here to fuck."

He half-smiled at that. The kind of expression cynics had when they can't believe a streak of good luck. He had a prominent erection and didn't even make an attempt at foreplay. He just pushed her knees wider apart and rammed it home.

She was ready for him.

He gritted his teeth in an almost painful smile as he fucked her. At first she'd thought that he might have false teeth, but she could tell now that they were real. He was totally into it. Totally focused. Maybe he was afraid if he didn't concentrate hard enough, he'd lose his hard-on.

Older men tended to try harder.

He felt good inside her. But that wasn't how she got off. For her, this was the foreplay. As he moved in her, she closed her eyes and concentrated herself, on his insides. On that region that was the deepest part of who he was. It didn't take her long to find the tender parts, the scar tissue inside. There was so much of it. She would have had to be blind to miss it. Like a beacon inside him, a flashing neon sign that said, *I am in pain and I want to die.* It was all a jumble, hearing his thoughts, feeling his emotions. She tried to block it all out and focus on her goal.

She had seen this hundreds of times before, but not always so severe. Who didn't have at least a twinge of a death wish? An open wound that refused to heal over? It was as if Ben Carroll was nothing *but* a walking death wish.

She hooked onto that soft spot and reeled it in.

She could sense that Carroll felt her inside his head, because he seemed to lose his concentration for a moment. The strange, skeletal smile faltered. He stared down into her face, her half-closed eyes.

And then, he started to die.

Somehow, she wrapped herself around those wounded parts of him and hugged them close, and she could feel what he felt, a strange warmth that bordered on drowning. Like there was fluid in his lungs, depriving him of air.

He started to come.

And that was when it got more intense and turned from fear to heightened sensation. The orgasm intensified and didn't end quickly. It was long and drawn out, making him shiver atop of her.

Meanwhile, she took what she wanted.

The sensation was so strong, he was gasping hard for air.

As he came, what he was, the personality and soul of Ben Carroll, sprayed forth from him into her, along with his semen.

And as he faded, drooping on top of her, that's when she started to come.

For all she knew, he was already dead, slumped across her belly. But that didn't matter at all. She was riding off her own furious sensations. Something that dwarfed what he had just experienced in every way.

Viv drifted in and out of consciousness during the waves of pleasure. They were stronger than they'd been in a while. It must have been Carroll's high level of pain. When it was over, she lay there on the bed, breathing hard, trying to regain her focus. The first thing she did was slide his body off of her.

Something about this time had really bothered her. She had caught some of his stray thoughts. He knew about some of the other deaths she had caused, and she could tell he was wondering if he had found the killer. The "blonde woman" he was looking for. And yet, there was another part of him, just as strong, that *wanted* to find her. That wanted her to take his life. She almost wondered if this had been a set-up, an attempt to somehow catch her in the act, but something in his thoughts had calmed her. He hadn't been trying to catch her in the act; he had wanted to become part of the *act* itself.

She arranged his body neatly on the bed and covered it with the sheet and blanket. Like tucking a child in for the night. She wanted to feel regret, but she really didn't know him. There was a time when she felt sadness for those who died in her presence, a time when she even felt guilty for what she was compelled to do.

But that time was long since gone. There was no use getting too wrapped up emotionally in it all.

Trying her best to ignore the corpse on the bed, she went about her usual routine, washing herself, cleaning the room. Once she was done and dressed, she put on her sunglasses and left.

She made sure to stay away from the manager's office. Luckily, Ben had taken care of getting the room. She didn't think anyone had seen her come or go. So soon after Maggie's death, this place made her very antsy. *No more motels for a while,* she thought. *And I'm definitely not ever coming back to this one.*

There were woods behind the motel, and she cut through them to get out to the highway. She walked for a mile or so before she started hitchhiking. It didn't take her long to get a ride.

CHAPTER FORTY-ONE

When Colleen got back to Jeremy's house by the beach, she really had no idea what she was doing. She paid the cab driver some exorbitant amount (and somehow she had enough money in her purse, thanks to Jeremy).

She went inside the house and wandered around aimlessly from room to room. Turning on lights and turning some off, trying to focus on what she was looking for, trying to think through the shock that numbed her.

Among her things in the drawers Jeremy had let her use, she found a straight razor. She used to joke that she used it to shave her legs, that it gave her the closest shave, but in reality it was something she had not used in a long time. Something she did not want to hold again, but which she had kept for a moment like this, when the pain was just too much.

She remembered back when she was a teenager, when she used to cut herself out of boredom and depression. But this was something more. This was pure horror, and an unbearable sadness. Emotions that threatened to swallow her whole. To crush her.

She needed something to bring her back to reality. To cut through the agony she was feeling inside.

She stuck her arm out in front of her and ran the edge of the razor across it, drawing blood. It had been a long time since she'd done it, but somewhere in the back of her mind she knew it would happen again.

She carved shapes into her arm, bringing more blood to the surface. She did not cut her wrist. Then she switched the razor to her other hand and stuck her other arm out in front of her.

The cutting helped, but she still couldn't get Jeremy's murder out of her head.

Blood dripped onto the bathroom floor. She'd somehow wandered there during her cutting, and now the floor was splattered with blood that flowed from both her arms.

She stared at herself in the mirror above the sink, unable to comprehend who she was, or why she was alone in this house.

* * *

Sam was having a hard time thinking as he drove down the street. He wasn't really sure where he was going. All he knew was that he was covered in blood and he wanted to get clean again.

How the hell did I get covered in blood, anyway? It was like he was experiencing a nervous breakdown. Like he was constantly living through a mixture of reality and dreams that was confusing and thick as fluid around him, forcing him forward on a current he could not comprehend.

There were things he thought he did, that he could not understand. Things that made no sense to him. He couldn't even be sure what was real anymore.

But this blood on him now, it was real. And if he was able to trust his memory—and he wasn't sure that he could—the reason why was a horrible one. One he refused to accept.

He'd seen another man torn apart in front of him. He could not determine who was doing the tearing, but it looked like the work of his own hands. But it didn't *feel* like he was doing it. He was an observer, forced to watch the horror of another man dying in front of him. The whole thing had such a dream-like quality to it. But here he was, and the blood seemed so real.

He saw the public beach coming up on his left. The weather was getting colder and it was deserted. *Water.* It was only a temporary answer to his problem, but he wanted so badly to be clean, and here was water in abundance.

He turned left and parked in the lot beside the beach. There didn't seem to be anyone around, for as far as he could see.

Sam got out of the car and ran toward the waves.

He didn't think about whether anyone could see him from the road, driving by. And he didn't look again, as he ran, to see if there were any spectators he might have missed on first glance. All he wanted to do was submerge himself. To wash the blood away.

He dove into the icy water and swam as fast as he could. He submerged himself, wanting to drown and end all this confusion he was feeling. It was almost like he was walking underwater all the time these days anyway, why not just do it for real?

Sam held his breath for as long as he could, and then found himself surfacing against his will. The instinct for survival was too strong. He broke the surface and gasped for air.

He looked in all directions. Luckily, the beach was deserted. It was probably too cold for most people. He scrubbed at his clothes with both hands, trying to get rid of the blood.

He submerged a second time.

The water was very cold and he fought the impulse to get out and go back to his car. Instead, he willed himself to go limp, to sink to the bottom. To drown.

His body refused to cooperate.

He broke the surface again, gasping harder for air this time.

There was something inside him that refused to let him drown himself.

I think I'm a murderer, Sam thought, and it was too much to fathom. It just didn't seem real to him.

He did not submerge again. Instead, he began swimming toward the shore. When he reached shallow waters, he stood up and walked back on land, toward his car.

Soaking and shivering from the cold water, he opened the driver side door and slid inside on the bloodstained seats. He'd failed to get all the blood off his clothes, but his arms and face were clean now. He checked himself in the rear-view mirror.

Sam was breathing heavily as he searched his pocket for his keys. They weren't there. They were still in the ignition. He turned the key and his car started, then he turned on the heat.

He sat there for a few minutes, letting the car idle, trying to get his breathing back to normal before he got back onto the road.

CHAPTER FORTY-TWO

When she got back to Jeremy's house, Viv noticed, despite her exhaustion, that the glass door had been left open. That wasn't all that strange in itself, if someone was home. But something about it triggered concern within her.

Why do I have such a bad feeling about this? She wondered.

Once she got inside, the feeling was stronger. Someone was in the house, and their pain was so strong she could not help but feel it too.

"Jeremy," she called out, running down the hall to his bedroom.

At that moment, Colleen had completely vanished from her mind.

There was blood on the carpet, and a bloody handprint on the wall. A bloodstain painted the bedspread as well. *What the hell happened here?*

It was then that she heard the crying. Viv went to the door of Jeremy's bathroom, across from the bed. The door was locked. There was blood on the knob, and a trail of it on the floor that Viv hadn't noticed at first, when she'd panicked and thought of Jeremy.

What the fuck is going on?

After she took a soul, an exhaustion always followed. Sometimes sooner, sometimes later. She could feel it coming on. She didn't have a lot of time before it engulfed her. Her panic had focused her for the moment, but she so badly wanted to collapse on the bed and huddle into a ball, bloodstains or not.

Viv knocked on the door, suddenly remembering Colleen's name, despite her fuzzy brain. The sobbing was decidedly feminine.

"*Colleen, you in there?*" Viv said, noticing the strange timbre of her own voice.

The sobbing stopped for the moment. Viv pounded on the door again. "Colleen! It's Viv. Come on out. There's blood everywhere." Her voice sounded normal again.

"Viv?" the voice was soft and scared.

"Come out of there. *Please?*"

There were a few minutes where nothing happened. And then the lock clicked and Viv didn't even wait for the door to open; she just pushed her way inside and grabbed Colleen by the shoulders.

"What the fuck is happening in here?"

Colleen stood there, naked and dumbfounded. Blood was dripping from her arms. From her legs, her body. Her face was an irritated red from crying. The blood seemed to be everywhere. In the sink, in the tub, in the toilet, on the walls. Viv couldn't avoid stepping in blood just coming into the room.

"Who did this to you, Colleen?" Viv demanded. "Where's Jeremy?"

Colleen tried to speak, made a physical effort, but the attempt didn't work at first. Viv saw the straight razor on the floor by the toilet and knew instantly that nobody had done this to her, that she'd done it to herself. Viv had seen this before. She had seen just about every manifestation of human pain there was at this point in her life.

It was then that she noticed that Colleen had carved words in her arms. *Help* and *Jeremy*, over and over.

Instead of demanding more answers, Viv pulled Colleen close, wrapping her arms around the girl.

"Take a deep breath, Col," Viv said, whispering in her ear. "You're safe now."

The sobs started again.

Viv did not let go.

But then there was the bleeding. Any desire to nurture Colleen and reassure her took a back seat to the need to stop this bleeding.

The wetness of it soaked into her clothes, touched her skin through her shirt. The blood embraced Viv's arms and neck.

"We've got to get you cleaned up."

Viv pulled away from her. It took some effort, because Colleen didn't want to let go at first. Viv opened the medicine cabinet and took down bandages and gauze and peroxide. She closed the toilet seat and made Colleen sit down, and then examined her wounds. There were so many cuts. They practically covered her arms and legs. There were more on her breasts, across her stomach. All were bleeding, but none of them appeared to be life threatening. Not yet, anyway.

Viv soaked a cloth in warm water and began washing the wounds, wiping away the blood. It just came back, but a little slower this time. Viv rinsed the cloth out and started again. She wiped at Colleen's tear-stained face, at her myriad wounds. Despite her feeling weak, Viv still felt some of the old hunger. If she hadn't just "eaten," she would have found Colleen's anguish impossible to resist. It was just too tasty for words. Luckily, she was able to maintain her willpower.

"You really did a job on yourself," Viv said softly, cleaning her.

"Oh, Viv," Colleen said softly.

"What happened to make you do this, Colleen?"

"Viv, it's Jeremy."

Viv stopped and looked her right in the eyes.

"What happened to him, Colleen?"

"He's dead," Colleen stopped to let out a long, gasping sob. "Oh my god, Viv."

Viv dropped her gaze and went back to dressing her wounds. "Tell me all about it," she said, trying to sound less demanding.

"It was the same guy. The one who killed Turney that night."

Colleen had never spoke to Viv about Turney before. But she'd told Jeremy, and Jeremy had passed the story on to her. Viv remembered Jeremy saying something about a friend of hers being torn apart right in front of her eyes. And this reminded Viv of the newspaper stories. Bodies ripped to pieces.

"The Shredder," Viv said, seeing the headline in her mind's eye. "He got Jeremy?"

"There was nothing I could do to help him, Viv. Honest. All I could do was run."

"Well, at least you had that much sense. Otherwise, you'd be dead, too. Not that you didn't try hard enough to do it yourself."

"I don't remember coming here, Viv. I don't remember anything after he got Jeremy."

"You've probably been working on autopilot since then. You instinctively came back to the one place where you felt safe. As for the cutting, this isn't the first time you've done it, am I right?"

Colleen looked more coherent now. She actually looked ashamed. "No, this isn't the first time."

"I could tell. You knew what veins to avoid. Funny how the mind reacts to trauma," Viv said. "We can't predict these things."

"Thanks for coming back, Viv."

"I just wish I came back sooner. I wish I'd been with you two. Maybe I could have done something."

"There was no way to stop him, Viv. He took us by surprise, like an animal. Ripping Jeremy apart with his claws."

"Where did this happen? In the city?"

Colleen nodded. Her eyes kept staring at the floor.

"All the blood," she said, softly.

"Don't worry about that now. You've got to think. You have to tell me where this happened."

"I don't know the address. We saw him on the street and I told Jeremy it was the guy who killed Turney. And he wanted to follow him. Find out where he went."

"Would you know how to get there again?"

"I don't know," Colleen said. Her breathing was more normal now. "I think so. But please don't make me go back there, Viv."

"You don't have a choice in the matter, Colleen. You have to take me there."

"Please, Viv."

"Once we get this bleeding under control, get dressed. I have to get a few things together, and then we're heading out."

Colleen started crying again, but it didn't sound as soul-wrenching this time.

"I know it's a lot to ask," Viv said, touching her cheek. "But this is Jeremy we're talking about. I can't just let someone kill him and get away with it. And I don't trust the cops on this. You didn't call them, did you?"

Colleen stared at her blankly.

"I didn't think so. You were so wrapped up in shock that it would have been the last thing on your mind. That's good. I want to handle this myself. And I need you to take me there. We can't just leave Jeremy mutilated like that, can we?"

"No."

"You get dressed and try to calm yourself down. I won't take long getting ready."

Viv left her and ran to her own room. It was strange how focused she was, so alert. So far she had been able to stave off the exhaustion that followed a feeding. She was so focused that it really hadn't even hit her what had happened. That Jeremy was dead.

That she would never see him again.

Once inside her room, Viv began to sob uncontrollably. The realization was finally setting in. She closed the door and tried to stop, but the tears overpowered her.

* * *

Sam was driving erratically. He was wet and cold and had no idea where he was going. He also was becoming increasingly convinced that he was somehow a murderer, although he had no memory of his actions.

How extensive is it? he wondered. How many deaths am I responsible for? *Did I have anything to do with Maggie's death?*

His first instinct was to go home. But he was sure someone was waiting for him there? Was it a friend or an enemy? He'd been driving aimlessly for a while now, trying to delay the need to make a decision. Maybe he should go back to his office. But it was late now and he would have to deal with security if he wanted to get upstairs, and that was something he'd rather not confront right now, with his soaked clothes and bloodstains. Besides, he didn't have a change of clothes there.

He was taking a left when another car hit him. He'd been so wrapped up in his thoughts that he hadn't even seen it coming. There was the sound of glass shattering and the airbag in the dashboard in front of him hissed as it inflated, lashing out at him.

One moment he was spinning, with sounds rushing in at all directions. And the next there was the throbbing of his pulse, loud in his ears, and nothing else.

"Are you okay?" someone was saying, out of Sam's line of sight. There were strange glaring lights that kept flicking on and off.

He grunted, and then something happened. He went into a kind of trance and watched as if from outside his body. *Is this what it was like to be dead?* But no, he could see himself struggling to be free of the twisted metal. And he could feel it, even though he felt detached from his body, too. He was wriggling like a grounded fish, pushing and pulling at the metal around him. Fighting to escape.

* * *

"Are you okay?" Alfredo Lima asked again, seeing movement inside the twisted car. The tarmac was aglow with a thousand bits of windshield glass. He was tense as he looked inside, but at least movement confirmed that the occupant of the damaged car wasn't dead.

But how was the driver was going to get out? This looked like one of those *Jaws of Life* moments. His car was pretty smashed up, but nothing like this one. He'd been able to walk away at least.

He sure hoped the person he saw struggling to get out was the only occupant.

He couldn't bear to think of what it meant if he'd killed someone. The fact that he already had two strikes against him for drunk driving didn't do much to calm his nerves. He didn't hear any sirens yet, but he already considered getting into his car and taking off before the police got there. There was no way this was going to turn out good.

He'd thought about calling 9-1-1 on his cell phone, but decided against it. Now that he saw the person in the other car was still alive, he felt a little better about that. Maybe he could help them before he had to leave. But it didn't seem likely. He'd already lingered long enough. Besides, he'd always seen in movies how there was the danger a car could explode in these kinds of situations. And he didn't want to hang around for something like that.

Even though he had to protect himself, Alfredo knew he would have a very hard time living with something like this on his conscience. He wasn't a cold-blooded killer, after all.

There was a siren then, in the distance. He wanted to make sure the person got out okay, but he couldn't stay any longer. He had to get away before the cops appeared.As he turned to go, something jumped up out of the wreckage. Something fast that landed a few yards away from him. Near his own car. Something that was kneeling on the road in front of him, and looked very much like a man wracked with pain.

"Are you okay?" he said again, as he approached the figure. "Someone's coming to help you. I can hear them. You'll be okay."

Alfredo tried to walk around the man. His only desire was to get back in his car. To drive as far away from the scene of this accident as he could, and to go into hiding for a while, until this all blew over. He just hoped his car would still start.

As he passed, the man lunged for him, grabbing his leg.

He tried to kick the hand away, but couldn't. The man pulled hard and Alfredo fell backwards, hitting his head on the tarmac. His could feel his teeth slam together.

Before he could get up, someone was on top of him, landing hard on his stomach. Fists were striking him in the head, over and over again, until something cracked and Alfredo Lima was dead.

* * *

In her bedroom, Viv found her gun. She didn't often have much reason to bring it places, but this seemed like a safe bet. She brought some other surprises, too, just in case. As she pocketed her cell phone, she toyed with the idea of calling Grif for backup. He couldn't have gotten very far by now. But she decided against it. She had never relied on him in the past, and she wasn't going to start now. She was his big sister. He came to *her* with problems. Not the other way around.

All her life, she had to be the strong one. It was ingrained in her.

Somehow she'd been able to sidestep the exhaustion. This whole thing with Colleen had given her a second wind. But she knew it wouldn't last. Sleep would not be denied for much longer. And it wouldn't do to keel over in the middle of trying to avenge Jeremy's murder.

Viv had a kit in her bag for just this kind of situation. She got it out and started prepping the needle.

"Are you ready, yet?" Viv called down the hallway, hoping that Colleen hadn't started making new grooves in her skin.

"Almost done," Colleen called out.

She took the shot and leaned against the wall, feeling it take effect almost instantly. It was a little pick-me-up she'd had made special for occasions like this. It was nice to know it worked.

She could feel her blood pumping. Her heartbeat was pounding in her ears for a few minutes, until she started to balance out and feel like herself again. Well, *almost* like herself. This wasn't an exact science.

She took a deep breath and went out into the hall. It was then that Viv noticed the television. If Jeremy had been massacred in the middle of the city, wouldn't it be on the news? Something like that wouldn't just be ignored.

She grabbed the remote control, and turned it on. She flipped to the cable channel that showed local news twenty-four hours a day.

A woman was talking. She looked distraught, but you could never tell these days. News people were becoming better and better actors. She turned up the volume.

"Police are on the scene," she said. "This seems to be another in a string of recent killings. So far, the police appear to have no leads, even though this violent act was committed in broad daylight."

The news switched to a reporter at the scene of the crime. First, the reporter's name flashed across the lower right hand corner of the screen. Then it was replaced with the location of the murder scene. The reporter was talking, but Viv didn't hear him.

The original news anchorwoman came back on. Behind her, a picture of Jeremy came up on the screen. She began explaining who Jeremy was, and how he'd died.

"God, I never thought I'd be watching Jeremy's obituary on TV," Viv said.

Colleen came into the living room behind her, dressed and ready to go. But she saw Jeremy's face on the television screen, too.

"Oh," she said. Her voice sounded like she was on the verge of tears again. "I didn't think he would be on the news."

"He was a high-profile guy. The fact that he's been a recluse the last few years makes him even more irresistible to the press. And the fact that he was torn apart in the middle of a major city, in broad daylight, doesn't hurt. This is the kind of story these people live for."

"Are we still going back there?"

"Frankly, I don't know what to do. I'd like to check the scene out, but it's swarming with cops now. And Jeremy's killer won't be anywhere near there."

Jeremy's picture faded. To be replaced with someone new.

"Oh my God," Colleen said. "That's him."

Viv still had her back to her. She didn't ask what Colleen meant, it was clear enough.

"One of the cars involved in the crash was registered to Dr. Sam Wayne, but police did not find him at the scene of the accident. Anyone with information as to the whereabouts of Dr. Wayne is requested to call the following number." A phone number flashed onto the screen below her. "The driver of the other vehicle, Alfredo Lima, was pronounced dead on arrival at County Hospital."

"Sounds like he's been really busy today," Viv said. "You're sure that's him, huh?"

"I'd bet my life on it."

"Well, at least we have a name to go on. And a face. I just hope we find him before the police do."

She pulled her cell phone out of her pocket and pushed buttons.

"Who are you calling?"

"I have friends who can find out information for me, quickly. It shouldn't take too long to get a lead on this Dr. Wayne."

Viv turned off the television and led Colleen outside. The number she called rang, but nobody picked up. That was okay. She had other numbers. She stopped a minute to turn to Colleen.

"You know, since I know where Jeremy was killed now, there's no reason you have to come with me."

"Please, Viv. I want to come along."

"Okay," Viv felt relieved. She didn't really want to risk leaving Colleen behind and maybe coming back to find that she'd cut herself to pieces, this time maybe for good.

Colleen followed her out to the garage. Viv's BMW was in there.

Viv got inside and turned the key. The engine came to life without hesitation.

CHAPTER FORTY-THREE

All he knew was that Dr. Wayne had brought him to a different place, but he had no memory of traveling.

Charlie almost had his hands free of the ropes that were tied behind his back, when the shrink returned. He could hear the door opening, and then closing. Slamming.

There was always the chance it could be someone who came to rescue him. Someone had been here before, ringing the doorbell incessantly. But they'd given up and gone away. Maybe they'd come back. There had to be hope. Except that it was fading fast. Despite a strong desire for it to be otherwise, he knew who it was.

Charlie thought about his mother and stepfather, slain in front of him. Of the fury he'd felt when he found out he was Dr. Wayne's prisoner. The desire to kill the man had been strong in his mind.

It wasn't so strong anymore. His anger, which seemed so important to Dr. Wayne, was dying out. It was replaced with something stronger now. Fear.

Charlie was in a bathtub, his arms and legs tied behind his back, like a calf at the rodeo. He'd almost gotten his hands free, then he could free his feet as well. He might even escape, if he had any more feeling in his limbs.

The bathroom door opened. Charlie saw someone's silhouette, standing in the doorway, through the transparent vinyl of the shower curtain. The person moved toward him, and slid the curtain aside, tearing some of the hooks free in the process.

From his angle, Charlie could barely see the man standing over him. But he saw enough to know who it was.

"It's time to go," Dr. Wayne said. His voice did not sound human anymore.

Charlie tried to respond, but the tape over his mouth prevented him from making real words.

"It's time to go," Wayne said again. "But you're not coming with me this time. I don't need you anymore. When you were angry, you were useful to me. But you've lost that. You're just a frightened little pup, now. And there are too many of those in the world already."

Charlie tried to get angry again. He knew that might buy him some time. Might make him worth something to Dr. Wayne. But he just couldn't muster it anymore. The sheer hopelessness of his situation had beaten it out of him.

"We have to part company," the man said. "I think people might know about me now. They might be coming. I have to get out of here before they get too close."

Charlie struggled, but it was a feeble attempt. He was too weak, too defeated by it all. There was no reason to fight anymore. He knew it was futile.

Dr. Wayne raised a booted foot above him, and the foot came down on him, hard. Charlie closed his eyes and held back the tears. There was no point now. Tears would win him nothing. The foot came down on him again and again. He could feel vomit and blood pushing up out of his mouth, but the tape over his mouth wouldn't let it out. He started choking. And still the foot came down. He could feel his ribs shatter beneath it. The foot moved up his body. His spine must have been crushed, because all sensation suddenly left his body. There was no more pain. Then the boot came down on his head. Once, twice. And it was over.

* * *

Sam kept stomping on the body, watching the blood flow down toward the drain at Charlie's feet. He was little more than pulped flesh and bones at this point.

"You're useless to me now," Sam said, when he'd stomped on the body a final time. "I have to get out of here."

He left the bathroom and went to pack his clothes and other things in a suitcase, but he moved slowly, like a man in a trance. He wouldn't have even thought to do such a thing, except there was a tiny part of his consciousness that made him think it was necessary. He was going on a trip. He needed a change of clothes.

When he was packed, he pushed a curtain aside and looked out the window. Nobody was out there yet. No police cars, no teams of people. He still had time. The only thing out there that seemed unusual was an unfamiliar car in front of the house next door. He couldn't tell if anyone was inside, or who they were. It didn't matter. They were no threat to him.

He grabbed his suitcase and looked around the house one last time, wondering if he'd forgotten something, but having no idea what it could be.

* * *

"Do you think he's in there?" Colleen asked.

"Who knows," Viv said, her hands still on the steering wheel, even though they'd parked. She'd made the right calls to find out where to find Sam Wayne's house. "I don't know what made me bring you along. You shouldn't be here. This guy's dangerous."

"He killed Jeremy. He killed Turney."

"I know. And he'll kill you if you get in his way."
"What about you?"

"I can take care of myself."

Colleen looked at her. "How can you be so sure? He could kill you, too."

"Maybe."

Viv reached into her coat and took out the gun. "Maybe not."

"You're going to shoot him?"

"I'm sure as hell not going to talk him to death."

Viv took the cell phone out of her other pocket. It was small enough to fit in her hand. She gave it to Colleen.

"Who do you want me to call?"

"Right now? Nobody. But if something goes wrong, I want you to call the police. I don't want him getting out of here. I don't want him killing anybody else."

"How will I know if something goes wrong?"

"I certainly don't want you to go inside with me. Let's give it fifteen minutes. If I don't come out in fifteen minutes, then call the police. Can you drive? I want you to drive away as soon as you call. Or maybe drive away first."

"What if he's not in there?"

"Well, there must be a phone in there. I'll just call the cell phone. If he's not there now, I'm going to have to wait for him. I didn't come all this way for nothing. You just stay out of sight, okay?"

"Okay."

"Wish me luck."

Viv opened the door on her side and got out. "Don't forget, if there's any sign of trouble, drive away and make that call. If I'm in there and he starts coming down the street, make some kind of noise so I know.

She grabbed the cell phone and made a quick call. She gave the address they were at and wrote down a number on a scrap of paper. Then she hung up. "Here," she said to Colleen. "If you see him approaching the house, call this number. It's for his phone. Just let it ring twice and hang up, so I'll know it's you. But don't beep the horn, whatever you do. That might tip him off."

"Okay."

"I want to get revenge for Jeremy. I want to do this myself. But if something goes wrong, I don't want him to get away."

"I know."

"Now scoot over and get behind the wheel."

Viv closed the door and started moving toward the house. Colleen watched her in the rear-view mirror. She went up on the lawn and walked around the building, heading toward the back.

Colleen held her breath and looked at the phone in her hand, hoping she wouldn't have to use it.

CHAPTER FORTY-FOUR

Viv jimmied the lock on the back door and quietly opened it. In her other hand was the gun, just in case someone was expecting her. You never know.

When she got the door open, the first room she entered was the kitchen, and it was empty. The light was out.

She slowly made her way to an adjoining room, a living room, with a couch and a television. That room was quiet as well.

It wasn't as dark in the living room, though. One of the shades was slightly open. She could see the furniture outlines in the faint light. It would be nightfall soon.

I should have brought a flashlight along, she thought. In her hurry, she knew she'd forgotten something. But maybe it wouldn't matter. If she got out quickly enough, she wouldn't even need it. There was no way she was going to turn on the lights, though. Not even for a minute. If he was in the house, it would tell him exactly where she was.

Viv thought how much easier it would have been to plan all this out. If she'd known beforehand who this guy was, she could have targeted him. Seduced him. Killed him with no struggle at all, and dined on his soul. This way was so much messier.

Jeremy had told her about this guy. About how Colleen had described him. He was like her. There was something otherworldly about him. Some kind of vision around him that only Colleen saw.

And all this time, Viv thought there was only one other one like her in the whole world. Grif. And now, to finally find another one. And have to kill him on sight.

It was kind of sad in a way. To find someone else like her and Grif and to find out he was a homicidal murderer who she had to stop. But then again, weren't Grif and she murderers, too? Maybe she had more in common with the monster who lived in this house than she realized.

She wondered, *have the police been here?* She'd seen the report on TV telling her that Wayne had been in a car accident, but the police had access to the same information she had. They knew who had been in that accident, where he lived. Chances are they'd been here before she had, checking to see if Wayne had come back home.

She was starting down the hallway, when she heard movement. He was nearby, in one of the rooms.

She didn't make a sound, or tried her best not to. She raised the gun, and removed the safety, ready for him to attack. The sounds got louder then.

He must be distracted, she thought. He wasn't even aware she was in the house.

She approached the doorway where the sounds were coming from. She didn't want this to go on any longer than it had to. The door was slightly open. Was he behind it?

It flew open then, and someone jumped out at her.

She leapt out of his way, and he slammed into the wall. It was a powerful crash. It sounded like he'd broken a hole right through.

Viv reached over and turned on the hall light. There was no reason to conceal herself in shadows anymore. She could see him now, but his face was blurry, indistinct, and red with rage. He didn't give her a chance to focus before he flung himself at her.

She aimed the gun at him and fired. There was no way she was going to give him a second chance to lunge at her.

He did not move, did not cry out, even though she was sure she had shot him in the chest. She raised the gun, aimed for his head. Fired again.

He darted to one side, avoiding the bullet, and hurled himself down the hall at her.

She fired one more time before he made contact, and threw her to the floor.

* * *

Colleen heard the gunshots. She heard someone cry out. Was it Viv? Should she wait here for Viv to come out, or was she in trouble? Colleen stared down at the cell phone in her hand and wondered if this was time to make the 9-1-1 call.

What if the police came and found Viv in there, after she'd killed the guy? she wondered. I don't want them to take her away. To arrest her for this. She's doing this for Jeremy. She's doing this for *me.*

Heaven knew she wanted Jeremy and Turney avenged. But there was no way *she* could do it. Viv was her avenging angel.

She waited. Viv had been in there for ten minutes by the time the gunshots went off. She'd agreed to wait fifteen.

She rolled up all the windows, and locked the doors. And waited. Ready to punch the numbers on the phone.

* * *

The gun was gone. Not that it had done much good, but she'd just felt better holding it in her hand. Now it was somewhere on the floor, just another failed attempt.

He had a tight grip on her, and kept slamming her into walls. Somehow, she'd stayed conscious.

She'd used her moves on him, taking advantage of her training over the years, but nothing seemed to stop this guy, or faze him in the slightest. If a bullet didn't slow him down, Viv was pretty sure that trying to stop this guy was a lost cause.

And so it continued. He kept hurling the both of them at walls, at furniture, making sure that she took the brunt of the impact. He was trying to knock her out. To crush her. But she resisted.

If we are alike, she thought through the haze, through the constant battering. *Then maybe I'm as tough as you are. Maybe I can take as much punishment as you can.*

But she knew that wasn't true. She couldn't survive a bullet to her heart. She'd been injured in the past. She'd been hurt. So maybe they weren't totally alike after all. But maybe she was just tough enough to beat him somehow.

He kept throwing her around rooms, and then she bounced off a bathroom wall, falling against a blood-splattered tub. She got her hands out in time, to prevent the porcelain from connecting with her head, and caught a glimpse of what was in the tub. Something that had once been human, and now was so much crushed flesh and bones and blood.

It was then that his foot came down on her. And any illusion she had of her toughness faded away with her consciousness.

* * *

As soon as fifteen minutes were over, Colleen punched the numbers. She was talking on the phone when a police car pulled up in front of Sam Wayne's house. They were already on their way, before she'd even called. A neighbor must have heard the gunshots and called.

Regardless, she told the woman on the phone that her friend was in trouble. That she'd been abducted by Dr. Wayne and that she'd heard gunshots from inside the house. Colleen said this because there were only two police officers getting out of the car and approaching Wayne's house, and she was sure that two wouldn't be enough. That they would need more. Many more. After what she'd seen him do to Turney, and then Jeremy, she knew that even a dozen cops might not be enough to subdue him.

She also knew that Viv was probably dead by now.

She sat in Viv's car, afraid to start the engine and drive away. Afraid to leave before she knew for sure. She didn't get out to say anything to the officers, to tell them what she knew. She just sat there, watching.

Waiting.

The police officers knocked on the front door and waited on the steps. They looked at the house and talked to each other. Maybe they were trying to decide what to do next.

Then the front door opened and someone grabbed the two men and pulled them inside before they even had a chance to draw their guns.

The door closed again.

Colleen sat in the car, frozen. Knowing now that it was time to go. That this was the evidence she needed to know that all was lost.

But she couldn't move. Not a muscle.

CHAPTER FORTY-FIVE

Colleen sat there in the car, watching the house, and time was as frozen as she was. She had no idea how much longer it took for the sirens, for the other police cars to pull up in front of Sam Wayne's house.

There was a lot of activity. Colleen started the car finally, and pulled away from the curb. She drove two more houses down, but she pulled over again and parked. She turned around in her seat and watched the house. Officers surrounded the place and some forced their way inside.

There were more gunshots. She thought she heard people screaming.

And then he was running across the lawn. Sam Wayne. He was carrying a suitcase as he made his way toward the police, and she thought it was a surreal moment, because he moved like an animal. He dropped his case as the police approached and grabbed an officer who got too close to him. He ripped the man apart as she and the other officers watched. He threw the pieces back at them.

Then he stopped where he was and stared at the others who surrounded him. They were watching intently, their guns drawn, waiting for his next move. For some reason, they did not shoot.

And then something began to happen. The officers stopped watching Wayne and turned their attention to each other. They began to fight, but it wasn't like anything she had ever seen before, in life or on television. It was worse than fighting—it was more like the way animals tore into each other with tooth and claw. As if the rage and violence inside of Sam Wayne was contagious, a virus that he could spread without effort.

They had lost all interest in him and were killing each other. There were more gunshots, but now cop killed cop. Some officers wrestled on the tarmac, trying to grab at guns just out of reach.

For just a moment, Sam Wayne stared in the direction of Viv's car, but Colleen wasn't sure if he could see her. She was terrified he might run toward her. She was about to start the engine again, in case she had to flee.

But he didn't move in her direction. He picked up his suitcase again, as if it were something he felt a need for, but could not comprehend why. Then he got into the nearest police car. There was a screech of tires as he drove away.

The police officers left conscious, or perhaps they were simply the ones left alive, continued to attack each other. It was an unending chain. When one killed another, he then went on to attack the victor of another skirmish, and so on, until there was no more activity on the front lawn of Sam Wayne's house.

Colleen sat in the car and watched. They had been as oblivious to her as they had been to Wayne. Their rage was that focused, that intense.

When she didn't see anyone else moving, she hesitated, then shut off the engine.

She got out of the car, and walked toward the house. Passing the abandoned police cars that still flashed their brightly colored lights. Passing the dead uniformed bodies at her feet, but not close enough to risk someone suddenly rising up and grabbing her. She'd seen enough horror movies to know to avoid that happening.

But no one moved as she passed them by.

She had to go inside the house. She had to see for sure if Viv was dead.

She walked up the lawn to the house. The front door had been broken in. She went inside. She moved like someone in a trance, in a dream. It didn't seem to be her at all.

She wandered from room to room, stepping over the unmoving shapes on the floor. She looked into each room, until she got to the bathroom down the hall. The light was on. She looked inside and saw Viv lying beside the tub.

The tub and the floor were thick with sticky blood. Colleen wondered how much of it was Viv's.

She knelt down beside Viv and tried to lift her by the shoulders, but she felt like dead weight.

Then Viv's eyes opened.

"You're not dead," Colleen said, though her mouth didn't seem to move.

"I'm not?" Viv asked her.

"No."

Viv tried very hard to get up on her own. She grabbed the edge of the bathtub, but her hand slipped on its bloody surface. Colleen tried her best to help her up, but Colleen wasn't very strong. Somehow, Viv was able to stand mostly on her own.

"Is he still in here?"

"No, the police came. He killed a lot of them, and he got away."

"I wasn't able to do the job," Viv said. "I tried to avenge Jeremy, but I failed."

"That's okay," Colleen said. "You're allowed to fail. Nobody can stop that man."

"I'll stop him," Viv said. "Although maybe not today."

"Let's get out of here," Colleen said.

Viv moved with a limp, but she did okay. Colleen guided her out of the bathroom and down the hall to the living room. Viv bent down to pick up her gun. Colleen maneuvered Viv past the bodies of dead policemen. She turned on lights as they moved, from room to room, trying to see where they were going.

* * *

Viv's eyes were open and she was aware, if sluggish. She could have moved on her own, but was thankful Colleen was there to lead her.

As they entered the living room, also littered with bodies, Viv noticed a picture in a frame on the coffee table. Something that triggered memories. She had been in this house before. It was strange she hadn't realized that until now. This was Maggie's house. Maggie, the one soul taken that she regretted. She'd felt something special for Maggie, something that could have grown over time. If only Viv had given it the chance.

So this monster was her husband, Viv thought, regarding the photograph. Maggie and Sam, so young and looking so in love. Their arms around one another. A snapshot from another time, when Maggie wasn't married to a monster. When he was just a man. Viv looked at him clearly. Engrained his face in her mind.

"What are you doing?" Colleen asked as Viv pulled her toward the table. "The way out is *this* way."

"I need something," Viv said, and when she got close enough to the table she grabbed the photograph, clenching her free hand around it hard. Her other arm was around Colleen's neck.

"I knew this woman," Viv said. "She was special, but she's dead now."

"Come on," Colleen said. "We can't stay here anymore."

She led Viv through the door that went out onto the front lawn.

They headed down the sidewalk to Viv's car. Viv got in on the passenger side.

"You can drive, right?"

"Yeah, sure."

"Then drive us away from here," Viv said. "Back to the house. I need to think about what to do next."

Colleen started the engine and drove them away.

PART FOUR

THIS OVERWHELMING RAGE

CHAPTER FORTY-SIX

The wind was pounding on the house, frantically trying to get in, but the walls held. Colleen was in Jeremy's room, rolled into a ball on the bed, crying again. She'd been doing that, on and off, for days now, once Jeremy's death finally seemed to sink in and she realized he wasn't coming back. Viv hoped it would stop soon. Well, at least she wasn't cutting herself anymore.

Viv was in the kitchen, leaning against the counter, drinking a glass of wine. Suddenly, the house was so quiet that she could hear Colleen's sobs without really trying, even though she was at the end of the hall, behind a closed door. Then the wind started its pounding again.

I'll have to go in there soon and hold her again if she doesn't stop, Viv thought. *Not that it helps much.* She looked at the phone and toyed with the idea of calling Grif again. When she first got home with Colleen, she'd been so wrapped up in taking care of her that she didn't even think about Grif. But now, she wanted to reach him and ask his advice about what to do next. She'd tried to call him several times, but he wasn't answering his cell, which got her wondering about what could have happened on his end. He was on the run, after all, or so he said. She had no idea where he was now, and she had no other way to get in touch with him. She'd left about ten messages on his voicemail, each more agitated than the last. Now all she could do was wait.

In this house.

Everything about this house reminded her of Jeremy. She'd wanted to move on, but Colleen refused to leave, and Viv didn't feel strongly enough to fight her on this, yet. Sure, it was uncomfortable staying here, but this was her home. Viv *had* lived here for the last five years. In fact, Jeremy told her that he would leave the place to her in his will.

It was funny, she thought the police might come here, but they hadn't. Maybe Jeremy really did keep this place a secret somehow, when he wanted to be a recluse. Maybe no one knew he had been living here. It was private enough. But someone had to have a record of this place—whoever took care of his financial matters. Someone had to show up here eventually, and she kept expecting visitors. It made her antsy.

This wasn't a time to roll up into a ball and shut out the world. The man who killed Jeremy was still out there, unchecked. No one had been able to stop him. Not even a squadron of armed policemen.

Not even *her*. And Viv had been so sure she could handle it. Like she'd handled so many other problems in her life. For once, she'd underestimated her opponent, despite the story Colleen had told Jeremy about her friend being torn apart in front of her, and the news reports of the other victims killed the same way. Viv was sore, and bruised, but it was nothing serious. She had been tougher than even she thought.

Somehow, Viv and Colleen had walked away from that house alive. They were the only ones who did.

But Sam Wayne was still out there. Still killing. It didn't sound like the police had many leads. Viv heard on the news that Wayne had abandoned the police car he'd swiped in a ditch somewhere off the highway, and nobody had seen him since.

Every time there was a news story about a riot, about someone going out of control, or some other horrendous act of violence, Viv knew there was a chance Sam Wayne was nearby, causing it.

And here they were in Jeremy's house, hiding from the world. Letting his killer run free.

I can't do this much longer, Viv thought. *I want to be here for Colleen, but I'm not used to this inactivity. I have to move on soon.*

She knew what she really needed.

She hesitated at the door to Jeremy's room. This was a lot like her relationship with Jeremy all over again. Someone who had frequent bouts of depression, someone who constantly tempted her to take a life. But also someone she cared about and wanted to protect. No matter how tempting Colleen seemed, Viv knew she had to fight her impulses, just as she had with Jeremy.

This meant another late night rendezvous with a stranger. There was no way around it. Somebody had to die, and Viv just wasn't strong enough to stop the process.

She remembered what Grif had told her about souls being less and less satisfying. How he'd needed to feed more and more often these days. It was true. She felt it, too. In the old days, a soul could last her a month or longer. Not anymore.

Which is why she was so afraid, standing outside the door, hearing Colleen sobbing on the other side.

"Colleen, are you okay?"

She didn't respond. Viv didn't move. She wanted so much to go in there and console her, but she was getting hungry and didn't trust herself anymore.

"I have to go out for a while," Viv called through the door. "I have to take care of a few things. I'll be back soon."

"Please don't go," Colleen said, her voice muffled by tears. But she didn't come out of the room to stop her. Viv was glad she didn't.

She grabbed her jacket and went out to the garage. Her car was still there, waiting to take her away from the beach house and Colleen.

CHAPTER FORTY-SEVEN

Colleen really wanted to die.

She kept seeing pictures in her head of Jeremy, of Turney. Of them dying in front of her. Of them being torn asunder by a madman with a bright red face.

Both times, she was helpless to stop their attacker. Both times she had somehow been miraculously spared.

The crying didn't stop anymore. Viv had given her some pills, and they made her fall asleep for a few hours at a time, but then she'd have to wake up again, and the pictures would start in her head, and they'd bring forth the tears.

She had never felt so miserable before. So alone. Sure, Viv was here, but Viv had her own issues. The few times she came in and held Colleen, Viv had seemed tense, anxious. Like she didn't want to be there, but was forcing herself.

When they first got back, after the siege on Sam Wayne's house, Colleen thought she might be able to nurse Viv to health. She seemed to be badly hurt by Wayne's attack on her. But the period of healing didn't last long. Viv was back to her old self in no time. Either she healed very quickly or her injuries weren't as bad as Colleen had thought. It was for the best, Colleen wasn't much help to anyone in her current state.

She knew Viv didn't want to stay here. The house must hold a lot of memories. But Colleen could not bring herself to go anywhere else. Not now. There was nowhere else she wanted to be.

Colleen sat up in Jeremy's bed. Viv had left a while ago. Colleen wondered where she was going this time of night. There was so much she didn't know about her. So many secrets. Her brother had kept secrets, too. Grif had looked so good, she'd almost fallen under his spell. If Viv hadn't walked in on them that night, there was a really good chance she might have cheated on Jeremy. It had nothing to do with love, because she realized now that she'd loved Jeremy very much. But lust had always played a big part in her life, and Grif almost made her revert to her old ways.

She wiped her sore eyes and got out of bed. For the first time in a long time, she was hungry. She opened the door and went down the hall to the kitchen.

The house was so quiet, now the storm had died down.

They'd gone to his funeral. No one noticed them at the back of the crowd. . The casket had been closed, and they hadn't seen his face one last time. But she didn't need to. His face was imbedded in her mind. His anguished face at the time of his death. She saw enough of that face to last her a lifetime, and even then it wouldn't go away. She loved that face and feared it, both at once. She wanted it to leave her brain forever, and dreaded that one day it would, and she might lose him.

There had been lots of people at the funeral. People she didn't recognize and a lot of faces she did. Famous people who had been his friends once, before the accident that changed him and made him feel less than whole. Before the time when he'd hid away from the world, convinced he was hideous and unworthy of their love.

Viv had stood by her the whole time, holding her up. Keeping her strong. She hadn't said very much through the whole thing, but her physical presence there essential to Colleen making it through the ceremony.

She opened the refrigerator. There were some cold cuts, some bread. Some salad in a glass bowl. She helped herself, glad to feel that she had an appetite again. She grabbed a half-empty bottle of red wine from the back and filled up a glass.

She turned on the CD player on the counter. Jeremy used to like listening to music when he cooked. He almost always played jazz.

And, as she played the CD that was in the player now, the sounds of Miles Davis filled the room around her, reminding her of him.

She thought of the old 45 record he'd played for her late one night, but it was too soon for that. It would be too painful to listen to now.

She stood there, at the counter, eating and drinking wine, letting the tears fall again, not trying to hold them back at all, and missing Jeremy very much.

This was *his* house. She hadn't lived here long, but she'd gotten to know him pretty well in the short time they'd known each other. They'd grown very close so quickly, like they'd known all along it wouldn't last, and they had to make every moment count.

She was glad she'd shared his life, if only for a little while.

Surrounded with the music Jeremy loved, she could almost feel him there, around her. Holding her close and keeping her safe.

* * *

Sam found himself in a narrow room, full of shadows. It had nothing in common with the house he'd shared with Maggie. He missed her intensely right now. He wasn't sure if this was better or worse than the long period of numbness he'd felt after she died.

But he felt so alone without her now. So lost.

How did he get here, anyway? He didn't remember much of how he came to be in this dirty room, in this filthy bed. But here he was. He could hear something on the floor and turned on the light. Roaches scurried out of sight.

He knew he was in danger. That people were looking for him. That he couldn't go back to the life he knew.

He opened his suitcase and looked inside. There wasn't very much that could tell him why he'd left. There were some clothes. They seemed to have been picked at random, but they'd last him a few days. And there was a photograph in a faux-gold frame of him and Maggie.

They were laughing in the picture. It made him realize that toward the end they didn't laugh anymore. In fact, her life had been in shambles and he knew about it, but he didn't do anything to save her. He was so busy debating what to do, that she slipped between his fingers and faded away.

He had been able to help so many people, but he hadn't been able to help his own wife.

He sat back in the creaky bed and stared at the photograph. God, she'd been beautiful.

I can't stay here, he thought. I don't belong here.

Sam walked over to the room's only window and pulled the shade down, and then let it snap up. It was so tense that he jerked his hand away at the sudden motion, and the shade spun up to the top of the window.

He looked out the streaked, dirty glass. There wasn't much to see. Across the way was the windowless wall of an old warehouse. He could see an alleyway, littered with garbage. There were a couple of people at the far end, but he couldn't see them clearly.

Where the hell am I? he wondered again. He had no memory of coming to this place, and yet here he was. And it didn't appear as if anyone else had brought him here. He must have come on his own.

He reached up and grabbed the shade, pulled it back down to block out the sun and the grim view outside.

What do I do now? he wondered. He had a distinct feeling that he was in trouble, that people were after him, but he had no idea why, or who they were.

No, that wasn't completely true. He had an idea why. There were memories that he had access to, but which were broken into fragments. He could remember horrific things. Things from his point of view. Things he himself had done. But he did not remember having the ability to stop these acts. To control his impulses. It was as if he were only an observer in someone else's body.

Did I really do those things? He wondered. Am I really such a monster?

And if so, what would stop him from doing it again?

There was a knock at his door. He stood there by the window, staring at it, not wanting to answer. He did not make a sound.

There was another knock. Then a woman's voice, "Hello?"

He didn't recognize the voice, but it did not sound threatening. And despite his fear, he yearned for some kind of human contact. And for answers.

Sam walked slowly to the door. Stood against it.

"Yeah?" he said softly, not sure if she'd hear him.

"Were you sleeping or something?"

"No," he said, his voice slightly louder. "I'm up."

He opened the door, wanting to see the face that went with the voice. Wanting to convince himself this wasn't another dream.

The woman reminded him of Maggie on first glance. She didn't really look like her, but she had the hard eyes of an alcoholic. Maggie had eyes like that toward the end. Picturing her in his mind's eye, he could see them begging him for help.

"Hi," the woman said. "I was just wondering if maybe you might have something to drink in there. Something you might like to share with somebody."

He looked at the bed. His suitcase. "No," he said. "I'm sorry. I'm not much of a drinker."

And then he thought of the visions he'd had, of the things he was sure he had done, and he wondered if maybe this wasn't the time to *start* drinking.

"Is there a bar nearby?" he asked.

"Yeah, there's one down the street," the woman said. A glint of hope in her eyes.

"I know," he said. "How about I buy you a drink? I feel like I could use one myself."

"That would be great," she said. "Let me get my jacket. It's getting cold out there."

"Sure," Sam said and watched her go down the hall. He closed the door for a moment and went to the bed. He put the photo of Maggie and him back in the suitcase and closed the case up. He put it under the bed, disturbing more roaches. He couldn't see them, but he could hear them.

He checked his pockets. His wallet was there. He made sure it was intact. It had some money left in it. He checked his other pockets until he found a key and locked the door to the dirty little room on the way out.

She was waiting for him in the hallway.

"Don't you have a jacket?" she asked.

"Naw, I guess I forgot to bring one."

"That's too bad," she said. "By the way, my name is Rachel."

"Nice to meet you, Rachel." He hesitated, wondering if he should give her his real name. "My name's John," he told her.

"Well, John, I really want to thank you for offering to buy a girl a drink."

"It's my pleasure," he said, leading her toward the stairs. There wasn't any sign of an elevator. "I guess I don't feel much like drinking alone tonight."

CHAPTER FORTY-EIGHT

Viv went cruising.

There was a certain stretch where prostitutes plied their wares. One of many. But Viv had been to this particular section before, and it had really worked out well in a pinch. Maybe it could again.

She drove by them slowly, listening to their catcalls, searching for just the right one. The one with the most pain in her face. Even though she wasn't a man, the hookers were very aggressive as she drove by. She certainly wasn't the first woman to cruise here. Some women came to find a suitable threesome for their men. Other women just wanted other kinds of kicks.

"You want me baby, you know you do," a tall blonde shouted at her, with a faint Southern drawl as she drove by. "I'll do whatever you want, sweetness."

Most of them were women, but some of them were clearly transvestites and transsexuals. Some of these had a lot of pain to give, and it was very tempting, but she also knew they would be resistant to making it with someone like her. She wasn't exactly their regular clientele. And Viv wanted someone who would be *very* receptive. Someone who wouldn't put up too much of a struggle.

"Over here," Viv said to a woman who looked a little older than the rest. Her guarded face lit a little at being picked out of the crowd.

"Get in on the passenger side," Viv said, waving her over. The others hooted and laughed. "Mary's gone got herself a looker."

The hooker got in on the passenger side and smiled as she sat down beside Viv. She had on a lot of makeup to cover her age. And her hair was peroxide blonde. It looked as if it would be brittle to the touch.

"You ready to go to heaven?" Viv asked.

"Shouldn't I be saying that to you?" the woman asked. "There aren't a lot of women cruising around here." The hooker had a husky voice. Too much whiskey and cigarettes. "But I'm game. I just love a little variety."

"Good," Viv said and stepped on the gas pedal, taking them away from the boulevard.

"What's your name?" Viv asked, feeling the hunger gnawing down deep inside her, but trying to maintain her composure. She didn't want to seem too desperate after all.

"Paulina. How about you?"

"Viv."

"What made you pick me out of the crowd, sweetheart?"

"There was something about you that just caught my eye. You looked so sad."

"Sad? Baby, I ain't sad."

"Sure you're not," Viv said. "We're almost there."

"And where might that be?"

Viv parked the car in a deserted parking lot. There were only a few lampposts, and where they'd parked it was pretty dark.

"You ready for some action?" Viv asked.

"I don't mean to talk business, but I like my money up front."

"Sure," Viv said, opening her purse and taking out some bills. "Is this good enough?"

Paulina smiled. "I'd say so."

"Good. Let's get in the back seat."

They both got out of the car and then got in back. "How do you want to do this?" Paulina asked. "Who's going to be on top?"

"I will,' Viv said.

Paulina hiked up her skirt. She wasn't wearing any panties, which came as no surprise.

Viv went down on her for a bit first, then, when Paulina was good and wet, she reached down on the floor of the car and lifted a little bag. She had a strap-on with a dildo that doubled as a vibrator. She tied it around her waist and turned it on and let it hum.

"Shit, this is going to be fun."

Viv rubbed it against her clitoris, and then, when Paulina seemed to be really responding, she slipped the head of the vibrator into her. Pauline let out a yelp as she took it inside her, and Viv smiled. She'd picked the right one. As if the dildo wasn't enough, Viv started probing the woman with her mind, seeking out the pleasure centers and massaging them. It didn't take very long before the woman was moving around beneath her, breathing hard and making noise.

When Paulina reached the verge of orgasm, Viv hurried the process, increasing the strength of her sensations. And then, in the midst of it all, she searched for the part of Paulina's mind that was damaged, shattered. Vulnerable. It didn't take long to find. She had been right—there was so much sadness in this woman. Viv almost started crying without even realizing it. When she found the core of it, she embraced it. All the while watching Paulina with an odd fascination. No matter how many times she witnessed this, it never got old.

"Oooh," Paulina gasped. She tried to form words but it came out as inarticulate grunts.

Viv embraced the damaged part of Paulina's soul and drew it out, devoured it, took it into herself.

The groans got louder for a moment. Paulina sounded like she was going to explode. And then, the sounds died away. She stopped moving beneath her.

Suddenly, the woman's bladder emptied onto the leather seat. Viv raised herself up on her arms to escape the flow.

Shit! Viv thought. *I was careless. Now how am I going to get rid of this urine stink?*

It was then that *her* orgasm began. She gritted her teeth and tried to keep from letting the urine touch her, but it was an impossible task.

When it was over, Viv stared down into the shadowy face beneath her. The glassy eyes. She could see them in the faint light from the street lamps further down the parking lot.

Viv got out of the car and slipped back behind the steering wheel. She started the car and drove across the deserted parking lot. There was a park nearby.

It was a short drive. There were a few kids sitting in their cars, drinking and making out. Viv drove past them, deeper into the park proper.

There was a bench at the end of the road and nobody nearby. Viv parked and got out of the car. She opened the back and slid Paulina out by her arms. Then she lifted the woman gently and put her on the bench. She brushed down the hem of her dress. Just another homeless woman sleeping on a park bench. There would be no sign of foul play.

She'd simply had a heart attack.

Viv got back into her car and drove away from the park.

She wiped her face with the back of her hand and half-wondered about disease. It wasn't something that bothered her much. She'd resigned herself to the idea a long time ago that she was not as susceptible to diseases as other people. But the faint worry lingered in the back of her mind. If she hadn't contracted anything by now, then she probably wasn't going to, but you could never know for sure.

The woman had tasted vile, though. She wondered about her hygiene. Which made her aware of the urine smell, again.

Which, in turn, made Viv regret even more what she'd had to do tonight. It wasn't like she always enjoyed these things. Sometimes they could be special, but more often than not they were just a means to an end. This time had been repulsive.

All that mattered, though, was that she satisfied the need, got rid of the ache inside her.

Now that she'd fed, the process had begun inside her. Her body would assimilate what she'd taken from the woman and replenish itself. She would need to curl into a ball soon and sleep it off.

She had just enough time to get home.

God, I hope I have time for a shower, she thought.

* * *

"When I went to see Dr. Wayne," Colleen read aloud. "I was full of anger I didn't understand and my temper kept getting me into scrapes. But after I saw him, the anger left me. It's like he just drained it right out of me. But I felt so weird afterwards, that I didn't want to go back and see him anymore. So, I just stopped going. But I swear I still see him every once in a while, like he's following me. Something about him scares me. Like he wants to hurt me or something."

So it was the same Dr. Wayne, Colleen thought as she closed Turney's diary. That must have been why Turney had seemed so anxious when he'd come to ask her for a place to stay, always looking over his shoulder

So maybe it wasn't a random act of violence that night when Dr. Wayne killed Turney right in front of her. He'd probably been hunting Turney for a while. After he took away Turney's anger, and left him hollow.

If only I could have known. If only there was some way I could have warned Turney before that fateful night.

It was such a waste. Turney had been so young. He was just starting to turn his life around. Then she thought of how she'd been trying to get Turney to move out of her apartment just before he died. She felt guilty about that now.

She put the diary under her pillow and walked down the hall to the living room. The television was black and silent, a square sentinel in the middle of the house, waiting to be brought to life with noise and color.

At the end of the other hall, leading away from the living room, was where Viv called home. She'd been inside that room before, but never alone. She had never *explored* it before.

I wonder where Viv goes, Colleen wondered.

She was always so quiet when she left in the middle of the night. Sometimes she'd take her car, and sometimes she'd find another mode of transportation. The bus. A cab. It all depended on her mood. But she usually left without a word and never explained afterwards. In fact, when Viv returned from these mysterious excursions she was usually exhausted to the point of near-collapse and locked herself in her room. Sometimes not emerging for days.

Maybe there are clues in there, Colleen thought. *Something to tell me where she goes on these mysterious trips of hers.*

She turned and looked through the sliding glass doors behind her that looked out onto the beach and its waves.

The moon was full and made the sand glow.

She turned back to face the closed door to Viv's room. The curiosity was too much. She went to the door and turned the knob. It was open.

Colleen took a deep breath and went inside.

She had seen the inside of this room before, but, even now, the starkness of it surprised her. The minimal furniture. The mattress on the floor in the far corner of the room. So much bare floor space.

She went over and turned on the compact stereo on the floor beside the bed and pushed the "play" button. Billie Holiday began to sing the song "Strange Fruit." Colleen had heard Billie's voice before, back when she was a child.

There must be some kind of clue here, Colleen thought. *Something to explain Viv's behavior.*

But there wasn't. In the bureau drawers, there was nothing mixed with her clothes.

Then there was the closet. The door was in the wall opposite the mattress.

Colleen just assumed there were clothes in there, but decided now she wanted a closer look. She went over and tried the door. It was locked.

She knew ways to unlock doors. She turned and walked toward the kitchen, to get some tools. She got as far as the end of the hall before she sensed someone watching her, and turned to see someone standing outside the sliding glass doors, looking in.

It was Viv.

She pounded on the glass with her palm. Colleen ran over and opened the door. Viv seemed to have to make a great effort to pull herself inside.

"Are you okay?" Colleen asked.

"I'm fine. I just need to get to my room and sleep."

"Let me help you."

Viv began to protest, then let Colleen move closer and help her toward the hallway. Colleen hoped she was too tired to notice she'd left the door to Viv's bedroom open.

They went inside the room. Billie Holiday was still singing. Now it was "God Bless the Child." Viv didn't seem to notice the music. Despite the fact that she was trying her best to stay awake, she was starting to become very heavy against Colleen's side. She could barely keep her eyes open. It must have taken all her effort not to collapse.

"The bed," Viv said, and Colleen led her to the mattress on the floor, where Viv allowed herself to drop.

Viv rolled onto her side and pulled the sheets up over her. "Please let me sleep," she said softly to Colleen. "And close the door."

Colleen was going to ask where she had been, but it was none of her business. She simply had to look out for Viv, as Viv had looked out for her the week before.

"Do you want me to help you get your clothes off?" Colleen asked.

"No," Viv said. "Please. Just leave me alone."

It wasn't an angry tone. It was the voice of someone on the verge of unconsciousness.

Colleen shut off the music, then the overhead light and closed the door behind her.

This wasn't the first time Viv had come home exhausted, but it was the worst instance so far.

I really want to know what's wrong, Colleen thought. She poured herself another glass of wine in the kitchen. *I'm going to ask her in the morning.*

It was about then that she realized she had finally stopped her crying jag. She drained the glass of wine and poured herself another one.

* * *

He wanted to ask her so many questions, but didn't know where to begin. And there was no guarantee she'd have any answers. As far as he knew, this was the first time they'd ever met.

"Can I ask you a really strange question?" Sam asked.

Rachel watched as the bartender placed her drink on the bar before her. Sam could tell she really wanted that drink, but she hesitated.

"Sure."

"Do you have any idea how long I've been here?"

"What?" she asked, clearly perplexed. She raised the glass to her lips and drank. "Don't you know?"

"Must have been one hell of a binge I was on," Sam said. "I don't remember much about how I got here."

"I thought you said you weren't much of a drinker?"

"Look, it's not easy to admit, okay? I was sober for a whole year and then I fell off the wagon." He gulped his whiskey. "It doesn't look like I'll be getting back on that wagon anytime soon."

"Sorry to hear it," Rachel said. "To have stayed sober for so long. It must be heart-breaking."

"The struggle's over at least," he said, trying his best to sound defeated, which wasn't that difficult, considering his circumstances. "Did you notice me before today? Have I been here long?".

"You really don't remember, do you?"

"It's a blur," he said, calling the bartender over. "Another round for me and the lady."

The bartender nodded and took their empty glasses away.

"I heard you yesterday. And maybe the day before. But I hadn't seen you until today. I wasn't sure who was in that room, but I got real thirsty, you know. And I guess I was hoping you were a kindred spirit."

"So I've been here at least two days?"

"That's as much as I know. I didn't pay much attention before that. I remember another guy, Rolph, he was in that room for a while, but I think he left about a week ago."

"It's worse than I thought," Sam said. "Two days gone. Now I have an even weirder question. Where the hell are we?"

"We're in Philadelphia," she told him, clearly puzzled by his questions. "That must have been some bender."

"Sure was," Sam said as the bartender returned with their drinks. "Keep a running tab," he told him.

He had no idea how he'd gotten here. Had he flown? He certainly didn't remember a plane ride. Had he gotten here by some other means? There was no way of knowing.

Sam lifted his glass. "Hair of the dog, I guess."

"You look like someone who could use a person to talk to. And I've got nothing but time," Rachel said and brought her glass to her lips.

"About a month ago, my wife died. I guess my life's been a shambles ever since."

"That's horrible. How did she die?"

"Heart attack," Sam said. "And she was so young."

"I'm so sorry," Rachel said.

"After her funeral, things kind of came unraveled. I don't remember much since."

"Don't you have people who will miss you? Did you have a job?"

"Nobody will miss me."

They were at the far end of the bar. Some new people came into the room and Rachel seemed uncomfortable.

"You know, why don't we go back to your room? We can get a bottle on the way. We can talk all night if you want."

"I wanted to get out of that place," he told her. "But I guess it doesn't matter much. There's as good as any place."

"Come on, let's go."

They drained their drinks and then he paid the bartender, and they left. Rachel kept her head down and didn't look around. Sam watched the new people moving toward the back of the tavern. Two men and a woman. He wondered why they scared Rachel so much. But he knew enough to take her hint. He didn't want any trouble.

On the way back to their building, they passed a small liquor store. They went inside and got a couple of fifths. Vodka and whiskey. And a six-pack of beer. Then they went the last block back.

When he got back to his room he turned on the lights and saw tiny shapes scatter across the floor, which made him wish they hadn't come back so soon. He was just starting to get the roaches out of his mind.

She sat on the bed and pulled the bottle of vodka from their bag. She broke the seal. Then she hesitated again.

"I have some glasses back in my room," she said. "I'll be right back."

"Okay."

She got up and went out into the hall. She closed his door as she left. He sat on the end of the bed and kicked his shoes off. He really needed a shower.

Rachel came back with two cheap-looking water glasses. "Sorry I don't have any ice."

"Don't worry about it," Sam said.

"What would you like?" she asked, unscrewing the top of the bottle she'd been fiddling with before.

"The vodka would be fine."

"Okay."

She poured some in both glasses and handed one to him.

"What was she like?" Rachel asked.

"Huh?" he said, lost in his own thoughts for a moment. Trying so hard to get his bearings back. Even though he knew he'd done something wrong and people were looking for him, things were still hazy. He took a pull from his glass and reached down and popped open a cold beer. "What was *who* like?"

"Your wife. Before she died."

"You know, we'd had some rough times, but I loved her very much."

Sympathy filled Rachel's eyes as she drank.

"She was beautiful."

"And she just had a heart attack, right out of the blue?"

He measured it all in his mind, wondering how much he should tell her.

"Yeah," Sam said. "I didn't have any idea it was coming. Neither did she."

It felt so strange sitting here on a strange bed, with a woman who wasn't Maggie. Like he was in a dream. Except that the room was all too real. The occasional scurrying beneath the bed made his skin crawl.

He was thinking about the roaches (or was it something worse?), when Rachel leaned forward and kissed him.

He must have had an odd reaction because she laughed. "Never been kissed before?"

"I'm sorry," he said. "I just wasn't expecting it."

"No kidding. That's why I did it. Besides, you looked so sad, thinking about her."

"Do we really have to talk about her? I really don't want to bring us both down. Why not just forget about it for tonight?" he grabbed the vodka bottle from where it rested on the bed and unscrewed the cap. "Hold out your glass."

He filled her glass halfway, then did the same for himself.

"I just want to forget about everything," he said. "That's why I'm here, isn't it? Because I wanted to forget?"

"You didn't have to come all the way here to do that," Rachel said. "A lot of people here, they've given up, you know. Sometimes I feel that way. I sure hope you don't."

"I can't tell you how I feel right now," Sam said. "All I feel is numb."

She kissed him again. "Even when I do that?"

It seemed like such a long time since he'd shared any kind of intimacy with another human being. His life had been such a jumble of fragments lately. Any kind of anchor in the storm appealed to him. And Rachel was the most appealing anchor he was aware of right now.

"I guess not," he said.

"If you want to forget so badly, why don't we forget together?"

This time when she kissed him, he responded. He could taste the vodka on her tongue. She sucked on his eagerly.

He felt her arms go around him. It was strange her taking the lead like that. It felt awkward to him. But he did not resist.

She suddenly stopped and went to the door. He thought she was going to leave, but instead, she locked it.

"Too many drunks around here," she said. "Sometimes they wander into the wrong room. I don't want anybody to wander in here."

"Okay."

She smiled at him as she started taking off her clothes. He sat on the bed and watched her.

When she was down to her panties, she plopped down beside him and drained her glass. Then she held it out for a refill.

He poured more for her.

He drained his glass and got up. He'd forgotten about the roaches by now, just as he'd forgotten about the peeling wallpaper and the cracked plaster. It was all so distant as he started pulling off his clothes. He needed so badly to make contact with someone. It was all that mattered right now.

CHAPTER FORTY-NINE

When Colleen woke up, Viv was still in her room. Or at least she assumed she was. Her bedroom door was still closed. Concerned, Colleen walked over to the door and slowly, quietly turned the knob. Viv was still on her mattress, wrapped up in her sheets. She didn't move.

I hope she's not dead, was Colleen's first thought.

Viv's clothes were scattered across the floor. She'd had enough energy left to get undressed at least. When Colleen had tried to undress her the night before, Viv kept rolling into a tighter ball.

Colleen stood there a moment, watching Viv sleep.

A phone rang.

It was a small, blue cellular phone on the floor beside the mattress. For a ring, it played Wagner's *Ride of the Valkyries*.

Colleen was afraid the ringing might wake Viv, and she instinctively snatched the phone up and left the room, closing the door behind her.

She opened the phone. "Hello?" said a man's voice on the other end. "Viv?"

Colleen wasn't going to say anything. *Who was she to answer Viv's phone?* But she recognized the voice. "Grif?"

"You're not Viv."

"Grif, it's me. Colleen. Remember?"

"Oh, at Jeremy's house, right?"

"Yeah."

"Is Viv there? She's been trying to reach me, and I finally got a chance to call back."

"I don't know. She's sleeping pretty heavily."

"Oh, she is?"

"Yep, I'd feel really weird waking her. I've never seen anyone sleeping so deeply."

There was silence, then, "You better not disturb her. She must have had a rough night."

"Do you want me to leave her a message? Is there a number she can reach you at?"

"She has my number. Just tell her to call my cell phone. I guess the battery was dead before. So how have you been?"

"Not so good," Colleen said. "Did you hear about Jeremy?"

"Yeah, I heard. It was on the news. Did they catch the bastard who did it, yet?"

"No. I don't think they will."

"Why not?"

She didn't know what to say. Then, "I don't think he's human."

He didn't seem to find that weird. "So how are you holding up?"

"I went through a crying jag for a while. It's been rough."

"What about Viv. How's she taking it?"

"She's been taking care of me. But I can tell it bothers her a lot. I don't know what she did last night, but I think she might have gone drinking. She could barely stand when she got back last night. That's why I think she should sleep it off."

"You're probably right. Definitely don't disturb her. Just tell her to call me when she wakes up."

"Okay."

"Hang in there," Grif said. "And I'm sorry about Jeremy. He sounded like a nice guy."

"He was pretty special."

"Got to go," Grif said. "Bye."

There was a dial tone. Colleen shut the phone; she put it on the kitchen counter.

She went and looked down the hall at the closed door to Viv's bedroom. She wanted so badly to wake Viv, but she resisted the impulse.

Suddenly, Colleen felt very alone.

* * *

When Sam woke up, Rachel was still in his bed, asleep. He could feel her breath on him, and the movement of her chest against his.

He remembered the night before. The two of them fucking. He had a sense memory of what it felt like, how her body felt to his touch. How she touched him. It was so vivid; it was like being transported back in time for a moment.

He tried to get up, but was so afraid of waking her that he didn't dare.

It was then that he realized why he'd been woken from sleep. There was shouting coming from another room. The building was so old and the walls so paper-thin that it could have been coming from anywhere. But it sounded softer at first and now it increased in volume. A man and a woman were shouting. The shouts were accompanied by occasional crashes, and poundings on the walls.

The sounds had a curious effect on Sam. He could feel his heartbeat quickening and adrenaline coursing through his veins. There was a sharp pins and needles feeling in the back of his head, and a sharp ringing in his ears, which, despite its pitch, did not block out the sound of the couple fighting.

The woman screamed. Her screech boring through the walls like a power drill.

Rachel stirred beside him then, but did not wake. She'd probably been living here long enough to get used to the sounds.

Sam closed his eyes and listened to the beating of his heart, the racing of his pulse. He tried to empty his mind, but the beating of his heart and the ringing in his ears and the shouting all conspired to undermine his attempts.

The ringing got louder then. So did the pounding of his heart.

Please let me get through this without my heart exploding, he pleaded, inside his head.

CHAPTER FIFTY

"You're finally awake," Colleen said. She just got back in from walking along the beach and was closing the sliding glass doors. It was getting cooler. She could smell the strong scent of the sea.

Viv was stretched out in front of the television, watching CNN. She didn't respond.

"Grif called this morning," Colleen said. "But I didn't want to wake you."

Viv looked at her then. Her eyes still looked very tired. "Which phone did he call on?"

"Your cell phone. I hope you don't mind me answering it. I was just scared it was going to wake you with its ringing."

"It wouldn't have woken me," Viv said. "Not in the state I was in. But thanks anyway. What did he want?"

"He said he was returning your call. He was sorry he hadn't called earlier."

"So he's available again. Did he say how to contact him?"

"He just said to call his cell. He said the battery was low before or something."

"Does he know about Jeremy?"

"Yeah, he knows. We talked for a minute or two. He heard about it on the news."

"That's good that he called. I've been trying to reach him for a while. I almost gave up."

"Are you going to ask him to come back?"

"I don't know what I'm going to do right now. I'm having the hardest time just waking up."

"You were so exhausted when you came home," Colleen said. "What were you doing all night?"

"It's kind of a long story," Viv said. "I'm not up to it right now."

"Please tell me what's going on? Are you okay?"

"I'm fine. And I don't feel like talking about it."

"You were in a real bad way when you came back. You could barely walk on your own. At first I thought you'd been drinking. Is that it? Were you on a bender because of what happened to Jeremy?"

"What kind of question is that?" Viv asked.

"Look, I guess you could say it's none of my business, but you'd be wrong. We're together here in this place and we're supposed to be friends. I had Jeremy torn from my life, and now I have no idea what's happening to you. I want to know what's wrong. Is it drinking? Drugs? Why can't you just share with me?"

"It's neither of those things. It's nothing."

"Bullshit," Colleen said. "Why can't you open up to me at all? Is it that terrible a secret that you can't confide in me? And you've been so distant since Jeremy was killed. There are like these moments when you really seem to want to connect, to share, and then you always pull away again. It's really aggravating. It's like you're here for me, but not a hundred percent. Like you're always afraid to get too close."

"Please, Colleen, I'm really too tired to fight about this."

"I am *not* fighting. I'm trying to communicate with you. To find out why the woman I live with, my only friend right now, has a secret life she can't share with me. I am not kidding about the way you were when you got back last night. You were on the verge of collapse. It scared the hell out of me."

"You really want the truth, don't you?"

"Yes. I do."

"It might not be too easy to take. It might be another burden for you to carry."

"Look, it can't be all that bad. You have no idea what my life was like before I came here, before I found you and Jeremy. There's no nice way to put it; I was a slut, okay? Sex was the whole of my existence. It was the only way I knew how to connect with other people. To feel wanted and desirable were the only positive emotions in my life. I'm not proud of it. Even when I was with Jeremy, I have to admit, I was tempted by Grif that time he was here."

"That's not surprising. Grif has that effect on a lot of people."

"No, it wasn't him. It was *me*. I guess I was able to turn myself around once I got here. Once I found Jeremy. But I don't know if that was because I really loved Jeremy, or I just wanted to believe I did, or if it was because we were isolated out here, away from the world and temptations."

"Why are you telling me this?"

"Because that's what people who care about each other *do*. They share. They bare their souls. I want to show you that I have nothing to hide. That I won't be shocked by anything you tell me. That I won't judge you."

"You say that now."

"What is it? Are you a drug dealer? Are you a prostitute? Are you a mass murderer like the man who killed Jeremy?"

Viv looked anxious at that. She didn't respond.

"You can tell me. I am dead serious about that. I will *not* judge you, and I won't push you away."

"It's not the kind of thing I tell people every day. In fact, Jeremy was the only one who ever knew. And it took its toll on him, I think. I don't want to place that same burden on your shoulders."

"I am telling you I *want* that burden," Colleen said. Then, "Are you a demon?"

Viv looked surprised at that.

She said it again. "Are you a demon?"

"What the hell are you talking about?"

"The first time I saw you, I had a vision," Colleen said. "It was similar to that man who killed Jeremy. Except when I first saw him, I saw this image of snakes biting. And there was something with claws and teeth and made of shadows, just out of sight. I only saw it for a moment, but it scared me. It turns out that I had every right to be scared, because right after that vision, he tore my friend Turney apart right in front of me.

"When I first met you, I saw another vision. But it wasn't an animal. It was like you were wreathed with vines. Ivy that flowed all around you. I can't really explain it right, because it wasn't really a plant image. But it wasn't serpents or anything either.

"These visions are new to me. It makes no sense why I see them, or what they mean. Well, I guess the one Sam Wayne had makes sense. But I have no idea what the one around you meant. But is there a link? Are you like him? Are you some kind of demon?"

"A demon," Viv said. "No, I don't think so."

"You don't sound very sure?" Colleen asked.

"I'm not sure of anything anymore."

"What was the secret that Jeremy knew about you?" Colleen pleaded. "Tell *me*."

"Demons are creatures from hell. Monsters. They corrupt human souls. They're just superstition; that description does not apply to me."

"Please, Viv, trust me."

"Look. I get these urges. I need to go out and find someone and fuck them. And when that happens, I take something from them, and they die, and my urge goes away, and I feel satisfied."

"So you kill them," Colleen said softly. She instantly hated herself for putting it that way, especially after she had promised not to judge her, but she said it before she could stop herself. Viv had an odd look on her face.

"Look, I shouldn't have said that. But I'm still tired, and you're so insistent. But yeah, I kill them. But it doesn't involve any violence, and they feel nothing but pleasure at the end. I give them the best orgasm they ever had before they leave this world. I know because I feel it, too. I can't justify why I do it. But the urge is so strong. It gets so bad that I feel that if I don't do something, I am sure I will die myself. It's something I have to do in order to stay alive."

"I saw the same vision when I first met Grif. Is he the same way?"

"He's my brother. Yeah, he's the same way. Except he likes to move around a lot more. He never found someone like Jeremy I guess. Jeremy offered me sanctuary, a place where I didn't have to run anymore. A place where I could hide and where I wouldn't have to exist if I didn't want to. He let me come and go as I pleased, with no questions asked."

"Jeremy was pretty special, huh?"

Viv nodded. "Like I said, I am not a demon. Not the way you meant. I am alive, I breathe. I need food and water and love, just like you."

"I said I won't judge you, and I won't," Colleen said. "I care about you, Viv. And I'll keep your secret just like Jeremy did."

"And that's why I've been so distant. Others' pain makes my urges stronger and you've been in a lot of pain lately. I don't want to hurt you, Colleen, and it has sometimes taken all my willpower to resist taking you into my arms and taking you away from everything, for good. But I can't do that. So I've had to go out and find other ways."

"Was it difficult with Jeremy?"

"Yes, sometimes it was *very* difficult. He went through periods of bad depression. After his plane crash, he didn't want to live anymore. He begged me to kill him, but I couldn't. I cared about him too much. He accepted me like no one else ever had, aside from Grif. It was painful living with him, so sometimes I had to leave for a while. But there were good times, too. Lots of good times."

"I knew that you wanted to go after Wayne when you got better. But you stayed here because of me. If those urges of yours are that bad, I must have been very difficult to be around."

"That's why I acted the way I did. It was a constant struggle."

"I'm sorry for that. I can't say I feel a lot better now, but I've stopped crying at least. I guess that's a good sign."

"It is."

Colleen sat down beside her on the couch and hugged her close.

"It's been a painful time for both of us. We both loved Jeremy."

"I know."

"But it's time for the next phase in our lives," Colleen said, fighting back the urge to start crying again. "Do you still want to go after Wayne?"

"I've been trying to keep tabs on him. Looking for any weird activity out there. Riots, acts of rage. I think I have a good idea where he is now."

"I'll go with you, if you want," Colleen said.

"You don't have to."

"I want to. I want to pay him back for what he did to Jeremy. And Turney."

"You'll come in handy. You can detect him quicker than anybody else, if you see this *vision* thing you mentioned. But I don't want to put you in any danger. You have to promise me you'll listen to me if we get too close."

"I want to help," Colleen said.

"Maybe I should call Grif back," she said. "And see if he's up to coming along with us."

* * *

When Sam woke a second time, it was later in the day. The arguing had stopped.

Rachel was no longer in bed beside him. He sat up, putting his feet on the floor. He listened for sounds. There were none. It was quiet and he was alone.

He felt sticky as he pulled his pants on. It was dark as he went over to the door. He listened for any sounds in the hallway, but there still wasn't anything to hear.

Slowly, he opened the door.

The first thing that caught his attention in the hallways was the puddles of blood on the grimy floor. He forced himself to walk around them, to move forward. To explore, hoping that it might jog his memory.

The second thing he noticed was the smell of death that was all around him. Not yet strong enough to be overpowering, but well on its way there.

As he walked down the hall, he noticed that all the other doors were broken in. Torn off their hinges. A few lay in the middle of the hallway; others were pushed into the rooms themselves. There was more blood on the doorjambs.

He looked inside one of the rooms and saw a human body in pieces on the floor. A hand. A head turned away from him. A coil of bloody entrails.

For some reason, he was not afraid. Despite the horrors that surrounded him, he did not feel as if he was in danger.

I did this, he thought. He had no memory of it, but he knew it was true. I killed everyone in this building. *I am the only one left alive.*

As he continued to move down the hall, there was a sound coming from one of the rooms. The soft humming of a radio. It was playing classical music. Beethoven's Sixth. *The Pastorale.*

He looked into the room. Two men lay on the floor, their faces blue, their dead hands around each other's throats. They'd choked one another to death.

The music played on. Sam made no move to shut it off.

He walked to the end of the hall, to where the staircase led down to the other floors. He did not have to explore the other floors to know there was more of the same downstairs. Death in every room.

Still, he forced himself to look down. Rachel was on the stairs, or at least the upper half of her body was. Her face was staring up at him, dead and unseeing. Just hours before he had marveled at the warmth of her body; surprised by his ability to still feel close to another human being.

But, I'm not human anymore, he thought, forcing himself to look at where her body stopped, where her entrails draped across the cracked marble stairs. He had no idea where her lower torso was.

Fighting back a violent shiver, he turned and walked back to the room he woke up in. He went back there and closed the door again, to block out the blood.

Sam sat down on the old, creaky bed and covered his face with his hands. But no tears came for the dead.

I have to get out of here, he thought. *I have to go far away from here.*

Sam put his hands down and stood up. First, he had to wash off the blood.

When he was done, he pulled his suitcase up from under the bed. He filled it with all of his things that he could find. Then he got dressed.

He made his way out of the building. Avoiding spilled blood and human tissue. Avoiding Rachel's remains on the staircase.

Gingerly stepping around her, his eyes avoiding her wide, accusatory eyes.

Sam had no idea how much humanity he had left, or how much longer it would last. But however much remained inside him told him to get away from this place and the carnage he had committed and forced others to commit.

He could not bear to see the fruits of his handiwork. Perhaps there was another part of himself that took satisfaction in such things, but there was enough of Sam Wayne left to know that he wanted to stop the slaughter. He just had no idea how.

* * *

"Grif's on his way here," Viv said, putting the phone down on the kitchen counter. "I guess that means we'll be leaving soon. Are you sure you still want to come?"

"Sure," Colleen said. "I don't have anything else to do. Besides, I want to get that bastard as much as you do."

"You can help us find him, but I don't want you getting involved when we move in. I don't want anything to happen to you."

"I know," Colleen said. She hesitated, then said, "Can I ask you something?"

"You know you can."

"Do you find me attractive?"

Viv smiled. "You're fucking with me, right? This is a pretty funny time to ask me that."

"No, I really want to know. You told me you've been with other women. I was curious."

"Yeah, sure. I find you very attractive," Viv said.

Colleen blushed. "This thing you do to people. Does it happen all the time? Can you ever have normal intimacy with anyone?"

"If you are asking if I could sleep with you," Viv said. "The answer is no. You've got a lot of pain in you, and I refuse to risk it. Sure, I've made love to people without taking their lives, but not often enough to feel comfortable with it. Somewhere in my mind, I am quite sure I equate sex with death. Let's say I find some pain inside you that I never knew about, something so serious that I just lose any sense of willpower. I would never forgive myself if anything happened to you. I never risked it with Jeremy, and I won't risk it with you."

"That sounds like a horrible burden to carry through life," Colleen said. "Always so afraid to be intimate with someone else."

"You could say that."

"Have you ever fallen in love, Viv?"

"Sure, a few times. It passes."

"Have you ever killed anyone you loved?"

"It's happened. Early on, I wasn't as knowledgeable about all this as I am now. I made mistakes. I still do, even now."

"It happened recently?"

"I don't know if I want to talk about it."

"Please, I want so badly to understand. I want there to be no secrets between us."

"Sometimes I wonder if I should have mentioned it before. But that time I went into Sam Wayne's house, intent on killing him, it wasn't the first time I'd been there."

"I know you took a photograph of him and his wife. You said that the woman had been special to you."

"To be honest with you, she was more than that. I had no idea who Sam Wayne was, then. I had no idea *what* he was. I never met him then. I met Maggie in a bar, and we started talking. I sensed so much pain in her, and it drew me to her. She made it so easy for me.

"At first, I let it play out. Like a cat toying with a bird. No, it was never really like that. I had feelings for her right away. And I questioned my motives constantly. I didn't want to hurt her. I wanted to explore the feelings I had for her. But it was too late by then. I was desperate for someone to devour, and it was too late to look for someone else. Besides, it seemed like I was using all my willpower to keep Jeremy safe, I didn't have enough for two people. By the time I was convinced I didn't want to kill her, I realized there was no other option.

"She was such a sad woman. She was an alcoholic by the time I met her. She felt isolated from her husband. And she had suspicions that there was something disturbing about him; that something about him scared her. She was beautiful and very fragile. My first instinct might have been to take her life, but once I got to know her,

I wanted to protect her. To save her. But you see, in these situations, my urges are so strong. They are a question of survival. I had no choice at the very end."

"And you feel horrible that you had to take her life?"

"Of course I do."

"So you are not a cold, emotionless creature at all. You are struggling with your emotions constantly."

"Colleen, I really don't like talking about this."

"I think it's beautiful that you cared so much about her. That you didn't want to kill her."

"Being in that house again, seeing her picture, it brought back so much. Knowing that had been her house was more painful than any injuries Sam inflicted on me."

"I really don't want to belabor this. But a succubus is a demon who seduces humans and then takes their lives. An incubus is the male counterpart. You and Grif…"

"Demons again."

"Just an observation. I am not judging you, just trying to help you understand what you are."

"You think you're helping, but it's not that simple. You're looking at this from some kind of religious mumbo-jumbo kind of viewpoint. But I didn't come from Hell. I was born just like you were. I breathe just like you do. I am alive. If I do things to survive that are kind of horrible, things other people do not do, then there has to be some kind of explanation. But I don't think this stuff about demons makes sense. Maybe it did back in the Middle Ages. Back then, they thought people who were insane were possessed by devils. And we know now that isn't the case."

"I'm sorry."

"One minute you say you want to be close. To have no secrets between us, and then you feel compelled to say stuff like this. I know you don't mean it that way, but it feels insulting."

"I'm really sorry. It's just a hard concept to understand. You tell me that you are responsible for the deaths of others, and I am trying so hard to understand why."

"I know it's not easy. Jeremy had a hard time understanding, too, but he let me stay here anyway. He said he'd always be here for me, which is why I could never risk hurting him. He accepted me unconditionally. Which is why he meant the world to me."

"I'm always here for you, too. I want you to know that. I never meant to hurt your feelings."

"I know it's hard to understand. I have a hard time accepting it myself a lot of the time. But you know, I had to make a decision early on. Either I accept what I am and live with it, or I kill myself. And I want to be alive too much."

Viv's eyes were moist, but she did not shed a tear. It was the closest Colleen had ever seen her to crying.

"I'm here for you," Colleen said, moving closer. She took Viv in her arms and pulled her close. She could feel the hardness of Viv's muscles in her embrace, as she tensed up, but Viv did not push her away.

"I know," Viv said softly into her ear. "And I know you are trying so very hard to understand, which is more than I can ask for. I'm asking you to forgive and accept a lot about me. I think maybe it would have been better if you didn't know any of this stuff. But now that you do, for you to still want to hold me like this. That really means a lot to me.

"I'm here for you, too," Viv said and gently kissed Colleen's cheek.

CHAPTER FIFTY-ONE

Sam got off of a Greyhound bus and began to wander. He had tried to sleep most of the trip, and wasn't even sure where he was. Not that it mattered anymore. He just had to get as far away as he could.

Now, he wandered the sidewalks, trying to figure out what to do next.

Sam found himself in the middle of a park, on a bench, wondering where he could go. It seemed like wherever he went, death followed. Because *he* was the cause of it. This was becoming much clearer to him now, even though he had no idea why it was happening.

I have to kill myself, he thought, looking out over the quiet duck pond in front of him. *There is no other choice. If I am the cause of all this violence, then I have to put an end to it myself.*

But *how?*

He wasn't sure where he was. What town? What state? He wasn't even sure what day of the week it was. He had to find a newspaper.

He ran his long fingers through his hair. How long had it been since he'd had a haircut? Since he'd taken a shower? Everything was a blur to him.

Sam looked down at the suitcase beside his leg. He hadn't taken much with him. Perhaps he hadn't been planning on leaving for very long. But something told him that it would be a mistake to go back home now. That his house would be crawling with police looking for him.

That clinches it, he thought. I have to put an end to this.

Sam grabbed his suitcase and stood up, convinced that he had to find an answer to his dilemma.

Up ahead, beyond the trees, there were skyscrapers. He could go to the top of one and jump off. But that could endanger someone below, and he'd already taken enough lives. He could throw himself in front of a speeding car, but that would endanger someone else as well.

He kept walking, out of the park and down toward the congested center of the city. It was there that he saw it, off in the distance.

I can jump off that *bridge*, he thought. It's perfect.

With this destination in mind, he walked with a new sense of mission in the direction of the suspension bridge.

* * *

"Is there anyone you should call before we leave? Who knows when we'll be back again?"

It was Viv's way of saying, *Maybe we won't be coming back.* Even though she knew Viv would do everything in her power to protect her, Colleen knew that something could go wrong. It would be very dangerous. She had seen Sam Wayne in action before, and she knew what he was capable of.

During the past couple of weeks, Viv had been watching the news channels intently and checking the Internet. Staying on top of any odd behavior. Riots, unusual waves of violence, sudden incidents of rage, as well as any particularly violent murders that involved people being torn apart limb from limb. Viv thought she had some solid leads, but there were several of them, and it might take awhile to check them all out.

Colleen stared at the phone, but couldn't think of one person she wanted to call. She hadn't talked to her mother in months and couldn't bring herself to call her now, just to say good-bye. Maybe forever.

After a while, Viv came back in. "Grif should be here soon. Are you all packed?"

"Almost. How long do you really think we'll be away?"

"It's hard to say. I have some leads, but who knows how hard it will be to follow them up? You better take at least enough clothes for a week. We could always do laundry out there."

"Out where?"

"Most of the suspicious behavior I saw was around Philadelphia," Viv said.

CHAPTER FIFTY-TWO

Sam stood on the edge of the bridge, looking down at the turgid waters below. It was a pretty long fall, and when he hit bottom, it should be easy enough to drown, if he didn't die on impact.

He closed his eyes and put his suitcase down beside him. He wouldn't be needing it for this particular trip.

Cars were passing him by on the bridge, beeping their horns as if encouraging him to jump.

This is the best way to stop the bloodshed, he thought, and took a deep breath.

He jumped.

He could see the water coming toward him, and then he lost consciousness completely.

* * *

By the time Grif reached the house, they were ready to go. Viv was sitting on the couch in the living room, her bag packed, her feet up on the coffee table as she watched the television. The news was on, as usual.

Colleen was in the room she had shared with Jeremy; she had just finished packing, too.

He looked in at Viv and knocked on the sliding glass door. She motioned for him to come inside.

"So you finally got here," she told him. "I was starting to wonder if you'd make it."

"I had a lot of things going on," he said, standing beside the couch and looking at the television. "But I dropped them all for you."

"Nice to hear it," Viv said. Then she called out, "Col, you ready yet? Grif's here."

"Is she coming with us?" Grif asked.

"Yeah. I tried to talk her out of it, but she won't listen."

"I'm serious," Grif said. "This sounds dangerous."

"I know," Colleen said, coming down the hall behind him, carrying her suitcase. "But I want to help you guys catch the guy who killed Jeremy. Viv's already explained to me how dangerous it is. I know all about it. Remember, I've seen him up close."

"She can detect him," Viv said. "She can *see* this *vision*, kind of like an aura, I guess. Or so she says. I'm thinking that means she might help us find him quicker. And the sooner we stop this guy, the better."

"Yeah, I can pick him out of a crowd quicker than anyone."

"If you were so good at detecting him, how come you weren't able to warn Jeremy?"

"He came out of nowhere. There's no way I could have warned him in time."

"Now look what you did," Viv said. "And she finally stopped crying yesterday."

"I'm not crying," Colleen said, holding back the tears.

"I'm sorry," Grif said. "I didn't know the details. Look, let's start over again. I really don't want to fuck things up right off the bat. I mean, it wouldn't be new for me, but I'd like to do things right this time. Can you forgive me, Colleen?"

"Yeah, sure," she said, but he could tell she was still trying to maintain her composure.

"So you got a car this time?" Viv asked.

"Yeah, if you want. It's comfortable enough. What's wrong with your car? It in the shop or something?"

"There was an accident. There's a horrible odor. I'd rather not use it for a long trip."

"Okay," Grif said, not sure if he should ask further. He decided not to. "You want to head out now?"

"Sure," Viv said. "Maybe you can help us with our bags."

It was then that something on the television caught her eye. There was a riot on the other side of the country.

"Well, looks like he's on the move again," Viv said. "Colleen, remember me saying it might take us awhile to find him? Well, it doesn't look like it will be so tough after all."

CHAPTER FIFTY-THREE

When he hit the water, instead of the life leaving him, it simply clicked up a notch. Whatever humanity Sam Wayne had left inside himself was pushed back into the hidden corners of his brain, and the other side of what he was came forward.

He went underwater, but quickly clawed his way up to the top again and swam back toward the bridge. Then he began climbing up the metal structure as quickly as he could.

There was a crowd of people above Sam, staring over the railing, as he climbed up toward them. He grabbed the closest ones and pulled them over the side, letting them fall to their deaths in his place. The others scattered, but they didn't get far.

The ones he didn't chase after, began to act strangely and started fighting. Striking out. Hands turned into fists or fastened around throats.

It was one big free-for-all.

There was a television van on the corner, and people were filming the scene. Sam, or what had once been Sam, watched them for a moment, then the reporter was striking the cameraman repeatedly with his microphone, and then the cameraman lifted his camera high and brought it down hard on the reporter's skull. The broadcast came to an abrupt end.

Cars had stopped on the bridge, and people got out of their cars to shout at one another. The shouting degenerated into more bloodshed.

And Sam was at the center of it all. His clothes still soaked from his brief dip in the river. His hands reached out for whoever he could grab.

A helicopter buzzed overhead. Another camera to replace the smashed one below. Another watchful eye to transmit the carnage to the people at home.

Sam stared up at the helicopter, wishing that his arms were long enough so that he could reach it and pull it down to the ground and crush the life out of its passengers. Even if he climbed up the sides of the bridge, he wouldn't have gotten close enough to get a hold of it. And even then, there was no guarantee he could have done the damage he wanted to. Flesh and blood was one thing, but metal and whirling blades were another. Not that he was clear-minded enough at this point to think that out completely.

Instead, he made his way across the bridge, grabbing people as he went quickly enough to smash their heads into railings, or into their cars. Or walking over people already dead or dying on the ground beneath him.

Sam Wayne wasn't really sure who he was, or what his destination should be. But he knew he wanted to get off the bridge. And he wanted to kill as many people as he could along the way.

* * *

The television screen showed an overhead shot from a helicopter of a bridge. Stopped cars and what appeared to be many bodies were on the bridge. Some people were fighting with each other. Several more appeared to be dead. Above it all, a man was walking across the tops of the vehicles.

"It's him," Colleen said.

"I have never seen anything like this," the news reporter was saying. "I really have no idea what to make of this situation. Police are trying to get to the scene now, but are having trouble because of the backed up traffic, which includes many abandoned cars."

"How do we deal with this?" Grif asked, watching the screen with amazement. "Do you have any kind of plan?"

"Not yet," Viv said. "But we have to confront him before he slaughters more."

"It looks like he's doing just that."

"I know. That's why we've got to stop him. The police won't be able to do anything."

"This is the guy who killed Jeremy?"

"And Turney," Colleen said. "A friend of mine. But he's killed a lot more than just them."

"I went up against him, Grif," Viv said. "His name is Sam Wayne and I confronted him in his own house."

"He's still standing?"

"He's not only still standing, but he was able to handle me pretty easily. We're not dealing with a normal person here, Grif. Not by a long shot."

"I can see that."

"Remember when I told you Colleen could sense him, that she saw some kind of *vision*? She saw similar visions around us. Do you think there could be a link?"

Grif stared at her, but did not answer.

"We could fly there," Colleen said. "Get there faster."

"Faster isn't necessarily better. We don't have a plan yet," Grif said. "Besides, we have no idea how much more havoc this guy might be up to. He might put an airport at danger at some point. No, we should drive there and try to figure out a solid plan along the way."

"I agree," Viv said. "In fact, that's why I wanted you to join us. I really need another head to think this through."

"You ladies already packed or do you have to get ready for our trip?"

"We're packed," Viv said, "and ready to go."

"My car's out front. We better get started. It will probably take us a couple of days to get there, if we don't make too many stops."

"You still coming, Col?" Viv asked.

"Sure."

"Are you really sure we should bring her along?" Grif asked. "That will just increase the chances that someone might get hurt."

"I told you, she has the ability to detect him. It will come in handy when we get there."

"I hope so."

"It will be tough leaving this place," Colleen said, looking around the room.

Viv shut off the television using the remote and stood up. "We'll come back, eventually. We're not going away forever."

"I hope not," Grif said under his breath as he grabbed their suitcases.

CHAPTER FIFTY-FOUR

Sam stood in the middle of a green field. When he first arrived, a bunch of guys had been playing touch football, but now they were involved in a free-for-all, pounding on one another with their fists. Kicking each other. Two men already lay on the grass, bloody and unmoving. The others, caught up in the fire of the moment, didn't seem to notice.

At the other end of the field were some trees and a duck pond. He remembered seeing a mother there with her small child, feeding bread to the ducks. Now, the mother was trying to drown her own child, who was furiously trying to fight her off. She succeeded in holding him under long enough to fill his lungs. Even the ducks were attacking each other. Feathered bodies floated on the pond's surface.

He watched as people filled the park. Runners, bicyclists, families having picnics on the grass. It didn't take long for them to get infected with the rage Sam spread like wildfire. Runners pushed a cyclist to the ground and stomped him to death before turning on each other. Families furiously tried to kill one another, staining picnic blankets red.

And it was all because of *him*. He could feel the rage building inside of him. He could feel it surging out of him, every inch of his body throbbing as it pumped pure hatred into the world, infecting everyone it touched. He no longer had an identity, although he still wore the body of a man. Now, he was something different. A beacon of pure, unrestrained fury, sending out waves of negative energy. He could feel his influence expanding, the waves reaching further and further out.

The rage seemed to feed on itself. As he infected others, he also fed off of them, creating a constant cycle that kept recycling itself, growing stronger all the time.

Everyone in his vicinity was trying to kill whoever was nearest. Whoever they could grab and strike and stomp to death.

Sam felt very good inside.

* * *

"The riots seem to be spreading. Incidences of looting and vandalism have run rampant. All actions by the police to squelch this madness seem to be failing, as police who come in contact with the rioters have been joining in the fray."

Viv looked at the car radio and then up at Grif behind the wheel. "It's started," she said. "I knew this would happen eventually."

"What do you mean?"

"He was a time bomb waiting to go off, and it's finally happened. Colleen and I saw this guy in action. He had cops killing each other on the lawn in front of his house. I even felt it to some degree when I came in contact with him, although it didn't take me over. It sounds like he's only gotten more powerful since we last saw him."

"So you've seen this guy more than once and lived to tell about it," Grif said to Colleen, who was in the back seat. He looked at her in the rear-view mirror.

"Yeah," Colleen said. "And every time was horrible."

"There's no turning back, now," Viv said.

"Well, have you girls thought this through?" Grif said. "How the fuck are we supposed to stop this guy when he's even making cops kill each other?"

"I got close to him," Viv said. "I wasn't able to stop him, because I wasn't prepared. I had no idea how strong he was. But if I got that close once, I can do it again."

"I got close to him, too," Colleen said. "Twice. I saw him kill two people right in front of me, but I didn't go crazy with rage, and he didn't harm me."

"That's right, isn't it?" Viv asked her.

"I don't want Colleen getting close to him again," Grif said. "I don't want to risk something happening to her. We have to take care of this ourselves, Viv."

"But don't you see, maybe I'm immune to him," Colleen said.

"What does that matter, Col?" Viv asked. "If you can get close to him, how does that help anything? You can't do anything to stop him."

"Maybe I could get some kind of bomb and get close."

"And blow the both of you up in the process," Grif said. "Stupid idea."

"We have to do *something* to stop him. Look at all the people he's killing."

"We're not going to do anything that would put you at risk," Viv said. "Grif and I already agreed about that. If you can help us find him, fine, but you are not confronting him."

"Why don't we just drop her off somewhere now?" Grif said. "We don't need her to find him. Hell, he's the top news story in the country right now."

"I'm not going anywhere," Colleen said. "I'm going with you."

"Sounds like it's a good idea we didn't fly out there, after all," Viv said, turning up the radio. The violence had spread to the airports. It was pure bedlam.

"How far do you think this will go?" Grif asked. "It just seems to be spreading more and more."

"I wish I had killed him when I had the chance," Viv said.

"It would have saved a lot of lives," Grif said. "But you had no idea what you were in for. You were lucky you survived your encounter with him."

"At least she healed up real fast," Colleen said. "I was worried that she was in real bad shape when I found her in that house."

"So we any closer to devising a plan?" Grif asked them. Then to Viv, "Or are you just going to go charging at him with a sword or something?"

"Last time I brought a gun, and I could have sworn I shot him, but it didn't stop him. Maybe I didn't hit him at all. Maybe it has to be a headshot or something. I don't know."

"Well, you have to get close enough to try," Grif said. "That sounds like the tricky part. Even if you get past the madness that he's surrounding himself with, there's no guarantee he'll let you get close enough to do anything."

"I have to at least try. Nobody else seems to have any solutions. We can't just let him run wild like this, killing whoever he wants, can we?"

CHAPTER FIFTY-FIVE

Sam sat atop a rock formation at the city zoo. The bears had just finished killing each other off. Four bloody carcasses lay on the concrete beneath him. Their throats ripped out. Blood formed thick pools beneath them, which spread to the filthy wading pool.

There was a time when it would have been suicide for him to be here, inside the cage. But now, it was lethal for the animals.

He looked outside the bars. There were bodies everywhere. Dead families, dead zoo employees, dead lovers on dates. All the animals had torn each other to pieces from the elephants to the snakes.

For as far as he could see, there was only death.

Sam had shed his clothes by now. There was no more reason for such things as modesty. Besides, he was the only one alive for miles. He was no longer subject to the rules of man.

There was the hum of a helicopter from above. Another camera crew no doubt, monitoring his progress. Sending back pictures to the waiting world of his latest carnage.

He stared up at it, wondering how far the waves of rage traveled. Sure, he was able to send the emotions out, infecting people around him. But could the waves emanate upwards to the sky?

Seemingly in answer, the helicopter began to waver a bit, as if it were losing control. Then it flew lower in the horizon, until it disappeared from view. There was a sound in the distance. Did it crash? He liked to think he had something to do with its descent, but he didn't care enough to go see. It was too far away.

He leapt down from the rock formation with its caves, that had once acted as a shelter for the bears. He passed the unmoving forms of the bears themselves and then grabbed onto the bars. They were just wide enough for a man to squeeze through. He slipped out and climbed the fence beyond.

There was such an overwhelming silence. This place had once been filled with sounds. People chattering, animals bellowing and roaring, hissing and cawing. And now, all of it was gone.

Sam passed the cage where the wolves had lived. They were dead as well. All the animals were. Sam threw his head back and let out a long howl, just to break the silence. Just to let this place know that he was the dominant one. That he was the king of this jungle.

* * *

"I don't know," Viv said softly. "I'm really having second thoughts about bringing her along. There's too much of a risk that she might get hurt."

"It was your idea to bring her," Grif said. "We could have just left without her."

"She insisted, and convinced me that she could be of some help, but even then I had to struggle with the idea. Now, as we get closer and hear about the horrific things happening over there. I'm convinced I made the wrong decision."

"It's not too late to change your mind," Grif said. "We could leave her here. She's asleep. We could go the rest of the way without her."

"No, she'd follow us somehow. I know she would, and then who knows what would happen to her? At least with us, we can keep an eye on her. Try to protect her."

"This is too much to handle," Grif said. "Have you been hearing the news reports? How are we even going to get close enough to do anything? It sounds like the entire western seaboard has gone insane."

"I know. Maybe none of us should go any further. Maybe this *is* a suicide mission, and we'll end up dead before we even get close enough to see him."

"Maybe."

"And I don't know about you," Viv said, "But I'm starting to feel pretty itchy. I really need to feed it."

"It's like you read my mind."

"The closer we get, the stronger the craving. It's actually kind of painful at this point."

"I know," Grif said. "Only too well."

"We've got to do something about that. We've got to be strong when we confront him."

"And we still have a ways to go."

"Let's go downstairs to the bar," Viv said. "There's bound to be someone down there. I can't put it off any longer."

Grif sighed deeply. "I was hoping you'd say that. It's getting tougher and tougher to keep away from Colleen. She's pretty tempting, you know."

"Just stay away from her."

"I told you I would, didn't I?"

"Well, you make sure of it. Here I am worried about protecting her from that monster, and it turns out *you're* the one I need to be wary of."

"I can handle it. I have more willpower than you think."

"We're both on edge, Grif. And it's only going to get worse. We need to do something about it."

They left.

* * *

Colleen could hear them close the outer door. She got out of bed and slowly made her way to the bedroom door. She didn't turn on the light. When she felt the knob, she opened the door a crack and looked outside into the suite room that connected the two bedrooms. Nobody was out there.

They've gone to find victims, she thought. *Sometimes I wish they'd just take me.*

She wasn't sure if she meant that. Did she really want to *die*? Sometimes she did. But another part of her wanted to believe there was a way she could help them stop Jeremy's killer. A way she could make a difference.

But, down deep, she felt this was a hopeless cause. They were all going to die. Wouldn't it be better to die here, in the arms of one of them, than to be torn apart by Sam Wayne?

Viv had told her that, upon death, her victims felt a kind of intense ecstasy. It wasn't painful at all. They were practically grateful to die for her.

That's the kind of death I want, Colleen thought. *I don't want to die in pain.*

She sat down in front of the television, turned it on and flipped through the channels with the remote control. Some of the stations had gone black. The others were filled with more horror stories. But now, they seemed more like speculation. Nobody was reporting from where things were happening anymore. Word was that troops had been sent in to set things right, but that there was no word from them yet. It was as if they had entered a black hole. No one could contact them.

What chance do we have? Colleen wondered.

CHAPTER FIFTY-SIX

Maggie was there, holding him. He was crying and she was kissing his cheek, telling him not to cry anymore. He could feel her arms around him. He could feel her, he could smell her. She was so real. He could smell her hair, and it made him tighten his hold on her.

"I've done so many horrible things," he told her. "It's all so out of control now. I have no idea how to stop it."

"Calm down," Maggie told him. "You're getting too upset. You've got to calm down."

"I've killed people, Maggie," he said. "I've killed so many people. There is blood on my hands, even now. How can you hold me like this after all that I've done?"

"There isn't any blood on your hands," she told him. "You haven't hurt anyone. You're just imagining it all."

He buried his head in her shoulder. His face was pressed tight against her flesh. He opened his mouth and kissed her, tasted her skin. It tasted just like he remembered. The taste, the smell. She was so real.

"There's no blood?" he asked her, wanting so badly to believe. "None at all?"

"No, you silly man. There isn't a drop."

"And you're alive again. You're really here with me?"

"I never left you, Sam. I don't know why you won't believe me."

"I saw you dead, Maggie. I buried you. It was the hardest thing I'd ever had to do in my life, saying goodbye like that. It was then that I realized how important you were to me. How much I needed you in my life to keep me sane."

She kissed his temple. "I won't ever say goodbye to you, Sam."

He tried to hold her harder, so hard that he might crush her, but by then the dream was fading and there was nothing to hold on to anymore. He tried to resist waking up with all his might, but he just couldn't. In his dream, he had felt so warm and safe. But there was no way it could last. Maggie was long gone now.

Sam woke up on the grass, in the middle of another field. This field was enclosed by a high metal fence. He could see the corpses of slaughtered deer scattered across the grass. Some of them had killed each other. Some had been killed by people, who also were stretched out on the grass, dead.

Sam felt very hungry and ran over to a deer. He picked up a piece of it and started to eat. He was so hungry that the raw meat tasted wonderful.

He closed his eyes and tried to conjure Maggie up again from the dream. Just her face, one more time, but he couldn't visualize it. She was lost to him again. Everything in his former life was getting harder and harder to picture in his mind's eye. There were walls going up inside him, separating then from now, and they were getting stronger.

* * *

Colleen could hear noises. People fucking. She lay on her bed, listening. When she'd heard them coming back to the room, she shut off the television and went back into her bedroom, where it was dark.

From what she could tell, one couple was in the suite room, on the couch, probably, and another was on the other side of her wall, in the second bedroom.

She wanted so badly to see what was happening. She wanted to see how they fed. What happened to the people when they died? She got up from her bed and went to the door. She listened.

Slowly, she turned the knob and looked out in the suite room. Grif was out there, on the couch, fucking a woman. She looked older than he was, her hair slightly gray.

Looking at her face, Colleen could tell that she'd been very pretty once.

Grif was on top of her, pumping away. The woman was making odd noises; her eyes were rolled back in her head. Colleen had heard sounds of passion before, but there was another sound that came from her. A kind of rattling from the back of her throat.

Grif's mouth was stretched in a tight grin. He continued moving, but his eyes were intently on the woman beneath him. She was gurgling now, her arms grabbing at him, pulling him closer, her body spasming beneath him.

She suddenly thrust her head up and kissed him. Colleen had never seen such a forceful kiss. It was as if the woman was trying to force herself into him, the way she grabbed at him with her hands and arms, the way she wrapped her legs around him, making it hard for him to thrust his pelvis.

And then, she spasmed again and stopped moving. She went limp beneath him. Grif wrapped his own arms around her then, and pulled her close, still pumping his lower torso. Colleen closed the door.

She went to the wall that separated her bedroom from the other one. She could hear Viv and her partner in there. There were similar sounds. The sounds of real passion, but the rattling, too. The gurgling. They were ugly sounds that were always on the outer edges of passion, punctuating the moans and hisses. Eventually, some of the sounds on the other side of the wall stopped, too. Colleen had her ear to the wall, and she was sure she could still hear Viv, groaning in ecstasy, riding out her own orgasms as her victim, too, stopped moving. Colleen didn't know why, but she was certain Viv was on top in there. That she was belly to belly with someone who wasn't alive anymore.

Something about the sounds scared her and excited her at the same time. To be so close to death, and yet to feel spared, safe. It was strange.

All this passion was contagious. Her hands performed the role of lover as she stretched out on her bed and listened to echoes of those sounds in her mind.

CHAPTER FIFTY-SEVEN

The closer they got to Sam Wayne, the more vivid Viv's dreams became. Not that they weren't already vivid enough to wake her most nights. But now, it was as if she were drowning in the imagery, in the flashbacks. Her life was playing out before her while she slept, the way lives passed before the eyes of people about to die.

Does this mean I am going to die soon? she found herself wondering, gasping for air in the darkness, in the bed where she'd taken someone's soul mere hours before.

Grif and her were so used to this, disposing of the bodies had become second nature. Everything was tidy and done in no time, the dead already forgotten. Well, except when she slept. Then they came back with a vengeance. They all came back eventually, no matter how nameless or faceless they had seemed when she took them. She could see every line of their faces, every nuance of their body language. She could hear their voices clearly, speaking to her. More often than not, asking for their lives back.

There were lots of faces. The first one was her father.

He'd started sneaking into her room when she was twelve. She only wanted it to stop. It was about the third or fourth time (who was she kidding, she knew it inside and out, it was the *third* time), and he was coming, and she reached out and felt his mind with her own, and even at that young age, she'd been strong enough to envelope his essence, his soul, and make it surrender to her. Sure, back then there was more of a struggle. It was like landing a marlin to her that first time, but she won in the end, and her father was dead, collapsed on top of her in the bed. She was pinned beneath him, helpless in the dark.

She had to cry out for her mother. Something her father forbade her to do when he made his secret visits, and she almost felt guilty breaking that rule, no matter how much she hated him, because she was confused, scared, not sure what she had done, but she knew that she was somehow responsible for why daddy wasn't moving. Why he was just a heavy, lifeless mound of flesh on top of her.

She didn't tell her mother what she'd done, because she couldn't bring herself to believe it herself. That it had been her handiwork. Even though she knew it was. Her mother had simply believed that, in the course of molesting her daughter, her husband had suffered a heart attack. Viv remembered getting dressed and helping her mother move him out into the hallway, because there was just too much shame leaving him on her bed. They somehow got him onto the big oval throw rug that was beside her bed, and dragged the rug, and him out of the room and into the hallway. It was then that her mother called 9-1-1, screaming into the phone about how her husband wasn't moving and she needed someone to come immediately.

She remembered Grif, who was younger than her and strangely quiet for a little kid, at the corner of the room in his pajamas, watching their mother with the biggest, saddest eyes Viv had ever seen. She went to him and hugged him close. He didn't ask what had happened to their father, even though he'd seen them drag him out into the hallway. He didn't make a sound.

After that night, her mother had never again talked to her about what her father had been doing to her. Her mother must have blocked it out of her mind, or pretended to, and Viv did not have the guts to bring it up herself.

Luckily, the hunger didn't start out strong. There was always a strange itching in the back of her mind, this need that always irritated her, but not strong enough to drive her crazy. She was able to resist it.

But down deep, she knew what it was. And how to satisfy it. Perhaps it was the terror of the memory of what had happened to her father that had given her the willpower to resist satisfying her hunger again for years.

She found herself very attracted to boys, and other girls, early on, in junior high, but she resisted. It took all her resolve to keep from doing what the other kids were doing. High school got worse. But it was in her sophomore year that she just couldn't resist any longer.

He was a senior and handsome, and he pursued her, a sophomore, and it had been years since her daddy and she was sure that it wouldn't happen again, *couldn't* happen again. That she'd just imagined it. And then some heavy petting in the back of a car led to other things, and this boy ended up dead, the victim of a "heart ailment" that hadn't been detected before. She'd somehow known enough to keep from getting pinned this time and was able to get away and get help. But everyone knew what they had been doing and not only did she have to live with the fact that she'd been responsible for his death, there was also the shame of being caught "doing it."

It got worse then. The hunger got stronger each time, and after her boyfriend died, it was harder to resist. But she couldn't act on it. She couldn't kill more people. She suffered in silence, doing everything in her power to keep from acting on her impulses.

She'd been able to resist for another six months or so, but then things got ugly. She started seeking out prospective *victims*, but it couldn't be anyone she knew, anyone she could feel guilty about or who could be traced back to her. This meant a lot of run-ins with very unsavory types. Perverts, mostly.

She always cried afterwards, even though she told herself that the men deserved it. Even though she felt that she really had no choice.

She didn't know when Grif found out he was the same way. It must have been later on, after she'd left, but she couldn't be sure. He didn't like to talk about it. For some reason, he'd seemed more mature back then, more capable. It almost seemed like he was going backwards sometimes, he was so much more reckless now.

After high school, she'd even joined a convent out of desperation. But it didn't work out. When another novice died because of her, she had to move on. Temptation was everywhere. She couldn't escape it no matter where she went.

When she was younger, she thought she was a vampire. Even though she never drank blood. And the succubus thing—the time Colleen mentioned it wasn't the first time it had crossed her mind. But she couldn't bring herself to really believe it. Vampires, demons, they were just make believe. And she was real, flesh and blood. She wasn't some kind of monster.

She just killed whoever she got intimate with.

There were lots of attempts to control it. Alcohol and drugs weren't any help. They simply made her lose control and increased the frequency of the incidents and some of them got messy. Meditation only seemed to help for a short time, and psychotherapy was out of the question. She couldn't tell anyone else about her secret. They would lock her away forever if they found out.

Maybe it will all be over soon, she thought, feeling the tension in her muscles. *Something* was coming, she was sure of that. *Something bad*.

Viv closed her eyes and tried to get back to sleep, despite her fear of what dreams might bring. As she drifted off again, she just hoped that she wouldn't see her father's face this time. It had been a long time, but he still scared her most of all.

CHAPTER FIFTY-EIGHT

Sam sat on top of an abandoned car; there were a lot of those now. It was dark, but he knew that there was no one alive anywhere near. There were no sounds at all, except for his breathing.

There was still the throbbing in the back of his head. The switch inside of him that had been turned ON wasn't showing any signs of shutting off anytime soon. He *seemed* calmer now, but he was not even close to being Sam Wayne again. His arms and legs were still tensed like tightly wound coils. He was a snake always on the verge of striking. He knew that the first sign of anything alive would set him into another rage.

He was actually surprised that his mind was clear enough to have coherent thoughts. It had all seemed so very fuzzy for a long time now.

He felt no guilt over what he had done. He was simply following his nature.

He felt sticky from the blood that covered him. None of the blood was his own.

It is my job to bring death to the world, he thought. *It's as simple as that.*

CHAPTER FIFTY-NINE

Grif woke up on the couch in the middle room of the suite. Someone was shaking him awake. He thought it was Viv. Sometimes when they were kids, she used to sneak into his room and ask if she could stay with him. She used to be scared a lot back then. She sure didn't seem scared now. In fact, ever since they'd been on their own, she'd been the toughest person he had ever known.

She'd left home when she was eighteen. She just took off, and he didn't see her for years. Not even on the holidays. Their mother used to cry a lot about that. Grif didn't cry, but he was very hurt about it, too. He felt Viv had abandoned him. He wanted so very badly to go away with her.

He knew what their father had done to Viv, even though she never spoke about it. He knew that if he hadn't died when he did, chances were good Grif would have received late night visits from daddy at some point, too. There were already signs by then that their father was considering it. In that respect, Grif felt lucky.

He always hated his mother for letting that happen. For refusing to acknowledge that their father could have been anything other than a good man. As he got older, he fought with his mother a lot. Maybe being left behind by Viv increased his anger. He started drinking young, and used to come home drunk. Sometimes his arguments with his mother got physical.

Grif wasn't proud of that.

He'd discovered his *malady*, the one he shared with Viv, later than she did. He was about sixteen, in juvenile detention after a particularly nasty run-in with Mom. Another, bigger boy had forced himself on Grif, and had ended up dead, and while nobody could prove he was responsible, the other kids stayed away from him after that.

He'd always been a troubled kid, but once he got out of lockup, he was determined never to go back. The first thing he did was leave his mother's house, intent never to go back there again, either. And, like Viv, he decided to try his luck on the road.

Their paths crossed about five years later. It was complete coincidence. Despite the bond they'd once shared as kids, they hadn't really known how to find one another again. But, ever since that chance meeting, they'd drifted in and out of each other's orbits. Never staying together long enough to set up any kind of routine. Just when they started getting close again, one or the other would leave without a word some morning. And they both understood.

Being like this, it was too easy to get dependent on one another. When they were the only two people like this in the world, that they knew of. But this was the kind of life where two people leaving a trail of bodies could draw just way too much attention.

It was hard enough handling things when you were alone. Keeping the heat off.

Too many deaths could draw too much attention. And Grif was determined to keep his promise to himself to never be locked up again.

Viv was smarter. She'd always managed to stay one step ahead of anyone curious. He'd been able to do it by sheer luck.

He tried to think of the first time they made love. What had prompted them to even try it? Were they that sure they couldn't harm one another, or were they so full of guilt for the lives they'd taken over the years that each secretly desired that the other would take *their* life?

"Grif?" a soft voice said in his ear. "Wake up."

He'd been lost somewhere between wakefulness and sleep, and now he opened his eyes. Not that it helped much. The room was dark.

"Colleen, is that you?" he whispered.

"Yeah," she said. She tugged at his arm. "Come with me."

"I'm trying to sleep," Grif said. "Can't it wait?"

"You can't sleep out here," she said. "It must be uncomfortable. My bed is so big."

"I can't," he said. "You know why. Viv told me you know."

"I don't care," Colleen said, tugging at his arm again. "Sometimes I think I want to go through with this, that I want to get rid of that Wayne guy. But I can't. I'm too scared."

"You don't have to come with us," Grif said. "You can go back. We won't stop you."

"No," Colleen said. "I don't want to go back. I don't want to do anything anymore. Now that Jeremy's dead, I don't want to live."

"You don't know what you're talking about."

"I do," Colleen said. "Believe me. I've thought about this a lot. I can't do this anymore. I just want it to end."

"Why me?" Grif said. "Why lay this on me?"

"Because the way people die with you and Viv, it sounds like such a good way to go. No pain. And I know you like me. We almost did it that night in Jeremy's house. The attraction was there. And now I don't have any reason to say no."

"I don't want to," Grif said. "I like you, Col. If I hurt you, I wouldn't be able to forgive myself."

Instead of arguing further, she stopped tugging his arm and crawled on top of him on the couch. She kissed him. He felt her soft tongue in his mouth and even though he'd satiated his hunger hours before, there was enough of an itch left to get stimulated by her attention. He'd noticed that the closer they got to where Sam Wayne was, the worse the need was. Viv had mentioned it, too. And it was so easy to get it started again.

He kissed her back and pulled her close to him.

"See," she said, stopping for a minute. "It's easy."

"But I really don't want to do this," he told her.

"Shhh," she said and started kissing him again.

He wanted so badly to push her away, but once he started getting into it, he lost all sense of judgment. It was an old cliché, guys not being able to say no and all, but in his case it was really true. He was a slave to his need, and he couldn't resist it when someone pursued *him* so rigorously.

"Come on," Colleen said in his ear. She licked his lobe. "I don't want Viv to hear us. Let's go to my room."

"She might still hear us through the wall," Grif said.

"I don't care," Colleen said. "I just want to do this so bad."

She hadn't made love to anyone since Jeremy died, and this, mixed with her desperation, made her as hungry as Grif was, in her own way. Not only was he her way out, it was the most pleasurable way out she could think of.

This time when she tugged his arm, he didn't resist. He got up and went with her.

* * *

In her dream, Viv saw Sam Wayne above her, holding her down on the floor. He raised his fist to strike her. She struggled beneath him, trying to push him off, but he had her arms pinned under his knees. She had never felt so helpless.

And then, he was no longer Sam Wayne; he was her father. Pinning her with his dead body. She was small and scared and no matter how hard she tried, she couldn't push him off by herself. So she started to shout. It wasn't that loud at first, because she was ashamed and scared, but then she realized that if no one heard her, she would never get free, so she started to cry out louder, and louder.

The door flew open and the light came on. Her mother was hysterical right from the start, shouting out questions but then wailing and crying too much to hear answers. She remembered her mother somehow pulled her father off enough for her to squeeze out from under him. She helped her roll him onto the floor, onto the throw rug. She looked up and Griffin was in the doorway, still a child. He stared at her with big eyes that tried to comprehend what was going on.

And then Grif was an adult, and he looked angry at her for some reason. He turned and ran down the hall. Ran away.

Viv woke. Her breathing was hard again. But she heard something else. The breathing wasn't all her own. And there were other sounds. Coming from the other side of the wall, where Colleen was sleeping.

She knew instantly what the sounds were, and she tensed, hoping it was a dream. Hoping that she hadn't woken at all and this was just the nightmare getting worse and worse. But she knew it was real. And she knew who was making those noises.

He couldn't resist, she thought. *He's going to kill her*!

She lay there, wondering what she should do. If she should try to stop them. But she couldn't bring herself to get out of bed. She wanted so badly to save Colleen, but she felt pinned there. As if her father's body had returned in the night and collapsed upon her all over again.

CHAPTER SIXTY

"I'm coming," Colleen said beneath him. She was on her belly now, and he was taking her from behind, and she was quivering beneath him. He was a very good lover, one of the benefits of satisfying his need on a regular basis, and it didn't take him that long to get her to this point. He didn't just stimulate her with his body, his mind knew how to stimulate the right parts of her brain, too.

Instinctively, and quite against his wishes, his mind sought hers out, stroked the gentle boundaries of her soul. Like a hand, his mind closed around what made her alive, one finger after another. With each closing finger, her sensations intensified, until he knew she thought she was going to black out. But she didn't. He kept her aware and kept cranking up the volume. It was almost more than she could bear.

She had a hard time thinking; it was all too much. But she faintly made out a thought, and he could hear her. *I'm almost there.*

And then she cried out beneath him. This wasn't new to him, but it scared him. If Viv didn't hear them before, she definitely would hear them now. Usually, people died when they got this far.

Colleen was shouting and writhing and he wanted to pull out of her; he wanted to run out of the room and get as far away from her as he could. *The whole building must hear her by now,* he thought,

- 354 -

but he couldn't bring himself to stop. He was so close. He could feel his mind around hers, ready to draw her in.

But he couldn't. She resisted. She surrendered to the most violent orgasms she had ever experienced, letting them rock her like a woman possessed, but she would not surrender her soul to him.

He came. Usually this didn't happen until the moment when the other person died, then he got release. But this wasn't a normal situation. Everything was different this time.

Colleen bit the pillow hard, trying to muffle her sounds. It was going on and on and Grif came harder than he ever had before. It just about sapped all the energy out of him, it was so severe, but she just kept squirming beneath him.

It was then that Viv came into the room. She turned on the light and stared at the two of them there, on the bed. Grif had lost his momentum, but Colleen was still writhing like crazy.

"Stop it!" Viv said, breaking the silence. "Grif, you have to stop!"

But he was already finished. He rolled onto his side and watched Colleen as she rode it out. Her movements slowly calming down. It looked so strange to him. This had never happened before.

"I'm done," he said, looking up at Viv, who seemed as shocked as he was. "I'm done. I'm done."

Colleen was hyperventilating and it took a while for her breathing to go back to normal. All the while, they watched her, dumbfounded, not sure if she was in danger of dying. Perhaps her heart would give out after all.

She sat up in bed, covered in sweat and her face was flushed red.

"Oh man," she said. "That was fucking *incredible*."

* * *

"It's spreading," Viv said, staring at the TV screen. They had not said a word about the night before. Grif was stretched out on the sofa, waiting to use the shower.

The violence was reaching further inland. More states were affected now.

"It won't be long now before we're in the thick of it," Viv said. "Chances are we'll never get close enough to even reach him. We'll be killed before then."

"Maybe we should turn back," Grif said. "This is starting to look more and more like a suicide mission."

"Where would we go?" Colleen asked, coming from the bathroom, wrapped in a towel. "No matter where we go, it would reach us eventually, at this rate. And who knows how much stronger he'll be then?"

"So how do you propose we get close enough to stop him?" Viv asked. "Assuming we can do anything if we reach him."

"I don't know," she said. "Just drive on in and hope for the best?"

"We could always leave the country," Grif said. "There has to be a limit to what this guy can do."

"I don't know why," Viv said. "But I think the more it spreads the stronger he gets. Eventually, it will spread everywhere. There won't be any stopping it."

"You think this is some kind of apocalypse?" Colleen asked.

"It could be," Viv said. "Unless someone stops it, I think this could be the end of all life."

"You know there's probably no way we can get to him," Grif said. "Might as well just wait here and let it happen."

"How can you be so sure?" Viv asked.

"It's spreading, you said so yourself. Who can say when it will stop? What proof do we have that it will?"

Grif looked at Colleen, wrapped in her towel.

"You know what?" he said. "At this point, I don't care. If you two don't care about living anymore, then I'm more than willing to ride this out with you. We can have a little fun before the end, at least."

"You've got it wrong," Colleen told him. "I don't want to die anymore. I don't know what you did to me, but now I want to live more than ever. It's like you opened up something inside of me that made me realize how important it is that we finish this."

It was true that she looked energized, refreshed. Viv had not seen her this way since the height of her relationship with Jeremy, when she last seemed truly happy.

"They haven't been able to get close enough to him to drop a bomb or do anything that could really stop him," Viv said. "When anybody tries, they're never heard from again."

"And nobody will hear from us, either," Grif said.

"There's something different about us," Colleen said. "You two aren't like other people. I don't think I am, either. There has to be a reason why we're wrapped up in this. Maybe there's a reason why he's attacked people I was with before, but never harmed me. Maybe he *can't* harm me."

"You have no proof of that," Viv said.

"Both times, I got away. When I turned back to look at him, he seemed distracted. Confused. But he could have killed me easily. I was right within arm's reach. And yet, he let me go."

"Could just be dumb luck," Grif said.

"And I can't explain it, but I feel full of energy after what happened with Grif," Colleen said. "I feel like a charged battery."

"It's called afterglow," Viv said.

"No, it's more than that," Colleen said. "I know we can stop him."

"The pep talk sounds great and all," Viv said. "But do you really believe it? How do we know he won't just kill us, just like he's killed everybody else?"

Colleen walked toward her and stopped just in front of her. "You know me better than that, Viv. You have to trust me on this one. Even that time at Wayne's house, when I went in to get you. The people he'd infected, who were killing each other, they didn't attack me. I was in the car, watching, and none of them came near me. When I got out and went toward the house, none of them tried to hurt me. I just walked on by, like they didn't see me at all."

"That's good for you, but what about us?"

"You survived him attacking you," Colleen said. "Nobody else can say that. When he's lashed out at other people, they die. And if you can survive a confrontation with him, that probably goes for Grif, too."

"We don't know anything for sure," Grif said. "It's all speculation. We could drive in there, and get slaughtered before we even find Wayne."

"We could," Colleen said. "And then maybe we won't. The only way to find out is to try."

"Crazy or not, somebody's got to do *something* to stop him," Viv said. "He's not getting any weaker."

"He's like a fucking god of war," Grif said. "Spreading his plague across the Earth."

"We have two choices," Colleen said. "We dive in and try to end this, or we get as far away as we can. But I'm starting to think we can never get far enough at this point."

"Do you think she might really have a clue as to what's going on?" Grif asked Viv.

"I don't know," Viv said. "So we drive right in and hope someone doesn't kill us along the way?" Viv said. "It just sounds too risky. We have to come up with a better plan than that."

"Well, we better decide on something soon," Colleen said, staring at the television. An overhead camera showed people hitting each other with whatever was handy. It looked like a Roman gladiator pit. Blood-smeared corpses littered the streets. "It sure isn't getting any better out there."

CHAPTER SIXTY-ONE

They were waiting to get up the nerve to leave. That's the only explanation that Colleen had for why they were delaying the final leg of the trip. It was as if everything had flipped. She was now more eager than ever to go on, to get this over with. But the other two, they seemed to have lost their desire to complete this.

This was especially strange because she knew that Viv was the one who had wanted revenge most of all. Back at Jeremy's house, she was all wound up and wanting to lash out at something.

She could hear them in Viv's room, arguing. There was something in the air, Colleen could feel it too. A kind of electricity that made her tense up. Viv and Grif were shouting. They were talking about *her*.

"You were insane to risk it," Viv was saying. "What if she had died last night? I told you not to do it."

"I couldn't resist. She begged me to do it. You know how it is."

"You never did have any willpower. Hell, you'd just fed a few hours beforehand. And even then you didn't have enough?"

"Something about her," Grif said. "I couldn't say no. What's the problem, anyway? Nothing happened. I wasn't able to do it. She's safe from us."

"Maybe it was just this time," Viv said. "Maybe next time it won't be so good. Could you live with her death on your conscience, Grif?"

He didn't reply. Colleen wasn't sure how to take that. She was sure that he'd done worst things in his past. She suspected that he could get over anything, given enough time. He didn't seem the type to linger on things too long.

Their voices were so agitated. Whatever was in the air was affecting them. Colleen went back to her bed and stretched out on it. Not knowing what else to do. She'd wanted to go outside and get some air, but this strange feeling she had. It scared her. She wouldn't feel safe if she left now.

As if to reinforce her fears, sounds started coming from outside. Pounding, shouting. There were other people in the hotel and they were experiencing it, too. They were even more vulnerable to the bad, churning emotions that filled the air.

Someone screamed.

Viv and Grif came out of Viv's room. They'd had the door shut while they argued. Not that it helped any. But now they were out in the suite. She could see them from her bed. Her door was open.

"What was *that*?" she asked.

Viv turned to face her. As if in answer, there was another scream. This one was louder and longer, followed by a sound that made them think of a thick metal pipe crashing into a wall. There was one more scream, and then silence.

"It's started," Viv said. "Whatever is happening. It's *here* now."

Colleen got out of bed and went to them. The noises were getting louder.

"The world's going fucking insane," Grif said.

"We have to stay here until it passes," Colleen said. Her voice sounded very sure. "As long as we stay here, we're safe."

"This madness is going to circle the globe," Viv said. "There's no way we can stop this."

And then a chorus of new screams filled the air. Colleen covered her ears with her hands.

* * *

At some point, Colleen brought Grif back to her room and they'd started fucking again. More to block out what was happening outside than anything else.

The way he made her feel, Colleen wanted to fuck Grif forever. He seemed totally astounded by the way she reacted. He'd clearly never met anyone who could match his stamina before. Hell, she didn't match him, she surpassed him. He was having a hard time keeping up with her.

She could feel her head tingling. He was trying to do something to her mind. She knew it. Maybe it wasn't something he had any control over. That's what she'd theorized about the two of them, that they had no ability to control what they did, once they were in the thick of it. Like vampires, they had needs and they were slaves to these needs.

Except they couldn't get what they wanted from her. She was immune. It totally baffled Grif.

The tingling in her head felt good. It heightened her sensations. It made her cum harder and more often. He hit her G-spot, and she found herself squirting all over him. Eventually Grif just wanted to stop, but she wouldn't let him. He tried to get off the bed, but she pulled him back. She had always had a strong libido, but something about him pushed it up a notch. *Two notches*. She felt like she was reverting to some animal state.

"I got to go," he said weakly, trying to get away again, trying to pull himself out of her, but she wrapped her legs tighter around him, refusing to let him go. She grabbed the wooden bars of the bedpost and held on for dear life, refusing to budge. Even after he came, she wouldn't let him go.

Despite the closed door, and despite their fucking, they could still hear the noise from outside. It reached a fever pitch and then started dying down. Whatever this thing was that Sam Wayne did to people, it was fast and furious and people killed one another quickly. It wasn't long and drawn out.

When it was completely silent, Colleen relaxed her legs and let Grif go. He seemed eager to get away from her. He was sweaty and weak and somehow ended up sitting on the floor, his back to the door, breathing hard.

"You never met a girl like me before, huh?" Colleen said to him. She was breathing hard, too.

"No," Grif said, half-smiling. His face looked skull-like for a moment. "You got that right."

"We have to go soon," she told him. Totally sure of herself. "It's safe to leave now, and we've got a mission to accomplish, before this spreads too far."

"I know," Grif said, but he didn't make any effort to get up off the floor.

* * *

Viv sat on the floor of her room, listening to them. She wanted to join in, but she resisted. She tried with all her might to clear her head. Between their sounds, and the sounds from outside, it was almost too much to bear, but she was able to at least partially empty her mind.

And after she'd just yelled at Grif for risking it, for fucking Colleen. Here he was, at it again.

At least *they* were preoccupied. The sounds from outside were getting increasingly disturbing. Strangely, nobody tried to break into their suite, though.

Viv tried to block out the sounds of anger and violence. She closed her eyes tightly and tried to concentrate on the sound of her own breathing.

It lasted less than an hour, and then all was quiet again. Everything was peaceful.

There was a knock on her door.

"Viv?" Colleen asked. "Are you okay in there?"

"Yeah," she croaked, as if she hadn't spoken in years and it was something new to her.

"Get ready," Colleen said. "We have to go soon. It's time to move on."

"Sounds like a plan," Grif said.

CHAPTER SIXTY-TWO

There didn't seem to be any other drivers on the road. There were a lot of abandoned cars, and dead bodies here and there. Viv wondered if everyone else in the world was dead.

Grif was driving. Viv was sitting on the passenger side, leaning against the window, looking out. For some reason she found herself thinking about Jeremy. She let her thoughts take her away.

They'd met when she'd been doing some modeling. She had heard about him before she actually met him. He'd dated a lot of the other models, girls she knew. She wasn't really close to any of them; she mostly kept to herself, but she couldn't help hearing about him.

She'd actually liked modeling, while it lasted. She'd had to earn money, and people seemed more than happy to pay her a lot of money to pose for pictures.

When they'd finally met, there was an obvious, mutual attraction between them, and she'd considered exploiting that. But it just didn't happen. Instead, they somehow found themselves in a different kind of relationship.

They'd flirted, always on the verge of moving forward to something else. But they didn't get close until after his accident. He'd gone into seclusion and she'd sought him out. Maybe at first intending to use his despair, perhaps she'd even wanted to end his suffering. But she couldn't bring herself to do it. She'd helped him come back from the edge. She'd been the only one to nurse him back to health. To nurture him. She swore she would never harm him, and she never did. One of the few promises she'd ever been able to keep to herself.

After the crash, he shut himself off from everyone but her. By that time, she was starting to feel overexposed and Jeremy was more than happy to offer her a way out of the business. He'd taken care of her financial needs. He let her use his credit cards, even her car was in his name. No one knew she lived there. They kept to themselves. She only went out at night. No one could trace her. That's why she had stayed with him so long. She told him everything and he still accepted her, still wanted to protect her. It was the first time she'd stayed in one place that long since childhood.

But like everything else, it had had a price. She'd had to resist him. No matter how much he'd beg her at times to take his life, she'd had to deny him. Sometimes it seemed more than she could bear, and she'd had to leave for days at a time. But she always went back. She couldn't leave him for long.

It was good when Colleen had entered the picture. She took the edge off, no matter how briefly. It would have been very hard for Viv to leave him completely, but with Colleen keeping him preoccupied, it made it easier for her to come and go. To have more of a distance from him. After years of intensity, it was nice to turn it down a bit.

But now, Jeremy was dead. She'd lost him. After years of taking care of him, helping him become himself again. It was so painful to lose him like that.

Colleen was in the back seat. She seemed very alert, looking out the back window.

"We're getting close," Colleen said. "I can feel him."

This was something new. She'd never said anything about being able to sense Sam Wayne before. While this was a helpful asset to their mission, it also made Viv uneasy. That and her ability to resist Grif's hunger. All this time, Viv had thought she was a normal girl, but it was clear that she wasn't. She was like them. Not exactly like them, she didn't have their urges, their needs. She was like their opposite. The one thing that could resist them. The snake charmer among the serpents.

"It won't be long now," Colleen said. She was behind Grif's seat now, whispering into his ear. "He's very close, now."

Viv turned from the passenger window to look back at Colleen. There was something different about her. Viv saw a kind of an aura around Colleen. It was as if someone had outlined her face in bright green. And then, as quickly as it happened, it was gone.

This made Viv wonder. Back at the hotel, had they been unharmed by the outside world because they were all immune to the violence? Or had they been spared because of Colleen's presence somehow? Viv remembered Colleen being so sure that no one would harm them if they stayed in their suite.

When they'd left the hotel, there had been bodies in the hallways. Bodies outside on the street. Viv remembered their tortured faces.

"I hope you're both ready," Colleen said softly. "Because this will all be over soon."

* * *

When they reached the bridge, they were low on gas. Not that it mattered much. The bridge was choked with cars and there was no way they could have driven across. They'd fueled up at abandoned gas stations along the way, but this was the end of the road.

"We have to get out there," Colleen said. "He's close."

"How can you be sure?" Viv asked, but Colleen was already out of the car and walking toward the silent, unearthly traffic jam. Grif shut off the engine.

"I guess we're following her, then?" he asked.

"What other plan is there? She seems to think she can detect him somehow. We've followed her this far. Why not go all the way with it?"

"I don't know," Grif said. "I guess there's no Plan B at this point."

"Not that I know of."

He took out the keys and opened his door. Viv opened the passenger door, and they both got out. There was a foul odor in the air. It didn't take much detective work to figure out why. Scattered between the abandoned cars were bodies, and pieces of bodies.

"This can't be real," Grif said.

"I'm afraid it is."

He went to the trunk of the car and opened it. They had more guns in there. He took out a pistol and slid it into the front of his pants. Then he pulled out a sawed-off shotgun.

"If he's capable of all this, do you think guns can kill him?"

"I don't know," Viv said. "But we've got to try, right?"

"I am really starting to regret coming along with you guys," Grif said. "But I guess I didn't have much choice. The way this thing is spreading, it would have caught up with me eventually."

"I wish I could be sure that we could stop this somehow," Viv said. "But I really don't have a clue. The only person who seems to have any kind of idea what's going on here is Colleen, and I'm not a hundred percent sure she's *all there* these days."

"She sure seemed all there in the bedroom," Grif said and smiled.

"That was a stupid risk," Viv said. "You had no idea she'd be able to get through it okay."

"She got through it fine."

"I really don't want to talk about this again."

"I think you're jealous. Why didn't you join in? It wouldn't have been the first time."

"We have more important things to do now than talk about this."

"Okay, okay. I'll drop it."

She made sure to take her own guns, and she checked to make sure there was a fresh clip in each of them, and that she had extra ammunition.

They looked out at the bridge. Colleen was walking on top of cars. She was halfway to the other side.

"Might as well catch up with her," Grif said.

They walked over to the cars and got up on top of one at the beginning of the bridge, then started walking across the roofs like Colleen was doing. The world seemed utterly still, except for the sounds they made. Not even the sound of a bird in the sky.

Even the water below them was silent.

There were bodies on the ground between the cars, on top of hoods, some inside the cars where they'd been locked in struggles while they killed each other. An incredible wave of violence had washed over them, and like mad rats they'd torn each other apart. But it was so calm now.

Viv and Grif picked up their pace to try and catch up with Colleen, but she was moving fast.

"Wait up," Viv called out to her.

Colleen did not turn around. Either she didn't hear Viv, or she pretended not to.

The bridge was long, and they hadn't even reached the middle of it yet.

"What's her hurry?" Grif asked, almost slipping off the roof of a Cadillac. Some of the cars were spattered with blood that was dried now. But you had to be careful.

He struggled to regain his balance and then moved on.

Viv stopped to wait for him.

"I don't know," Viv said. "It's like she's going to meet someone she can't wait to see again. There's something strange going on here."

"She doesn't have any weapons, does she?" Grif asked.

"I don't think so."

Colleen was walking over the trapped cars as if she were walking on air. Never a misstep, never a wrong move. She picked up her pace as the others struggled to keep up.

"Colleen," Viv shouted, but she didn't turn to look back at them. She seemed not to hear.

"She's like a woman possessed," Grif said.

"I've never seen her act like this," Viv told him. "It's kind of scary."

They kept walking along the car tops, and then Colleen leapt down and disappeared from view. She'd reached the other side.

"We're almost there," Viv said. "Maybe we can get her to listen to reason once we get off this bridge."

But it didn't make much sense. Colleen had gotten a head start. Once they got off the bridge, she'd be even further away. She was probably running by now. Viv had the urge to turn back. Colleen was their way to find Sam Wayne; otherwise, it would be like finding a needle in a haystack. But if Colleen wasn't going to cooperate with them, then there wasn't much point in going on.

"Are you thinking what I'm thinking?" she asked her brother.

"I don't know. Are you thinking we should give this up?"

Viv looked back. "We've come too far now. I guess that's not an option."

"Yeah, we're almost there," he said.

They reached the last car, finally, and climbed off. There were more cars in front of it, but once they'd gotten off the bridge, there was no longer a need to walk in a straight line. Viv and Grif went to where there was some open space. They stopped to survey the area.

"Where is she?" Viv asked. "I thought we'd see her."

"There she is," Grif shouted and pointed. Colleen was running across a green field up ahead. The grass was littered with corpses. Viv caught sight of her, then Colleen disappeared behind some trees.

"She must be going to him," Viv said. "There's no other explanation."

"But so eager? It doesn't seem real. It's like this is some kind of weird dream. Doesn't she know he'll kill her if she gets too close?"

"I don't know," Viv said. "She's been right in front of him twice already, seen him kill two people right in front of her. And yet she got away untouched."

"What does it mean?"

"I don't know, but maybe we'll finally find out."

They started running toward the field.

They stopped when they reached it. Colleen was still far ahead of them. There was death all around them, but there was also something moving down at the other end of the park. Not something, *someone*.

Sam Wayne turned in their direction. He just stood there, watching them approach.

"Is that him?" Grif asked.

"It must be," Viv said. "Nobody else is alive. I guess this is it." She pulled out her gun. "This is your last chance to turn back."

"And go where?" Grif said. "If we don't stop him now, there's nothing to go back to."

CHAPTER SIXTY-THREE

They got closer, but Sam did not move from where he stood, watching them.

His mind was kind of hazy, hovering between the rage that had taken over, and the last vestiges of who he had been. There was a tingling sensation in his head, in his arms and legs, like something was coming out of him. Some kind of energy. And while it was generating, his mind was almost on hold. That was the only way he could have explained what he felt, if he'd wanted to.

If someone had asked.

But whenever anyone got close enough, he lashed out at them. He was a kind of beacon, it seemed. And nothing could get in the way of the message he was sending out into the world. Nothing.

He couldn't feel whether it was hot or cold. Because of the tingling, he couldn't even really feel his own body, although he knew it was there, beneath him. Otherwise, he'd just drop to the ground.

He didn't look down at himself, though. It wasn't important for him to know his body was still there. To *see* it.

Sam felt like a man at the bottom of a deep, deep ocean, water filling his ears and deafening him, making it hard to really see things clearly. Making it hard to move.

And, always, the crazy tingling everywhere. It was almost painful.

She was the first to reach him, but he couldn't see her.

That wasn't exactly true. He could sense that someone was there, in fact it was almost as if he could briefly see the faintest outline of her, but when he tried to focus on her, she would disappear.

This was a familiar feeling. He *knew* this person. He wanted to lash out at her, to kill her, but she was invisible to him. And, the more he tried to concentrate on her, the fuzzier his mind got. He found it difficult to remember what he was looking for.

* * *

Colleen stood over to Sam Wayne's side and watched him. His face was bright red and the veins bulged on his neck. He was moving his head back and forth, as if he was looking for something. She was amazed she could get so close. But then, this had happened before. When he'd killed Turney and Jeremy, she had expected him to kill her too, but both times he'd seemed too distracted before he could. As if he couldn't really see her at all.

Colleen had felt a kind of magnetic pull, drawing her to him. She'd tried to resist it at first, but the closer they'd gotten to him, the more impossible it was for her to turn back. As if whatever came out of him that was infecting the world with violence was also what drew her to him.

But now that she was here, not ten feet away from him, she didn't know what to do. She thought it would be clear to her when she finally reached him, but it wasn't. Colleen just stood there, watching Sam Wayne looking for her; obviously feeling her presence but unable to pinpoint where she was.

I can't just stand here, she thought. He's bound to find me eventually.

* * *

To Viv, Sam was a disappointment. He didn't look like someone who was responsible for thousands of deaths. He was just a naked man, smeared with blood.

She did feel the tension. The pins and needles in the back of her neck. But that was as far as it went. She was able to resist the rage that emanated from him, and it was clear that Grif could, too. Maybe if they hadn't succumbed to the wave of rage back at the hotel, it wasn't going to take control of them now.

"What's wrong with his face?" Grif asked, as they got closer.

His face was odd. To Viv, it was blurred. Like the molecules couldn't stay still long enough to form his features, like they were constantly moving.

"I don't know," she said.

"So that's definitely him?" Grif said and raised the shotgun.

"It has to be," Viv said. She thought back to Wayne's house, the one where Maggie had lived, too. His face had been blurry that time too, when he'd pummeled her. It was only in photographs that she'd seen him normally. He hadn't looked all that impressive. A mildly attractive man, but not extraordinary in any way.

From what Colleen said, only she could see his face clearly when he was like this.Sam was looking around, distracted, trying to find Colleen. She was close, standing very still. He clearly could not see her.

"So, if we stop him, then everything will go back to normal?" Grif asked, and it struck Viv that he was stalling.

"*Shoot him,*" she said.

* * *

Grif aimed and fired. The hollow-point bullet buried itself in Sam's chest. He barely moved. The bullet seemed to have no effect. Grif fired again.

It was then that Sam Wayne leapt forward and grabbed Grif. It was amazing how quickly he moved. He closed the gap between them in seconds. The shotgun dropped to the grass, and Grif's legs gave out from under him. He was down on the ground, with Sam on top of him. He could smell the man's breath; it smelled of blood and decay. But even up close he couldn't get any better view of his face. It was even more blurred.

Sam slammed his head into Grif's. Hard. Somehow, Grif stayed conscious and struggled, trying to push Sam off him, trying to fight back, but Sam overpowered him. Grif had never felt so helpless before. He had always thought he was stronger than normal men. There had never been a fight when he hadn't had the upper hand. But now, there was no way he could break Sam's grip. No way to get free.

Sam's hands grabbed Grif's biceps and pulled outwards, ripping his arms free. Grif could feel them tear away from him; he heard the sickening sounds of his body being torn apart. Grif began to scream, and Sam put his hands on both sides of his head, and there was intense pressure and pain.

* * *

Sam tore Grif's head from his body, flinging it out into the tall grass.

It had all happened so fast. Like a spider that stays very still in one part of its web, and then suddenly pounces and eliminates its prey.

Viv didn't have much time to react. By the time she realized what was happening, Grif was already dead. She grabbed his shotgun up from the ground and began pounding Sam in the back of the head with it. But he didn't seem to notice.

She looked up for a second, and saw Colleen a few yards from them, just standing there. She looked horrified, staring at what was left of Grif.

Viv turned the shotgun around and aimed it at Sam's head.

If Grif died so easily, Viv thought, staring down. What chance do *I* have?

This seemed much worse than the last time, in Sam's house. He had at least seemed somewhat human then, even if he was totally psychotic. But now, he didn't anymore. There were strange growths on his limbs, bizarre tumors that made him look sick and diseased. And his movements, they were no longer the movements of a man.

"Viv," Colleen cried. "Look out!"

Sam was up from the ground in a flash and had pounced on Viv, knocking the gun aside and wrestling her to the ground. Grif's shotgun went flying out her hands, and her own guns seemed a million miles away.

She could feel his fists pummeling her again. Could feel him tearing at her clothes. She tried with all her might to stay conscious beneath the barrage.

And then his blurred face was pressed beside hers, cheek to cheek, and he was forcing her legs apart. She could feel him forcing his way inside her. It all happened so fast. She struggled, but she wasn't strong enough to push him away.

She could see Colleen just over his shoulder, in the background, moving from foot to foot, almost dancing, looking terrified and helpless.

With his cheek so close, Viv knew his ear had to be as well, and she tried so hard to speak. She almost choked on the word. "Maggie."

He didn't stop what he was doing to her, but he made an odd sound. A questioning sound. So she forced herself to say it again, even though she could feel that he had injured her jaw. Blood filled her eyes and mouth.

"What about Maggie?" she asked him.

And then, as he raped her on the grass, she could feel her own mind reaching out to his, trying to find a way in. And the way in was Maggie, beckoning her, showing her the secret entrance into a mind long ravaged by madness. He let his guard down enough so that she could work her way inside, penetrating his mind as he penetrated her body. It was mostly chaos and pain, like she had taken a journey into hell, but there was a tiny sliver of Sam Wayne left inside there still; a human fragment that still mourned for Maggie. Viv used this opening to insinuate her mind into his, and then she could feel what he felt, could feel his rage, even as he was on the verge of orgasm. And she went along for the ride, letting his sensations flood her, letting a rhythm coexist between them.

And then, she found what was left of his soul and wrapped herself around it, pulling at it, trying to absorb it into herself.

The sliver of Sam Wayne was scared and wanted to die. It was lost in the creature he had become and didn't want to continue being. Viv embraced that part of him and pulled him to her.

From the corner of her eye, she could faintly see Colleen. She had grabbed the shotgun where it had fallen on the ground and lifted it up. She tried to aim it at Sam, but she clearly didn't want to hurt Viv. She stood there aiming the gun, hesitating.

Viv squirmed to get her arms free. She'd been enhancing his sensations as he raped her, and he was just preoccupied enough so that she could get her arms free and grab his head. She lifted it up.

Colleen had fired a shotgun a few times before. On the way out here, Grif had given her lessons. She didn't have very good aim. But now, with Sam right in front of her, she didn't have to. She could practically press the gun against his skull before she fired.

But she was just standing there.

"Do it!" Viv said.

And at that moment, Sam came, and Viv swallowed the essence of who he was. Who *Sam* was, the human part of his psyche. She sucked it clear out of his head, but she was afraid that it was not enough, that it wasn't all that was inside his mind, now that he was something different.

But it must have been enough, because the violent creature that raped her suddenly went limp, just for a moment, and in that moment, Colleen fired the gun, splitting its skull in two and splattering Viv with blood. The bullet tore through the beast's bone and brain matter, and then buried itself in the ground mere inches from Viv's own head. The sound was thunderous.

"Oh my God," Colleen shouted. "Viv, are you okay?"

She only heard the words faintly, but she saw Colleen's mouth moving.

Sam had collapsed on top of Viv and it took all her effort to push him off her. She couldn't help but think of her father. But she wasn't a little girl anymore. He rolled to one side. His cock had still been inside her. He'd ripped her up down there; and she was bleeding. There was a lot that would need healing. But somehow she had made it through alive.

Colleen went to her and knelt beside her.

"He's not moving anymore," she said. "I think we killed him."

Viv could barely hear her. It was like Colleen was talking at the end of a long tunnel. Her ears were still ringing from the shotgun blast.

We killed him, Colleen had said. As if she was well aware that Viv was doing her best to kill him her own way. *From the inside.*

Viv was sore and bloody as she sat up. Colleen was embracing her, but she got a clear view of Grif, or at least some pieces of him, and she started to cry. All his life, Grif had felt angry and confused.

Even when he'd figured out what he was, what *they* were, and learned to accept it. He never really had any sense of peace.

This sure was an awful way to find peace.

I guess we weren't totally alike after all, Viv thought. *Somehow I made it through this alive, and you didn't.*

Viv hadn't cried in a very long time and it felt strange to her. Unnatural.

Colleen was crying, too, and held her close.

"Grif's dead," Colleen said softly. "I'm so sorry."

Viv gently pushed her away and somehow got to her feet.

"We have to bury him somehow," she said.

But there weren't any tools around, and the ground was hard here. She tried to dig up dirt with her hands, but her hands started bleeding and Colleen stopped her.

"We have to get out of here," she said. "You're hurt and bleeding."

"I'll live."

Viv stopped digging and got to her feet.

"Let's go back."

"We need his keys," Colleen said.

"They should be there," she said. The lower half of Grif's body was nearby, caked in gore. "In his pocket."

Colleen stared at the pants that held half of Grif. She didn't move.

"I'll do it,' Viv said. She got down on her knees and crawled over to them. She searched his pockets. There was a tinkling sound as she pulled out the ring of keys. "Here."

Colleen came over and helped her back up to her feet. Viv leaned on her for support. She considered trying to lift Grif and bringing him back with them, but she knew she would never make it. She felt all used up.

They walked slowly over the bridge again. This time, Colleen did not run away from her, but stayed beside her, helping her. Despite her injuries, Viv was strong.

It seemed to take forever to get to the end of the bridge, walking over the tops of abandoned cars. Then they had to find Grif's car. Viv recognized it.

When they reached it, Viv slid into the driver's side seat and put the key in the ignition.

"Where are we going?" Colleen asked.

"Anywhere, away from here," Viv said slowly.

She noticed the gas tank. "We'll have to find more gas."

There was another car nearby, with almost a full tank of gas and keys in the ignition. Instead of trying to siphon the gas out, it was easier just to take it. Luckily, it wasn't blocked in completely. Viv slid behind the wheel and started the engine. She tried her best to avoid the scattered bodies and body parts as she headed toward the highway that would take them away from all this, but it was futile. Body parts were everywhere. At least they couldn't feel it as they crunched beneath the tires.

At one point, as she navigated her way past an obstacle course of bodies and abandoned cars, Viv heard a buzzing from above and looked out her window to see a plane in the sky above them.

EPILOGUE

CHAPTER SIXTY-FOUR

The television was on, and they were watching the morning news. Whatever had happened in the city was still a mystery, but at least now it was over. The body count was still undetermined, but speculation was that it was going to be in the millions. Nobody offered any answers. The entire world was still in shock.

The pictures on the television screen looked like footage from the Holocaust. Piles of bodies for as far as the eye could see.

"It's horrible," Colleen was saying. "If we hadn't killed him, it would have spread. It would have killed everybody."

"I know."

They didn't think of themselves as heroes. They had been scared and knew the source of the violence, and either they did something about it or they didn't. It wasn't much of a choice.

There had been a time back there, when Grif died in front of her, when Sam first pounced on her, when Viv was sure she would die that day. There did not seem to be the slightest chance that she wouldn't. To be alive now seemed hollow, unreal.

I died back there, Viv thought. *I know I did. One of those bodies on the TV screen is mine. I'm just too stupid to realize it.*

Colleen was on the bed beside her. She was wrapped in a towel, having just come out of the shower. Her skin was warm.

Viv rubbed up against her.

"You feel so good."

Colleen laughed. It wasn't really a giggle, but it was close. She was holding back slightly. They hadn't gotten far enough from the carnage for her to really giggle.

Colleen leaned forward and kissed her.

"I wanted to thank you," Colleen said. "For everything."

"You did just as much as I did. There's no reason to thank me."

"I feel like I should," Colleen said. "There's no way I could have done anything myself. As it is, I'm not sure how much help I was."

"You helped plenty."

"We really don't have to talk about this. I made him vulnerable, but you pulled the trigger. We couldn't have done it without each other."

"When I pulled the trigger, he was already dead. I saw it. He was limp. I knew you'd done it to him. I just pulled the trigger to make sure."

Viv kissed her again. "Don't talk anymore. Please."

Viv hugged her close.

"I better take a shower myself," Viv said. "Do you want to get my back?"

"Sure."

* * *

After Viv's shower, they made love. It was something they both were anticipating for a long time. Since Jeremy's death, in fact. Colleen had felt such a strong attraction to Viv; it had taken her almost all her willpower to resist acting on it. What she didn't know at the time was that it had been much the same for Viv.

Unlike Viv, Colleen hadn't been worried about killing someone else with her intimacy, though. She'd simply been afraid. There had been some drunken threesomes in her past, but Colleen had never been with another woman who she really cared about before. And Viv had sometimes seemed so distant in Jeremy's house, she hadn't wanted to pursue anything and risk pushing her away completely. For a while there, they were all each other had.

Viv told her that when Grif had been able to make love to Colleen, and didn't kill her, it had filled her with a hidden sense of joy. But, even then, she had been too scared to act on it. Even if it had worked for Grif, what was to say it would be the same for her? She wanted Colleen badly, but would never forgive herself if something horrible were to happen.

But that was before Viv had seen the green aura around Colleen's face, back at the bridge. There was a reason why she had survived sex with Grif. A reason why she had been able to stay alive when she was near Sam Wayne. There was something different about Colleen, too. She was one of them. When Viv told Colleen that she had an aura, too, she was incredibly happy.

* * *

And now, in the bed, Viv did not hold back. The wounds Sam Wayne had given her were mostly healed now, even the psychological ones seemed far away, and she was able to make love with total abandon, giving of herself as she never had before, not even with Grif. Finally, she had met someone she could seriously consider a soul mate, and it felt wonderful.

She gently massaged Colleen's mind, as they got deeper into pleasing one another. Grif had done it and had made Colleen feel wonderful. Viv was determined to surpass it, to make Colleen feel more pleasure than she ever had in her life.

She had her fingers inside Colleen and was kissing her hungrily. Colleen was moaning softly beneath her, her mind tingling from Viv's abilities.

"Oh my God," Colleen said when they stopped kissing for a moment. "This is so wonderful."

Viv smiled and kissed her again. Then she slid down and used her mouth on Colleen.

As her tongue explored Colleen's sex, her mind penetrated deeper into Colleen's mind, to the pleasure centers of the human brain, and Viv started to trigger waves of sensation that started to overwhelm Colleen. Her body was becoming like an instrument, and Viv was the virtuoso who knew every string to pluck, every note to hit.

* * *

For a moment, Colleen hovered outside of consciousness, and she could see Jeremy there. He was laughing at some joke, and it was like he was alive again.

Then Colleen's voice, in her own head, cried out *Oh my God, he's dead!*

The image of Jeremy's death flashed through Colleen's mind, and with it came anger and sadness. It had been locked away in there, and Viv's prodding had opened it up again. It hadn't been easy to find. She was sure that Grif wouldn't have known where to look.

Colleen came back to consciousness and found herself engulfed in sensations. "Ohhhh," she cried out. The pleasure was getting too strong.

* * *

I'd better pull back a little, Viv thought, and tried to remove herself from Colleen's mind, but it was too late. She was too deep inside, and something was happening. Viv could feel Colleen's soul, and felt herself wrapping around it.

No!

There was still a sad, vulnerable part of Colleen that was filled with pain. That wanted to die. It had healed over for a time, but now it was open again. Raw. Viv tried, but could not resist it. It was her addiction, her need. It overpowered everything else.

And, combined with her need, there was something new. A growing anger.

She used every ounce of willpower to force herself out of Colleen's brain, but it wouldn't work. The more noise Colleen made, the more Viv knew they were getting into very dangerous territory.

She could feel herself absorbing Colleen's essence. Who she was. Her very soul.

NO!

Viv pulled away, but Colleen was grunting and wriggling on the bed before her, lost in pleasure. Viv was trying so hard to stop it, but it was too far gone. As Colleen's sensations came to their peak, she began to die, and her essence flowed into Viv.

"You can't die, Col," she said. "Please don't die."

But it was too late. One moment, Colleen was convulsing beneath her. The next, she was limp and lifeless.

The room got very quiet.

CHAPTER SIXTY-FIVE

I t was dark now.

Viv went out to the car. Colleen was in the back seat, wrapped in the sheet. Viv would find a good place to bury her.

An anger burned within Viv over what had happened. *Maybe I didn't escape from Sam Wayne,* she thought. *Maybe he left a piece of himself inside me, after all.*

She started the engine and pulled away from the motel parking lot. She had no idea what direction to go in, so she left it to chance.

She turned on the radio. A haunting song filled the car. A song she hadn't heard in a very long time.

There are stairs. That go upstairs. Only, there's nobody there.

Tears welled up in her eyes as she drove.

That was *Jeremy* singing. Back when he had been young and innocent. And *alive.*

She had never felt so alone in all her life.

-THE END-

ABOUT THE AUTHOR

L.L. Soares was born in New Bedford, Massachusetts. Dozens of his short stories have appeared in magazines like *Cemetery Dance, Gothic.net, Bare Bone* and *Horror Garage,* and anthologies like THE BEST OF HORRORFIND 2, RAW: BRUTALITY AS ART and ZIPPERED FLESH: TALES OF BODY ENHANCEMENTS GONE BAD! His story "Second Chances" received an Honorable Mention in the sixteenth annual edition of THE YEAR'S BEST FANTASY AND HORROR, edited by Ellen Datlow & Terri Windling.

In the fall of 2010, his first story collection, IN SICKNESS (featuring stories by himself and writer Laura Cooney), was published by Skullvines Press, and BREAKING EGGS, a novella written with Kurt Newton, was released by Sideshow Press.

He is an active member of the Horror Writers Association (HWA) and a former chairman of the New England Horror Writers (NEHW).

He was nominated for the 2009 Bram Stoker Award for co-writing the humorous horror movie review column, Cinema Knife Fight, which now has its own website and a full staff of writers at cinemaknifefight.com

He lives in the Boston area with his wife and pet iguana, Pippi Greenstocking.

Made in the USA
Middletown, DE
29 July 2015